Peter Watt has spent time as a soldier, articled clerk, prawn trawler deckhand, builder's labourer, pipe layer, real estate salesman, surveyor's chainman, private investigator, police sergeant and advisor to the Royal Papua New Guinea Constabulary. He speaks, reads and writes Vietnamese and Pidgin. He now lives at Maclean, on the Clarence River in northern New South Wales. He is a volunteer fire fighter with the Rural Fire Service, and also serves with the Volunteer Rescue Association and Queensland Ambulance Service.

Peter Watt can be contacted at www.peterwatt.com and on Facebook at 'Fans of Peter Watt Books'.

Author Photo: Shawn Peene

Excerpts from emails sent to Peter Watt

'Have just finished reading *And Fire Falls*. Mate! How good was that. Bloody marvellous. The story just keeps on getting better.'

'I felt there were three themes that you could only appreciate if you had read all the books. The first was the continued presence of Wallarie looking after the good and keeping an eye on the bad. The second was Jack Kelly rescuing Jessica. Very clever storytelling. After the *Papua Trilogy* we probably thought we had lost him forever. And last, the cottage at Manly and the drawings of Fiona from the early books. Who would have thought that after about 100 years, Sarah and David would have followed in the footsteps of Fiona and Michael.'

'Your description of the jungle and the privations suffered by the soldiers in New Guinea was brilliant. It reminded me of the few, and rare, times my father spoke of his time at Milne Bay during that period of the war. I have to admit, I had tears in my eyes when you referenced the airfield in Milne Bay, with the fighters taking off under withering fire.'

'Thanks for writing such books, mate. They mean a lot to people such as myself. My father would have loved to have read it, I'm sure. It's a shame he's not around anymore. After reading your book, who knows - he may have opened up even more.'

'I must say how much I enjoy your terrific books set in the colonial era. I find however that my dictionary is totally inadequate in expressing my full appreciation and wonder at your skills in capturing and presenting the atmosphere of life in those historic times. I would love to be able to read more of your amazing literature, as would the legion of fans you have here.' (UK reader)

'I am just writing to let you know that I don't do reading. However, I have just read the entire *Frontier* series in three weeks. Thank you very bloody much! The lawn looks like a jungle, my swing has gotten worse and my beloved Wallabies still can't beat the All Blacks! All this I place squarely at your feet you cad. Did I mention that I don't like to read! You even have me writing to an author! Many thanks. Keep up the good work, just hurry.'

'I have just finished reading *War Clouds Gather*. Like all your yarns (and I have now read them all so far) it is a cracking read and the Duffys and Macintoshes now seem like part of the family.'

'I am an avid reader of good historical and fictional novels. Peter has the ability to combine both of these concepts in a very rare way. He can transport the reader to the time and place where events are in process. That takes talent. We are indeed very fortunate to have a world class writer of Peter's calibre in Australia.'

PETER WATT

Beneath A Rising Sun

PAN
Pan Macmillan Australia

First published 2015 in Macmillan by Pan Macmillan Australia Pty Ltd
This Pan edition published in 2016 by Pan Macmillan Australia Pty Ltd
1 Market Street, Sydney, New South Wales, Australia, 2000

Cataloguing-in-Publication entry is available
from the National Library of Australia
http://catalogue.nla.gov.au

Typeset in Bembo by Post Pre-press Group
Printed by IVE

For Naomi
For her love and support

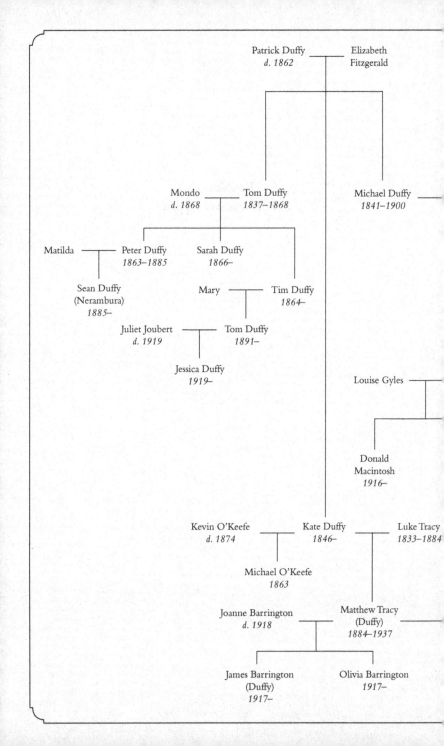

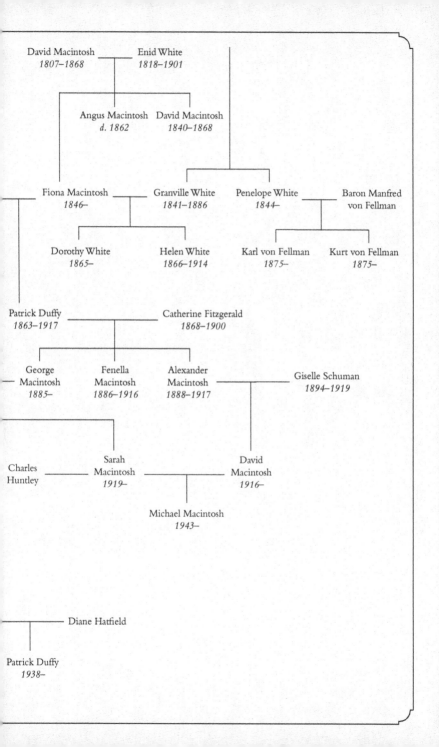

PROLOGUE

Sydney, Australia, 1943

Lieutenant Tony Caccamo, a former member of the New York Police Department and now an officer in the American military police, was about to kill a man in cold blood. He could feel his body tremble – not so much with fear, although he felt afraid, but with extreme apprehension. He was about to assassinate a high-ranking British officer.

The semi-automatic army-issue .45 pistol hung loosely in his hand as he stood in the darkness watching the front doors of the harbourside mansion. He had been given his orders back in General MacArthur's HQ in Brisbane, and his commanding officer had informed him that the man he now waited to kill was a dangerous traitor, in league with the Japanese. When Tony had questioned why the Australian authorities had not detained the suspect, he had been informed that without irrefutable evidence the Brit was too well connected to British aristocracy for that to happen. He was slated for a position in signals intelligence, which would give him access to the Allies' deepest secrets, and this could not be allowed to happen.

Tony had been given forged papers and was posing as a Canadian merchant seaman, which had allowed him access to the city's less salubrious society over the last couple of months, giving him an opportunity to track his prey.

His target, Lieutenant Colonel Albert Ulverstone, had just inherited his family title with the death of his esteemed father, and that now made him the new Lord Ulverstone. The Prime Minister of Great Britain, Winston Churchill, had previously interfered in MI6 investigations into suspected traitors amongst British aristocracy, and this left only one option for Britain's most important ally, the Americans. What was one more death in a war claiming millions of lives?

Despite the cold autumn night, sweat clung to Tony's skin under his rough garb. He had been tracking the British lord's movements around the city and had noted that he was a regular visitor to the home of a very wealthy Aussie entrepreneur, Sir George Macintosh. Ulverstone was a creature of habit and usually dined here at Sir George's home on Monday evenings. He would be vulnerable when he stepped out of the house into the darkness to walk to his private sedan parked twenty yards away in the driveway. It was then that Tony would close the distance and fire straight into the man's head. The .45 bullet was known for its massive impact, and the second shot into the man's chest would ensure his death.

Tony could feel the sweat on the palms of his hands. He could hear the distant clatter of bells on buoys in the harbour and a dog barking somewhere in the distance, but little else disturbed the silence of the night. He had planned his escape, and if all went well the assassination of the British officer would forever remain an unsolved murder case for the Aussie police.

The front door opened and Tony could see Ulverstone framed in the doorway, Sir George Macintosh standing behind him. He could hear the two of them exchanging pleasantries. Tony waited for the door to close so that there would be no witnesses. Ulverstone was already walking to his car and Tony could hear the crunch of fine gravel underfoot. He gripped the pistol, raising it ready for action, and stepped from the shadows.

He was halfway to Ulverstone and now exposed in the open. Within seconds he would be on top of the British officer.

Suddenly Tony was aware that the door to the house had opened again and a voice called, 'Old chap, you forgot your hat.'

Tony froze. In the open he knew he could be seen and without hesitating he turned and sprinted into the darkness.

*

'Good God, man!' Sir George yelled to his friend. 'I think someone was about to do you a mischief. That fellow, running away over there.'

Albert Ulverstone spun around and just caught sight of a man disappearing out of the driveway onto the street. He looked back to Sir George Macintosh still standing in the doorway with a hat in his hand.

'I could have sworn that chappie had a gun,' Sir George said in a shocked tone, and Ulverstone felt a shiver of terror. The first thing that came to his mind was that the man was an agent of the British secret service organisation, MI6, or perhaps even the Secret Operations Executive, the deadly covert organisation of the British wartime government. Ulverstone knew that he would have to take precautions if that was so.

★

Many miles west of Sydney, on the other side of the Great Dividing Range, a life had just been born into a world at war. On the outskirts of the large country town of Goulburn, the weakened mother lay back against the soft pillows. The farmhouse was large and comfortable, and a fire flickered gently in the bedroom hearth.

Sarah Huntley – nee Macintosh – had come to the property, one of the many in her family's estate, to await the birth of her first child. She had done so reluctantly, as this had meant leaving the family businesses in the hands of her brother, Donald Macintosh. The birth was three weeks premature, but the child was delivered safely by the experienced midwife.

'You have a grand-looking boy,' the elderly midwife said, holding up the baby who was already bawling his anger at being removed from the warmth of the womb. 'Your husband will be proud of his son.'

Sarah bent her head forward to see the life she had brought into the world. He was slimy and wrinkled, and she sighed as she fell back against the pillows. All that pain and time away from her beloved companies to produce something more alien than human, she thought. What she could not tell the midwife was that the child was not that of her husband, Charles Huntley, but that of her cousin, David Macintosh.

The midwife went about the business of cutting the umbilical cord and cleaning the baby before placing him in a swaddling cloth beside his mother. 'Do you have a name for the wee one?' she asked, perusing Sarah for any possible signs of postnatal fever or injury.

'Not as yet,' Sarah answered.

'I will have the doctor call in tomorrow morning to carry out a routine examination,' the midwife said as she packed her medical bag.

The woman left and the housemaid, a young woman in her late teens, stepped into the bedroom. Her face brightened at the sight of the baby.

'Mrs Carey said that you have a boy, Mrs Huntley,' the girl said with a wide smile. 'What is his name?'

'Michael,' Sarah said in a weary voice.

'If I may ask, is there any special reason for the name?' the maid asked, going to the baby beside her employer.

'To be honest,' Sarah said with a frown. 'It just came to mind a few seconds ago. I would like you to remove the baby to your room tonight, so that I am able to get a good night's sleep,' she instructed, and the maid willingly scooped the baby up into her arms and took him away.

The logs burned away in the bedroom fireplace, casting eerie shadows on the wall. Sarah began to doze off but woke almost immediately with a sudden wave of terror. She found that she was staring at a shadow of a man with a spear dancing on the walls. She tried to scream but no sound came out. For reasons she could not explain, the name Wallarie filled her head. She had heard about Aboriginal corroborees, and she felt as though she was no longer in the sleepy pastoral village of Goulburn but much further north in the arid country of the brigalow scrub plains, in the presence of an ancient people her family had massacred three-quarters of a century before.

A burning log slipped and the Aboriginal dancer was gone, leaving her wide-eyed and in a lather of sweat.

The words of her father, Sir George Macintosh, echoed in the silence of the room: 'There is a blackfella curse on our family.'

*

My name is Wallarie and some of you know me. I am a Darambal man of the Nerambura clan. I am long gone from your earthly world, but sometimes the old ones let me return to the places I once hunted for the kangaroo and goanna. I return because there is a curse on a couple of whitefella clans for what they did to my people.

If you go to the bumbil tree on a whitefella place they call Glen View and sit in its shade, and if you listen to the sound of the wind blowing across the parched brigalow plains, you might hear me whisper in your ear the story of the Duffys and Macintoshes.

Maybe if you look up into the blue skies you will see a great eagle drifting above. That will be me watching you in the shade of the bumbil tree.

Maybe I am not real and you will hear nothing of this story.

Part One

Winter in the Southern Hemisphere

1943

Part One

Winter in the Southern Hemisphere

1941

ONE

Sergeant Jessica Duffy quickly scribbled down the essentials of the decoded Japanese signal. The Allied report had been transmitted from an aerial reconnaissance of the Bismarck Sea north of the island of New Guinea. She could see a picture emerging, but it was not her job to analyse information into intelligence.

The American signals intelligence office in General MacArthur's Brisbane HQ was a hive of activity and manned by predominantly American service personnel. A year earlier Jessica, a sergeant in the WAAAF, had been appointed as a liaison officer in the highly sensitive area of codes and intelligence. She had top secret clearance and had come to impress the American colonel in charge of her section with her understanding of the strategic implications of the signals that passed across her desk.

As she worked away, Jessica became aware of the heavy

scent of cigar smoke: her boss, a gruff, slightly overweight man who never seemed to be without his trademark cigar, was standing behind her.

'What do you think it all means, Sergeant Duffy?' he asked with his Texan drawl.

'I am not an intelligence analyst, sir,' Jessica said, turning in her swivel chair.

'You have a good instinct for what you see crossing your desk, Sergeant Duffy,' the colonel said, standing over her. 'Give me your best guess.'

'I think that the Japs are planning to reinforce Lae and Salamaua,' Jessica said. 'It seems obvious from what we know of their naval formations of transport ships, escorting war ships and a heavy aircraft cover to protect them.'

'And in your analysis, what does that mean?' he continued.

'If they succeed,' Jessica said, 'to put it in military terms, we could be up the creek without a paddle.'

The colonel snorted a laugh through the cigar clenched between his teeth. 'Mac has to dislodge the Japs from any plans he has to go after the little yellow bastards, on his route across the north of New Guinea, on his way to the retaking of the Philippines,' he said. 'A battle in the Bismarck Sea will decide the outcome of the Japs' future in this part of the world. Well done, Sergeant Duffy.'

With that he walked away, leaving Jessica to reflect on the picture she could see emerging from the flow of information from both the enemy and their own sources. She had already calculated that the battle in the Bismarck would prove to be critical and, if lost to the enemy, could cause the war in the Pacific region to drag on a lot longer. Since the American naval victory at Midway Island over a year earlier, the Japanese defeat by the Australians at Milne Bay and the subsequent victory by the Americans at Guadalcanal, the Japanese had been forced to stop advancing and instead consolidate the territory they already occupied. However, it had come at a terrible cost in Allied lives as the Japanese chose to die to a man rather than surrender.

Jessica returned her attention to the pile of communications forms on her desk, searching for those that needed to be transmitted to RAAF HQ for action. When she'd first started working in the Brisbane HQ she'd caused quite a stir in the male-dominated intelligence office. She was a beautiful young woman and her olive skin and jet-black hair gave a hint of her Aboriginal blood. These days everyone was too consumed by the urgency of decoding the Japanese radio intercepts to pay much attention to her. Besides, her thoughts were with Lieutenant Tony Caccamo, a friend who had been mysteriously absent from the department since Christmas. Tony seemed to be some kind of troubleshooter for the colonel's office and she worried about where he was and what he might be doing.

Tony was not the only one living a life of subterfuge. Jessica had been asked by Prime Minister Curtin himself to spy on the Americans, or at least to ensure they were not withholding information from their Australian allies. It was the patriotic thing to do, Jessica knew that, but if her American colleagues ever found out about it, she would likely disappear without any questions being asked. It was a disconcerting thought.

★

In a small obscure cafe of lino-covered floor and well-worn artificial marble topped tables in Sydney's central business district, two well-dressed men met and ordered tea and sandwiches for lunch. The younger of the two was in his mid-twenties, tall and good-looking. His tailored suit had cost more than the man sitting opposite him would earn in a month. The older man was in his mid-forties and had the pallid complexion of an office worker.

The cafe was empty except for two young sailors sitting in a corner, talking loudly and consuming meat pies covered in tomato sauce. They paid little attention to the two men sitting by the doorway.

'Good to catch up, old chap,' the older man said. 'Canberra feels that you are doing a good job in lieu of your brother-in-law, Charles.'

'How is Charles faring?' Donald Macintosh asked as the waitress, a young girl barely fifteen, placed a pot of tea and two cups and saucers on their table. She withdrew before the man Donald knew as Allan Saxby answered.

'Your brother-in-law is doing well,' Saxby answered. 'I believe he is flying a Beaufighter out of Milne Bay. I have been informed that your sister, Sarah, has made you an uncle.'

'Not much you don't know, Mr Saxby,' Donald said, turning the pot to mix the tea leaves which he suspected would be few and far between thanks to severe rationing.

'Well, we know just a little more thanks to our contact in Mac's HQ in Brisbane,' Saxby replied, glancing at the noisy young sailors on the other side of the room. 'We would like you to go up to Brisbane and have a chat with Sergeant Duffy as soon as possible. The PM is concerned about this thing in the Bismarck Sea. He is not sure if Mac is keeping him fully informed about affairs to our north.'

'From what I have been able to glean it is just another military engagement,' Donald began pouring the coloured hot water into the cups as the waitress returned with a small jug of milk. He glanced up at her. 'Do you have any sugar?'

'Sorry, mister,' she said, placing the jug on the table, 'our ration ran out. But for two bob I might be able to lay my hands on some.'

'Never mind,' Donald responded. 'We will take our tea without sugar.'

'Ah, it is good to see that enterprise still thrives in these difficult times,' Saxby sighed when the waitress had left to fetch their sandwiches.

'You mean the black market,' Donald growled.

'Not that the family of Sir George Macintosh would know about such shortages,' Saxby said in a sly tone. 'Your government contracts supplying our American friends have proved to be very lucrative.'

Donald did not reply. He knew the comment was a way of reminding him why he had agreed to cooperate with the representative of the Australian government sitting at the table with him. Donald had not wanted to act as the intermediary between Sergeant Jessica Duffy and the government contact, as he had been in love with Jessica before the war. He had convinced himself it was all over when she had taken vows as a Catholic nun, but she had unexpectedly reappeared in his life the year before – and she was no longer a nun.

'Does Curtin think we might still be under threat from invasion?' Donald asked, forcing his thoughts away from Jessica.

'He does,' Saxby replied. 'But he feels that the outcome of a clash in the Bismarck Sea might decide the future. If we win he feels that the Japs will be forced to concede any real hope of remaining in New Guinea. It is vital that the PM has all the intelligence coming out of MacArthur's HQ.'

'You know what you ask of Sergeant Duffy is dangerous,' Donald cautioned.

'I believe that she is a patriotic Australian and as such accepts the risks,' Saxby said. 'We all have to make sacrifices.'

Donald looked at the well-fed public servant with contempt. Saxby was not risking his life; he led a safe and comfortable existence. Donald did too, but he felt guilt for his own protected role in Australia. He was fit enough to serve in the armed forces but his father had ensured his job had been classified as essential, exempting him from military service. As time had gone on Donald had come to accept that his father had been right. Donald had been instrumental in the organisation of provisions for the American allies sent to Australia. It was true that this had proved to be extremely lucrative, but it was still an essential role. Nothing was black and white in his world, and it was in the grey areas that the Macintosh financial empire thrived.

The two men ate the sandwiches of devon and tomato sauce when they were placed before them, and Donald was glad that he would be going home to a hearty steak at the end of the day, washed down with a bottle of good champagne.

Saxby finished his tea and sandwiches, reached for his hat and bid Donald a good day, leaving the young man to consider his upcoming meeting with Jessica Duffy. He was fortunate that Olivia Barrington, the woman who had shared his bed, had been posted back to the United States in her role as a Red Cross nurse. It made life less compli-cated if he did not have to lie about who he was meeting in Brisbane. They had parted more friends than lovers, and both knew the affair had run its course.

*

The heat of the tropical day shimmered like water across the hard-packed earthen airstrip where Pilot Officer Charles

Huntley's twin-engine Beaufighter was parked, ready for action. Milne Bay was not Charles's choice of postings as it took him far from the comforts of his old life in Sydney. As he sat in the shade of his tent he held a letter that made the terrible isolation even harder to bear: he was now the father of a healthy baby boy. As he had not received a single letter from his estranged wife since he had enlisted, he was not surprised that the correspondence had come from his brother-in-law, Donald Macintosh. Charles felt a wave of relief at the news. He had had a terrible suspicion that David Macintosh was the father of his wife's child, but the date of the baby's birth proved he could not be as, by Charles's calculations, the man had not been in Sydney at the right time. The boy must be his.

A fellow RAAF pilot ducked under the tent he shared with Charles and flung his cap on his own camp stretcher, plonking himself on a stool beside his cot.

'Good news, I hope,' he said, observing the expression on his friend's face.

'I have just been informed that I have been promoted to fatherhood,' Charles answered with a broad smile. In his late twenties, Charles was almost a decade older than most of the pilots in the squadron, and his colleagues had already starting calling him Dad for that reason.

'Jolly good show, old chap,' his tent mate said, rising to slap him on the back. 'That means you will have to shout the mess. Nothing much else happening around this hell-hole at the moment.'

Just then a young orderly room clerk poked his head into the tent. 'You are required immediately at the briefing tent. Big flap on.'

The two pilots glanced at each other quizzically. Charles shrugged and they both ambled over to a larger tent set back in the jungle. Charles had heard bits and pieces at the intelligence briefings that suggested the Japanese were mustering a substantial naval force to reinforce their garrisons in New Guinea. The last he had heard was that American fighters and bombers had clashed with the Japanese navy and air force over the Bismarck Sea. He guessed that this urgent briefing would have something to do with that.

He went to reach for the letter that informed him of his son's birth, then realised with superstitious dread that he had somehow dropped it in the scrub on their way to the briefing tent. Charles experienced a sharp pang of apprehension, as the piece of paper had suddenly taken on the status of a lucky talisman. Pilots were a superstitious lot, and many strange objects became lucky tokens to them.

Already he could see the armourers dragging heavy belts of 20 millimetre explosive bullets to the aircraft parked along the strip. Bombs, too, were being loaded onto small trolleys as airmen stripped down to their shorts worked feverishly to arm the deadly snub-nosed, twin-engine bombers the enemy had come to nickname 'the whispering death'. This was because the sleeve valves in the engines were quieter than the poppet valves of other aircraft. The relative silence of a swooping Beaufighter caught the unsuspecting enemy in a hail of nose-mounted cannon shells and machine gun bullets fired from the wing.

*

The rain had not abated all week, but Major David Macintosh did not mind. At least he and his company were able to shelter from the deluge without fear of being shot at. The battalion's return from the New Guinea campaign for respite and training had taken them out of the firing line. Now they were posted to the highlands of far north

Queensland, west of Cairns, in camps of sturdily erected tents and semi-permanent buildings of timber that housed the quartermaster's stores, battalion HQ and the vital cookhouse.

David was in the large tent he had established as company HQ. He sat at a small folding table, poring over reports submitted to him from his platoon commanders and those sent down from battalion HQ. David's promotion had been authorised just before the battalion had withdrawn from the heavy fighting of the New Guinea theatre of operations, and he had been given command of a rifle company and awarded a Military Cross for his actions in North Africa.

When the rain eased David and his men would go back to clearing the heavily forested land to build a parade ground that would also double as a football field, and David was fortunate that in his company were many northern New South Wales soldiers who had been timber cutters before the war.

The posting back to Australian soil meant a chance for men to recover from lingering illnesses such as malaria and scrub typhus, and the Regimental Medical Officer had noted that many of the men were recovering an average forty pounds of weight which they had lost while fighting in the mountains of New Guinea, and then down on the mangrove plains, pushing the Japanese off the large island. In the fighting at Buna, Gona and Sananda more men had been lost in a few weeks than had been killed in all the months on the Kokoda Track. David's company had lost men he had served with in the deserts of North Africa and the rugged hills of Greece and Syria. It all seemed a lifetime ago but was in fact less than a year.

In one corner of the tent was his company clerk, Corporal Lansing, who also examined the soldiers' pay books, ration sheets for the catering section and the quartermaster's stores list for replacement equipment.

The rain pounded on the canvas and ran in rivulets under the duckboard floor, as well as dripping through tiny holes in the tent. Both company commander and clerk suffered damp uniforms, but at least they were not soaked to the skin as they had so often been in New Guinea.

The flap of the tent was flung open and a rain-drenched soldier wearing his gas cape as a raincoat dragged in a large canvas bag full of mail. He also had a small bundle of paper which David knew was the routine orders from battalion HQ, to be posted on the noticeboard outside the tent. The corporal clerk immediately dropped his clerical duties to open the bag and begin sorting the mail into platoon allocations.

'Got one for you, boss,' the corporal said, passing a letter to David.

David also knew immediately who it was from because of the neat handwriting. He opened the letter eagerly and unfolded the two pages. It was from Allison in Sydney, and an image of her face immediately came into his mind. He could visualise the beautiful young woman with her startling green eyes, alabaster skin and raven hair cut stylishly short. Her first piece of news was that his cousin Sarah had given birth to a baby boy. He felt that her estranged husband would be pleased. At least Charles had got something from being married to Sarah – a son of his own blood.

Although their letters had never gone beyond the bounds of friendship, David hoped to see a lot of Allison if and when he was in Sydney again. They had met at a party at the Macintosh residence to celebrate his return from the Middle East the previous year; her husband had been killed flying in the battle to save Milne Bay. Allison now worked as a legal secretary for none other than his beloved 'Uncle' Sean Duffy after she had transferred to his legal practice six months earlier. At the end of the letter Allison mentioned that Sean was not a well man, and she hoped that David could return to Sydney to see him. David was upset to read this news as the man had been the only father he'd known for as long as he could remember. However, only a miracle would get him leave to travel to Sydney at this stage of the return as they established their battalion area.

Just then David saw the miracle staring him in the face – in the freshly delivered RO's on his desk. Amongst the list of names of battalion personnel to attend courses was his own. He was to be sent to Sydney to attend an officers' course, substantiating his promotion to major. David wanted to whoop with joy but knew that was not conduct becoming a company commander; instead he simply broke into a broad smile that creased his rugged, weather-beaten face. He was only in his mid-twenties, tall, broad shouldered and physically tough, but his eyes told a different story. His eyes were those of an old soul.

TWO

Death came whispering over the Bismarck Sea to strike the Japanese fleet. It also flew high above with the big, four-engine bombers and American P38 Lightning fighters.

Charles Huntley's stomach-churning fear was gone as he made a sweeping turn to drop down and level off at five hundred feet. In his gun sights was the stern of a Japanese destroyer and he was vaguely aware of the tracer rising towards him and tiny men running around on the deck of the enemy fighting ship. A hundred yards away he opened up with his cannon and machine guns, aiming at the bridge of the destroyer. His strafing run took him from stem to stern, raking the ship with gunfire, causing his own aircraft to shudder from the heavy recoil. The objective of the head-on attack was to inflict damage on the ship and obliterate anyone on the bridge, putting the ship's command out of action.

Charles pulled on the controls to rise just above the ship's mast. He could feel the slight shudder of incoming small-arms fire hitting the fuselage. He needed to avoid enemy fire from other craft in the sea which was crowded with destroyers and troopships whose decks were packed with soldiers preparing to disembark in landing craft.

Charles was startled as fuel drop tanks hurtled past his aircraft from the higher flying American fighters. They discarded them for more manoeuvrability in dogfights with Japanese fighter aircraft sent to disrupt the Allied attack on the invasion convoy.

'Look at that, skipper!' Charles heard over his headset. It was the voice of his radio wireless operator, Sergeant Ted Reid, who was busily reloading the aircraft's cannon with 40 pound drums of ammunition, behind him in the cramped aircraft.

Charles swung around to see American B25 light bombers skimming across the sea. From their noses poured a deadly hail of machine gun bullets as their two 500 pound bombs were released to skip across the waters and slam into the sides of Japanese ships with devastating explosions. The sea was boiling with death as missiles from high-flying bombers caused huge columns of water to spout, nearly engulfing the low-flying RAAF Beaufighters and B25 light bombers. Enemy ships were exploding, burning and slowly sinking, and the sea was full of the bobbing heads of Japanese sailors and soldiers who had abandoned their doomed vessels.

Where ever Charles turned his attention beyond the cockpit he could see aircraft swooping, wheeling and diving. He shuddered when he noticed the great red circle on fighters above and realised that the Japanese fighters were engaging in the fight, attempting to intercept the low flying light bombers and Beaufighters. But the American fighter pilots fought desperately to prevent the interference.

'Look out, skipper, Jap fighter three o'clock high,' Charles heard his observer scream down the intercom headset.

Charles swung his head and could see the deadly Japanese Zero firing its 20 millimetre cannon at them. He executed a desperate manoeuvre, tipping his fighter bomber on its right wing as the stream of tracer ripped past to splash in spouts in the sea only five hundred feet below. He knew that he could not outfly the faster, lighter Zero and was stunned to see it suddenly ripped apart in an exploding fireball. From the corner of his eye he saw an American Lightning fighter swoop past, and Charles found himself saying a heartfelt thankyou under his breath.

In a Beaufighter not far from Charles's own aircraft a war photographer balanced his camera on the head of the pilot, standing behind him without a harness and filming the battle through the nose cockpit. Damian Parer's short documentary would be in Australian cinemas within weeks under the title *The Battle for the Bismarck Sea*.

'Time to go home, Sergeant Reid,' Charles called to his crewman through the intercom.

Already other Beaufighters were peeling away, ammunition spent, and navigating back to Milne Bay. Time had lost all meaning during the battle and only now, with the loud drone of the twin engines either side of him, did Charles have time to reflect on how close they had come. Already Sergeant Reid was reporting that they had taken a lot of small-arms fire and were lucky to be in the air at all. Charles prayed that the luck he had had today would stay with him and he would one day return home to hold his newborn son in his arms.

★

Many thousands of miles south in the sleepy country town of Goulburn on a property just outside of town Sarah Huntley stared down at the sickly baby in her lap. His premature birth had left the baby boy teetering on the verge of death, and only urgent medical intervention had kept him alive. But he now appeared to be growing stronger if his loud bawling was anything to go by. Sarah gazed down at the baby in her arms as he suckled on her breast and felt nothing but frustration and resentment at his existence.

'Valery, take the baby,' Sarah commanded to the woman hovering anxiously nearby. Valery Keevers was an experienced nanny who had been hired to care for the newborn baby. She was a single woman in her early thirties and her face was etched with concern. She stepped forward and gently took the baby from Sarah's arms.

'I will engage a wet nurse for Michael,' she said, rocking the crying boy in her arms. 'There is a young mother in Goulburn who has lost her baby and needs the money. Her husband has been killed in the war.'

'I will trust your judgement,' Sarah said, buttoning her blouse and wondering why she could feel no maternal bonds with this new life. In fact, she had come to resent the baby's demands for attention when she knew that her real role in life was managing the considerable family fortune from its base in Sydney. For the last two months of her confinement in the rural backblocks she had received reports that her brother Donald was being looked to by the shareholders as the centre of power in the Macintosh companies. She bridled at being left out of the important decision-making all because of a squalling infant. She needed to return to Sydney as soon as possible. Valery Keevers could act as a de facto mother to Michael: she seemed to have a bond with the infant already. The fact that Sarah's estranged husband Charles considered the baby his was an asset, as she could always use Michael as a means to control him in the future – should he survive the war.

The cold had begun to sweep the plains around Goulburn and soon it would bring snow to the villages higher up in the hills, but Sarah was warmed by the thought that she could now return to Sydney and resume her role as the future leader of the Macintosh financial empire.

*

The railway journey across the vast Nullarbor desert from west to east was an exhausting ordeal. The carriages were uncomfortable and crowded with khaki-uniformed Australian soldiers and white-jacketed sailors. Sleep was impossible as the train clack-clacked loudly, throwing off coal smoke as it traversed the steel rails that spanned the nation.

Amidst the passengers was a small group of civilians, and amongst those non-military passengers was an older Canadian man, a young Chinese woman holding a baby girl, and a European boy around five years old. Cyril Blacksmith had been an aircraft engineer but was now retired. His Chinese wife, Po, was considerably younger, and he had become a father later in life. Their daughter, Lan, was a beautiful child of Eurasian appearance and could have passed as a life-sized doll. She had attracted admiring attention from some of the older servicemen travelling on the train, men who had not seen their own children in years. The little girl was a reminder of what they had left behind in order to serve their country in its darkest hour, fighting for its very survival.

So far 1943 had not seen any real change in the Pacific war, although newspapers reported that the Germans were taking reverses on the Eastern Front against the Russians. Late last year the church bells had rung out across Britain for the first time in years to celebrate Montgomery's great desert victory in the second battle of El Alamein. The Germans under Rommel had been defeated and pushed back across the top of North Africa.

The young boy on the train, Patrick, was not Cyril's son but that of his former employer, Diane Duffy, now a prisoner of the Japanese in Changi prison at Singapore. Cyril had promised Diane that he would get her son safely to Australia, and he was to be taken to Sydney, to a prominent lawyer, Sean Duffy, who would be able to arrange his welfare. Cyril had also arranged for employment in the aircraft industry, as he had excellent qualifications now in great demand by a country at war.

Cyril glanced at the boy staring out of the window at what seemed to be endless plains to the horizon. Since his birth he had been raised in the Far East with its noisy, crowded cities, green paddy fields and mountains covered with lush vegetation. The country he now gazed at was harsh and dry with very few features.

'We should reach Adelaide in the morning,' Cyril said, sensing the boy's frustration at being cooped up on the train for so long. 'You will be able to stretch your legs and have a bit of a look around.'

Patrick turned to Cyril and sighed. 'I wish Mummy was with us.'

'She will be one day,' Cyril said, reaching out to grip the boy's shoulder reassuringly, but privately wondering if she would survive the horrors of Japanese imprisonment. Already stories were leaking out concerning the appalling way the enemy treated prisoners. What the Japanese had done in China before the war was well known in the west, the atrocities recorded on file and in print by eyewitnesses.

'Is Mr Duffy a nice man?' Patrick suddenly asked.

'I suppose so,' Cyril answered, releasing his grip on the boy's shoulder. 'Your mother has spoken highly of him, and I am sure that he will be very kind to you. Auntie Po, Lan and myself will not be far away in Sydney,' he added. 'He sounded very keen to meet you when I was able to speak to him on the telephone.'

Patrick returned to staring out the window and Cyril leaned back in his seat to gaze at his daughter in his wife's lap. She had her thumb in her mouth and slept blissfully unaware of the horrors of a wider world to the north of her new home.

*

Lieutenant Tony Caccamo checked into the merchant seamen's boarding house located in the infamous Rocks section of Sydney Harbour, overlooking the city's Circular Quay. The building was rundown and in need of repairs, but the tiny room he had to himself was clean enough. Beside his single sagging bed he had a rickety chair and a tall wardrobe. He had not achieved his mission to execute the rogue British officer, and as he lay on his bed staring at the fly-specked ceiling, he cursed himself for accepting the covert mission in the first place. Since his failed attempt to shoot Ulverstone at the residence of Sir George Macintosh, he had spent his days wandering the city, frequenting insalubrious hotel bars around Sydney's dock areas. Only once had he made contact with his commanding officer, when he had come down to attend a meeting in Sydney. They had arranged to meet in Hyde Park, and Tony had briefed the American intelligence colonel on what had occurred.

'I trust in you to come up with a solution, Lieutenant Caccamo,' the colonel had replied, chomping on his cigar. 'I heard you were one of the best back in New York.' Tony had wanted to say that he had been one of the best at arresting murderers, not becoming one himself. He had bitten back his retort because he knew that in time of war all the rules went out the window.

The colonel had spat a remnant of the loose tobacco on the ground and stared at the pigeons fluttering around a great water fountain. 'I can tell you that what we are doing is sanctioned by the limeys' MI6. They have gone behind Churchill's back on this. They are as frustrated as we are that Ulverstone has not been arrested as a traitor. But lords seem to be untouchable in the British system. So the Brits have left their dirty work to us . . . or should I say, to you.'

Tony knew exactly what the colonel meant. Should he be caught, the American government would disown him, with the excuse that he was a deranged soldier acting on his own. The former New York detective knew that his boss was smart enough to have already written up the papers declaring him a deserter with mental problems in the eventuality of his being caught.

'I will need some more time,' Tony said. 'He is not an easy man to get alone. I blew my chance with him when he was visiting Sir George Macintosh.'

'When you finish with Ulverstone we should get you to knock off the Aussie's goddamned Prime Minister, Curtin,' the colonel said with a short laugh. 'He turns a blind eye to his longshoremen sabotaging our supply system on the wharves.'

'They call them wharfies in this country,' Tony said. 'I have heard stories from some of the merchant seamen about how the sons of bitches have been dumping supplies meant for our boys in the harbour. Most of their union are made up of commies.'

'Well, if we can't get rid of their commie-loving prime minister, we might be able to arrange for a few of these Aussie wharfies to end up in the harbour.'

Tony turned to glance at the colonel sitting beside him, and wondered if he was simply joking. But he did not see any humour in his face and shuddered. All Tony wanted was to get the job over with and return to his normal posting back at MacArthur's HQ in Brisbane where he could be close to Jessica Duffy. It had been a long time since he'd seen her, and these weeks alone on the secret operation had given him ample time to confront the fact that he was falling in love with her.

'Is there anything else, sir?' Tony asked, and the American officer shook his head and strolled away through a flock of pigeons.

Tony had felt very much alone as he had watched his commanding officer disappear into the crowds of other uniformed men on the sidewalk opposite the park. He had reconciled himself to the fact that what he was doing was morally right, but he would never have guessed that his war would turn out to be fought on the streets of Sydney. Here in this city, if he was convicted of killing a high-ranking British officer, he would be hanged for murder.

*

Sarah's appearance in the Macintosh boardroom in Sydney was like a lightning bolt. The murmuring of the grey-haired men sitting around the great table in the smoke-filled room ceased as she appeared wearing a chic blouse and skirt ensemble that showed off her trim figure. Her brother

Donald was just as startled as the other ten men in the room but he rose to greet her courteously.

'Sarah, what a surprise to see you here today,' he said from the head of the table. 'I am sure that I extend my congratulations, and those of the board members here today, on the birth of your son, Michael. We did not expect you back so soon.'

'Thank you, Donald, and thank you, gentlemen,' Sarah responded in a clear voice of command. 'My baby is with his nanny and is well tended to. This has allowed me to return to my duties on the board of management, where I belong in these difficult times.'

She stepped to the end of the table opposite her brother and a board member rose to politely pull the chair out for her. She thanked him and sat down, removing her long gloves. Donald resumed his seat, and for a moment there was a silence as if he was gathering his thoughts.

'I hope I have not caused you to forget what is on the agenda for today, Donald,' Sarah said sweetly, knowing that her unexpected appearance had done just that. 'Glancing at the papers before me, I gather we were talking about beef production.'

'Yes, yes,' Donald said, shuffling the papers in front of him.

The meeting continued but Sarah did not contribute anything to the discussion. Her aim was simply to remind the board members that she was back.

When the meeting ended and the other members had left, Donald walked up to his sister. 'I have to be honest and say that I think you have returned to work too early.'

'I don't think so,' Sarah retorted, rising from her chair and slipping on her expensive gloves. 'As you are quite aware, I'm sure, not once while I was in Goulburn did I receive any company reports.'

'You were having a baby and I thought that would be your main preoccupation,' Donald answered with an exasperated look. 'After all, is it not the role of a woman to have babies and look after them?'

'The war has changed a lot of things, big brother,' Sarah said, staring into Donald's eyes. 'My baby is well looked after, and I have the brains to run our family enterprises as well as you – if not better. I have already met with Father and he supports my decision to return. So I shall go to my office and see if it is as I left it.'

With that, Sarah turned on her high heels and walked away, happy in the knowledge that Donald was both angry and frustrated that she was back.

THREE

Sergeant Jessica Duffy sat in a Brisbane cafe with a cup of tea before her. The only customer at this time of the morning, she was deep in thought when a man wearing an expensive suit sat down opposite her at the scratched, formica-covered table. He was in his mid-twenties, with aristocratic good looks, and he had the strong physique of the Macintosh men, an inheritance of their Irish Scots ancestors.

'Hello, Jessie,' he said warmly. 'It has been a while since we last met.'

Jessica returned the smile. She had been in love with this man before the war, before she had taken vows as a Catholic. She had since left her order, and now she was a single woman working for the war effort.

'Hello, Donald,' Jessica responded. 'You are looking well.'

There was a slight awkwardness between the two of them, which they both did their best to ignore.

'I can see that you have a cup of tea,' Donald said. 'I should also order.' He rose to go to the counter where a heavily built Greek man with a five o'clock shadow took his order.

'I would like to tell you that the Prime Minister's Department was very pleased with the information you passed on to me at our last meeting,' Donald said, sitting down again and speaking softly so as not to be overheard. 'It confirmed suspicions that our American allies do not tell us everything.'

'From what I have overheard at HQ,' Jessica said quietly, 'MacArthur considers Australia a weak target to be exploited by the Japs. He does not seem to have a very good impression of us. He considers that he has secured the South West Pacific, but now the real threat is from the northern areas of Australia.'

Donald had learned from his contacts close to the PM that Curtin still harboured a private fear that the Japanese might invade the country, although he did not declare this in public.

Jessica continued with other snippets of information she had overheard or seen in transmissions between the Americans. She was able to provide information about the personalities of highly ranked American officers; the petty jealousies between them, and the internal politics that drove their careers.

Donald did not take written notes but listened intently to each name she mentioned. It was as important to know your friends as it was to know your enemy in the Machiavellian world of global politics.

That year, 1943, had opened with some victories in the Pacific, but the Japanese were far from beaten, and had the potential to counterattack with great force. Donald was also aware that the American government had thrown most of its war resources towards the European theatre of conflict, with the philosophic global strategy that the Nazis had to be defeated first.

'There is someone else on the staff at HQ,' Jessica said finally. 'He is an American military policeman, Lieutenant Anthony Caccamo. He seems to have dropped right out of sight. I am hoping that your contacts might have some information about his whereabouts.'

Donald frowned. 'He would not happen to be the man I saw you with at the PM's Sydney conference late last year?'

'Yes, about the same time I saw you with that American woman,' Jessica retorted.

'Touché,' Donald said with a small smile. 'Does he play an important role on Mac's staff?'

'Tony is a bit of a mystery man,' Jessica said. 'I get the impression that he is an odd-jobs man for the Americans, although of course he never speaks about his work. I tried to find out if he had been posted overseas but that does not seem to be the case. From what I can gather he is still somewhere in the country.'

'I will see what I can find out about your man,' Donald said just as the cafe owner delivered a pot of tea and chipped cup and saucer to the table.

'Will you be staying in Brisbane?' Jessica asked after the burly man had retreated behind his counter and begun to wipe down the benchtop.

'I am afraid not,' Donald replied. 'I have to return to Sydney on the train tonight. I am fearful of my sister returning to work.'

'That does not sound as though it's anything to worry about,' Jessica said.

'You don't know my sister,' Donald said, screwing up his face. 'She appears to have been born without human feelings for others – including her new baby. She's a chip off the old block and she is out to take complete control of the family enterprises.'

'I thought that you might wish to rush back to your lady love,' Jessica said, sipping the last of her tea.

'It was you who broke your promise to me,' Donald said in a low, angry voice. 'You did not tell me that you had resigned from being a nun. I had given up hope. As it is Olivia and I have tacitly chosen to separate.'

Jessica knew that he was right, but could not stop the feeling of his perceived betrayal. Then she also remembered how she had felt the attraction to the former New York policeman, and regretted her jibe. Jessica was confused at her own feelings. She had always thought that Donald was no longer of interest to her romantically, but every time she was in his presence she felt a small spark that threatened to grow into a fire. 'I harbour fears that Tony's life may be in danger, and he is a good man,' she said.

'Nothing more?' Donald asked but Jessica did not reply. 'I will see what I can do. I know that what you are doing for us comes at a cost. No doubt you feel you are betraying the trust of your colleagues and friends at Mac's HQ, but the defence of this country must always be our priority.'

Jessica did feel guilt at what she was doing, as she had come to love the generosity and openness of the Americans she knew. She was also aware that they could be ruthless when it suited them.

'I should go,' Donald said, rising from the table and leaving his tea untouched. 'I will pass on what we have discussed here, and we will meet in about a month's time. Keep up the good work.'

'I will do my best,' Jessica replied. 'But I can't promise results.'

Donald looked down at Jessica sitting at the table. 'You are an extraordinary woman, Jessica Duffy,' he said, donning his hat and stepping away to walk outside into the bright winter sunshine.

★

Sydney solicitor and Great War veteran Sean Duffy leaned on his walking stick in his city apartment. Beside him stood a young boy staring apprehensively at the closed door.

'Who is it, Uncle Sean?' he asked as the door opened and a tall man stepped inside, wearing an army uniform and carrying a kitbag over his shoulder.

'David!' Sean exclaimed in joy. 'It is good to see you, son.'

Major David Duffy stepped forward with a broad smile across his rugged face and embraced the older man in a great bear hug.

'Uncle Sean, great to see you too,' he said and turned to glance curiously at the young boy standing beside Sean, gazing up at him with a mixture of awe and fear.

'David, this is Master Patrick Duffy,' Sean replied, limping over to a settee to sit down and ease the burden on his tin legs. 'He has come to stay with me until I can sort something out for him.'

'Another in the clan, by the sounds of it,' David said, crouching down to inspect the grave face of the little boy. He extended his hand and the boy shook it shyly, intimidated by this giant who smelled of tobacco and sweat.

'Young Patrick here is a distant relative of yours,' Sean said. 'He is the son of your cousin Matthew. His mother, Diane, is currently in Japanese captivity in Changi prison.

It seems Diane named their son Patrick in honour of the original Patrick Duffy, who came to the colonies way back in the 1850s. Sadly, Matthew never got to see his son, as he was killed by some fanatic in Iraq before the war.'

'I remember hearing about his death,' David said straightening up and turning back to Sean. 'What are you going to do about young Patrick?'

Sean shook his head. 'I was shocked to hear that he was on his way, but he is blood, and it is my duty to look after him until his mother returns.'

'Aren't you getting a bit old to look after kids, Uncle Sean?' David asked.

'I bloody well virtually raised you,' Sean snorted. 'You were a handful, and I think young Patrick might prove to have more manners than you did.'

'Ah, point taken,' David grinned. 'I guess you and Uncle Harry did keep me on the straight and narrow.'

The man Sean referred to as Uncle Harry was Harry Griffiths who was also a Great War veteran and ran a boxing gym in Sydney. Harry had worked for Sean as his private investigator, as he had been a policeman before the outbreak of the Great War. He had enlisted and, like Sean, been wounded on the Western Front. Harry had turned David into a very good heavyweight fighter who might have had a chance of representing Australia in the Olympic Games. But war had changed everything. Instead of in the ring, David had fought in the Spanish Civil War, the deserts of North Africa, the mountains of Greece and Syria, and now the green hell of New Guinea.

'I believe that congratulations are in order for your MC,' Sean said, gazing at the purple and white riband on David's chest.

'Yeah, the army throws the odd one out occasionally,' David said. 'I know you have one or two like it yourself.'

'Well, as young Patrick is too young to join us at the pub, I thought we might eat in tonight and have a beer together,' Sean said, rising to his feet with the assistance of his cane. 'I made up a good old-fashioned Irish stew for us – more vegetable than meat, of course, thanks to rationing.'

'That sounds grand, Uncle Sean,' David said, propping his kitbag against a chair. Patrick was watching his every move. 'Come to think of it,' David continued, 'I might have something in my kit that the young fellow would like.'

David pushed his hand into the top of the sausage-shaped kitbag to retrieve a small brass aeroplane made from empty bullet cartridges and scrap bronze. It had been crafted by a soldier in the workshops and David had purchased it from the enterprising young man. The soldiers also turned the leaf springs from vehicle suspensions into Japanese Samurai swords and sold them to naive Yank servicemen for a good price. David had been planning to give the aeroplane to Sean as a paperweight, but given the expression of delight on Patrick's face when he handed the heavy object to him, David didn't think his uncle would mind.

'Thank you,' Patrick said reverently, gripping the brass aeroplane as if it were made of gold.

'You can call me Uncle David,' David said. 'I like the sound of that as I don't have any kids of my own.'

The three sat at the table in Sean's clean and neat flat with the plates of steaming stew before them. A loaf of fresh white bread sat on a wooden board beside a small tub of dripping, and Sean poured two glasses of beer, along with a glass of cordial for Patrick.

When Sean glanced from David to Patrick he experienced a strange feeling of joy and sadness. He had lost the love of his life last year when Louise, the estranged wife of Sir George Macintosh, had died of cancer. Her death had made him question the very reason for living, and he had even considered suicide. He had drowned in many bottles of strong liquor to dull the pain, but the news of Patrick's arrival had given him the feeling that he had something to live for after all. He had never been a father, but he had raised David and now he must raise another, at least until his mother returned to claim him. How long that would be depended on many things, and one of those things was winning the war so that Patrick's mother could be liberated from Japanese captivity. In the meantime he could only hope she managed to survive the harsh conditions of the camps.

'I know there is one young lady who has been counting the days until you return,' Sean said to David with a smile. 'She bothers me every day whether I have heard from you.'

'Allison,' David said, returning the smile. 'Her letters have kept me going, but she has never expressed any romantic interest in me.'

'I have come to learn a little about Miss Lowe since she took up her position with my law firm,' Sean said. 'She is very reserved. She has reverted to her maiden name, which I suspect is her way of putting behind her the tragedy of losing her husband and baby, but I think she is afraid of losing anyone else close to her. So I don't want you to go upsetting a young lady I like a lot.'

'I can reassure you, Uncle Sean, that given this bloody war does not look like ending soon, I am in no position to make plans for romance.'

'I can tell you, my boy, that it's bloody near impossible to resist the right woman when she comes into your life, no matter how hard you might try. Believe me, I know from experience.'

'I hardly know Allison,' David said.

Sean smiled and shook his head. He raised his glass of beer as a salute. 'To love and war,' he said, leaving David to reflect for a moment on the two women in his life – Allison and Sarah.

★

Sir George Macintosh stared at the wall in his office. It was adorned with the Aboriginal weapons collected from Glen View after the massacre of the native people who had once lived there peacefully. That peaceful time had changed eighty years earlier, when the Native Mounted Police had descended to 'disperse' Wallarie's clan. Wallarie had been the last of his people and his death a decade earlier should have ended the curse on the Macintosh family, who had authorised the killing of the men, women and children that terrible morning so long ago. However, to Sir George it seemed that the curse had persisted. He had just returned from an appointment with his specialist, who had informed him that the new wonder drug penicillin could be used to cure syphilis. However, Sir George's sickness was too far gone for treatment, and the disease was entering its terminal stages. Damn the disease, thought Sir George, he had too much left to do to ensure the family's future to die.

The sun was setting outside and the shadows crept across the floor of the dimly lit library. It was time to turn on the lights.

A knock at the door broke Sir George's melancholy thoughts.

'Come in,' he called.

Sarah walked inside and kissed him briefly on the cheek. He noted how cold her kiss was.

Sarah sat down on a divan by a large French window overlooking the white-stone gravel driveway leading up from the great wrought-iron gates of the mansion.

'I believe your appearance at the board meeting rather took everyone by surprise,' he said by way of greeting. 'Are you well enough to resume your management roles?'

'I had a baby, Father, not a life-threatening illness,' Sarah replied.

'I gather you named him Michael,' Sir George said. 'You know that is a name not welcome in our family. Why did you do that?'

'It was a whim,' Sarah said. 'I don't think a name has much to do with anything.'

'It does when it is linked with the Macintosh name,' Sir George said.

'Well, that is ironic,' Sarah said bitterly. 'Especially when you and I know the baby's father is also a Macintosh. At present he does not appear to resemble either his namesake or his father. He is weak and sickly.'

'Jehovah has punished you for lying down with your cousin,' Sir George said, and Sarah laughed.

'Who are you to speak of God when I have never seen you do one charitable thing in your life – unless it was meant to further your reputation as a philanthropist. No, Father, it was my desire for David that brought about the birth of this baby, not your Jehovah.'

Sir George seethed at the thought that his grandson was of the blood of a man he had done everything possible to eliminate. Still, he had to admire his daughter's guts. She was not afraid to stand up to him, and he had discovered this was a rare quality when a person held as much power as he did. His only son Donald was a weakling in comparison, and Sir George had long come to realise that it would be his daughter who would rule the Macintosh empire when he was gone from this world. She had already abandoned her married name and resumed her maiden name of Macintosh, and her son would be known as Michael Macintosh.

'One of the servants informed me that there was a disturbing incident here a few weeks ago,' Sarah said, changing the subject. 'I was told that a man was loitering in the grounds with a gun.'

'We are not certain that the man had a gun,' Sir George said. 'And since then there have been no other problems.'

'Do you think you might have been the target of the intruder?' Sarah asked.

'If you think that it was some jealous husband on the rampage, I can assure you those days are long behind me,' Sir George said with a half-smile. 'No, I suspect that it was some criminal intending on breaking into our house to rob it.'

'Would that not be too risky?' Sarah countered. 'Considering that we have servants on the premises, and you have a pistol by your bed. Surely a burglar would not chance such a risky venture.'

Sir George pondered on his daughter's words. He had dismissed the incident as an attempted robbery, but perhaps there was a different explanation. Was it possible that Lord Ulverstone had been the intended target? If so, why? He knew that the British aristocrat had been linked to Fascist causes in England before the war, and he suspected that the links went much deeper, but Ulverstone was one of Britain's esteemed upper class and surely not capable of outright treason.

'You can sleep soundly,' Sir George lied to his daughter, 'there is nothing to worry about.' In fact she had caused him to reassess the whole incident, and he thought again about the long-dead warrior, Wallarie, and the curse he had laid upon the Macintosh family. This kind of mischief was surely his doing.

If the younger generation did not believe in the ancient curse, Sir George Macintosh certainly did.

FOUR

Sir Colin Archibald Sinclair, KBE, MLC and current president of the highly elite and prestigious Australian Club in Sydney's Macquarie Street, might have asked Sir George Macintosh to depart the premises had he known about the conversation taking place between Sir George and his guest, Lord Ulverstone – whose presence was authorised because of his reciprocal membership of the Brook's Club of London.

The Australian Club had been established to cater for wealthy and influential gentlemen in the early part of the nineteenth century as a home away from their vast pastoral holdings and industrial empires. Its mahogany panelling, glass-fronted bookcases, priceless artworks, crystal chandeliers and deferential staff made it a cathedral to money and power. Within its walls business was discussed – despite the rule that this should not be. Membership was not only by wealth but also by connection to society's elite. Subjects verging on treason were definitely not acceptable to gentlemen of the Australian Club.

Sir George settled back in a comfortable leather couch, Lord Ulverstone opposite him. Between them they sipped on the finest Scotch available in Australia.

'You should be my guest at the Imperial Service Club in Barrack Street when we meet, old chap,' Ulverstone said, raising his crystal tumbler to sip his Scotch. 'After all, I believe that your father and brother both served the empire with some distinction.'

'They were both fools,' Sir George replied. 'And both dead in a war that was supposed to end all wars.'

'That might have been so had it not been for the damned Jewish Bolshevik conspiracy to rule the world,' the British peer growled. 'What we have had since 1918 are weak so-called democratic governments. Only Germany and Japan have had strong government, and see how both have swept the world virtually unopposed.'

'I should point out that Herr Hitler does not seem to be sweeping Russia any more after his defeat at Stalingrad,' Sir George said. 'From what I have read, Germany lost a complete army in their failure to capture the Bolshevik city.'

'It is only a temporary setback,' Ulverstone replied quickly. 'Hitler will consolidate and counterattack in a spring offensive. You will see the Bolsheviks reel back in defeat. Mark my words.'

'How do we explain Rommel's defeat in North Africa?' Sir George asked. 'Another front that Hitler has lost.'

'The damned Eyties let us . . . Germany down,' Ulverstone said, correcting himself. 'It has never been the Führer's intention to conquer that part of the Mediterranean. That was Mussolini's domain.'

'Any way that you look at it, the war for the Axis powers of Germany, Italy and Japan has slowed considerably, albeit they are not defeated,' Sir George said, glancing around for a waiter to refill his glass.

'True believers are needed now more than ever to assist the crusade to stamp out the Jewish Bolshevik threat to Western civilisation,' Ulverstone said quietly.

'I am not a traitor,' Sir George said. 'I may have financial interests in Germany but so too do the big American companies – despite being officially at war with Hitler.'

'We English do not have the same pragmatic attitude as our American cousins,' Ulverstone replied. 'The Americans are smart enough to recognise they should not confuse waging war and making money. But we have a code of honour that says we must differentiate between the two. So, as far as the King's law is concerned, you are a traitor simply for dealing financially with the German government.'

The statement stung Sir George. He had little time for military affairs and had always tried to convince himself that what he did was simply make money, despite the political differences between his own country and those considered the enemy. After all, wars came and went, and in the end what counted was who was in a position to put food on the table of workers and give them roofs over their heads.

'I would never consider assisting the enemy,' Sir George said.

'You are already, old chap,' Ulverstone warned. 'Your interests in German industry are building the infrastructure for Herr Hitler and his Nazis. But that will prove to be the best thing you can do for your family's enterprises in the long run, when the Axis powers eventually win this war. Who will the victors look to to provide leadership in the new world order? It will be men like you and I.'

'I would rather not discuss this subject any further,' Sir George said, looking about nervously. 'The reason I invited you to the club today was to discuss the incident at my house some weeks ago.'

'I presume you are referring to the burglar,' Ulverstone answered.

'I don't think he was a burglar,' Sir George said. 'Burglars in this country rarely carry guns, and I am sure that I saw a pistol in his hand, and that you appeared to be his target. Is there something you might like to tell me?'

The British officer shifted uncomfortably in his seat. 'I will be truthful with you,' he lied. 'I did recognise the man. He is the husband of a woman I have been seeing. I suspect he was attempting to settle the score with me.'

Sir George frowned. Ulverstone's explanation had the ring of truth; in his early years he too had confronted the angry husbands of women he had seduced. 'I would advise that you report the man to the police,' Sir George said. 'He may not be finished with you.'

'Steady, old chap,' Ulverstone said. 'That could expose me to a scandal, and as an officer wearing the King's commission, I could be court-martialled for conduct unbecoming an officer and gentleman. I do not wish to bring attention to the situation, and I have since terminated any contact with the married woman in question.'

Sir George stared into the eyes of the English lord and thought he could detect the hint of deceit. But the man's explanation had logic, and frankly if the betrayed husband did catch up with him it might not be a bad thing; Sir George strongly suspected that Ulverstone was a full-blown traitor to the Empire. It did not pay to be in such company in times of war, when hanging was the sentence for traitors in Australia.

★

Allison Lowe was breathless. She stared at the message taken by one of the law clerks and felt her face flush. It was a request from Major David Macintosh to be his date for an evening of dining and dancing at Romanos nightclub tomorrow.

Allison had heard about the legendary nightclub where only the wealthy could afford the high cost of food and beverages. Located in the basement of the Prudential Insurance building in Sydney's Martin Place, it was said to be a sumptuous and elegant place with subdued lighting to set a romantic ambience for the patrons. It was also a place where ladies wore evening dress, and Allison did not have such a dress.

Allison glanced at the big clock on the wall opposite and noted that it was 9.30 am – plenty of time to organise a dress if she could get the day off. She rose from behind her desk and went directly to the Major's office – as Sean Duffy was warmly known by all those who worked for him.

She could see that he was alone, poring over legal documents, and she knocked lightly. Sean glanced up, 'Yes, dear,' he said.

'Major Duffy, I was wondering if I could have time off today for something very important.'

A broad grin spread across Sean's face. 'It wouldn't have something to do with Major Macintosh's invitation by any chance?' he asked and was pleased to see the startled expression on Allison's pretty face.

'How . . . You have seen David, haven't you?' she said, a little annoyed that he had not told her David was already in Sydney.

'He would have asked you in person, but the army have him tied up with duties at the moment,' Sean answered. 'From your request, I gather you have accepted his invitation to Romanos.'

'Yes,' Allison said. 'And I need time to find an evening dress for the occasion.'

'Take the rest of the day off,' Sean sighed, knowing how this young woman could easily steal the heart of any red-blooded male. 'But I expect you back at work tomorrow morning.'

Allison broke into a radiant smile. She would have liked to give Sean a hug, but she knew he was a man who rarely displayed emotion in public, so she thanked him warmly instead, then hurried away, her thoughts full of David and the evening to come. She would contact the one woman she was sure would have an evening gown she could borrow – her best friend, Sarah Macintosh.

Allison caught a taxi the few blocks to the building that housed the headquarters of the Macintosh enterprises. She paid the driver and went into the foyer to speak to the receptionist. A phone call was made and Allison was cleared to head up to the Macintosh offices.

There she was greeted by a radiant-looking Sarah who showed no signs of having just had a baby. Allison had sent a small layette as a gift when she had heard about Michael's arrival, but she had not seen Sarah for many months. In fact she had been rather surprised to hear that her friend was returning to work so soon after giving birth; even so, she was pleased to see her and she embraced Sarah warmly.

'I must apologise for not calling on you when I heard about your return to Sydney,' Allison said, disengaging from the hug. 'But it is good to see you again, and looking so marvellous too.'

Sarah gestured to a comfortable settee in the corner of her office, and Allison sat down. 'You do not need to apologise,' she said with a sweet smile and settled into a large leather armchair. 'Since my return I have been too busy to catch up with anyone. How are you? I have been told by a little birdie that you are working for the enemy.'

'Major Duffy could not be called the enemy,' Allison said. 'He is one of the sweetest men I have ever known. David loves him as he would love a father. As a matter of fact, David is currently in Sydney on a military course.'

'David is here!' Sarah exclaimed.

'I thought you knew,' Allison said, taken aback slightly.

'No,' Sarah said. 'The last I heard of him he was somewhere up in north Queensland. Where is he staying?'

'I'm not sure,' Allison answered. 'I guess with Major Duffy in his Sydney flat – or the barracks.' She was beginning to realise that coming to Sarah to request an evening gown for a date with David had not been the wisest of ideas. She knew that the baby Sarah had borne was David's child, but Sarah had assured her that their relationship was well and truly over and she no longer had any feelings for him. Perhaps foolishly, Allison had believed her, and seeing Sarah's reaction to the news of his being in Sydney, she suspected that her friend had been lying about how she felt.

'I suppose David will contact Donald and myself when he gets settled,' Sarah said as if brushing off the subject. 'Now, tell me, to what do I owe the pleasure of your visit?'

Allison was sure now that she had made a mistake in coming here, but she did not know how to extract herself from the situation without offending her friend. 'I know I am asking a big favour but I need the loan of an evening dress, and as you and I have swapped clothes in the past, I was wondering if I could borrow one from you.' She only hoped that Sarah would not ask why. She held her breath waiting for the reply.

'I have a couple of old evening dresses at home,' Sarah said. 'I can send them around to your flat today.'

'Thank you, Sarah,' Allison responded with a great feeling of relief. 'I owe you a big favour.'

'What are girlfriends for if they can't share,' Sarah said archly.

They chatted for a few minutes, and all the while Allison was itching to leave. She was starting to feel very uncomfortable around her old friend, and she did not think it was purely because of David. She noticed that Sarah was smoking cigarette after cigarette, and not once did she mention her baby son. She knew that Sarah could be ruthless in business, but she had always been kind and thoughtful towards her. Allison did not want to think ill of her friend, but she was beginning to think that perhaps she was not so kind and trustworthy as she had thought.

*

True to her promise, Sarah had two very fine evening dresses delivered to Allison's city flat. Both dresses fitted perfectly, and Allison selected the newer one. She regretted that she had no fine jewellery to wear with the long, body-hugging dress; all she had was a set of delicate earrings her husband had given her before he was posted to the Pacific. She held them in her hands and for a moment felt the deep sadness of his death and the loss their unborn baby, then she placed his gift carefully back in the small jewellery box and turned away.

Right on time, David arrived wearing a finely cut civilian suit and hat. Allison saw him from the window of her second-storey flat. He was standing on the pavement below, talking to the cab driver. She had forgotten how broad his shoulders were. Her stomach was in knots as she went down to the front door to greet him. She did not know why but she felt extremely nervous. Was her hair and make-up just right? Had she applied too much lipstick? Would he find her attractive? This was silly, Allison told herself, so she took a deep breath and opened the front door.

'Hello, Alli,' David said, and she was vaguely aware that he was holding a bouquet of colourful flowers towards her.

'David! What beautiful flowers,' she said, accepting the gift from him. 'I should put them in a vase immediately.' She walked quickly up the stairs and placed the bouquet on the dining room table, not bothering to locate a vase but instead hurrying back down to David.

Out in the cool evening he noticed her shiver so, without a word, he removed his coat and placed it around her shoulders before they stepped into the waiting taxi. Allison found that she was very aware of every feature of his tanned face: his grey eyes, broken nose and the many small scars displaying a history of violence in his life. He was not handsome in any classical sense, but he had a rugged, reassuring face that made Allison feel secure.

The taxi dropped them off at Martin Place and they walked from there to the nightclub. Inside, in the foyer, Allison noticed a marble bust of Napoleon, which struck her as almost out of place. As the maitre d' escorted them to their table Allison looked around in delight. It was an elegant and sumptuous place, quite different to everyday Sydney which seemed to have grown drab with the privations of war. The place was filled with men in uniform and smart civilian suits, and women in expensive gowns and jewellery, and Allison spotted many prominent Sydney identities, including the commissioner for police.

Allison chatted easily with David as they waited for the prawn cocktail entree to be served at their table. She could not help but marvel at the cost of the evening, but David was a Macintosh and money was like water to that family.

When the food arrived, he raised his glass of fine hock to eye level. 'To being in the company of the most beautiful woman in Sydney,' he said with a warm smile.

'I don't know of a night I did not wonder where you were and how you were faring,' Allison responded. 'It is so good to see you safely home.'

'I am not sure I would consider Sydney home,' David said, extracting a prawn with a small fork from the side of the tall glass they were served in. 'I guess the decision as to where home is will come with the end of the war.'

Allison was a little disappointed at this; it seemed David was still restless. Sean loved to talk about this man he considered a son and she had learned a lot about his past. He had grown up in the old German New Guinea on a copra plantation and had attended boarding school in Sydney under the watchful eye of the Major, who had been appointed his guardian under the terms of a will. He had been imprisoned in the infamous Dachau concentration in Germany in 1936 and had escaped only to go on to fight in Spain against the Fascist General Franco. His German-Jewish grandmother had been the only female figure in his life, as his mother had died during the terrible influenza pandemic of 1919. His father had been killed in action on the Western Front in the Great War, and he had never known him. David had proved to be a very good heavyweight boxer with aspirations of a title, but he had found himself instead fighting for Australia as a soldier. He was an interesting, well-travelled man, but when Allison looked deep into his grey eyes she saw a lot of pain. Yet there was also a sense of gentleness in this tough, dangerous man.

'What will you do when the war is over?' Allison asked.

'I am not sure,' David said. 'My first priority is to survive.'

His statement jolted Allison as she knew from experience how fragile these men's lives were. Her husband had died flying a Kitty Hawk fighter plane over Milne Bay.

'But I have a proven record of being hard to kill, and right now all that concerns me is being in your company. There was not a night in the jungle that I did not think of you too. Your letters kept me sane.'

Allison was suddenly aware that his hand was touching hers across the table.

'How about we have a dance before the next course,' David said. 'Although it has been a long time, so I will apologise in advance for being a bit clumsy.'

They made their way to the polished wood dance floor and took their place amongst the other couples. The band was playing a slow number and David took Allison gently in his arms. She could feel his strong, warm body pressed against her own. Despite his confession of clumsiness he was light on his feet, and she felt herself swept along by him.

She placed her cheek against his chest, and for now there was no war, no possibility that the man who held her in his arms might die on a faraway battlefield; they were just two young people caught up in the moment. Allison realised with a jolt that she would always love this man no matter where in the dangerous world he might be. She also knew that loving him was not the same as sharing his life. She recognised that he was a restless soul and he might never settle down.

That night David took her to her flat – and Allison took him to her bed.

FIVE

Tony Caccamo slid back the top receiver on his .45 pistol, ensuring that the movement was smooth and lubricated. Confident that it would not jam, he reloaded the magazine and pushed it into the handle until it clicked into a locked position. He then loaded a round into the chamber, and wiped his hands of excess gun oil. The weapon was ready but he had doubts about himself. For weeks he had shadowed his target in a dreary job of hanging out in the back streets of Sydney, rain, hail and shine. But his tedious task of tracking his prey had appeared to bear results.

After his botched job of shooting the British traitor weeks earlier, he had been able to keep a low profile tracking Ulverstone who appeared to avoid returning to the Macintosh mansion, but had a habit of occasionally dining at the Imperial Service Club and the Australian Club in the company of Sir George Macintosh. Ulverstone had beefed up his protection, as Tony now noticed his army driver was armed whenever he drove him from Victoria Barracks where Ulverstone was attached on the staff of army intelligence.

On this cold and rain-filled night Tony expected his target to be dropped off at the Imperial Service Club for dinner. Tony stood in an alleyway about twenty paces from the entrance to the elite club for commissioned officers of the armed forces and their guests. Tony wore the rough dress of a merchant seaman and a beanie cap on his head. His hands were thrust into the pockets of a tattered military greatcoat, and he could feel the grip of the deadly .45 semi-automatic pistol.

He watched as smartly dressed military officers entered and exited the club, oblivious to him in the shadows. Tony had surprise, speed and concealment on his side in a city that was blacked out against enemy air raids.

It was around 7 pm, the time Ulverstone usually arrived at the club to dine. Sure enough, a military staff car pulled up in front of the club and Ulverstone alighted as his driver opened the rear door for him, an umbrella at the ready. Tony waited as the driver hurried back into the car to escape the rain. Then he stepped from the shadows and began to walk towards the unsuspecting British officer.

He slipped the pistol from his coat pocket and brought it up to fire. He was only fifteen paces away and Tony had the mass of his target in his sights. He fired and the shot reverberated amongst the concrete canyons of the darkened street. Ulverstone crumpled at the bullet's impact, and Tony stepped forward to deliver a shot to the head. But he had made one mistake and not allowed time for the military chauffeur to drive away, and he suddenly realised that the loud crack he heard was the driver firing wildly at him.

In a split second he had to make a choice: fire on the driver or finish off Ulverstone. He knew he could not kill an innocent soldier doing his duty, so he chose to fire three shots in the general direction of the armed driver, causing him to take cover.

A whistle blew from somewhere and Tony knew from his police experience that it had to be an Aussie cop sounding the alarm. He glanced down to see that Ulverstone was crawling for cover under the car; so the shot had not killed him, then.

The former New York policeman knew that he had no choice but to flee the scene, and he cursed himself for being so close and yet so far from achieving his mission. He turned on his heel and ran as fast as he could down the street in the teeming rain. The armed driver did not fire after him and Tony gave a quick prayer of thanks, but then he saw the outline of a big and burly police officer running towards him, waving a small baton. Tony swung around to take a path down another deserted street, and in doing so felt his leg go from under him on the slippery surface. He crashed into the concrete, hitting his head and seeing a shower of red stars swirling in the night, before he felt the crunch of the police baton strike the back of his head.

Everything went dark, and Tony knew nothing more until he awoke in a hospital, handcuffed to the bed. As his eyes began to focus he noticed a figure wearing civilian clothes sitting opposite his bed. Tony groaned and the man put down the paper he was reading, stood and walked over to him.

'I see that you are alive, sport,' the man said and Tony could tell from experience that he was a hard-nosed detective. 'I can now officially tell you that you are under arrest for the attempted murder of one of Britain's finest.'

Tony regretted that the charge was only attempted murder and not murder. He knew that his government would not come to his rescue. He was alone to face the wrath of the New South Wales justice system.

★

Sean Duffy still loved taking on criminal cases. As such he was well known to the desk sergeants at the inner city police station close to his law firm and was on good terms with most of them.

It was Sean's day to visit the station with its holding cells, and possibly solicit business for his law firm, Levi and Duffy. He stepped into the musty foyer of the station and was greeted by a robust old first-class sergeant, a former soldier from the Great War. Senior Sergeant Keith Ward was berating a young uniformed constable for not entering property details in his notebook.

Sean limped over to the counter. 'Sergeant Ward, top of the morning to you.'

'Major Duffy, would I be right in guessing you're here for our star prisoner this morning?' the jovial police officer asked.

'And who would that be?' Sean asked curiously.

'We copped one last night outside the Imperial Services Club in the process of shooting some Pommy lord,' the sergeant said, turning over a page in the large charge book and running his finger to the entry. 'A Canadian merchant seaman took a dislike to one of Britain's gentry and shot him in the shoulder. It appears that the Pom is also a lieutenant colonel working out of Victoria Barracks in some hush-hush department. The stupid galah we have in the cells has not said a word since we brought him from the hospital, and is due to be shipped out to Long Bay this afternoon to await his trial. I presumed you had heard about the incident.'

'Nothing in the morning papers,' Sean shrugged, leaning against the front of the counter. 'I guess it will hit the afternoon papers. But having said that, I am prepared to take his case on. Any chance of talking to my client?'

Ward shrugged, reaching for the keys to the cells, then opened the door to the inner section of the police station and escorted Sean to the dank cells below. Their proximity was heralded by the stench of urine, smoke and rotting things better not identified.

Sean turned his gaze on a man of medium build standing holding the bars of his cell door. The prisoner's head was bandaged and he stared blankly back at Sean.

'This is merchant seaman Peter Campbell . . . according to the papers we found on him,' the big police officer said. 'He's not real talkative.'

'Thank you, Sergeant Ward,' Sean said. The police officer ambled away to make himself a cup of tea and finish the morning paper, leaving Sean alone with the only prisoner in the small cell block.

'I am Sean Duffy, solicitor,' Sean said. 'If you need representation I am prepared to take you on.'

'Thanks but no thanks,' the prisoner said, still gripping the bars to his cell door.

'I know American accents, and I know that you have one,' he said quietly. 'You are not a Canadian citizen.'

The man froze and turned back to Sean. 'You are a lot smarter than the average Aussie, who does not know the difference between us and the Canadians.'

'You have to remember that it goes both ways, as you Yanks can't tell the difference between us and Kiwis, when we speak.' Sean could see the slightest hint of a smile on the man's face.

'And you don't hold yourself like any merchant seaman I know,' Sean continued. 'You have the bearing of a soldier.' He could see that he had the man's attention. 'You realise that the charge you face is pretty serious. Attempted murder can pull the same sentence as actual murder in this country. You need to have a barrister represent you in court.'

'Are you a barrister?' the man asked.

'No, I am a solicitor, but I can brief any barrister who is hired to defend you.'

'You are presuming I will be asking for legal assistance,' the prisoner said. 'The local cops have me wrapped up. They have the gun, and a witness to me shooting the limey colonel.'

'So you knew who the man was that you took a pot shot at,' Sean said. 'Not every day we get cases of Yanks posing as Canadian seamen trying to kill high-ranking British officers – although in the last lot I would have liked to shoot a few Pommy officers myself. So what reason would you have to go after the man?'

The prisoner turned his back, walked to the far wall of the cell and sat down. 'There is nothing I have to say on the matter,' he said.

'There is a lot,' Sean countered. 'For a start, who are you really? Is Peter Campbell your real name?'

'Thanks, Mr Duffy, but there is nothing else to say.'

Sean shrugged and walked away. What motive would an American have to kill a British officer? And why wouldn't he speak out to defend himself? It was a mystery, but if the man was determined to keep his secrets there was little Sean could do.

★

'He is a fighter,' the doctor said, bending over the cot where Michael Macintosh lay looking up at the world with curious eyes. Valery Keevers, his nanny, was also looking down at the small baby with loving eyes.

'In my experience baby Michael is a miracle child,' she said. 'He has defied the odds that said he should have died soon and he's growing stronger every day.'

'I don't suppose that you have heard from his mother,' the doctor growled, putting a stethoscope back into his medical bag.

'Mrs Macintosh is a very busy woman,' Val said, attempting to defend her employer. 'She knows that Michael is in good hands with me.'

'Oh, I know that you are an excellent nanny,' the doctor said. 'But a baby needs to be nursed by his natural mother and not some wet nurse.'

Val reached down into the cot to retrieve Michael and held him close to her chest. She rocked him gently, crooning soft words, and noticed that it was time to change his nappy.

'Well, I have another visit to make,' the doctor said. 'But do not hesitate to call me if the baby shows any signs of illness or distress.'

'Thank you, doctor, I will do that,' Val said and watched as he left the nursery.

Val went about changing the nappy, and fed Michael with warmed breastmilk, saved in a bottle. As she fed the baby she fumed at the almost total silence from the boy's mother. Only once had she telephoned to ask about the baby's progress since she had left him in Val's care. Even then there was little love expressed for Michael. How could any mother be so cold? Val asked herself. She gazed into the face of the little boy and thought that he was smiling at her.

'Well, young Michael,' she said, 'you may not have your mother but you will always have me, I promise you that.'

Outside the sprawling farmhouse the winds rose, bringing cold sleeting rain. Inside the house a log fire brought warmth to the nursery.

★

The roar of the twin Beaufighter engines subsided as Pilot Officer Charles Huntley prepared to exit his aircraft on the sun-baked airstrip at Milne Bay. Through the perspex of his cockpit window he could see the squadron commander chatting to another pilot, and when Charles finally stepped into the shimmering heat the squadron leader signalled for him to join him at the edge of the landing strip.

'How did it go?' the squadron leader asked.

'Not much to report,' Charles answered. 'I think our bash at the Japs over the Bismarck Sea has taken the wind out of their sails. We didn't see a single target of opportunity on which to use up a bit of ordinance.'

'Well, you can provide our intel people with any details at the briefing in half an hour,' the squadron leader said. 'Right now I would like to have a little talk with you, Charles.'

Charles immediately wondered what he had done wrong to have the respected squadron leader wish to talk to him outside the briefing.

'Don't look so worried,' the squadron leader said with a smile. 'I received a signal while you were out on your sortie that the RAAF wants one of our chaps to transfer to flying Spitfires, for the defence of Darwin. I do not want to lose you as you are one of the best pilots I have, but I have to bend to the needs of our service. Would you be interested in the transfer? It would mean going to Sydney to do an aircraft familiarisation course before flying out to Darwin.'

Charles well knew the reputation of the famous British fighter planes, which had been firmly established in 1940 during the Battle of Britain. 'It is hard to give up flying the Beaufighter,' he replied, but the posting would put him back on Australian soil, close to the son he had not yet seen. Besides, after the Battle of the Bismarck Sea, flying patrols in empty skies had become somewhat boring, especially when he knew that Darwin was still copping Japanese air raids on a fairly regular basis. It was a chance to get back into the shooting war. 'But I wouldn't mind having a bash at flying Spitties, sir.'

'Good chap,' the squadron leader said. 'I will inform our orderly room that you are to fly out tomorrow for Cairns. Lucky chap, you will be able to have a cold beer back home. No doubt you will also be granted some local leave. I believe that you are from Sydney.'

'It has been my home,' Charles said. 'I actually hail from Canberra.'

'Ah yes, the home of our wonderful war makers,' the squadron leader said with a hint of sarcasm in his voice. 'Well, I will see you at the debrief, but first join the others for a quick cuppa. No doubt it will be your shout in the mess again tonight, this time to celebrate getting out of here and back to civilisation.'

'Thank you, sir,' Charles said, saluting his commanding officer.

Charles stood for a moment taking in the implications of the transfer. He had originally been reluctant to serve his country in the armed forces, but when he had done so, he had made a full commitment to do so. He was already credited with shooting down four enemy aircraft, and one more would make him an ace. The Spitfires were perfect for bringing down Japanese Zero fighters and Betty bombers.

Charles turned his head to look at the squat but deadly Beaufighter. He would miss her, but he was going home and would soon get to hold his son in his arms.

SIX

Sarah was fuming. She had naively lent Allison a good evening dress, only to have her throw herself at David Macintosh in it. Had she known why Allison wanted it, she would have refused to lend it to her.

Sarah sat in her office with little thought for the reports piled up in front of her. Allison had said her only interest in keeping contact with David was that of a dutiful and patriotic Australian woman, giving support to a soldier on the battlefront. But rumours had reached Sarah that David had been seen in almost constant contact with Allison since his return from New Guinea. The two had been seen dining and dancing around the city's most prestigious establishments. She was so furious at this betrayal that she barely noticed her brother step into her office.

'I have had a request for you to action a report on your desk,' he said. 'It seems you are distracted from your work.'

'Did you know that David was back in town?' Sarah asked, glancing up at her brother with an expression of dark anger.

'Of course,' Donald shrugged. 'We have met for a couple of beers at the pub. He looks to be in good shape, considering the rigours of the campaign up north.'

'Why has he not made contact with me?' Sarah asked.

'I suppose it is because you are a married woman with a child, and David may not want to cause any rumours that might bring your reputation into disrepute.'

'But we are cousins,' Sarah said. 'What harm is there in us meeting?'

'I guess David has been a bit occupied with his course, and seeing your best friend,' Donald said with full knowledge that this observation would upset his ambitious sister. The war between the siblings raged unabated for the absolute control of the family fortunes upon the death of their father. 'You are surely not upset that Allison is seeing David?' Donald smirked.

'No, no,' Sarah dismissed the question with a wave of her hand. 'I will give my attention to that report now,' she said.

'Good,' Donald said. 'I will see you this afternoon at our board of management meeting.'

'By the way,' Sarah said as Donald was about to leave her office. 'How is your American Red Cross lady friend, Miss Olivia Barrington. I heard that she returned to the States to visit her sick grandfather, James Barrington Senior.'

'She left a few weeks ago,' Donald replied, realising that his sister was needling him. 'We remain good friends.'

Sarah smiled for the first time, and Donald knew it was simply because she had caused him a small hurt. Olivia was more than simply a girlfriend. He was on the verge of asking her to marry him. He had been in agony to do so because just one small matter had held him back, and that was his contact with Jessica Duffy. He had tried to tell himself that he no longer loved her but a tiny, ferocious fire still burned, deep in his feelings for her. It was the only real issue in his life he could not make a decisive decision on.

'I will see you at the meeting,' he said again as he left his sister's office.

Sarah did not immediately attend to the report she was supposed to action but instead stared at the wall opposite. She had an overwhelming desire to see David again – despite all common sense saying this was not right. Just for a fleeting moment she thought about her baby. Would she tell David he was the father? Sarah considered the question for a moment. No, she was establishing a reputation in a business world dominated by middle-aged men who already resented a young woman holding so much power; a scandal like this could be used by them to erode her position, and she would not allow that to happen.

But Allison Lowe was now an enemy she could go after with all her energy. No one – not even a best friend of many years – came between her and David Macintosh.

★

War stress, combat exhaustion, battle fatigue . . . no matter the term, Captain James Duffy, United States Marine Corps aviator, guessed that this had been stamped in his medical file after the battle for Guadalcanal in 1942. He had been treated in New Zealand for his physical injuries, and had also been seen by a psychiatrist before being granted medical leave in Australia, where he had been able to catch up with his twin sister, Olivia, who went by their family name of Barrington. James had chosen to adopt his father's family name of Duffy to honour the man he had come to know later in his life, and lose just as quickly to an Iraqi assassin's bullet back in 1936.

At the end of his leave he had expected to rejoin his squadron on the *Big E* – the aircraft carrier USS *Enterprise* – which had seen more action than any other single carrier in the Pacific seas. Battered and bruised from numerous attacks by Japanese aircraft, she had remained afloat to fight back, and had even been awarded a Presidential Citation from Admiral Chester Nimitz.

James, however, had not been aboard the carrier when the prestigious award had been bestowed on her, as he was living the life his marine comrades could only dream about. James had been detached to assist the government raise war bonds in Hollywood. He had been informed that with his leading-man looks, silver star on his chest and aviation wings as a fighter pilot, the public would love him.

James thought this was simply an excuse to get him out of the skies. He knew that his superiors considered him a mental wreck and thus not trustworthy to fly operations for a long time, if ever, and the frustration of being away from the flight deck of the ship he considered his home was slowly killing him.

He sat on the balcony of his Los Angeles hotel in the warmth of the summer sun, wearing a T-shirt and slacks and gazing out across the city. He held a rum and ice in one hand, although it was only nine in the morning, and considered whether he should just get falling-down drunk. Today he was supposed to be an advisor to a film about marine corps pilots flying courageous actions against the treacherous Jap bastards he had fought in real life. A car was scheduled to pick him up in an hour and James thought that was enough time to get well and truly blasted. He had friends fighting and dying in the skies over the Pacific, and here he was – a pretend hero.

James knocked back three good slugs of rum before dressing in his pressed summer-issue uniform in time to be on post in the foyer for his ride to the movie lot. Getting wildly drunk wasn't really a possibility – he could not afford a bad report if he had any hope of getting back into the cockpit of a Wildcat fighter. He had to carry out this duty and prove that he was not suffering battle fatigue. Still, the rum had helped take the edge off the morning.

His driver arrived, a young Italian kid employed by the studio to chauffeur clients and actors. He opened the door and threw a salute at James. 'Welcome aboard, Captain Duffy,' he said, sounding for all the world like a naval officer in a movie.

James made no comment and climbed into the rear seat to find a newspaper waiting for him there. The headlines were about the fighting in the very northern Aleutian Islands against an entrenched Japanese force. Japan had actually occupied United States sovereign territory, and that was a serious blow to American pride. Thankfully the news was good, though, as American forces fighting in the bitter cold of the sub-Arctic islands were slowly dislodging the tough Japanese soldiers. He skimmed the rest of the news, but did not see much about the war in the Pacific. The paper was more intent on distracting its readers with Hollywood gossip, real estate prices and the joys of drinking Coca-Cola.

'You a fighter ace, Captain?' the young driver asked over his shoulder, and James glanced up from his paper. 'Or someone famous, like Frank Sinatra?'

'Yes to the first question, and no to the second,' James

answered irritably. The kid was a punk who should have been in uniform rather than in a cushy job like this.

'Hey, that's great about being an ace,' the kid said with genuine admiration in his voice, and James chided himself for being so surly towards the young man.

'What's your name, kid?' James asked.

'Angelo Valentino,' the driver replied. 'My pals call me Angel, because the girls fall over me like they did the man himself.'

James knew he was referring to the famous silent-movie heart-throb, Rudolph Valentino. 'Yeah, I can see that,' James said with a slight smile. 'I suppose you took this job so that one day you will be noticed and become a famous filmstar like your namesake.'

'Na,' the boy said. 'I enlisted in the marines last week, and I'm off for training in a week. I got two brothers in the army. But the army is for sissies.'

James was taken by surprise; he had clearly underestimated the kid. Maybe Hollywood was not all it seemed after all.

They arrived at the studios, and after passing through the security gates found themselves weaving in and out of hordes of Indian braves, Civil War soldiers and a couple of crews of pirates streaming from the huge sheds that housed the film sets.

'This is your one, Captain,' Angelo said, stopping before one of the sheds. 'Hope you have a good day.'

James extracted himself from the vehicle and walked around to the driver's window. He leant in. 'Son, I just want to shake your hand and wish you all the luck in the world as a gyrene.'

Taken by surprise, the young man accepted James's firm handshake. 'Thank you, sir,' he said. 'I heard the girls go for a man in uniform.'

James looked at him, and for a moment he had a flash-back to the terrible fighting on the ground and in the air at Guadalcanal. He saw the smashed bodies of young men around the age of this boy, bloating under a tropical sun. They would never get to wear their fancy dress blues to impress their hometown girls. They would just be names etched in stone on some memorial. Yet here in his homeland the conflict felt as though it were taking place on another planet. It was only the great numbers of military uniforms on the streets of Los Angeles that reminded citizens they were at war.

Angelo drove away, and James walked through a side door into the cavernous building cluttered with lights, cameras, stages and sets. He could see a portion of a Wild Cat fighter and knew that only a part of the plane was used in filming so that the cameramen could place their equipment to take close-ups of the actor in the cockpit.

'Excuse me,' an annoyed female voice said from behind him, 'but aren't you supposed to be dressed in your flying gear?'

James turned to see two big eyes watching him from a pale, elfin-shaped face. The woman had long dark hair flowing around her shoulders, and she held a clipboard to her chest. He guessed she was barely in her twenties, and her accent had a touch of the South.

'Who, me?' he replied, turning to get a better look at her. She only came to his chin, and James saw immediately that she was pretty, but not with the staged beauty of the female stars he had come into contact with during his brief time with the studio.

'Yes,' the young woman replied, approaching him and then stopped a couple of paces away. 'Oh, I am so sorry,' she said. 'I thought that you were our lead in the production. I should be wearing my glasses.'

'Well, if you thought I was the star, then I am flattered,' James said with a grin. 'I am Captain James Duffy.' He reached out his hand and she shook it. It was small, and he sensed her shyness.

'My name is Julianna Dupont,' she said. 'I'm from New Orleans.'

'French name and all,' James said, and his flippant observation seemed to annoy the young woman.

'It is an old and honourable family name,' she said defiantly, and despite her diminutive stature there was fire in her almost violet-coloured eyes. 'I am not one of those Cajuns you Yankees make fun of.'

'How did you know I was a Yankee?' James countered.

'Because of your accent,' she answered. 'I would guess that you come from one of the states close to the Canadian border.'

'Very good, Miss Dupont,' James replied.

'It is my job to know things,' Julianna said, lifting her chin. 'I am the script assistant on this film, and one day I will write the scripts myself.'

'So you are not only beautiful but you also have brains,' James said and saw Julianna blush at such a forward statement.

'I have to speak with the script editor,' she said, and turned on her heel.

James watched her go, then turned back to the film set, which was filling with technical people setting up lights, cameras and sound microphones. He saw a handsome young man step forward and begin to talk to a man wearing a sleeveless jumper and beret. He had to be the director, because behind him was a folding chair with the word *director* stencilled on it.

'Good morning, Captain Duffy,' a voice said behind him, and James turned to see his military chaperone, Lieutenant Guy Praine from the army public relations department. 'I am pleased to see you here.'

'But what the hell am I doing here?' James asked.

'It is just a PR job,' the American officer said. 'The director would like you to comment on the scene he is about to shoot with our hero taking on four Jap fighters over the Pacific. I believe you know what that feels like.'

'Yes, but not in a mock-up of a Wild Cat. I was in a Dauntless dive bomber at the time.'

The older lieutenant shrugged. 'This is Hollywood, we don't let the facts get in the way of a good story. The actual enemy aircraft will be later superimposed on the screen. I had a few years here before the war, working in this studio's management.'

James watched men leaning down with levers below the sight of the cameras, and suddenly it was time to shoot. Smoke from a wind machine was blown at the mock-up, and James could hear the voice of the actor calling out over his pretend radio: 'Take this for Uncle Sam, you Jap murderers . . .'

The cockpit twisted and turned for the camera angles, but James's attention was caught by Julianna, who was standing on the other side of the set. She was looking down at her clipboard, and he noticed that she was wearing glasses now. At one stage she looked up and caught him staring at her. She quickly returned her gaze to the clipboard, pretending not to notice his attention.

The shoot of the scene was complete when the director called, 'Cut!' and the actor portraying the hero was helped from the cockpit, complaining that it was so cramped he had barely had a chance to move about in any dramatic way.

'Time we earned our pay cheque,' Lieutenant Praine said, guiding James over to the director who was in a conversation with the actor.

'This is Captain Duffy,' Praine said to the director, who glanced at James then returned his attention to the actor, a handsome young man in the prime of his life.

'Captain Duffy,' the director finally said. 'What were your observations of our dogfight?'

'Well, I have never known any of my comrades to make a statement about fighting for Uncle Sam,' he said with a sarcastic smile. 'Mostly we are so frightened that we are calling out enemy aircraft in high-pitched voices because we are scared shitless that a Jap 20 millimetre round is going to rip us apart.'

'Thank you, Captain,' the director said with a scowl. 'But this is how the audience want to see things and not what you may have experienced. This movie is far more important than anything you may have done for the war effort.'

James suddenly felt a red rage come over him and he felt his whole body tense. Lieutenant Praine sensed his anger and guessed that he might just punch the director.

'Captain Duffy has an appointment at a factory lunch break to address the workers in the war bonds drive.' He took James by the elbow and steered him tactfully away from the director.

'What would that goddamned son of a bitch know about aerial combat?' James snarled. 'This is nothing but a joke, me being here.'

'It's called PR, and it helps win wars,' the lieutenant said as they walked out of the huge shed. 'A lot of mothers and fathers, wives and sweethearts have boys overseas, and they want to be able to go and see a movie where their boys are being heroic in the face of terrible things.'

James stopped and turned to gaze back at the film set where he could see Julianna talking to the director. 'Do you know who that girl is talking to the son of a bitch I should have laid on his back?'

Praine focussed his eyes into the gloom of the massive building.

'Julianna, yes I know Julie,' he said. 'Smart gal, she has avoided most of the pitfalls of the industry and made it on her own talent as a scriptwriter. Why the interest?'

'I met her before the shoot,' James shrugged. 'Nothing in particular.'

'Julie is on roster at the Hollywood Canteen tonight,' Praine commented with a wry smile. 'And you happen to have the night off as our next appointment is not until seven tomorrow morning when you will be addressing a Rotary meeting breakfast.'

'Thanks, Lieutenant Praine,' James said. 'May I call you Guy, and you call me James, when we are out of earshot of others?' James added, as he had come to like this older man he guessed in his late thirties.

'Thanks, James,' Guy said. 'I am afraid I might be wearing the uniform of a commissioned officer, but I still feel very much like a civilian.'

It looked like he'd be visiting the legendary Hollywood Canteen tonight, where the biggest names in Hollywood volunteered to mingle with the uniformed soldiers awaiting their postings overseas. Maybe he might even get an opportunity to share a coffee with the intriguing young lady of French blood.

SEVEN

The day commenced as usual for Sergeant Jessica Duffy. Her pass to the secret and classified intelligence section in General Douglas MacArthur's Brisbane HQ was checked by the guard who let her into a windowless room filled with desks, clattering telex machines, bright lighting and a subdued but busy mix of military men and women mostly in American uniform.

Jessica sat down at her desk and was barely ready to receive the first message filtered to her when she smelled the acrid aroma of her commanding officer's cigar.

'Sergeant Duffy, report to my office,' he said and Jessica left her desk to follow him into his room. Many thoughts swirled through her mind, including that she had been discovered leaking American information to agents of her country.

The colonel laid his fat cigar in an ashtray fashioned from the base end of a brass artillery canister. He reached down for a newspaper on his desk and held it up to her. 'I thought that you should see this before you got the news from any other source,' he said.

Jessica peered at the front page and the first thing she saw was the face of Tony Caccamo. The headline read: *DERANGED CANADIAN ATTEMPTS MURDER OF BRITISH LORD.*

Jessica gasped in shock. Tony had been absent for some months, and all she had gleaned from him when he had said goodbye was that he might not see her for some time.

'Just as I figured,' the colonel said. 'Talk around here was that Lieutenant Caccamo was soft on you. So I thought it best for me to caution you that any knowledge you have of Lieutenant Caccamo is never to be divulged to anyone – not even those you work with. Are you clear on that? You can read the article if you wish.'

'Yes, sir,' Jessica dutifully responded, still reeling. She took the proffered paper and read the article. 'But how could Tony . . . Lieutenant Caccamo . . . be accused of attempting to kill a British officer? It does not make sense.'

'The Aussie coppers believe that he is a Canadian merchant seaman by the name of Peter Campbell, and that is all they have to know. If I hear that you have mentioned his name outside of this office I can promise you that you will regret it,' he said, reaching for his still smouldering cigar. 'The matter is of the utmost national security level, and it is in all our interests that we let justice take its course.'

'Sir, in this country even attempted murder could result in being sentenced to hang,' Jessica said in a desperate plea. 'I am sure Lieutenant Caccamo is innocent. There has to be something you could do for him.'

'Sergeant Duffy,' the normally gruff intelligence officer said in a softer tone, 'I liked the boy a lot, and wish I could help him, but he was fully aware of the consequences if his mission went wrong. We cannot afford to draw attention to his case – it could cause a major rift in the Aussie-American relationship, which we both know from working here is tentative at times.'

Jessica understood what her superior was saying, and working here she had found herself torn between loyalties. She knew her own country relied on the support of the vast American resources of men and war machines, but she also accepted that meant kowtowing to men like the arrogant and vainglorious General MacArthur.

'Sir, may I ask what Lieutenant Caccamo has been doing for the last few months?' Jessica asked, knowing her question had taken her across the line.

'You must be aware, Sergeant Duffy, that I cannot disclose to a foreign national anything concerning our operations,' the colonel replied sternly. 'You are dismissed.'

Jessica left the room and went back to her desk, slumping in her chair and thinking over all that had transpired in the office. It was obvious that Tony had been on a covert mission, but why would the Americans want to assassinate a high-ranking British officer? It did not make sense. The newspaper report also mentioned that the accused man had refused legal counsel. Jessica knew how dire Tony's situation was, and the name of Sean Duffy crept into her mind. He had fought for years to have the Queensland property of Glen View sold to her father. Sean was in Sydney where Tony was incarcerated at Long Bay Gaol, according to the newspaper report.

Nobody had forbidden her from contacting a lawyer on Tony's behalf. She would contact Sean to see if he could help. She needed to be careful, though; she did not want to be seen making unusual phone calls. She would wait and call from the telephone box at the end of her street.

After her shift Jessica did just that.

She lined up in the early evening behind a small queue of people, and after twenty minutes it was her turn to use the phone. She stepped inside the booth just big enough to take one person and lifted the warm handpiece. The box smelled strongly of sweat and cigarette smoke. Dropping coins in the slot she heard the telephone exchange operator come on the line, and as the number she requested to be dialled was a trunk call, the operator asked her to place more coins in the slot.

After a minute or two the call was put through and Sean's voice answered at the other end.

'Duffy speaking,' he said.

'Mr Duffy, this is Jessica Duffy calling from Brisbane.'

'Jessie!' Sean exclaimed. 'It has been a while since I last saw you. How is your father?'

'From his last letter he is fine,' Jessica replied, anxious to move on to the subject of her call. 'My time is short and I need your help on a matter in Sydney.'

'I have not dropped the matter of the purchase of Glen View,' Sean said.

'No, no, it is not that,' Jessica said. 'It is about a man by the name of Peter Campbell. He has been accused of attempting to kill a British officer in Sydney. He –'

'I have met Mr Campbell,' Sean cut in. 'I offered to represent him, but he firmly declined my offer.'

'His name is not Peter Campbell,' Jessica said, pressing her mouth closer to the telephone receiver and lowering her voice. 'His name is Anthony Caccamo, and he is a lieutenant with the American army.'

There was a short pause before Sean spoke. 'How do you know this, Jessie?'

'I cannot say how I know, but I do,' Jessica answered. 'Please help him. Tell him that I sent you.'

'Are you extending . . .' the voice of the operator cut in across their conversation and Jessica realised that she was short on coins.

'No, I will hang up,' she said. 'Please, please promise to help him,' Jessica said before the click of disconnection sounded.

She put down the phone back on its cradle, pushed open the door and stepped out into the serenity of the Brisbane evening. Tony's life now depended on the legal skills of Sean Duffy. She could only hope he was as good a criminal lawyer as he was said to be.

*

Doors clanged and heavy boots echoed in the corridors of the dreaded Long Bay Gaol as Sean Duffy was escorted to a room to meet with the prisoner by the name of Peter Campbell.

Inside the small interview room, the prisoner was seated at a battered table. He was in manacles and he seemed barely to notice the entry of Sean and the guards.

'I would like to have a private discussion with my client,' Sean said to the two burly prison officers.

'He is in for attempted murder, Mr Duffy,' one of the guards said. 'You think it wise to be alone with him?'

'Mr Campbell and I have met before, and he did not offer me any bodily harm then,' Sean said, taking a chair opposite the prisoner.

'As you wish,' the guard shrugged. 'We will leave the door open and be just outside if you need us.'

When the two guards had departed, Sean leaned over the table and spoke softly so their conversation could not be overheard.

'Jessica Duffy has asked me to help you, Lieutenant Caccamo,' he said and he could see that his statement had taken the man off guard. 'As a matter of fact, I spoke to her on the phone last night. She rang from Brisbane.'

'She knows that she should not get mixed up in any of this, Mr Duffy,' Tony hissed. 'It has nothing to do with her.'

'So you are an officer in the Yank army,' Sean said. 'What the hell is a commissioned officer doing trying to kill a Pommy officer of some standing in the English gentry?'

'That is classified, Mr Duffy. I failed in my mission and now I have to accept the consequences.'

'It is fairly plain to the eyes of the law that you are a common criminal, and considering who you tried to kill I do not expect our judiciary to be lenient towards you. You could even hang.' Sean could see an agonised expression on Tony's face.

'I wish I could tell you a lot more, Mr Duffy, but I have sworn an oath of secrecy. One of the prisoners told me that you are the best in Sydney, and that you were an officer in the last war. If I needed a defence lawyer I would hire you.'

'Then let me be your voice in court,' Sean said. 'If nothing else, I could plead diminished responsibility. It might save you from the gallows.'

For a long moment Tony leaned back in his chair and stared at the manacles around his wrists. 'What if I told you the man I tried to kill is a goddamned traitor, Mr Duffy?' he said quietly, glancing at the open door.

'You would have to elaborate, Lieutenant Caccamo,' Sean replied. 'That is a very grave accusation.'

'I am off the record, and nothing I tell you can ever leave this room. Will you give me your word on that?'

'I will,' Sean said. 'We have the same lawyer–client privilege you enjoy under your American legal system.'

'Good,' Tony said. 'I want at least one person to know the truth before I am sentenced. I feel I can trust you, and when the war is over and Ulverstone is exposed for a traitor, you will be witness to the fact I was a loyal soldier.'

'I can promise you that, but I will also fight to reduce any sentence imposed by our courts,' Sean said. 'Tell me about Lord Ulverstone.'

'Ulverstone was communicating with the Japs back in Singapore before it fell. We intercepted his messages, and an investigation by our intelligence section traced them back to him. MI6 know of his treachery but cannot touch him because of his political influence in London. They do not want the scandal of one of their aristocrats with a seat in the House of Lords being revealed as a traitor. So our government had no choice but to quietly remove him from the scene before he could do any more damage to national security.'

Sean had no reason to doubt what the young American officer was telling him. He figured that what he was hearing was a breach of the man's oath to his country, but he also knew the young man did not want to be thought of as a common criminal when the appropriate time came for such revelations to be known to a peace-time world.

'What were you before the war broke out?' he asked.

'I was a New York cop,' Tony answered. 'I guess I have proved to be a failure when working on the other side of the law.'

'Did the name of Sir George Macintosh ever come up in your brief for the job?' Sean asked.

'It did,' Tony frowned. 'And I asked Jessie about him.'

'Jessie,' Sean said. 'It appears you know the young lady fairly well.'

'She is a friend from when I was working at Mac's HQ in Brisbane,' Tony answered.

A faint smile crossed Sean's face. 'I think I can guess the rest,' he said. 'It is no wonder she called me.'

'I don't want her name coming up in any of this,' Tony growled. 'She knows nothing.'

'I understand,' Sean said. 'The young lady is a distant relative of mine – and like a daughter to me in many ways. I was with her father in the Great War.'

Tony looked surprised. 'I knew this country had a small population, but I did not know you were all related!'

Sean smiled at the joke, and warmed to the young man who had found himself in a terrible predicament. 'Well, I need some time to put a case together and register myself as your counsel. I will also need to see a King's Counsel friend of mine to represent you at the court case. In the meantime your secret is safe with me.'

Sean rose and limped to the door. The guards stepped inside to return Tony to his cell.

Outside the forbidding walls of the Long Bay Gaol Sean walked towards his car, thinking about the ironies of Sir George Macintosh's relationship to the British traitor. His old enemy might have a dark secret that would see his downfall if it was proved that he was an accomplice in treason with the British officer. Oh how grand would it be, to see Macintosh finally brought to his knees.

★

Sergeant Tom Duffy, as a member of the North Australian Observer Unit, was deep in the mangrove country of the Gulf of Carpentaria. On horseback, in four or five man patrols, the unit ranged Australia's desolate north. They were accompanied by Aboriginal guides and their task was to act as the eyes of the nation against any Japanese landings. The men had been selected because they were true bushmen. It was not an army unit that put much emphasis on traditional discipline, as the men were used to working alone on sprawling properties. Tom himself had worked the cattle properties of central Queensland after the Great War, and was now the owner of several of them. But in time of war he felt his duty was to his country, despite his age, and he had accepted the role as the patrol commander.

This time the bushmen had a young signals soldier with them. Private Andrew Paull had been seconded to the unit because of his skills with communications. He could ride and shoot, but he had lived all his life in Melbourne. The land around him was so different to what he knew of the crowded city; the silence was broken only by the wind and bird calls; the heat was oppressive, the terrain seemingly featureless, and they were utterly isolated from the rest of the world. It was this isolation that was hardest to bear. He was physically tough enough to endure working with the so-called Nackeroos, but out here the world looked so big and he felt so small, it would be easy to be dwarfed by insignificance. He felt it at night when the stars above were so multitudinous in a vast inky-black sky. Private Andrew Paull had expected to be posted to the Pacific campaign but had been transferred to this commando-style unit, thousands of miles from Melbourne and everything he was familiar with.

The sun was high overhead now and Tom called his patrol to a halt to find shade and partake of a midday meal. The heat shimmered across the flat landscape of stunted trees and red earth. Billy, the local guide, wandered off to ensure they were well away from the feared saltwater crocodiles inhabiting the mangroves. They had had an incident weeks earlier, when one of the great crocodiles had made its way into a tent pitched too close to the rising tide, and the men in the tent had been forced to kill it. It had made a good meal, but Tom was keen to avoid another such hair-raising encounter.

'Have you got the radio set up yet?' he asked Private Paull.

'Yeah, boss,' Andrew replied, having taken the cumbersome set off the pack mule they travelled with. 'Just going to send a locstat.'

'Good man,' Tom said, patting the lad on the shoulder as he squatted over the vital instrument of communication with the unit's HQ in Katherine. The unit only numbered around five hundred men all up, with around sixty local Aboriginals attached.

Tom was about to speak with the rest of the patrol when he saw Billy running back from the mangroves, his eyes wide with surprise.

'Bin find tracks,' Billy said, coming to a halt. 'Not tracks of people here.'

The patrols had reconnoitred the Top End for a long time without any sign of the enemy, but Tom could see from the expression on Billy's face that this was different. The rest of the patrol had overheard the exchange and quickly picked up their rifles.

'Let's go and have a bit of a look,' Tom said. 'You stay with the radio,' he instructed Andrew.

The patrol followed Billy on foot to the edge of the great mangrove swamp, and Billy stopped to point to the faint imprint of a shoe.

'Sandshoe,' Tom said, looking carefully. 'Jap sailors wear sandshoes. How long?' he asked Billy.

'Maybe one fella day,' he said, staring back into the mangroves. 'Not any more.'

The hair rose on the back of Tom's neck. Were they in the vicinity of a Japanese military unit? He guessed it would be the trace of a Japanese submarine crew member, as any surface ship would have been spotted by coastwatchers.

'Okay, boys,' Tom said quietly. 'We get this report straight back and go looking for any other tracks.'

Andrew was given the message but was frustrated to find that his radio was not working. He could not send the signal to Katherine, so for the first time since he'd joined the Nackeroos he might be facing some action at last. He swapped his radio for a rifle and joined his patrol to track down the possible enemy Japanese on Australian soil.

EIGHT

James visited the Hollywood Canteen whenever he had a night off from his PR duties. He would stand back and observe the sea of uniformed soldiers, sailors and airmen who came to listen to the music provided by some of the best known bands in the USA. He would watch starry-eyed kids in uniform gaping at actors and actresses they had only been able to worship on the silver screen in the small rural towns they had grown up in. At the Canteen they might even be lucky enough to catch a personal word from a big star, or even a dance with one of Hollywood's most glamorous actresses. It would be a memory they could take across the Atlantic to Europe – or into the battlefields of the Pacific. On the wall were photographs of stars such as Jimmy Stewart and Clark Gable who were serving in combat overseas.

James was only really interested in one face amongst the crowd, the face of a young woman serving free food to the mass of military men. He did not know quite why he was so attracted to Julianna Dupont, but occasionally he caught her glancing at him across the crowded room and he felt his heart lift with the thrill of it.

One night as the place was winding down and James was swallowing down the last of his drink, Julianna crossed the floor to join him.

'You have been here every night but you do not come to my counter for food, why is that?' she asked with the hint of a smile.

'I get well fed back at the hotel,' James said. 'I come here for the music and entertainment.'

'I do not see you dancing with any of the girls,' Julianna observed. 'You do not like girls?'

James felt his face flush, and then realised that she was teasing him. 'Maybe just one here,' he replied, recovering his composure.

'And which one would that be?' Julianna asked, glancing around at the pretty girls dressed in grass skirts who were just finishing a hula dance.

'The one I would like to ask to have a coffee with me now,' James said. 'Have you finished for the evening?'

'Thank you, Captain Duffy,' she said. 'But I must go home as I have an early shoot tomorrow at the studio.'

'It does not take long to drink a cup of coffee,' James pleaded. 'I can then make sure you get home safely.'

'Thank you again,' Julianna repeated. 'But I have my reasons for not joining you.'

'Oh, I am sorry,' James apologised. 'I did not realise that you had a man in your life.'

'I have no one in my life, Captain Duffy,' she said. 'But it is a personal choice not to go out with men who could be shipped out to the war and never return. I know that sounds selfish but I have already lost a brother to this war, and I do not want to lose anyone else I might come to care about. Guy tells me that you have seen a lot of combat and could do so again in the future.'

'That is not likely,' he said, half believing his own words. 'I will probably see out the war here in Hollywood, and in that case you and I will be bumping into each other all the time.' He watched her face and could see a flicker of indecision.

'One coffee,' she relented. 'And then I must go home – alone.'

'Hot dog!' James said. 'I know a place down the street that has good coffee.' He offered his arm and Julianna accepted his gesture with only the slightest reluctance.

The coffee lasted for two hours as they found themselves caught up in each other's company and conversation. Julianna was late getting home – but she did so alone.

★

Sarah Macintosh was stunned to see her estranged husband standing in the doorway of her office.

'Hello, Sarah,' Charles said, stepping into the plush office and closing the door behind him.

'How are you, Charles?' Sarah finally asked, feeling uneasy in his presence.

'Still alive,' Charles smiled. 'Despite what you might wish for my future.'

'Why are you here?' she asked in a frosty tone.

'I thought it was only right I should visit my wife – and the mother of my son,' he said, taking a seat. 'Speaking of my son, I was informed he is still in Goulburn in the care of a nanny. Don't you think he is a bit young to be separated from his mother?'

'I have a company to run,' Sarah retorted. 'The baby is in good hands.'

'You mean our son, Michael,' Charles said in a cold voice. 'He does have a name.'

'Yes, yes, Michael,' Sarah dismissed. She took in his air force officer's uniform with an approving eye. 'You are looking well.'

'Flying suits me,' Charles said. 'You did me a favour when you arranged for me to go to war.'

'You have no real skill in private enterprise, Charles,' Sarah said. 'Your expertise was in public service.'

'That may be so,' Charles answered. 'But you are the coldest person – man or woman – I have ever had the misfortune to meet. Maybe we should arrange a divorce.'

'You know that would not suit either of us at this stage,' Sarah said.

'More convenient that I get shot down and leave you the grieving widow of a war hero,' Charles stated. 'I intend to survive this war and come back to take my son from you.'

For a moment Sarah was tempted to shatter her husband's smugness by informing him the baby was in fact David Macintosh's, but she refrained and glared at him instead. She could not feel anything for this man; he was a stranger in her life.

'He is my son,' Sarah said. 'He belongs to me, and I will ensure you never have him.'

Charles rose from his chair. 'I am going to Goulburn to see Michael,' he said. 'I just came here to tell you that.' He was about to leave Sarah's office when Donald appeared.

'Charles, old chap, I did not know you were back in Australia!' Donald exclaimed. He held out his hand, and Charles accepted the gesture with a firm shake.

'Good to see you, too, Donald,' Charles said. 'I will not be staying in Sydney for long. I have been transferred to Spitties destined for Darwin. But I thought this visit would give me the opportunity to see my son for the first time.'

Donald glanced at his sister; he could see the frown on her face. He guessed the meeting had not been very cordial. 'I am having a beer with David Macintosh this afternoon after work. Then we are heading to Haydens in Pitt Street. You are welcome to join us,' Donald said. 'That is, if you have no other plans.'

'Sounds like a bonzer idea,' Charles replied.

'Good chap,' Donald said, and the two men walked out of the office feeling Sarah's glare boring into their backs.

★

As arranged, the three men met at Haydens nightclub. Charles wore his uniform and the wings on his chest attracted admiring glances from several young ladies. Haydens was known for its dancing and music, and was a venue where young women were able to meet servicemen who were in the mood to spend money on them. The Americans attracted most of the attention because they had more money than the Australians, had better manners and were generous with gifts of nylons and chocolates.

David and Donald wore elegant civilian suits and the trio made a handsome and striking picture.

'I heard you were up at Milne Bay,' David said to Charles when their drinks arrived.

'I heard that you were on the track,' Charles said, and in their identification of the theatres of their service the two men forged a bond common to men who have known combat.

Donald felt a little left out of the conversation that followed as the two servicemen exchanged stories of good and bad commanders, the political strategy of the ongoing war in the Pacific, and how they thought the war could be won.

'I should raise a toast to the splendid job our army and air force are doing in the Pacific,' Donald said, to include himself in the conversation.

'Better not forget the navy,' David said, and the three men silently raised their glasses.

'Donald told me that you are off to Goulburn tomorrow, Charles,' David said. 'Your temporary transfer has given you a wonderful opportunity to see your son.'

'Yes,' Charles replied. 'My wife called him Michael – which is not a name I would have chosen.'

'Why not?' David asked.

'I suspect she named him as a tribute to the man she is obsessed with, although he has been dead for almost half a century.'

'Michael Duffy,' David said quietly. He felt a touch of guilt for betraying Charles, whom he had genuinely come to like. He and Sarah had had a night of passion before Sarah had married Charles. Even then Sarah had talked about the mysterious Michael Duffy, whose life she had been able to piece together through the diary of her ancestor, Lady Enid Macintosh. Photos found of Michael Duffy had an uncanny resemblance to David – down to the broken nose.

'If I had had my choice I would have named my son Andrew or perhaps Edward,' Charles said. 'Good Anglo-Saxon names.'

'Well, Michael is kind of a family name,' Donald said, defending his sister's choice. 'Albeit, he was a Papist ancestor.' He hesitated to say more as he remembered that David was of Jewish descent through his mother, although David did not act like any Jewish person Donald knew. 'Let's drink and not mention my sister,' Donald said. 'I am at war with her at present. The election for vice-president of the board is due soon and I know she aspires to the position.'

'I doubt the board would choose a woman over a man,' Charles said. 'I am sure you will retain the seat.'

'Thanks, old chap,' Donald answered. 'I realise that things are a bit strained between you and Sarah. After the war you can be assured there will be a place for you on the board.'

Charles smiled grimly. 'Not if my wife has a say in it. Besides, you will no doubt be taking up your role as equal partner in the Macintosh enterprises, won't you, David?'

'I'm not sure,' David said, staring at his glass of beer. 'I might apply to stay on in the army and collect my generous allowance to stay out of management.'

Both men looked at him.

'I can see boom times after the war,' Donald said. 'There will be houses to be built for returning servicemen, and products they will need to fill those houses. We have already made inroads into any industries we see as potentially profitable postwar. You would be mad not to have a piece of the action.'

'We haven't won the war yet,' David said. 'Both Charles and I still have to face the Japs in the Pacific, and they are far from beaten. We may not even live to return home, which is a reality that every serviceman has to face.'

Charles nodded uncomfortably and for a long moment a silence fell between the three men.

They eventually parted company late in the evening. David returned to Sean Duffy's flat, quietly opening the front door lest he disturb Sean or young Patrick. He was surprised to see Sean sitting fully dressed at the kitchen table, poring over thick law books, a tumbler of Scotch on hand.

'Hello, David,' he said, looking up. 'Help yourself to a drink.'

David poured himself a Scotch and sat down opposite Sean. 'Bit late to still be working on a case,' he said, taking a sip of the excellent whisky.

'I have a very difficult case of attempted murder,' Sean said. 'The committal hearing has already established a case to answer in the court. My only hope at this stage is a diminished responsibility plea. The interesting thing about this case is that it has a link to Sir George Macintosh.'

The mention of the loathed person of George Macintosh pricked David's interest. 'In what way?' David asked.

Sean leaned back in his chair and rubbed his eyes. 'The man my client attempted to kill is a close associate of Sir George.'

'I read something about an English lord shot outside the Imperial Service Club. It sounded like the shooting was random. So, the Pommy aristocrat is a friend of Sir George?'

'It was not random,' Sean said. 'But I cannot say any more than that.'

'Uncle Sean, I can't sleep,' came a small voice. Both men turned around to see Patrick in the doorway; he was in his pyjamas and had clearly just woken up.

'What is it?' Sean asked.

'I miss Mummy,' Patrick answered. 'Why can't we get Mummy to come and live here?'

Sean glanced quickly at David, who shook his head sadly.

'Hey, young fella,' David said. 'How about I put you back to bed so that you can get a good night's sleep. Tomorrow Allison and I will take you to the flicks, and we will eat ice-cream.'

Patrick walked over and put his arms around David who lifted him easily and took him back to bed.

That night David lay staring at the ceiling. He was having trouble sleeping as fragments of his brief time with Sarah Macintosh swirled around his head. Was it possible that Michael was his son? David did not think so or surely Sarah would have told him. Besides, the timing was not quite right. He tried to dismiss the idea that the baby was his, but for some reason he could not dislodge it from his mind.

*

The tracks ended at a small beach lapped by blue-green tropical seas. Tom Duffy gazed at the horizon but could see nothing unusual.

Beside him Billy said, 'Jap man gone.'

'Yeah, it looks like it,' Tom replied. He turned to look at his patrol and he could see the disappointment on their faces. 'Well, boys, about all we can do is report what we have observed here, and let the navy know they might have a Jap sub in the waters of the Gulf. I think it is time we returned to camp and put on a brew.'

The men slung their rifles and trudged back through the mangrove swamp, wary to the presence of the giant saltwater crocodiles as they went. Back in camp Private Andrew Paull was still unable to get the radio operational and so the report was not passed on.

That evening the patrol sat under the seemingly endless parade of stars as orange embers rose into the moonless sky. Andrew brooded that he had come so close to seeing a bit of action, but it had fizzled out as quickly as it had started. He knew that his friends in the Signals Corps in the Pacific campaign were seeing a lot of action, and here he was wandering around mangrove swamps while the important stuff went on elsewhere. He felt that he was wasting his time here. Andrew lay back against an abandoned termite nest and listened to the men laughing and chatting in the dark. They talked about cattle stations they had worked before the war, pubs that had banned them from service because of their riotous behaviour, and realised that he had little in common with these former stockmen.

Tom noticed the young signaller sitting away from the rest of his patrol and he walked over and sat down beside him. 'Anything up, Andy?' he asked.

'Yeah, boss,' Andrew replied. 'Can you get me a transfer out of here to the real war?'

'Only if we get another sig to replace you,' Tom answered. 'You are bloody good at your job, and despite what you might think, our role out here is vital. We are the eyes and ears of this country against Jap incursion from the north.'

Tom reached for a stick of timber from a small pile that had been collected during the day and suddenly he felt a sharp pain in his left wrist. He knew immediately that he had been bitten by a snake.

'Bloody hell!' he yelped, grasping his wrist.

Andrew saw the snake disappear out of the light cast by the campfire and recognised it. 'Hey! Fellas!' he yelled. 'The boss has just been bitten by a snake. A bloody taipan.'

The men of the patrol jumped up and rushed over. Each and every one of them knew that the Gulf harboured only the most dangerous snakes in the world. Even with medical treatment the chances of surviving a taipan bite were almost zero. Tom Duffy had survived two wars, only to find himself facing death by snakebite. The tough men standing around him simply shook their heads and tried not to catch his eye. All they could do now was try to make him comfortable until death claimed him.

NINE

At first there was no pain at the site of the taipan's strike. Andrew had leaped forward to assist Tom, and in the glimmer of firelight he could see blood oozing from the twin lacerations. Both men locked eyes and Tom knew that he was a dead man. No one had ever survived a taipan bite that he knew of. The others of the patrol had already gathered around their stricken leader to see him off into death.

'Grab an axe,' Andrew shouted, and one of the men stumbled away to return quickly with a razor-sharp axe.

'Sorry, Tom,' Andrew said and looked up at the men standing around him. 'Hold him down,' he commanded, and four of the soldiers quickly grabbed Tom, forcing him to the warm earth. One of the men quickly shifted a small log under Tom's arm.

Andrew lifted the axe above his head, teeth gritted, and with all the strength he could muster swung down halfway between the wrist and elbow. Tom screamed as the lower part of his left arm was severed, flopping in the dust.

Already one of the men was wrapping a length of leather strip as a tourniquet around the bleeding arm, to stem the flow of blood. How far had the venom run in Tom's veins was the question in each soldier's mind as they moved to reassure their much liked and respected leader that he would live.

Andrew broke away to try the radio one more time. There was no reason that it should suddenly start working now, but he had to give it a go. Unexpectedly it hissed into life, and he was able to transmit a message that they were taking Sergeant Duffy to the nearest homestead for urgent medical attention. Already the other men were organising horses for transport.

Andrew watched as Tom was helped into the saddle. One of the mounted soldiers led his horse and another two rode closely along each side to ensure that he did not fall from his saddle in the dark. Tom was conscious and knew that he must remain so if he were to live. Andrew glanced at the bottom section of Tom's arm lying on the ground and was overwhelmed by nausea. He buckled over and vomited. He had no idea whether or not he had done the right thing. He knew that Tom would have died from the snakebite long before they could get him help; severing his arm was his only chance, although he did not hold out much hope that it would work.

When the party had been swallowed by the vast panorama of the night, a dingo howled its forlorn song in the darkness. Andrew suddenly noticed that his hands were sticky with blood, and he glanced down to see that they were trembling. It had been a miracle that the radio had suddenly come to life, and for a moment he had sensed something that he could not explain in rational terms.

At the edge of the campfire's glow he had thought he had seen an Aboriginal warrior standing and watching him as he fiddled with the radio to bring it to life. He was an old man and for a moment their eyes had locked. Andrew had seen that the man had scars on his chest, and a long white beard. He had also held a long spear and Andrew could swear that he had asked for tobacco.

Andrew took a burning stick from the fire now and walked over to where the Aboriginal man had stood. He crouched to examine the place for footprints, but there were none.

'You see Wallarie,' Billy said softly behind Andrew, causing Andrew to almost jump out of his skin.

'I saw a blackfella just standing here staring at me,' Andrew said, unsteadily standing up straight. 'But there does not seem to be any indication he was here.'

'Tom tell me 'bout Wallarie,' Billy said, peering into the night fearfully. 'He a spirit man look after Tom. Spirit man live up there.' He pointed to the night sky and the mass of twinkling stars.

With his observation made, Billy walked back to the campfire to pour a strong cup of tea, leaving Andrew baffled. There had to be a logical explanation, he thought. He did not believe in blackfella superstition. Dead people could not appear to the living.

*

The men escorting Tom reached the homestead before first light and were met by the station manager holding a lantern. 'I got a call on the radio that the doctor will be here shortly,' he said by way of greeting.

The soldiers assisted Tom inside the building and into a bed in a spare room, and there he lay wavering in and out of consciousness. He experienced a violent headache and stomach cramps, and the pain from his severed arm swept over him in waves. He wanted to cry out but forced himself to swallow the pain. Sweat beaded his forehead, and the bandage around his stump oozed dark blood. Eventually Tom lost his fight with the pain and fell into a strange world of swirling stars and darkness. He was hardly aware of who he was, and the voices around him faded into silence.

So, this was death, he thought, as the stars flickered out and he was left alone in the absolute blackness. In the distance a tiny light burned and Tom was suddenly flooded by the memory of a place he knew so well. He was sure that he stood on a hill surveying the brigalow plains under a rising sun. 'You come home to us, Tom,' the voice said and Tom turned to see a young Aboriginal man standing beside him. More surprising was another man beside the young warrior, a European dressed in clothing reminiscent of the Victorian age of colonial bushmen. 'You come home to me and your grandfather,' said the Aboriginal man. 'We hunt together, and you meet your grandmother, Mondo, who is with the women by the waterhole on our land.'

Before Tom could respond, the picture faded, and he felt as if his body was weightless. A female voice came softly to him, 'Sergeant Duffy, do you need water?'

Tom slowly opened his eyes and became aware that he was in a small room lit by a kerosene lantern. He focused on a face peering down at him and felt a soothing wet cloth on his brow. Tom was so thirsty that he could not speak, and nodded his head. Water was brought to his lips and he sipped gratefully.

The woman assisted Tom to sit up, and he became acutely aware of the pain that throbbed in his left arm.

Tom winced, and the woman seemed to understand, placing pain killer tablets in his hand.

'Take these,' she said.

Tom popped them in his mouth and instinctively reached out to take the glass of water. Suddenly he realised that his left arm was missing from the elbow down. For a moment he stared at the swathe of bandages covering the stump.

'The doctor was forced to remove what was left of your arm to your elbow,' the woman said. 'You were in a deep coma and none of us thought that you would survive.'

'How long ago?' Tom asked weakly.

'Three days and two nights,' the woman answered. 'Your men have returned to their patrol, and I am here to look after you until you are fit enough to get back on your feet. I am Miss Abigail Frost,' she said. 'I was a governess on the station, but with the evacuation of the family down south to Adelaide, I have been without any real work here. Mr Luland has kindly kept me on as a cook until I can find employment elsewhere.'

Tom gazed at the woman. She had a strong face that had its own beauty, and he guessed she was in her late thirties. Her long dark hair was tied in a bun, and he could hear the strong English accent when she spoke. It was an educated accent, and Tom could sense that she was a gentle woman by the touch of her hand and tone of her voice. 'Well, I am glad that you are here at this time, Miss Frost,' he said.

'Thank you, Sergeant Duffy,' she said with a hint of a smile. 'I am glad that you were able to get through the worst of the fever. I am afraid one or two of your men had a bet that you would not survive.'

Tom grinned. He liked the fact that his men were prepared to put money on his survival – it was the Aussie way of coping. 'That is not nice,' he said. 'They did not give me a chance to bet any money of my own on whether I would survive.'

For a moment Abigail did not realise his joke, but then she laughed. 'I am sorry, Sergeant Duffy. I agree, that is not nice.'

Tom joined her with a chuckle. 'I think you should call me Tom,' he said. 'May I address you as Abigail?'

'Certainly, Tom,' she replied, laying her hand on his good arm. 'I would like that.'

In her company, Tom was able to ignore the pain racking his body. He remembered how quickly young Andrew Paull had reacted to the taipan's bite by removing his arm, and that this had probably saved his life. He owed the young man a great debt.

★

As soon as Lord Ulverstone had recovered from the bullet wound to his shoulder he telephoned Sir George Macintosh for a lunch meeting at his club.

Over a gin and tonic, his arm in a sling, the British army officer said quietly, 'In a previous discussion, old chap, you told me that you had someone working inside the firm of Levi and Duffy.'

Sir George swilled his single-malt Scotch, watching the small blocks of ice drift in the tumbler. 'That is correct,' he said. 'It pays to know what the opposition is up to.'

'You may not be aware that the blaggard who tried to kill me is a client of Major Sean Duffy.'

'That bastard,' Sir George spat. 'Despite my strong dis-like for the man, I have to admit he is an excellent criminal lawyer. He could get the devil himself off a charge.'

'I was afraid of that,' Ulverstone sighed. 'If the matter goes to court I am afraid some very sticky questions might be raised. I daresay that your name would crop up too.'

'What are you trying to say, Albert?' Sir George asked. 'Is this some kind of blackmail?'

'Oh no, old chap,' Ulverstone said smoothly. 'I may be a little clumsy in asking for your help.'

'What help can I offer?' Sir George asked.

'Inside knowledge from your source in Levi and Duffy about the man who tried to kill me.'

'What does it matter?' Sir George said. 'He will be tried and no doubt found guilty of the attempted murder of a peer of the realm. I am sure the judge will view that very harshly.'

'It might be better for all if the man does not reach the courtroom,' Ulverstone said. 'It would save the legal system a lot of time and money were the accused to suffer an accident.'

Sir George looked sharply at the British officer. 'You mean if the man were killed before he gave evidence.'

'George, I suspect that with your contacts, and the rather vast means at your disposal, you could get access to the man in prison.'

A crooked smile crossed Sir George's face. He sensed that Ulverstone was a desperate man, and desperate men were easy to manipulate. 'If . . . and only *if* I could arrange something,' Sir George said, leaning forward in his chair, 'I would expect such a big favour to be returned.'

'You may ask your price,' Ulverstone replied, taking a swig from his gin and tonic. 'I am sure you would appreciate another title from the mother country when the war is over. Possibly even a seat in the House of Lords.'

Sir George slumped back into his big leather chair. 'We will see,' he said.

'Ah, but there can only be a deal if the man in prison does not make it to the first hearing in court,' Ulverstone reminded.

Sir George raised his glass and Ulverstone responded. The deal had been sealed. Tony Caccamo – alias Peter Campbell – was a dead man.

★

Signalman Andrew Paull pulled off his slouch hat and stepped inside the small bedroom to see Tom lying back against pillows.

'G'day, Tom,' he said. 'I heard that you were getting better.'

'Good to see you, Andrew,' Tom said with a smile. 'Your visit gives me a chance to thank you for saving my life.'

Andrew shifted uncomfortably. 'It was all I could think of at the time. I remembered stories about canecutters in north Queensland who would use their cane knives to cut off limbs if they were bitten by taipans.'

'You did the right thing and I owe you one. By the way, what happened to my arm?'

'Well,' Andrew said, clearing his throat. 'We, ah, we dug a grave and said a service over it the next day, just in case you didn't make it. The boys then had a drink and said good things about you.'

'Wish I had been there to hear them,' Tom sighed. 'By the way, who scooped the pool when I didn't join my arm in the ground?'

'I did,' Andrew said sheepishly. 'I knew you were going to live because Billy told me some old blackfella by the name of Wallarie said you would.'

'You know that's just blackfella superstition,' Tom said with a faint smile. 'Wallarie has been dead for years.'

'Yeah, I was told that by Billy,' Andrew answered. 'But funny things happen out there on those plains that I don't think anyone would believe unless they had been there.'

'So you saw him?' Tom asked.

'I didn't say that,' Andrew quickly responded. 'But I will admit that odd things happen to a man out there.'

Tom realised that the young soldier was not going to admit to seeing anything otherworldly lest he be marked as having gone troppo – a term used in the north for the madness that could come upon a person too long exposed to the loneliness of Australia's far north. 'If there is anything I can do for you, lad, you have only to ask. I am in your debt.'

'There is something you could do,' Andrew said. 'You could get me transferred to a unit in the Pacific. I've heard from the boys that you have some influence about the place.'

Tom gazed at the young man standing at the end of his bed twisting his battered slouch hat in his hands. Wrangling him a posting to an infantry unit fighting in New Guinea might be what he wanted, but it could also be a death sentence. Tom could see the pleading in the signalman's eyes and sighed in defeat.

'I will promise you that I will do everything in my power to get your transfer,' he replied. 'But remember, your job with the boys up here is vitally important.'

'I know that,' Andrew said. 'But I just want to have a go, before the war passes me by and one day my kids ask me, Daddy, what did you do in the war?'

Tom shook his head. That attitude had cost so many young men their lives, but who was he to try to persuade the lad to keep safe rather than risk his life for his country?

For himself, he knew that the loss of his arm meant he

was no longer physically fit to serve in the armed forces. He would return to his properties in Queensland and take over the running of them. His war had come to an end in the strike of a taipan snake. But he was still alive, and a strange thought crept into Tom's mind that Wallarie had let him live for a deeper purpose.

When Andrew had left, Abigail stepped into the room with a cup of tea and a plate of freshly baked scones. Tom had come to learn a lot about Abigail Frost over the weeks of his recovery. The civilian doctor who visited once a week had grunted that Tom was ready to return to whatever life lay ahead of him now. Somehow Tom hoped that the woman standing by his bed with the mug of tea would have a role in his life. He was becoming more than fond of his English nurse.

★

Sir George Macintosh had a man in the police force who had once worked with his old contact, Jack Firth, before his unsolved murder a few years earlier. The detective was cut from the same cloth and he regularly supplied damaging information on Sir George's business rivals, information that could be used to blackmail favourable business deals.

The policeman and the business tycoon sat in the corner of a busy Sydney hotel.

'So you want that Canadian we have in custody done away with?' Detective Sergeant Lionel Preston said, gripping his glass of beer.

'It will pay well,' Sir George said.

Preston leaned back in his chair. 'I can arrange it but it will not be easy as he is currently holed up at Long Bay. You will have to pay this much to get the job done,' he said, pushing forward a coaster on which he had scribbled down a figure. Sir George looked at it and nodded, pushing the coaster back to the detective.

'Consider it done, cobber,' the detective said, holding up an empty beer glass. 'Your round, Sir George.'

TEN

Captain James Duffy did not want to get out of bed. The dinner he had attended the night before to raise war bonds had virtually stretched to breakfast time. That is, if the consumption of bourbon was counted as part of the meal. He was weary of smiling all the time and having men slap him on the back, congratulating him on sending many sons of Nippon to their heaven with his fighter plane's guns.

He rolled over and was not overly surprised to see the naked back of a young lady beside him. James groaned when he tried to remember what had happened last night. There had been a young woman with aspirations to break into movies, and James racked his memory to recall if he had promised her introductions to the many directors and producers he had met over his weeks in Hollywood.

James had almost given up hope of getting Julianna to agree to taking their relationship further than a shared coffee. She had remained aloof from his advances, and the alcohol he had consumed the evening before had fed his despair until the young lady now in his bed had latched on to him some time in the early hours.

The telephone rang beside his bed, and James reached over the sleeping woman to answer it.

'James, the car is waiting for you out the front of the hotel,' said Guy Praine. 'You have an appointment at a munitions factory to speak to the workers.'

James groaned and the girl next to him stirred from her sleep. 'Give me fifteen minutes,' he said to Guy. 'Just need to shower and dress.'

James placed the phone back on the receiver and turned to the girl. She was very pretty, with blonde hair and blue eyes. He could not remember her name.

'I have some bad news,' he said as she sat up, the sheet barely covering her breasts. 'I have an appointment in a short time.'

'Do you have to go?' the girl said, pouting her disappointment.

'Yeah, the war needs me,' he grinned as he slid from the bed and walked into the bathroom where he reached for his razor and shaving soap. The girl followed him and he could see the outline of her curvaceous body in the mirror.

'Will I see you tonight?' she asked, wrapping her arms around his chest. 'You promised that I would get the chance to meet that new director at RKO.'

James did not remember the promise. 'Give me a number and I will call you,' he lied. The girl returned to the bedroom and dressed in her sleek evening dress that enhanced her figure to the fullest, whilst James quickly donned his best dress uniform displaying his medals for bravery. When James was ready to leave the girl took his arm and they walked out to the elevator. The operator cast admiring glances at James's escort as they rode down to the foyer.

The lift door opened and James and the young lady stepped out together. Directly in front of them was Guy Praine, and beside him was Julianna, who immediately turned on her heel and walked towards the hotel entrance.

'I think you are in a spot of trouble, James,' Guy said, looking the young woman up and down. 'Julianna said on the way over that she was planning to cook you a real home-style meal tonight.'

James knew the chances of that happening now were about as likely as him getting an immediate transfer back to the Pacific.

★

It was a bleak place and Sean Duffy felt a certain sympathy for the men incarcerated behind the great walls of Long Bay Gaol. He waited in a small, dank room with a table and two chairs. Sean had placed a packet of cigarettes on the table for his client, and after a short while Tony was escorted into the room by two burly prison guards.

Tony sat down and took a cigarette from the packet, then Sean leaned forward to light it.

'I don't normally smoke,' Tony said, sucking in the nicotine. 'But before I came here there were a lot of things I did not do.'

'How have they been treating you?' Sean asked, glancing back to ensure that the guards had closed the door behind them and he could not be overheard.

'Well enough,' Tony replied. 'But I don't look forward to spending the rest of my life here.'

'If you admit why you attempted to execute Lord Ulverstone, I am sure your government will corroborate your story.'

Tony looked at Sean as if he were a schoolboy. 'I don't know how you Aussies do things, but I can assure you that Uncle Sam is not going to support any story I have to tell about a British traitor. I knew from the beginning that if I failed I would be thrown to the wolves.'

'If we at least declare your true identity to the court, that would cause questions to be raised, even if you refuse to say anything else. It will shake the tree, and who knows what might fall out.'

'I am sorry, Major Duffy, but I stand as Peter Campbell and take my chances,' Tony said, shaking his head.

'You don't leave me much for your defence,' Sean sighed. 'I might try an insanity defence.'

'No defence would be better,' Tony said grimly.

'Is that what Jessica would want you to do?' Sean countered and could see that he had hit a nerve.

'Her name is not to come up at any time,' Tony said with some force. 'It is bad enough that she contacted you, but the people I work for would make sure she disappeared if they thought she was supporting me. No, I want to let things proceed as they are.'

'You leave me with very little for your barrister,' Sean said. 'If nothing else, is there anything I can do for you in here?'

'I am pretty right, thanks,' Tony said and Sean rose from his chair. He reached out and shook Tony's hand.

'Good luck, old chap,' he said and went to the door to indicate to the guards that his interview with his client was over.

The two guards entered the room once Sean had left and Tony suddenly started to feel uneasy.

'Get up, prisoner,' one of the guards said, an Englishman with a coarse face. Tony rose to his feet only to feel a club smash him to the concrete floor. 'What? Having trouble standing up?' he hissed as Tony lay curled up with his hands covering his head. 'Not so tough now are you,' he said, hauling Tony to his feet.

Tony could feel the pain ricocheting around his head from the vicious blow. 'Try to kill one of''is majesty's finest. You colonials never learn. Maybe you won't be makin' it to court.'

His uneasiness grew as he saw that the second guard was just looking on, clearly without any intention of intervening. Something had changed in the atmosphere of the prison in the last few days, and Tony knew danger when it surrounded him. He felt like a dead man walking.

★

Sarah had tried to convince herself that David Macintosh meant nothing to her, but that was not working. She did not know why, but the idea of possessing him was all consuming. She had to have him.

Sarah had heard that David and Allison were often seen at Romanos nightclub, and she knew through her sources that David was on leave this weekend. No doubt he would be at Romanos tonight, and Sarah asked one of the Macintosh staff to escort her there. Ryan was a good-looking young man who fancied himself and he jumped at the invitation, as Sarah had known he would – especially given she was covering the cost.

That evening they were ushered to a table just as the band struck up a popular romantic tune, 'Dearly Beloved', originally sung by Dinah Shore. The young woman covering the song was doing a grand job of imitating the American singer.

Sarah had her chair pulled out for her by a well-dressed waiter and Ryan sat down opposite her.

'Do you come here often?' he asked awkwardly and Sarah ignored the naive question. Ryan was only a year older than Sarah but unworldly. However, he looked good on her arm, and that was all that mattered for the evening.

Ryan ordered drinks and Sarah looked about expectantly. She was not disappointed when a few minutes later she saw David and Allison arrive. They were arm in arm and as David passed his hat to the young lady at the cloakroom he said something to make her laugh. The head waiter met him with a broad smile and it was obvious to Sarah that David had been to the club often enough to establish a rapport with the staff.

As the waiter ushered them past her table, Sarah saw that David had noticed her. She was satisfied to see him look startled.

'Hello, David, Allison,' she said with an icy smile when David stepped forward with Allison on his arm. 'It has been some time since I last saw you. I rather expected you to inform me that you were back in Sydney. After all, we are family.'

'My apologies,' David said, still off balance at seeing his cousin. 'I was planning to catch up before I shipped out again.'

Sarah turned to her old friend. 'Hello Allison, it is good to see that my dress suits you very well.'

Allison reddened a little, but then she rallied. 'I must thank you for your generosity, Sarah. I have had plenty of use out of the dresses you lent me.'

Sarah knew exactly what Allison meant, but she did not want to let her anger show. 'I should introduce my escort for the evening,' she said sweetly. 'David, this is Ryan. Ryan, meet David Macintosh.'

Ryan's eyes widened. David was a soldier of wide renown and his colourful story was legendary around the Macintosh corridors of power; he was, after all, a part owner of the vast family enterprises.

'Mr . . . Is it Captain or Major Macintosh?' he said, rising to his feet and extending his hand.

'Just David,' David said, shaking the man's hand. 'Do you work for the Macintosh business?' he asked and Ryan nodded. But when the young man turned to Sarah he received a withering look for his admission.

'So, I presume that you do not come here often,' David said, putting together the elaborate ambush his cousin had set.

'No,' Ryan answered. 'Sarah invited me to escort her here tonight.'

David looked at Sarah's face and could see that the guile was there but had been revealed unwittingly by the young man at her table.

'Well, Sarah, it was good catching up,' David said. 'I think our man wants to seat us at a table. I hope you enjoy the rest of the evening. The food here is excellent – as is the music.'

David left Sarah fuming. He and Allison were seated a few tables away, and when the waiter left them Allison leaned forward with a serious expression. 'I don't think that your cousin being here was a coincidence,' she said. 'Sarah is up to no good.'

'I would not concern yourself with her presence here tonight,' David said. 'Sarah likes to play games, but this is one she is not going to win.'

Allison gazed at David in the dim light and wondered if he was aware that Sarah's baby was in all probability his son. Sarah had virtually admitted this to her when she had discovered she was pregnant. Allison knew that Sarah could be a dangerous enemy to anyone who stood between her and something she wanted. She strongly suspected that the iciness that had crept into their friendship was because of David. Allison glanced over at Sarah's table and shuddered. There was something about her friend that worried her.

*

The door to Tony's darkened cell clanged open and he sat up on his bunk in surprise. It was the middle of the night and there was no reason for a visit from the guards.

'Get up, prisoner,' the guard growled, and Tony realised it was the coarse-faced guard who had hit him so brutally after his meeting with Sean. The guard was on his own and this in itself was highly unusual.

'Step outside your cell,' the guard said. 'Time for you to have a shower.' He shoved Tony in the back with a small hardwood baton.

'It's the middle of the night,' Tony protested, and received a vicious shove in the kidneys from the guard's baton.

'Just do what you're told,' the guard said, and Tony stepped forward uneasily.

Something was amiss but he was powerless to retaliate. To do so would invite a swarm of guards to assault him. All he could do was go along with the guard's commands. He walked down to the shower room, which was in total darkness. He knew now that his life was in dire peril and his every sense was sharpened by the threat of danger. He felt a hand shove him through the entrance to the showers and suddenly the room was flooded by light. Tony found himself at the centre of the changing area, and when his eyes adjusted to the bright light he could see three prisoners in a semicircle around him.

'Nothin' personal,' the largest of the men said, and stepped forward to lunge with a short blade that caught Tony just below the rib cage. The searing pain caused Tony to gasp, then he felt another sharp blade penetrate the back of his neck.

He desperately attempted to ward off his attackers, knowing that he would receive no help from the prison guard who had escorted him to the showers. Blood pumped from his carotid artery and he realised that resistance was now futile. The darkness came to him and he slumped to the floor, where his blood ran in a rivulet across the concrete.

ELEVEN

Sergeant Jessica Duffy passed through the security check at MacArthur's HQ in Brisbane to enter the top secret office. As soon as she did she sensed a sombre mood amongst her workmates.

'The colonel wants to see you,' a captain said, and Jessica went to his office, knocked and was told to enter.

Jessica stepped inside and could see the colonel of her section sitting at his desk, puffing on a cigar.

'Sergeant Duffy,' he said, removing the cigar from his mouth. 'I am not sure if you have heard, but Lieutenant Caccamo was killed in prison last night, down in Sydney.'

For a moment Jessica wondered if she had heard correctly, and as the news began to sink in she found that it was hard to remain on her feet. The colonel saw her swaying and left his desk to pull up a chair for her.

'I am sorry to have to tell you the news, but it is fairly well-known around here that you were close to the lieutenant.'

Jessica's mind seemed to be working in slow motion. 'How did it happen?' she asked eventually.

'From what I have been briefed he was killed by unknown person or persons in the prison shower room late at night,' he said. 'I am authorising you a forty-eight hour leave pass as from now, so I suggest that you return to your billet and take some time out. You of course realise that you are to remain in Brisbane for the period of your leave.'

'Yes, sir,' Jessica answered, rising from her chair and walking out of the office as if in a dream. She was aware of the sympathetic expressions on the faces of those around her, but no one said anything and she felt disconnected and alone.

At her house in Toowong birds were singing in the winter sunshine, but Jessica hardly heard their song as her mind was swirling with thoughts. The only person who could help her now was Sean Duffy. She was acutely aware that she was about to break all the strict rules by defying her commanding officer.

She quickly changed out of her uniform and packed a small suitcase. She called a taxi to take her to the Roma Street railway station, where she purchased a one-way ticket on the next train south. She had broken one order, and in forty-eight hours, when she had not returned to work, she knew she would be listed as absent without leave. Considering her very sensitive posting, her absence would not be treated lightly. She knew that soon enough she would be a wanted person.

★

Sean Duffy stood in the office of the gaol's governor, his expression dark.

'How could my client get himself murdered?' Sean asked, leaning on his walking cane. 'What is wrong with your security?'

'I am sorry, Mr Duffy,' the governor answered. 'I have initiated an enquiry into the circumstances of his death. That is all I can do.'

Sean knew the governor would protect his staff if they were involved. After all, it hardly mattered if a criminal was killed when so many innocent men were losing their lives on the battlefields around the world.

Back in his own office Sean slumped down at his desk despondently. The death of the young American officer was outright murder, and Sean suspected many of being complicit in his demise. Had the American government decided it was too risky for him to go to trial lest he reveal his real identity and why he had attempted to kill the British aristocrat? The Yanks were the most obvious suspects, but Sean was a canny lawyer and knew that the first rule was not to jump to conclusions.

He got up from behind his desk and went to his filing cabinet, sliding open the big metal drawer to thumb through a list of names of clients. He stopped when he found a name and ascertained that his client was to be released from Long Bay Gaol the following day. Sean would ensure he was there to meet him, to see what the man had heard about the murder from the inside.

★

On the other side of the Pacific, Captain James Duffy stood outside a florist shop in the balmy Californian morning examining bouquets of flowers. He settled on a bunch that was a mass of colour, paid and then walked back to his chauffeur-driven car.

'I think it will take a lot more than flowers,' Guy said from the back seat. 'I think you will have to grovel, suffer for a while, and then try again to show that you are not going to leave.'

'What makes you an expert?' James said as the driver set the vehicle in motion.

'I've been married three times,' Guy answered. 'But I have learned one or two things along the way. The first and most important thing is that women are emotional creatures. You might have to take acting lessons to be able to display true remorse. I think flying combat missions has dulled your emotional expression.'

'The goddamned woman showed no interest in a relationship with me,' James said angrily. 'So I slip up once and she refuses to talk to me.'

'You have yet to learn, old boy, that women need to be chased – until they catch you. It has been that way since the dawn of time,' Guy smiled. 'Trust me, Julianna has always been attracted to you, but she needs you to show your total dedication to her before she gives in.'

'It is easier flying operations against an enemy whose only aim is to kill you,' James said, staring out the window at the steady stream of automobiles travelling in the lanes of the highway.

Their ride ended at the gates of the studio lot, where James was to have lunch with the production staff of a film set against the Pacific war. He was supposed to praise them for their artistic efforts in portraying the war for the viewing public, but he knew nothing on the silver screen could ever convey the real horror of the war. The films did not show the blood, pant-pissing fear or reality of what a 20 millimetre explosive bullet did to a man's body. The actors had not been there, and that made a big difference. James knew that Julianna would be on the set today and he checked to make sure the flowers he had purchased were not damaged as he and Guy strode into the cavernous building where the filming was taking place.

He saw Julianna standing near an actor wearing the uniform of a navy fighter pilot.

'Good luck,' Guy said quietly as he peeled off to find the set manager.

Feeling just a little awkward, James mustered all his courage and walked over to Julianna, who was deep in conversation with the handsome young actor. She turned to see him approaching.

'James,' she said frostily, 'I am surprised to see you here today. I thought you would be back at the hotel enjoying yourself.'

'I will see you later, Julianna,' said the actor. 'I hope you will consider what we discussed.'

James stood awkwardly with the flowers in his hand. 'I know I screwed up,' he said when the actor was out of earshot.

'The flowers will not help you,' Julianna responded. She made as if to walk away, then turned back to him and said, 'Look, James, you are a very attractive man and I like you a lot, but I lost my brother in the Pacific and I never want to grieve like that again. It might have been different if you were not a marine, flying combat missions, but I suspect that you are one of those men who always wishes to be back on some godforsaken island fighting the Japanese.'

'All the same,' James said, 'I think the marine corp will leave me in Hollywood until the war is over. There is little chance of me being killed in combat here.'

Julianna touched James on the arm. 'If I could believe that was going to happen I might consider that something more serious could happen between us. I am sorry, James. But I will accept the flowers. They are beautiful.'

'I know what you saw at the hotel, but I was drunk, nothing happened,' James lied feebly, only to receive a look of contempt from Julianna.

'I hope you never have to swear on your life about that,' she said, but she did not take her hand from his arm. 'I guess you will have to prove that I can trust you before we can go any further.'

James nodded his agreement and Julianna withdrew her hand from his arm.

'I have to go to a meeting,' she said and turned to walk away, leaving James with the flowers. He watched her leave and felt nothing but confusion.

'I could not help watching you two,' Guy said, walking over to James. 'I have a feeling that Julianna had the last word.'

'Goddamned women,' James said in frustration. 'I don't know where I stand with her. She said that she would accept the flowers but she walked away without them. Is that some kind of secret female signal? If it is, I don't understand what she is saying to me.'

'For a single man who could have any beautiful unattached woman here, you look more like a married man who has returned home late at night smelling of liquor and cheap perfume,' Guy said. 'You are probably thinking that life was better back in the Pacific when you were just surviving from one day to the next.'

'I think you deserve these flowers,' James said, thrusting them into Guy's hand. 'You seem to know more about women than I do.'

★

121

The following day Sean arrived at his office, placed his hat on the rack and limped to his desk.

'Major Duffy,' a young articled clerk said through the doorway, 'there is a young lady here to see you, but she does not have an appointment. Her name is Miss Jessica Duffy.'

'Send her in immediately,' Sean said, and within a few moments Jessica appeared.

'Jessie! What a wonderful surprise to see you here,' he said, rising from behind his desk and embracing her with one arm, the other leaning on his walking stick.

'It is good to see you, too,' Jessica said, breaking gently from the embrace. 'I guess you know why I am here.'

'Take a seat.' Sean gestured to a chair near his desk. 'I can only offer my condolences. From the little that I knew of Lieutenant Caccamo, I sensed that he was more than just fond of you.'

'We might have had a future together,' Jessica admitted, taking a seat. 'Instead he has been murdered in cold blood, and I want justice.'

'From what I know about your current posting in MacArthur's HQ, and given that your young man worked for the same organisation, I can only think that your superiors had Mr Caccamo silenced,' Sean said.

'That is a strong possibility,' Jessica answered. 'But if anyone can get to the bottom of this, it is you, Major.'

'Do you have leave to be down here in Sydney?' Sean said.

'I did have leave,' Jessica replied. 'But it ran out about an hour ago in Brisbane.'

Sean raised his eyebrows. 'So you are absent without leave,' he said. 'That is pretty serious.'

'How could I continue working with people who might have been possibly responsible for having Tony murdered?' Jessica countered. 'I realise that taking unauthorised leave makes me a fugitive from the armed forces, but I have to know who killed Tony. Not just for my sake, but for the sake of his family back in New York.'

'I understand,' Sean said. 'Do you have anywhere to stay in Sydney?'

'My father has a place over at Strathfield,' Jessica answered. 'I will stay there.'

'I know the place,' Sean said. 'It is currently tenanted by a couple of young ladies working in a factory. I am sure you will be able to take up a room there, but you will have to use an alias.'

'I will,' Jessica said. 'I had a lot of time on the train to think of ways of keeping one step ahead of the law.'

'You sound like one of my clients,' Sean grinned. 'Do you have money to keep you?'

'I am sure that father can help me there,' Jessica said. 'But I would need to have the money come from you, and have Dad pay you back.'

'Very wise,' Sean said. 'I can arrange that. Have you heard from your father lately?'

'I received a letter from him to say that he has been discharged from the army, and has returned to one of our properties adjoining Glen View.'

'I was saddened to hear that your dad lost the lower half of his left arm,' Sean said. 'I have been in contact with him about one of his men who wants to be transferred out of the Nackeroos into active service. I was able to get David to agree to a posting in his battalion. But I digress,' he continued. 'I have a meeting with a man being released from Long Bay this afternoon, he might be able to help me get my investigation going into Tony's murder.'

Jessica looked surprised. 'I did not think you would care so much about his death,' she said.

'His family deserve the truth about why he died in this bloody war,' Sean said. 'He was a patriotic soldier doing his duty, and he should not be dismissed as some deluded criminal attempting to kill one of Britain's finest.'

'Thank you,' Jessica said, tears welling up in her eyes. 'You have always been there for all of us.'

'You look as if you have not had much sleep, my dear, so I suggest that you head off to your father's place over in Strathfield. I will telephone ahead to let the tenants know you will be joining them. But first, you need another name.'

'I thought that Joan Campbell would be my alias,' Jessica said, and Sean nodded that he understood.

'Then I will arrange that the appropriate identification papers be drawn up,' he said.

Jessica glanced at the man who was more than just her family solicitor. 'Is that not illegal?' she asked.

'When you have been defending criminals as for as long as I have, it comes somewhat naturally to adopt some of their practices,' he answered with a broad smile. 'Now, go and get a good meal and a long sleep, young lady. I will keep you up to date with my investigation. You can call me on my number at home.'

Jessica rose from her chair, walked around to Sean and threw her arms around his neck. 'Thank you, Major,' she said with tears in her eyes. 'If anyone can get justice for Tony, it will be you.'

After Jessica had left the office Sean sat considering her faith in him. He knew that if the Americans were involved there was very little chance he would be able to get justice for Tony through the usual legal avenues. However, Sean had long ago learned that the law and justice were not the same thing. If he had to, he would find other, less conventional ways of prosecuting this case.

TWELVE

Major David Macintosh had completed his company commander's course and had been transferred to a training command as an instructor. He was disappointed not to have been returned to his unit in north Queensland, but he had been assured that the current posting was only temporary. At least it gave him the opportunity to see Sean, Patrick and Allison more frequently.

It was mid-June and he was sitting at the kitchen table listening to the radio broadcast of the Prime Minister declaring that the imminent threat of Australia being invaded was finally over. On the European front the war had reversed Germany's initial overwhelming drive against Russia, and now they were on the defensive as the Red Army secured a few vital victories.

'Good news,' Sean commented.

'Unfortunately that does not mean the war is over,'

David said, sipping tea from a delicate china cup. 'By rights, I should be back with the battalion.'

'Enjoy the break whilst you can,' Sean said. 'I see that you and Allison are getting along nicely. She arrives each morning with a rose in her cheek.'

'Careful, Uncle Sean,' David chuckled. 'Not information a young lad should be privy to.' He reached over and ruffled Patrick's hair playfully.

'What do you mean, Uncle David?' Patrick asked, looking up at David from his homework. Sean had enrolled the boy in a primary school run by nuns just down the road from his city apartment, and Patrick was startling to settle into his new life.

'I will tell you one day – when you can shave,' David said with a broad smile.

Sean stirred sugar into his tea and gazed at the tall, broad-shouldered soldier and the young boy sitting at his kitchen table, and reflected on the past. He had never married, nor had children of his own, but he had raised David, and now he seemed to be raising Patrick. The Red Cross letters, when they came, indicated that Patrick's mother was still alive in Changi prison. Sean knew that he was no substitute for the gentleness of a mother's touch, but the boy seemed to be coping with the separation. The nuns at Patrick's school had informed Sean that the boy was a good student, but prone to daydreaming during classes. A couple of the bullies at school had picked on him because he did not have a mother or father in his life, but Patrick had stood up for himself, even knocking down one of the older boys. Needless to say Sean had been summoned to the school, after Patrick had been given the strap for fighting, and he had found the boy sitting outside the mother superior's office with a defiant expression on his face, and a black eye.

'I had to fight, Uncle Sean,' he said when he saw Sean. 'They said bad things about my mother.'

'I know you did,' Sean reassured. 'Did you win?'

Patrick looked with surprise at Sean. 'There were two of them, but I knocked out Daniel Murphy's front teeth. He ran away crying.'

Sean tried to hide his smile of satisfaction for the boy who carried the fighting spirit of the Duffy clan. 'Well, Sister Mary has informed me that you were not completely at fault in the fight, but she was forced to give you the strap for not apologising to Daniel Murphy for knocking his teeth out. I think the matter has now been resolved. I am going to make sure that next time two boys try to take you on, you will be able to knock out both boys' teeth.'

Patrick had given Sean a quizzical look. He had not yet been exposed to Harry Griffith's gym for boxers.

'I have a date tonight,' David said now, rising from the table. 'Allison and I are going off to the flicks.'

'What are you going to see?' Sean asked.

'*The Life and Death of Colonel Blimp*,' David replied. 'I believe it is about your generation of soldiering.'

'Yes,' Sean said. 'I knew a few Colonel Blimps in the last lot. Have fun but don't keep my girl out too long. She has a big day tomorrow helping me prepare briefs.'

David bid Sean and Patrick goodnight, and Sean was able to drop his pretence of being relaxed. He looked to the telephone and waited for it to ring. It had been three weeks since he had tried to make contact with his client being released from Long Bay, but the man had been released earlier than expected and had then promptly disappeared. Sean had put the word out that there was money in it if the released man contacted him, and finally he had been informed that the man would call his home this evening.

The telephone rang and Sean jumped up to answer it.

'I hear you want to talk to me, Major,' said the male voice on the other end.

'You made a rather quick exit from the Bay,' Sean replied. 'I was waiting to talk to you, but they said you had been released a few hours before your allocated time.'

'Yeah, the governor's a real nice bloke,' the former prisoner said sarcastically. 'Extra time off for good behaviour.'

Sean suspected that the prison officials did not want him to speak to anyone present in the gaol when Tony had been murdered and had spirited his client away before he could speak to his lawyer. But avarice was a strong motivator, and the reward was generous enough to persuade the man to make contact.

'What do you know about the killing of the Canadian prisoner?' Sean asked without further niceties.

'You give me the reward and I will tell you,' the man said.

'So you don't know anything,' Sean answered. 'It would be a waste of time paying you.'

There was a pause and finally the voice said, 'Detective Sergeant Preston put them up to it. You deliver the money to the pub tomorrow and I will give you the names of the bastards who did the Canadian in.'

Sean knew his source was reliable: the man had helped him in the past with inside information. He cared less about the prisoners who had actually killed Tony than the man who had put them up to it. He needed to trace back to the source, and the name of the police officer rang a bell.

'I will leave a package with Mabel at the bar,' Sean said. 'Better that we aren't seen together.'

'Good thinking, Major,' the man said. 'You had better watch your back if you are snooping into Preston,' the man cautioned. 'He is a bad bastard who would sell out his own mother if there was a quid in it.'

Sean thanked him and placed the phone on the cradle. Detective Sergeant Preston . . . now he remembered! It was rumoured that the crooked police officer occasionally assisted Sir George Macintosh. But as far as Sean knew, Sir George had no link to Tony, so the crooked policeman must have taken his orders from someone else. From what Sean had learned from Tony, that had to be the British traitor, Lord Albert Ulverstone, who must have suspected that Tony was the attempted assassin.

Sean ushered Patrick off to bed, and when he returned to the kitchen he took down the bottle of good whisky and poured himself a stiff drink.

Sir George was the link, he felt certain of that. Ulverstone would not have had contact with Preston otherwise, and it was well known that Macintosh and Ulverstone often dined together at the Australia Club or the Imperial Services Club.

Sean took a deep swallow of the fiery liquid. He was walking on dangerous ground if he was going to link a well-known police officer, a respected Australian knight of the realm and a British lord to a conspiracy to commit murder. He would have to tread very carefully from here on.

Sean was asleep slumped at the table when David returned from the movies. He gently woke Sean, and assisted him to his bed.

*

Sarah paced her office, her thoughts consumed with the fact that Allison was occupying David's leave time. What if she told him that he was Michael's real father? Would that bring him back to her? No, that was not an option for her.

The scandal would destroy any hope she had of taking sole control of the family enterprises.

'Your father is here to see you, Miss Macintosh,' her secretary said from the doorway.

'Show him in, Anne,' Sarah said, composing herself. 'Sit down, Daddy,' she said, ushering him to a comfortable leather chair.

Sir George eased himself into the chair. 'I have just had an interesting talk with your brother,' he said, and Sarah experienced a twinge of annoyance. She was acutely aware that her father liked to pit her against Donald; it was his way of manipulating them. Still, she understood him; she had inherited his desire for control.

'I doubt that Donald could have had much to contribute,' Sarah snorted, taking a cigarette from a gold case and lighting it.

'He thinks we should throw our weight behind Curtin and his Labor Party in the next elections.'

'What?' Sarah exclaimed in shock. 'The Labor Party is full of communists. They gave tacit support to those stupid women munitions workers in Melbourne who went on strike for equal pay. I have always suspected that Donald is a communist sympathiser. It will bring us down one day.'

'You exaggerate,' Sir George said. 'He thinks we should throw our lot in with what he expects to be the winning side in the August elections. After all, we have benefitted a great deal from government contracts and we do not wish to lose them with a change of government. After some consideration, I agree that we should be sympathetic to the Labor cause – at least until the end of the war.'

Sarah puffed heavily on her cigarette. Her brother had just usurped her position again and her father had been swayed to his side.

'I believe that your husband visited Goulburn to see your son,' Sir George said, changing the subject. 'I question whether your leaving him is such a good idea. My sources tell me that he has proven himself a sterling pilot and officer. Such a man by your side can only enhance your station in Sydney society.'

Sarah strode to the window of her office to stare out at the cascading rain. The winter of 1943 had proven to be wetter than usual, and the rain was affecting production in the agricultural sector of the Macintosh industries. Flooded roads and drowned crops had caused vegetable shortages.

'I might consider having him back,' she said, gazing at her refection in the window. 'But not into my bed.'

'You need to show the world that you are not only a competent businesswoman but also a good mother and wife,' Sir George said. 'The business world is not ready to have a divorced mother in such a significant role.' Sir George rose from his chair. 'I have a lunch appointment, so I will say goodbye.'

After her father left, Sarah remained standing by the window, and for a moment wondered where her estranged husband was at this time. The thought was fleeting, and she walked back to her desk to consider two important matters: how she could assert herself over her brother, and how she could destroy her best friend.

*

Sir George Macintosh sat in his library brooding over the file he had received from a clerk in his law firm. In actual fact, it was a file of copied notes passed to a contact in his law firm from an articled clerk inside Sean Duffy's own law practice, who had found living on a legal apprentice's salary insufficient for an interesting and diverse social life.

For a generous fee, the Duffy clerk had been tasked with acquiring any information that pertained to the Canadian merchant sailor recently deceased at Long Bay Gaol. The clerk had found a wad of scribbled notes that included various names, and amongst them Sir George saw his own name, along with those of Lord Ulverstone and Detective Sergeant Preston.

Sir George passed the file to the man sitting opposite him.

Lord Ulverstone read the file and looked up at Sir George. 'Do you consider this solicitor any real threat?' he asked.

'I have known Major Duffy for many years, and I regret to say that he is a tough and dangerous man, despite his physical disabilities. He appears to have linked the three of us to the killing in Long Bay.'

'From what I can glean from his notes he does not have any evidence to substantiate that link,' Ulverstone said, passing the file back to Sir George. 'I do not think there is any need to worry about some minor city solicitor.'

'You do not know Duffy as I do,' Sir George cautioned. 'He will not stop until he has evidence, and he has many contacts in the criminal class of Sydney. You might have noticed in the copy of his notes he mentions a contact recently released from Long Bay who gave him Preston's name, and how Duffy linked that to me and completed the circle by including you as an acquaintance of mine. We don't know how much the Canadian told him about his attempt on your life. As a matter of fact, you have not even told me very much about why some lunatic would want to kill you.'

'Better you do not know, old chap,' Ulverstone said. 'But if this solicitor might be a threat to us, do you have any ideas of how we can smother the matter before it goes too far? Can the man be bought?'

'Not Duffy,' Sir George answered. 'The only way he can be stopped is if he has a serious accident.'

For a moment Sir George reflected on this option. He had tried many years earlier to kill Sean Duffy, and might have succeeded had he not lost his initial contact in the police force, Inspector Jack Firth. Sir George strongly suspected that Sean Duffy, aided by his friend Harry Griffiths, had murdered the disgraced policeman. Sir George had learned some respect for Duffy after that.

'Can you arrange that?' Ulverstone asked.

Sir George looked sharply at the British aristocrat. 'I have already stuck my neck out for you,' he said. 'And it might just end up in the hangman's noose if Duffy succeeds in gathering evidence against us.'

'I appreciate what you did,' Ulverstone said. 'But matters have taken a bad turn for us both, and if we let the matter continue I will be joining you on the scaffold. Permanently removing Duffy is our only option. When the Canadian was killed, the police informed me that their investigations indicated a prison argument and nothing else. As far as they are concerned, the matter is closed. We need to ensure it remains that way.'

'I will think about it,' Sir George said. 'I am sure that Preston will have an interest in Duffy's demise when he sees what is in the file.'

Ulverstone rose from the leather chair. 'I will leave it with you, then.'

Sir George did not reply. Getting rid of Sean Duffy was something he should have done a long time ago. This time there would be no mistakes. He promised himself that.

THIRTEEN

James Duffy's persistence in wooing Julianna did not seem to be working. She had not returned his calls, and she avoided him whenever he was at the studios where she worked. He was surrounded by beautiful aspiring actresses and several had made it known they would like to become more closely acquainted, but James had eyes only for Julianna.

On his evenings off James would attend the Hollywood Canteen where Julianna continued her voluntary work. James would stand back in the crowd, sipping coffee and watching her whilst enjoying the entertainment of the big names in the town that created dreams.

On one of his evenings off he attended the Hollywood Canteen wearing a civilian suit. The doormen knew him well by now and they greeted him with respect and let him in. He ordered his usual coffee and glanced at the queue where Julianna was serving doughnuts to a young marine. She caught his eye and frowned her disapproval at his attention.

James shrugged and disappeared into the crowd, spending the evening jitterbugging with the beautiful young ladies from the studios. When it was time for Julianna to finish her shift and leave, James followed.

Outside on the busy street he saw Julianna standing at the kerb waiting for a taxi, and he also noticed that a couple of large drunken men dressed in army uniform had stopped to talk to her. He picked up his stride and when he was around twenty paces away he could hear their raised voices and Julianna's protests.

'Hey, buddy, leave the lady alone,' James shouted.

The soldier, who was obviously attempting to steal a kiss from Julianna, turned with a scowl to confront James.

'Push off, sport,' he said. 'We don't take orders from yellow-bellied civvies.'

James could see that neither man wore any combat ribbons and guessed that they were barrack-room heroes.

Julianna was wide-eyed with fear. 'It is okay, James,' she said, as if pleading for him to go away.

'This pretty boy your boyfriend?' the soldier asked. 'Why would a pretty gal like you waste your time with a snivelling civilian not man enough to be in uniform?'

'Captain Duffy is a marine fighter pilot who has the Navy Cross,' Julianna said, and noticed that the information made the belligerent soldier blink.

'I hate marines,' he said and swung wildly at James, who saw the punch coming and stepped aside. The big soldier followed his punch and went down in the gutter. His comrade bent to pick him up. He was just a fraction more sober, and with some difficulty hefted the first soldier to his feet.

'Time we got home,' he said as he helped the drunken soldier down the busy street.

'Are you okay?' James asked Julianna. He could see she was trembling.

'I thought they might hurt you,' she whispered.

James broke into a broad smile. 'So you do care about me,' he said.

'Of course I do,' Julianna said with a weak smile. 'I always have, but you betrayed me.'

'We were only friends at the time,' James said in his defence.

'You might be a fighter ace,' Julianna replied, 'but you have a lot to learn about how women function, Captain Duffy. I have to return to the studio to prepare notes for tomorrow morning's shoot. Would you like to share a taxi with me?'

'It would be my pleasure,' James said. 'I have never had the opportunity to see how you work.'

'We have a good supply of coffee and, according to your schedule, you do not have any commitments until tomorrow evening,' Julianna said.

'How . . . You have been speaking with Guy,' he said.

'Guy keeps me up to date on your busy schedule,' Julianna replied with a mischievous grin.

It was gradually dawning on James that he had served his period of penance and now Julianna was giving him another chance. He could not stop a big smile from spreading across his face.

At the studio the security guards greeted Julianna warmly, as they were used to seeing her working late at night. James followed her to the building where she shared offices with other scriptwriters and editors. A Hispanic female cleaner greeted her with familiarity, and Julianna responded in fluent Spanish. The two women laughed at a shared joke, and James was impressed with her knowledge of the language.

'I didn't know you could speak Spanish,' he said.

'I also speak French, Italian and have a fair grasp of the English language.' Julianna opened the door to a large room filled with tables, typewriters and rubbish bins overflowing with crumpled paper. 'My desk is over there. Welcome to my world.'

On the wall behind Julianna's desk was a row of studio portraits of silent-movie stars. James gazed at the photos and recognised many. His eyes fell on one in particular: a beautiful young woman by the name of Fenella Macintosh.

'Fenella Macintosh,' James said. 'I remember seeing a movie she was in when I was a kid.'

Julianna stood back, looking at the portrait. 'She had an interesting life. She was an Aussie, a well-known actress in her own country. When she came to Hollywood she was just starting to make a name for herself when she was murdered at her home up in the Hollywood hills.'

'I know her family!' James exclaimed. 'Her brother is Sir George Macintosh. I spent last Christmas Day with Sir George and his family in Sydney; he is an associate of my grandfather.'

Julianna looked at James in surprise. 'What a coincidence,' she said. 'I have been toying with the idea of writing a script about her. There were rumours that her own brother plotted to have her killed.'

'Sir George?' James said. 'I met him, and he does not strike me as a killer. Maybe a ruthless businessman, but not a man capable of having his own sister killed.'

Julianna shrugged. 'How can you tell what anyone is capable of? You probably did not think you were capable of killing before this war began.' She gazed at the face of the woman long dead. 'In my research of Fenella's life I came across the name of a young man, Sean Duffy, who seemed to be linked to her somehow. There was also a young man named Matthew Duffy who I have traced as far as his flying career in Palestine in the Great War. From her diaries it seems they were linked romantically for a short while at the beginning of the century. Apparently Matthew Duffy was the son of an American prospector and ran away to enlist in the war in South Africa against the Boer farmers.'

James paled. 'That had to be my father,' he said quietly. 'It could be no other person.'

'What?' Julianna gasped. 'Are you sure? I can hardly believe it.' She shook her head. 'Here I am with an interest in Fenella's life, and all the time she is linked to your life.' Julianna sat down in her shock, and picked up the framed portrait of Fenella Macintosh to stare into the expressive eyes of the former Hollywood actress. 'What a tragic life you had,' she whispered and looked up at James. 'I could almost believe that her ghost destined us to meet.'

James and Julianna gazed in silence at Fenella's portrait and James felt Julianna's hand slip into his own. When James departed for his hotel in the early hours of the morning, he kissed Julianna gently on the lips.

His commitments kept him apart from Julianna for a couple of days, but eventually they were able to meet at his hotel for dinner. James was in his dress uniform and Julianna was wearing a stylish silk dress, and heads turned to admire the handsome fighter pilot and the lovely young lady on his arm as they were escorted to a table.

When they had ordered James lifted his glass of champagne in a toast. 'To the most beautiful creature God ever put on this earth,' he said with a warm smile. Julianna blushed.

She lifted her own flute. 'May God protect the most precious man in my life.'

'I thought that after dinner we might go to my room for a nightcap,' he said.

Julianna frowned. 'James, I do not think that is a good idea.'

'Sorry,' he said, realising he had been a little forward. 'It is just that every part of me wants to be so close to you.'

'James, I feel the same way, but I was brought up to believe such things are sanctified only in marriage. I know it may be difficult for you to understand, but I was raised a strict Catholic and I cannot defy the laws of my religion. I realise that many of the girls you have known in the past may not have held the same beliefs.'

James blinked. He had never really considered religion an issue – until now. He had been reared by his grandfather, a staunch Protestant. He was vaguely aware that his father, Matthew Duffy, had been a Roman Catholic. Other than that, religion did not play much of a role in his young life. 'Does your religion forbid you to kiss before marriage?' James asked.

'No, no,' Julianna hurried to reassure. 'It is just that the most precious thing I can give you is my body, and then only in the holy sacrament of matrimony.'

James wanted to groan. He glanced around the dining room at the other young couples and wondered what they would be doing after their meal tonight. 'Maybe God turns a blind eye in time of war,' he said in an effort to make her smile.

'I am frightened, James,' she said. 'What if you return to the war and I never see you again? I could not survive that kind of grief after losing my little brother. You have done more than enough in this war, and you have nothing to prove to anyone. Guy tells me there are grounds for you to be honourably discharged. Or, if you wished to remain with the marines, you could ask for a training or administrative posting stateside.'

The champagne in James's stomach suddenly soured. Even though the chances of returning to combat flying seemed remote at the moment, he had not given up hope that his public relations stint in Hollywood would come to an end and he would once again find himself in the cockpit of a Hellcat fighter on the decks of the *Enterprise*.

'That would be a difficult choice for me,' James said. 'I think I might be in love with you.'

Julianna reached across the table, taking both James's hands in her own, and there were tears in her eyes.

'Oh, James, you don't know how much I have wanted to hear those words from you,' she said. 'I love you, and that is the problem, because I am terrified I will lose you to the war.'

'The way things are going I doubt that is any great possibility – unless I die of food poisoning or boredom.'

Julianna tried to laugh but she could see the pain in his eyes. She knew she was demanding a lot of James, but how was it that men could be so stupid as to choose the possibility of being killed over love and a life of peace?

That evening as they parted the long lingering kiss between them sealed an expression of desire and hope.

James returned to his room and was about to take off his jacket when he noticed a telegram on the table by the bowl of fruit. He picked it up and read the terse lines. It was from his sister Olivia. His grandfather had suffered a stroke and James was needed urgently back in New Hampshire. Everything had changed again in the blink of an eye.

*

Jessica was keeping in touch with Sean Duffy by telephone, consulting with him in his investigation of Tony's murder. There had been little to report since Sean had disclosed his suspicions about the collusion between Sir George Macintosh, Lord Ulverstone and a crooked police detective.

Jessica was growing frustrated. She was determined to get justice for the young American officer she wished she had shown more love for. The war had brought him into her life from across the Pacific, and it had taken him from her. She was growing bored of sitting around the house listening to the radio, reading and cooking for her two housemates. Occasionally she would go to the movies or visit the shops to browse the few goods still on the shelves. Rationing was biting, but people were still able to live a near normal life, albeit bereft of luxuries.

The phone rarely rang but this afternoon it did and when Jessica answered she recognised Sean's voice at the other end.

'I want you to put on your best hat and go and see a movie tonight at your favourite movie theatre,' he said.

'Why?' Jessica responded.

'Because you will meet someone there I consider a friend to our cause,' Sean replied. 'It is important, so please be there.'

'Who is the friend?' Jessica asked.

'You will know him when you see him,' Sean said. 'I do not want to give his name over the phone.'

'This is as mysterious as an Agatha Christie novel,' Jessica said. 'But I will be there.'

'Good, Miss Campbell,' Sean said and hung up.

Jessica sat by the telephone staring at the hand piece. Sean was careful not to identify her when using the telephone, and Jessica's past role in intelligence work made her appreciate his caution.

That evening Jessica dressed up warmly against the bitter cold of winter and caught a train into the city, where she walked a block to the theatre. People were huddled in lines awaiting entry out of the cold and Jessica scanned the queues of men and women. She drew a sharp breath when she recognised a familiar face.

Donald Macintosh was wearing a trenchcoat and his hands were thrust into his pockets. From his demeanour Jessica could see that he was expecting someone – and that someone had to be her. Their eyes met and he nodded his head, walking away from the entrance to the movie theatre. Jessica took his gesture as a signal to follow him. He walked to a small cafe nearby, and the two of them slipped into a booth together.

'Ah, Jessie,' he said by way of greeting. 'What have you gone and done?'

'I don't know what you mean,' Jessica said.

The cafe was warm and Donald removed his hat and coat. 'I will order a pot of tea and a round of sandwiches,' he said. 'I know everything, so there is no sense in you hiding the truth from me. Major Duffy has briefed me on his investigation.'

Jessica was stunned. Why would Sean brief the son of the man he suspected of being complicit in Tony's death?

As if reading her thoughts Donald said, 'I know about Major Duffy's suspicions concerning my father, but Sean has been more of a father to me than my own. There is a rottenness in our family, but despite my strong dislike for my father, I pray that Sean is wrong about his part in Lieutenant Caccamo's death.'

'So you know about Tony?' Jessica cut in. 'What else do you know?'

'I know that you could soon be classified as a deserter, and that carries very heavy penalties in wartime,' Donald said quietly. 'Even the PM is aware of you leaving your post. He is very disappointed.'

Jessica was stunned to hear that her absence from MacArthur's HQ in Brisbane had reached the Prime Minister's Department. Jessica had met John Curtin briefly and she admired him. To disappoint the leader of Australia hurt Jessica more than any military penalty could.

'You know I have my reasons for taking unauthorised leave,' she said. 'For all I know my own department could have been responsible for his death.'

'From the little that I have been able to glean, the Yanks were actually working in the background to quietly secure his release. They were just as stunned to learn of his murder. But I also suspect they are not overly disappointed that he has been silenced.'

'That just leaves the Major and myself to care about justice for Tony and his family back in New York,' Jessica said bitterly.

'And me,' Donald corrected her. 'I am in a position to help.'

'Why did you meet me tonight?' Jessica asked.

'I wanted you to know that I am on your side, Jessie,' he answered. 'You are still someone that I care about a lot.'

Jessica could see in Donald's eyes there was no guile behind this statement, and for a moment the days in western Queensland before the war came back to her in a gentle wave of memories. But so much had happened in the last couple of years and the two of them were now worlds apart.

'I appreciate your concern,' she said. 'I presume that you have my telephone number, should you need to contact me.'

Donald nodded. 'This is my number in case you ever need help,' he said, passing Jessica a slip of paper.

Donald ordered and then the two chatted as if they were back at Glen View and had just come in from riding their horses. That was a lifetime ago when the world knew peace.

FOURTEEN

The tranquillity of summer in New Hampshire brought back a host of memories for James Duffy as he drove up the tree-lined avenue to his grandfather's mansion. He had grown up in one of New Hampshire's wealthiest families with all that money could afford a young man, and before the war it had seemed his life would turn out to be just like his grandfather's, one built on power and privilege.

James alighted from his sports car and was met by his grandfather's old black butler at the front door. The two men greeted each other with fond familiarity, and the old servant led James inside. Olivia, his twin sister, came bowling towards him and threw her arms around his neck.

'James!' she said. 'It is so good to see you.'

James hugged her fiercely, then stepped back to look at her properly. She was dressed in a tennis skirt and had obviously just come off the court. Beside her was a tall and handsome young man James knew from his days at his exclusive high school. His name was Edgar Wilson and James did not like him. It was rumoured that his wealthy and influential politician father had found a way to have him exempted from the draft.

'I have heard a lot about your exploits,' Edgar said without offering his hand. 'Olivia has told me that you are a fighter ace. What's it like to be a hero?'

James was wearing his marine uniform, with the Navy Cross riband on his chest. 'Just been lucky,' he replied. 'How is Grandfather?' he asked, turning to his sister.

'He has recovered well,' she answered. 'He is upstairs in his library and will be thrilled to see you. He has been asking all day when you will arrive.'

'Well, better go and announce my arrival,' James said, leaving his sister and her despised boyfriend downstairs.

James climbed the broad turning staircase to the upper storey. The library door was open and James walked in to find his grandfather, James Barrington Senior, dressed in his pyjamas, dressing gown and slippers, sitting at his great polished timber desk. He glanced up at James and for a moment his face lit up with love and joy. The normally dour man rarely demonstrated emotion, so James was surprised and touched at his reaction.

'Hello, sir,' he said, wondering if he should go over and hug the old man.

'James, it is very good to see you,' Barrington said, attempting to rise.

James could see that he was physically weak from the stroke and quickly stepped in to help him. When he did his grandfather took James's hand and shook it. He helped the old man to a comfortable divan in the centre of the room and sat him down.

'It is good to see how well you have recovered.'

'Take a seat, James,' his grandfather said, patting a spot beside him. 'There is much to discuss while you are here. My sources on the west coast have told me that you are doing a fine job raising war bonds, but I suspect you would rather be back flying your Wild Cats.'

'You are right there, sir,' James answered. 'I have done everything that I can to get back into the war, but all my requests have fallen on deaf ears.'

'I will confess that I have used my friendship with the President to ensure that you are kept out of harm's way,' Barrington sighed. 'You are the only male member of my blood line, and even though you have adopted your father's family name, you are still my grandson. Look around you,' he continued, waving his arm. 'All this means nothing if it cannot be passed on.'

'There is Olivia,' James reminded him.

'Olivia is a woman,' Barrington snorted. 'She will find a man and follow him. As a matter of fact she appears to be very keen on that Wilson boy. Good family with a good pedigree.'

'I thought that my sister and Donald Macintosh were a sure thing,' James said. 'In my opinion, Donald was a far better deal than Wilson.'

'Your sister has a lot more sense than you,' Barrington said. 'She was not prepared to live so far away from home.'

'Well, I suppose I should cross off romance as a strong feature of my sister,' James sighed.

'She inherited the common sense from my side of the family,' Barrington said. 'Your reckless and impulsive acts appear to be in the Irish blood of your father.'

'At least the love of flying I got from my father,' James said. 'I know that it is in your power to speak to people in

Washington, and have me sent back to active service flying,' James said.

'That would be reckless,' Barrington countered. 'I need you here by my side. The next stroke may end my life, and I want to know that everything our family has fought for will continue when I am gone. I will not beat about the bush, James, I want you to resign your commission and return home. There is a position on the board for you, and I think with your public exposure as a war hero you could possibly end up with the governor's job.'

'I'm not a hero,' James said. 'Do you know how scared I get when I am in the cockpit, waiting to take off? I have to fight not to piss myself.'

'Despite that, you have proven yourself hero enough to be awarded the Navy Cross for valour,' Barrington said. 'What the voters will see is a handsome and dashing young man whose reputation for courage cannot be questioned.'

James could see that his grandfather was going to use all his considerable influence to keep him out of the war. Maybe he was right, James thought. He had done his bit, but then the memories of all those other men he had seen die – from the skies in the Pacific to the hell of Guadalcanal on the ground – came back to him. Yet if he accepted his grandfather's wishes he could go back to Julianna and tell her he was leaving the marines and the war behind. That would please her, and they could start planning a future together.

'If I accept your offer,' James said, 'it would have to include a woman I am in love with and hope to make my wife.'

'That is excellent news,' Barrington said. 'A man standing for public office is more favourably looked upon if he has a wife and family. Do I know the lady in question?'

'I doubt it,' James said. 'She is from New Orleans and works in Hollywood. Her name is Miss Julianna Dupont.'

'Dupont,' Barrington echoed. 'I know of the New Orleans Duponts,' he said and James could see a dark cloud come over his grandfather's face. 'As far as I know they are a strong Papist family.'

'They are Roman Catholics,' James said. 'I believe that her family rivals our own when it comes to money and capital in the South.'

'You cannot entertain the idea of marrying a Roman Catholic,' Barrington said. 'Get the foolish idea out of your head. There are plenty of eligible girls back here in New Hampshire from good families.'

'With or without your permission, I intend to propose to Julianna,' James said firmly.

Barrington rose from the divan and walked on unsteady legs back to his desk where he slumped into his chair. 'I can pick up the telephone right now and call Washington. A word from me and you would find yourself back in the cockpit of a Hellcat. I know you would use what little common sense you appear to have and delay any idea of marriage until the war is over.'

'I would, Grandfather,' James said, shocked that his grandfather would rather see him dead than married to a Catholic.

'I will call friends in the War Department to arrange for your return to active service – if you promise me that you will not go ahead with any foolish ideas of marriage to that woman.'

'You have my word,' James answered. 'At least until the end of the war. I think that I should catch up with my sister now that we are both clear on how things stand between us.'

'James, you have misread me,' Barrington began to protest. 'I love you and only have the best intentions at heart.'

'My best intentions or yours, Grandfather?' James said. 'I have always respected your wishes, and I am grateful for all that you have given Olivia and myself over the years. You forget, however, that my mother, your daughter, fell in love with a Roman Catholic, and I carry his blood and name. I love and respect you, but I cannot denounce who I am. Good afternoon, sir. I will see you when we dine tonight.'

James left the library and walked slowly down the stairs, reflecting on how his flesh and blood would rather risk losing him in combat than see him marry a Catholic. It was strange that back in combat no one really cared about a man's religious beliefs. Each was a brother to the man fighting beside him, and somehow James felt that the same thing should occur at home. He would keep his promise to his grandfather, but he would also marry Julianna when he returned from the war and hung up his wings. All he had to do was lie to Julianna and say that the marines had decided he was needed back in the Pacific. Hopefully she would accept that matters were out of his hands and promise to wait for him. He knew he was walking a dangerous tightrope.

*

The message written on the sheet of paper in Sean's hands shook him to the core. He looked at young Patrick standing with his school bag slung over his shoulder and shuddered.

'Who gave you this piece of paper?' Sean asked, fighting to keep calm.

'A man outside the schoolyard said he knew you and he wanted me to give you the letter because it was important,' the boy said.

Sean reread the threat: *The boy carrying this message to you could have a bad accident if you do not stop asking questions about the death of the Canadian.*

'What did the man look like?' Sean asked and the boy shrugged.

'He was old,' he said.

Anyone over eight years of age was old to Patrick.

'If you see the man again, run back to school and tell Sister Mary he is trying to hurt you,' Sean said, knowing full well why Patrick had been given the message. It was a way of showing how vulnerable the boy was. How in hell did anyone outside a trusted few know about his investigation? He did not suspect Jessica or Donald. There was obviously a leak, and it had to be inside his own law firm. Was it worth continuing this investigation if Patrick's safety was at risk? Sean gazed down at the schoolboy with paternal fondness. It was time for a talk with Jessica and Donald, to discuss what they should do from here.

A meeting was arranged for the next day. They would individually take ferries to the popular beachside suburb of Manly and then catch a ferry straight back to Circular Quay together.

When Sean's ferry pulled into the wharf he saw Donald reading a newspaper, whilst Jessica sat on a bench throwing chips to the swarms of seagulls. The three immediately boarded the next ferry returning to Circular Quay across the windswept harbour. The ferry dipped and rolled through the heavy seas pouring in from the harbour's heads. The other passengers were mostly servicemen from America, and a few from Australia. In many cases they were in the company of young women. A few of the older civilian passengers frowned at the fraternisation of the American servicemen with Aussie girls as the little ferry passed between the hulls of the great warships anchored in the harbour.

'I have had a threat delivered to me,' Sean said when the three were together inside the cabin. 'Had it been directed at me personally I would not be worried, but the threat was against young Patrick.'

'You have to be a low bastard to threaten a child,' Donald growled. 'Do you have any suspicions as to who may have been behind it?'

'I think the most obvious person would be Detective Preston,' Sean said.

'It might be best if you stop your investigation,' Jessica said. 'It is not worth Patrick's safety – or yours.'

'How will you get justice for Tony if I desist now?' Sean asked.

'I will finish Tony's mission,' Jessica said quietly, causing both men to look sharply at her.

'Do you mean killing Ulverstone?' Donald asked in horror.

'That was Tony's mission, and it is the only way we will get any justice for him. I doubt that we will ever be able to collect enough evidence to expose him as a traitor. He is too well protected by the system,' she said with quiet certainty.

'Jessie,' Sean said sternly, 'you have been a nun, and the Ten Commandments tell us that to kill is a mortal sin. Besides, killing a man is not as easy as it may seem.'

'Major, we are at war and Ulverstone is an enemy – a traitor. What is the difference between shooting the enemy in New Guinea or in Australia?'

'It's a stupid idea,' Sean grumbled. 'Forget it. What you should be doing is worrying about your position as a deserter, not going after a man with legal protection.'

'Ulverstone is about to be appointed to a committee on our defence strategy,' Donald said. 'That would allow him into the most secret meetings we hold with the Americans. I was in Canberra a couple of weeks ago when the Americans protested his appointment, but it fell on deaf ears with our people.'

'All the more reason why I should finish Tony's mission,' Jessica said.

'You are not with the Special Operations Executive,' Sean cautioned. 'That is something they would do. Besides, it is preposterous – a former nun executing a man on Australian soil. If you are caught you will probably face the same fate as your young American officer. I doubt that if he were alive he would condone your harebrained idea.'

'I am a member of the armed forces,' Jessica said, 'and I am prepared to put my life on the line to defend this country. My father has done so many times, as you have, Major.'

'A very stirring, patriotic speech,' Donald said sarcastically. 'But you have to have a watertight plan to carry out such a mission.'

'I have,' Jessica replied. 'And I will need your help, Donald.'

Donald blinked his surprise as the ferry plunged into a wave trough, forcing the three to grip a rail in the cabin. 'How can I help?' he asked warily.

'You are in a position to get close to Ulverstone,' Jessica said. 'You have told me that you have met the man at your father's place, and I believe you have occasion to mix with him at a professional level. All you have to do is arrange for me to meet Lord Ulverstone and I will take it from there.'

'I am not sure if Ulverstone is inclined towards the fairer sex,' Donald said.

'Then find out,' Jessica said firmly. 'If all goes well, you two will be out of this conspiracy after I meet Ulverstone. You will have alibis if you are ever questioned, which will be very unlikely. Oh, Major, I will need a pistol. I used to practise with my father's Webley & Scott on the station when I was young. I can assure you that I am very capable with a revolver. Can you do that?'

'I can,' Sean answered. 'But I am reluctant to support your plan to kill Ulverstone. There is no such thing as the perfect murder. Believe me, I have seen many people try and fail in my career as a criminal defence lawyer.'

'This is not a murder,' Jessica said. 'It is an execution of a dangerous traitor. Besides, if things go wrong I know the best solicitor in Sydney.' She tried to give him a reassuring smile.

'Jessie, Jessie,' Sean said, shaking his head. 'This is madness. There has to be another way.'

'I hate to admit it,' Donald said, 'but I think Jessie could be right. There is no other way to remove Ulverstone. What Jessie and I must do is plan this out to the very smallest detail. I have always felt guilty that I allowed my father to keep me out of uniform, but if I help get rid of Ulverstone I will be playing my part in the war.'

Sean's shoulders sagged as he realised that the young woman almost as dear as a daughter had made up her mind. She was very much like her father, Tom Duffy: stubborn and proud. He did not know whether to applaud her bravery or chastise her recklessness.

FIFTEEN

Flying officer Charles Huntley checked his control panel as the powerful engine of the Spitfire growled into life. The heat of the north shimmered on the airstrip, and around him other Spitfires came to life. The RAAF radio stations located along the coast were tracking the Japanese aircraft flying towards Darwin, and reports relayed indicated a force of around twenty bombers escorted by the same number of Zero fighters. Charles wondered if he would be up against the earlier version, the single-seater monoplane Zeke, or the improved version, the Hap, with its squared-off wing tips. Experienced fighter pilots from the European theatre, such as Group Captain Caldwell, had warned new Spitfire pilots that the nimble Zero fighter could run rings around the Spitties at low altitudes and that the war in the skies over Darwin required different tactics to those in the skies over Britain and France.

The Japanese air raids had been constant since 13 June but this would be Charles's first time taking them on from the cockpit of a Spitfire. He knew that the sweat rolling down his face was not simply from the heat of the tropical north. The waiting was the worst. Charles could hear his fellow pilots over his headset; everyone was jumpy, he could hear it in their voices. The locals had informed him that there had been around fifty to sixty raids on Darwin since February 1942. The Japanese usually attacked in the daylight hours for a clear view of their targets, but a consolation to Charles was that reinforced batteries of 3.7 inch AA guns were forcing the Japanese pilots to fly higher, and above 20,000 feet the Spitfire came into its own against the infamous Zero fighter.

Finally the command came to become airborne; they needed to reach their preferred height before the enemy aircraft appeared over Darwin. Charles throttled up and his fighter plane rolled onto the airstrip. Then it was time to fully open up and take off. The Spitfire was designed to be part of the pilot, and Charles experienced the exhilarating force push him back in his seat as the aircraft danced into the air, levelling off at around 27,000 feet to test the guns with a short squirt of valuable ammunition. Even as he did so the glint of the sun on metal aircraft skins indicated the moment had come and Charles watched as the enemy aircraft slid under him. The order was given to engage.

Charles was wingman to a more experienced fighter pilot and followed him down to attack a twin-engine bomber. He could see tracer fire arcing up at them both from a gunner on the bomber, but already bullets were spewing from the Spitfires' eight .303 calibre wing-mounted guns, and Charles could see the bomber shudder under the impact. Smoke began to pour from one of the engines, indicating that it would soon be crippled. While his commander concentrated on bringing the bomber down, Charles swept the skies for any threat, and he found it. A Japanese Hap fighter had locked onto the commander's plane and was manoeuvring to get on his tail. Charles called out his warning to the pilot following the stricken bomber down to finish it off.

Charles knew he must somehow get behind the Japanese pilot, and he pulled hard on the controls to lift the nose of his aircraft for a vertical climb. He was fortunate that the enemy pilot was fixated on wreaking revenge on the Spitfire commander, and Charles was able to roll over and dive down to level off a thousand yards behind the enemy Hap. He was still too far out to engage, so he put on as much power as he could to close the distance. The Japanese pilot realised the new threat on his tail and rolled sideways to avoid it. Charles followed his lead and suddenly realised that his foe was not an amateur as he was taking Charles to a lower height where the Hap could out-turn him and get on his tail. All Charles could think of was to roll over as he climbed, so that he could position himself to get a straight shot at the diving Japanese fighter plane. His tactic worked, but he found himself further away when he straightened up in the dive to pursue the enemy to a lower altitude. Charles put on all the power he had and felt the g-forces press against his body with crushing weight. He was suddenly oblivious to all the voices in his headset and felt for the trigger on his guns.

The enemy pilot suddenly began to level off and make a tight right turn, endeavouring to outmanoeuvre the Spitfire. Charles knew he was in real trouble now. He could see the calm green and azure sea below him and around him a brilliant blue sky with just a dusting of fluffy white clouds. In desperation he pulled on his controls to engage in the tightest turn he could. The g-forces had almost brought him to the point of blacking out, but through his tunnel vision brought on by the massive strain on his body he noticed in a split second that the enemy aircraft was below him and Charles had been able to get his nose up. In desperation he fired ahead of the Hap, praying that the enemy would fly into the stream of .303 rounds. He was hardly aware that his bullets had riddled the enemy fighter until it suddenly burst into flames and exploded violently. The Japanese fighter planes had sacrificed life-saving heavy armour protection in favour of manoeuvrability and range.

Charles hurtled past the fireball spiralling towards the water and knew that he must level off before he joined his opponent in the Arafura Sea. When he did he could see that he was just above the water and his training immediately kicked in. Charles glanced around and off to his left he could see the tiny dots, smoke trails of downed aircraft and swirling fighters of both sides. Now he was aware that his commander was calling him and in as calm a voice as possible Charles declared that he had downed one of the enemy.

Within minutes he was flying back into the melee, but it was already breaking up as the surviving Japanese aircraft turned for home. One or two stragglers were pursued for further kills, but eventually the squadron returned to the airstrip in Darwin, where Charles brought his Spitfire in to land. He taxied to a designated position and watched, physically and mentally exhausted, as his ground crew came running towards him. It was time to leave the cockpit, and Charles reached for a very precious talisman – a photograph of his baby son pinned to the side of the cockpit.

Charles slid open the cockpit canopy and felt the rush of warm air hit his face.

'The Nips have lost nine bombers and five fighters,' his armourer yelled up at him. 'A bloody good tally for the day, skipper.'

Charles nodded his head, acknowledging the enthusiasm of his ground crew now joining the armourer beside the Spitfire. He gripped the photo of his son, then realised that he hardly had the strength to leave the cockpit.

★

Major David Macintosh appreciated that his training role kept him in Sydney near to the people dear to him, but he found himself yearning for command of a company engaged in fighting the war against the Japanese. He had been an acting company commander up in the jungles during the desperate struggle along the Kokoda Track, and he dreamed of returning to that role.

He was sitting in his office making his way through training reports when his orderly room clerk poked his head around the corner.

'Sir, you have a telephone call from Brigadier Johnson.'

'Thanks, corp,' David said, remembering with fondness his old battalion commander who had now been promoted to the rank of brigadier.

David lifted the receiver. 'Major Macintosh speaking, sir,' he said.

'David, how the devil are you?' the brigadier said. 'Enjoying your stint with training command, I hope.'

'Well, boss,' David said, 'I would rather be back with the boys in the battalion.'

'I was hoping you would say that,' the brigadier said. 'The battalion is short a company commander and I immediately thought of you.'

David felt like standing up and saluting, such was his joy at the news. 'Sir, just name your favourite whisky and I will have a case delivered.'

The chuckle at the other end of the line brought back memories for both men when they had sat together in the rotting undergrowth of the New Guinea forests, discussing life back home – colonel and captain. 'No need for rewards, Major Macintosh,' the brigadier chuckled. 'Just do a bloody good job of keeping the boys in your company alive, and bring them back home in one piece. Your replacement is already on his way to take over your training command. You have forty-eight hours to get him up to speed, and then you will have a week's leave before you head off to join the battalion up north. Your orders will arrive tomorrow, so good luck. Your battalion will be part of my brigade.'

'Sir, that is bonzer news,' David said, still reeling from his stroke of good luck.

He replaced the telephone on the cradle and stared at the wall of his office. Outside the building senior noncommissioned officers bawled orders at potential young officers, treating them as if they should have stayed home with their mothers instead. In the distance David could hear the crackle of rifle fire as the trainee officers practised marksmanship with their .303 rifles. A magpie warbled a song from the tall gum tree just outside David's Nissan hut. It all sounded so peaceful and such a contrast to what he had experienced on the battlefields of North Africa, Greece, Crete and Syria. The New Guinea campaign was a hell all of its own, it required so much physical and mental strength just to stay alive.

As elated as he was, David was sobered by the fact that he would have to inform Sean and Allison that he was once again being transferred to the war zone of the South West Pacific. He wondered who he would break the news to first, and decided that it would be Allison.

That evening around six-thirty David arrived in uniform at Allison's apartment. She was surprised to see that he had not changed into his civilian suit, as was his habit when they went out. He was also carrying a bouquet of flowers, which she took from him and placed in a vase.

'They are beautiful,' she said, arranging the stems. 'You don't have to keep buying me flowers, my love,' she added, looking up, and for an instant a chill ran through her body. She could see in David's eyes that something was different.

'You are going back to the war!' she gasped. 'When were you going to tell me?'

'I was going to tell you at dinner tonight,' David said sheepishly. 'I am being posted back to the battalion up north, but it is still in training, so I will not be going directly on to active service.'

'But you will be sent back to fight eventually,' Allison said as tears welled up in her eyes. She sat down and placed her head in her hands. 'I have lost one man from my life and I don't think I can lose another.'

David moved awkwardly to her side and placed his hand on her shoulder. 'You know I am a soldier and have to do my duty,' he said gently.

'If I know you well enough, David Macintosh, you would have jumped at any opportunity to get back with your battalion. What is wrong with men like you?' she said, looking up from her hands. 'Sean told me that your training command could have been a posting until the end of the war.'

'The battalion needs experienced company commanders,' David said lamely. 'Men depend on me to keep them alive.'

'And who will keep you alive, David?' Allison countered.

'The thought that I have you to return to,' David said.

Allison threw her arms around his neck. She was sobbing, 'David, David, I cannot bear to think you might not come back to me.'

David held her gently until the sobbing subsided. He felt guilty because he knew he could have declined the brigadier's request.

'When do you go?' Allison said, wiping away the tears from her face with the back of her hand.

'I have a week's leave before I head north,' David said. 'I thought you might ask Uncle Sean to grant you a week's leave too and then we can have a holiday up in the Blue Mountains.'

'I do not want to go out tonight,' Allison said. 'I would rather spend every hour I can in your arms.'

David felt the same way and he wondered why he was driven to put his life on the line when he could stay at home with the woman he loved. It was a question every soldier had asked himself since man first took up the profession of soldiering, and there was no answer to it.

*

Thousands of miles across the Pacific Ocean a similar story was being played out. James Duffy sat in the studio canteen surrounded by people dressed in a variety of costumes as they came off the sets to have lunch. Julianna sat very still opposite him, staring into her coffee.

'I don't know where or when I will be shipped out,' James said quietly.

'I suppose you expect me to wait for you to return,' Julianna said bitterly. 'Just as I waited vainly for my brother to return.'

James reached out across the table to take her hand, but she withdrew it. 'Jules,' he said, using her pet name. 'It was not my choice to return to the war.' He was lying, and it seemed to him that the woman he loved could see that.

'Do you think I don't know that you are jumping out of your skin to return to flying,' she said. 'It is written all over your face.'

'Other men have to leave wives and children behind,' James pleaded. 'I can't stand on the sidelines while they risk their lives.'

'You could have done so much back here for the war effort,' Julianna said. 'Not every man has to risk his life to win the war.'

'Maybe I'm not every man,' James said in his defence. 'My father flew in the last war and I want to do my bit in this war.'

'From what I know of your family history, your father survived the war,' Julianna retorted. 'That is not a guarantee you will do the same.'

'We have the Japs on the back foot now,' James said. 'And I am a goddamned good pilot.'

For a moment a silence fell between them, then suddenly Julianna stood up. 'I will think of you, Captain Duffy,' she said. 'But don't expect me to be here when you return.'

Stunned, James watched her walk away and out of the canteen door, leaving him alone with the many oddly dressed figures taking their break from their movie sets. He spotted a table of men dressed in marine pilot uniforms, and one of them came over to him. 'We haven't met,' the young actor said. 'Are you a stand-in?'

James looked up at the man pretending to be a fighter pilot. 'I wish I was,' he said and swallowed the last of his coffee. 'But I'm the real thing.'

The actor blinked when James stood up, and walked towards the entrance.

SIXTEEN

It was Miss Abigail Frost, the new governess of Tom's cattle station located north of Glen View, who saw the blue-uniformed rider approaching the homestead. She stood on the verandah of the sprawling mudbrick building, shading her eyes against the late afternoon haze.

'Tom,' she called back into the house. 'I think there is a policeman approaching.'

Tom joined Abigail and watched the rider enter the yard bordered by fenced-in vegetable gardens. 'I know him,' he said and stepped off the timber verandah to greet the mounted policeman. 'Sergeant Clements, what brings you so far out these ways?'

'Mr Duffy,' the police sergeant said, dismounting stiffly from his horse. 'It's a bloody long way all right.'

'I hope you are not here on business,' Tom said, reaching out with his right arm to shake the man's hand.

'Sorry about yer losing yer arm,' he said, feeling Tom's firm handshake. 'Heard yer tangled with a snake up in the Gulf.'

'Yeah,' Tom said. 'And the bloody snake got to live.'

'I have an awkward question for yer, Mr Duffy,' the sergeant said. 'Yer wouldn't have seen young Jessie lately, would yer?'

'No,' Tom frowned. 'As a matter of fact she has not written to me for a while. I am a little concerned about her.'

'Sorry to be the one to tell you, Mr Duffy, but Jessie has been posted as AWOL from her unit. Seems she has been gone for around a month or more. The military contacted us, and I was sent out to see if Jessie was here.'

'I can assure you, Sergeant Clements, that I have not seen my daughter for a long time. Not even when I came back from New Guinea,' Tom said, frowning. 'Are you sure you got it right about her being AWOL?'

'Sad to say, the matter of her shooting through is true,' he replied. 'They even posted a photo up to us, and you know that I have known Jessie since she was a barefooted kid running around here.'

Tom nodded. He was stunned by the news that his beloved daughter, who had always proved to be so responsible and diligent, had deserted her post. It just did not make sense. 'Do you need a place to stay over tonight?' Tom asked.

'Thanks, Mr Duffy, but I have to push on to Glen View. One of the boys working there has a few questions to answer about some missing property in town. The manager there will be expecting me.'

'You will be well looked after at Glen View,' Tom said as the police officer swung back into the saddle. 'I know the Macintosh manager, he's a fair-dinkum bloke.'

'If you happen to see Jessie,' Sergeant Clements said, 'tell her to come and see me in town before those bloody military police get to her.'

'I will do that,' Tom said and the police sergeant rode away.

'I heard your conversation,' Abigail said when Tom returned to the verandah. 'From what you have told me about your daughter, it seems very much out of character that she should desert her post.'

'Something very serious must have happened to make Jessie go AWOL,' Tom said. 'No wonder I have heard so little from her in the last month or so.'

'Come inside and I will make us a pot of tea,' Abigail said gently, sensing Tom's concern. 'Whatever has happened, I am sure Jessica is well.'

Tom followed Abigail inside the house and sat down at the kitchen table. In the distance he could hear his stockmen shouting and whooping as they brought in a few head of cattle they had rounded up from a back paddock. Tom puzzled over his daughter's absence from her military posting and he racked his memory for where she could possibly be. There was one place she might go in Sydney, a house in Strathfield that was part of his real estate portfolio. He also remembered that it was connected to the telephone, but there was no such luxury on his cattle station. At least it would be a starting point for his search for his daughter.

'Abigail,' Tom said, looking across the table at the woman he had come to love. 'I will have to head off for a few weeks.'

'Does this have anything to do with Jessie?' she asked.

'Yes,' Tom answered. 'But I don't want to tell you any more because I don't want it coming back on you.'

'I understand,' Abigail said, reaching across the table to hold Tom's hand. 'Just be careful. You know that I love you.'

Tom grasped Abigail's hand and held it firmly. 'I will brief Brendan on what is required,' he said eventually. 'He is a good manager and things will run smoothly while I'm gone.'

'Promise me you will keep in contact with me,' Abigail pleaded. 'I have come to learn that you are a man who does not run from danger.'

Tom looked with surprise at Abigail. 'Why do you think there is any danger in my search for Jessie?' he asked.

'Call it a woman's intuition,' Abigail said. 'But I feel there is danger out there waiting for you. I had a dream that there was a pool of muddy water and a great flock of crows squabbling over something dead.'

Tom squeezed Abigail's hand to reassure her. 'You have been too long in this part of the world. It is the isolation that brings on such dreams.'

But Abigail was not so sure. It was said that the women in her family had a gift for seeing the future. Her own grandmother in their small English village had been whispered to be a witch.

That evening Tom packed a suitcase with clothes and essentials. He walked over to the wall and took down the .303 Lee Enfield hanging there. With his functional arm he stripped the weapon down and packed it carefully in the large suitcase. Next to the rifle he placed a box of cartridges. He did not know quite why he was taking his rifle, but he did not feel comfortable leaving without it.

The next day Tom briefed his manager and kissed Abigail goodbye. A sulky had been prepared, and one of the station hands took the reins. Abigail watched the sulky take her man from the property, remaining on the verandah until the following dust cloud swallowed him from her view. He would reach the nearest large town with a rail head, and from there travel by train to Sydney.

★

Jessica Duffy had spent many sleepless nights, tossing and turning, desperately trying to work out a plan to execute the British traitor. She knew that she would need help but the other two conspirators could not be expected to be physically involved in the deadly mission. For Jessica this was not only an act of revenge but also a vow to finish what Tony had started under orders from his government.

She telephoned Donald Macintosh and they arranged to meet at a small cafe a couple of blocks from his city office. Jessica arrived first. The weather was wet and cold and that had kept many workers indoors in their office buildings. The cafe had only three other patrons: three young women wearing overalls, workers in the small automotive shop nearby. Jessica overheard them enthusiastically discussing car mechanical systems. The war had changed so much; what would their futures be like when the men returned, Jessica wondered.

When Donald entered the cafe Jessica watched as the three young women snatched admiring glances at him. She could hardly blame them: he did look handsome in his raincoat and expensive three-piece suit. He sat down and ordered a pot of tea and a devon sandwich with cheese from the very young and pretty waitress hovering nearby with a small notebook and pencil at hand.

'You look like you could do with some sleep,' Donald said to Jessica.

'You could be right,' she answered. 'I haven't slept well since our meeting on the ferry.'

'I hope you have come to your senses and have dropped your crazy idea of going after Ulverstone,' Donald said.

'Why would I?' Jessica countered. 'Ulverstone is a danger to our security.'

'You are not an SOE or a Yank OSS operative,' Donald said. 'You should leave the matter to others. I think you should return to your unit back in Brisbane and throw yourself on their mercy. I am sure that Mr Curtin will be able to pull a few strings to keep you in the Yanks' good books. If not, I can arrange to visit you in Long Bay Gaol and bring a cake with a file in it.'

Jessica smiled at Donald's clumsy effort at humour. 'I like chocolate cake,' she said. 'With sugar icing topping, but somehow I doubt you are a very good cook.'

'You are right about my cooking skills,' Donald sighed. 'But seriously, Jessie, I am the last person who wants to see you get into any serious trouble. You mean a lot to me.'

Jessica frowned. A short silence fell between them while the waitress placed a plate with a sandwich on it before Donald. 'The tea is on its way,' she said and left them alone again.

'The Yanks are pretty angry about your disappearance,' Donald said. 'It seems that you carry many valuable secrets with you.'

'I would never disclose what I know to anyone,' Jessica replied. 'What I have briefed you about in the past had nothing to do with the coded messages I dealt with.'

'We know that, Jessie,' Donald reassured. 'You only passed on the politics of Mac's staff.'

'I asked to meet with you here today to float an idea,' Jessica said, changing the subject. 'I want to have you set up a social meeting with Lord Ulverstone – if you can.'

'Why?' Donald asked, placing the half-eaten sandwich on the plate. 'What do you have in mind?'

Jessica stared over Donald's shoulder at the three young motor mechanics leaving the cafe. They were laughing, and umbrellas popped as they stepped out into the rain. How she envied their simple aspirations in life: probably to meet some handsome young man and marry him. She thought only of taking a man's life, and risking her own in a mission she had now made hers alone.

'I need to gain his trust,' she answered and saw Donald break into a broad smile.

'That is not going to work,' he chuckled, shaking his head.

'Why not?' Jessica questioned. 'Don't you think I am attractive enough to catch a man's eye?'

'Jessie, you are the most beautiful woman in the world, but Ulverstone prefers the company of young men,' Donald said.

'What do you mean by that?' Jessica asked.

'He came through the ranks of the best English public schools and acquired a taste for the touch of other men. Do I have to spell it out?'

'Oh,' Jessica said. 'I think I know what you mean. You mean like Mr George Bernard Shaw.'

'And others,' Donald said just as his pot of tea was placed in front of him. 'It is something many turn a blind eye to because it is a crime to be so inclined in our society.'

'I see that my idea will not work, then,' Jessica said. 'I will have to think of another way to get to him.'

'Jessie,' Donald said and she was aware that he had reached over the table to take both her hands. 'I am begging you to drop the idea of killing the man. It is too dangerous.'

Jessica could feel the old stirrings she remembered when she had met Donald for the first time and felt herself deeply attracted to him. She had tried to ignore his hints about how he felt towards her, but it was obvious now in his eyes. The flicker of a flame could easily turn to a raging fire if she let it.

'I appreciate your sentiments, Donald, but I am also a member of our armed forces and, as such, committed to seeking out the enemies of my country,' she said.

'Leave that to the men on the battlefield,' Donald said. 'This mission was not one meant for you.'

'Is Ulverstone no less a danger to our country than any Japanese soldier or airman bombing the northern towns on the coast?' Jessica replied. 'Just because I am a woman I should not be prepared to put my life on the line?'

'I did not mean that,' Donald said. 'Maybe I can figure out a way to expose Ulverstone.'

Jessica withdrew her hands from his. 'I think we should finish our conversation now and I will take time to think of another way of getting to the man,' she said, rising from the table. 'I will call you when I have a new plan.'

Donald watched her pay her bill and then step outside onto the wet streets and flip open her umbrella. He did not finish his tea; it had begun to leave a sour taste in his mouth.

*

Jessica arrived at the Strathfield house and walked up the big painted concrete steps. She shook her umbrella and left it outside the front door, then stepped inside. She knew immediately that she was not alone in the house: there was the instantly recognisable scent of pipe tobacco wafting down the hallway. Her heart leapt in her breast as she stepped into the kitchen and she saw her father sitting at a table, a mug of steaming tea before him.

'Hello, Jessie,' he said, rising from the chair to sweep her up with his good arm. The crushing embrace left the young woman speechless, until he put her back on her feet.

'Dad!' she exclaimed. 'How . . . when?'

'This morning, on the train from Brisbane,' he said, holding his beloved daughter at arm's length so he could examine her. 'You look awful.'

Jessica broke into tears and wrapped her arms around her father, acutely aware that the lower part of his left arm was missing. 'Oh Daddy, it is so good to see you again,' she said between sobs. She felt as though she was once again a little girl in the arms of the tall, strong man who was her loving father, that she was safe and protected with him.

'I think you need a good strong cup of tea,' he said gently.

'I would prefer coffee,' his daughter replied.

'You have been with the Yanks for too long,' Tom said with a laugh.

'How the dickens did you know to find me here?' Jessica asked as her father pulled a jar of coffee down from the shelf.

'I was not sure where I would find you,' Tom said, placing the jar under his armpit and unscrewing the lid. He was becoming very adept at managing with only one arm. 'But this was as good as any place to start. According to our agents, I believe that you have a couple of other tenants staying here.'

'Yes, but they will not be returning from work until later this afternoon,' Jessica said, taking the jar from her father and finding a cup.

'Are you going to tell your old dad why you went AWOL?' Tom asked.

Jessica stood for a moment holding the coffee jar. 'It's a long and complicated story,' she said.

'As you are a complicated woman – like your mother – I would expect no other kind of story,' Tom smiled grimly. 'Sit down and tell me.'

Jessica placed the jar on a bench and sat down opposite her father. 'While I was at General MacArthur's HQ in Brisbane I met an American officer, Lieutenant Tony Caccamo,' she said.

'Yes, I know the name. You mentioned him a couple of times in your letters. I got the impression you were a bit smitten with him,' Tom said.

'I think I loved him,' Jessica said. 'I would have been sure if I had had the opportunity to get to know him better, but he was murdered.'

'Murdered,' Tom said with surprise. 'How and when did this happen?'

Jessica told her father the American officer's mission, arrest and subsequent murder in prison by agents of Lord Ulverstone or, worse, his own government.

'I feel that the only way to get justice for Tony and his family is to finish his mission.'

'What! Are you saying that you plan to kill this Pommy lord?' her father asked in utter surprise. 'Is this why you have deserted your post?'

'What would you have done in my shoes, Daddy?' Jessica asked in despair.

Tom drew a long breath and sighed. He stared at his daughter and could see utter defeat. Oh, how much he could see her mother in her expression. 'I want you to promise me that you will do nothing foolish,' he said. 'I will go and see Major Duffy and sort something out.' Tom could see relief etched in Jessica's tired face. 'I am booked into a hotel not far from Sean's office, so I will call him as soon as I get back. In the meantime, as your father, I suggest that you get some sleep and let me worry about fixing your problems. You and I will go out to a good place to eat tomorrow, and you will fill me in on all that has happened since we were last in contact.'

Jessica rose from her chair and flung her arms around her father. 'Thank you, Daddy,' she said, not really knowing, or even caring at this moment, what her father planned to do. She had to admit to herself that talking bravely about executing Ulverstone had been easier than actually going through with it.

Tom gave his daughter one last kiss and hug before stepping out into the rain. He unfurled his umbrella and walked to the railway station to catch a train to the city. As he walked he thought about the rifle tucked away in his suitcase. It was obvious that his war was not over.

SEVENTEEN

The two old soldiers met at their favourite pub around the corner from Sean's legal office. It had just opened for the morning but was already filling with men in uniform. Tom Duffy and Sean Duffy stood at the bar, one man missing part of his arm, the other missing his two legs, veterans of the battlefield now cast as spectators in this new war.

'So you found Jessie,' Sean said after greeting Tom warmly and ordering a round of drinks. 'I am sorry that I could not tell you she was down in Sydney – she made me swear to keep her whereabouts a secret even from you.'

'I can accept that,' Tom said, taking a swig from his beer. 'You are, after all, her solicitor.'

'I am also your legal advisor,' Sean countered. 'I should have told you.'

'No matter,' Tom said, taking a swig from his beer. 'The main thing is that I have found her and, all going well, will be able to convince her to give up on this bloody stupid idea of killing the Pommy lord.'

'I presume she has briefed you on Ulverstone's traitorous activities,' Sean said. 'I guess you also know that the American soldier murdered in the Bay was very special to her.'

'Yeah, pity I didn't get to meet him,' Tom said. 'He must have been a bloody good bloke to win Jessie's heart.'

'I did meet him, and I can see how Jessie would have fallen for the man,' Sean said. 'He was a good bloke.'

'How do I stop my daughter from doing something she will regret for the rest of her life?' Tom asked. 'She is no killer.'

'Cobber, unless someone else finishes the job for her, I very much doubt you will be able to stop her,' Sean answered. 'She may not be my daughter but I have watched her grow up, and I know that once she makes her mind up, not even her father can stop her.'

'Then the only solution is for someone else to do the job for her,' Tom said quietly.

'I am afraid that you are right, and knowing you, Tom Duffy, I understand what you are saying.'

'Who else knows about Jessie's intentions?' Tom asked.

'Donald Macintosh,' Sean replied.

'Young Macintosh!' Tom exclaimed. 'How the bloody hell has he got himself tangled up in this?'

'I strongly suspect that Ulverstone had Sir George's assistance with the murder,' Sean said. 'I have known Donald for a few years now and I will vouch for him. He is not, as they say, his father's son. Besides, I think he has direct links to the Prime Minister himself and may be well placed to help us.'

'Whatever I am planning, I don't intend to involve you,' Tom said.

'Too late, cobber,' Sean grinned. 'The fact that we are even discussing the idea puts us back in the war, but this time a bit of behind-the-lines work, like we did on the Western Front in no-man's-land. We carried out dangerous missions then with little expectation of coming home alive. This is just the same thing but in a different time and place.'

'I'm sure you can understand that what we have discussed here today cannot get back to Jessie,' Tom said. 'She might get the impression that I am taking over and excluding her.'

'I know what you are saying, old chap,' Sean answered. 'She might worry about you.'

'Something like that,' Tom said, taking another swig of his beer.

Sean raised his glass and tapped Tom's. A pact was sealed in the simple gesture, and two old soldiers were once again active in the war. But this time they had more than their lives at stake. To fail could bring about national outrage, and absolute disgrace to the Duffy name.

★

Sitting behind her desk in her office, Sarah Macintosh hardly heard a word uttered by her manager as he delivered his report on the Macintosh agricultural production quotas. She had just been informed that Major David Macintosh had been posted north to Queensland to rejoin his battalion.

Work pressures had distracted her from seeking out the man she was obsessed with, and soon he would be out of her reach. By all accounts a love was blossoming between David and Allison, and that simply would not do, as David belonged to Sarah, despite his rejection of her. Well, the only way to disrupt any romantic relationship was to go on the attack. Allison was no match for the resources Sarah could muster to drive a wedge between the two lovebirds.

Sarah was determined to crush her best friend in subtle ways that only a very devious woman could conjure.

'What do you think, Miss Macintosh?'

The question caught Sarah off guard. 'About what, Mr Anderson?' she asked, snapping out of her daydream.

'About getting our beef production up,' the manger said. 'The Yanks love their big steaks, and we are in a position to satisfy their demand.'

'Yes, yes,' Sarah responded quickly. 'I trust that you will be able to produce a plan to do that.'

'Yes, Miss Macintosh,' Anderson said, rising from his chair. 'I should have something in concrete before the next meeting.'

'Good,' Sarah said and watched him leave the room. Already her thoughts had returned to her planned assault on Allison, and she smiled for the first time that day. By the time Sarah had finished with Allison, David was sure never to want to see his girlfriend again.

★

This scene had been repeated ever since the invention of the first troop trains almost a hundred years earlier when women had first stood on railway stations bidding their men goodbye in the knowledge that this embrace might be the last they would ever share, when the powerful locomotives steamed and huffed their way from the sidings, to deliver their fragile cargoes to faraway battlefields.

In the gloom of the winter's night, Major David Macintosh held Allison in his arms, gently reassuring her that he would return. Sean leaned on his walking cane nearby, with young Patrick beside him watching with a certain amount of understanding of the sadness and urgency that was all around him. It had been a steam train that

179

had taken him from his mother the year before in Malaya, leaving only a fading image of a woman's face streaked with tears. Now this big man that Patrick had come to accept as an uncle was going away too, and Patrick wondered if he was going to the place where his mother was far across the sea.

'I will be back before you know it, old girl,' David said. Steam hissed from the locomotive nearby, and already coal smoke was rising from the stack as the engine readied to pull its load of khaki-coloured passengers north. 'And I promise to write every chance I get.'

'Be careful and come home to me,' Allison whispered between her tears. 'I love you very much.'

'I made it this far and I don't have any intentions of going away when I next return,' David said, disengaging himself from the embrace to turn to Sean.

'Well, Uncle Sean, I guess this is goodbye again,' he said, extending his hand, then he felt Sean's arms around him in a rough embrace.

'Be bloody careful, David,' Sean hissed. 'I made a promise to your mother many years ago that I would look after you. I made that promise on my life.'

David stepped back with a sad smile. 'You have been the only father I have ever known, Uncle Sean,' he said and looked away to Patrick lest Sean see the tears forming in his eyes. 'I want you to look after Uncle Sean, young Patrick,' he said, crouching down to the boy.

'I will, Uncle David,' Patrick replied.

'Good man,' David said, standing up and patting Patrick on the head. 'Time to get aboard.' He squared his shoulders and walked towards the carriage door. He felt as though he was walking to his execution. He could not tell those he loved most that he had a bad feeling about what lay ahead.

He stepped up into the train and was immediately assailed by cigarette smoke and the heavy scent of men in uniform: brasso, boot polish and nervous sweat. David made his way to the first-class sleeper section reserved for officers, and for a moment stood by the window of the railway carriage door, gazing at the only three faces he wanted to see. They were covered in tears – except for young Patrick who waved gravely to him. A whistle blew, the train lurched, and suddenly the three faces disappeared as if the platform had raced away.

As the troop train pulled away from Sydney's Central Station and David made his way to his cabin, he realised that his hands had begun to tremble again. There was no going back now. The jungles of the north awaited him; he could hear them whispering that he was on his way and that they were preparing to cover his dead body.

*

Twenty-four hours later Allison received a telephone call from Sarah. Sarah explained that she had acted rather rudely towards her and was very sorry. As a matter of fact she had planned a party at her home on the harbour for the following Saturday night and she would be very disappointed if Allison did not come. Allison hesitated but Sarah's sweet tone seemed genuine. Maybe they could put aside their differences over David and resume their old friendship. Allison said she would attend.

Sarah put down the phone and smirked. It had been so easy.

*

She towered over the wharf and the many men moving around her. In the early morning Captain James Duffy stood in the chilling mist that came down from the rugged mountains and swirled around the naval base. He stared up at her with mixed feelings. The *Big E* – the aircraft carrier *Enterprise* – sat in the Puget Sound naval dockyards under-going an outfit before her return to the Pacific war. Sparks flew from welders, and the hammering of rivets punctured the peace of the morning.

A naval officer of equivalent rank to James appeared from the mist and walked over to him.

'Are you part of the *Big E*?' he asked.

James turned to him and could see from his insignia that he was a weapons officer. 'I was with her up until Guadalcanal,' James said. 'I was transferred to the Cactus air force on the island – but she and I are back together again. Just got shipped out from California.'

'You will miss the sunshine and girls,' the naval officer grinned. 'The name's Kent Kowalski. I'm with her also.'

'James Duffy,' the marine pilot said, extending his hand.

'I heard that we were getting a pretty boy from Hollywood,' Kowalski grinned. 'I'll take you aboard and we can see if there are any other flyboys around for you to meet. They will no doubt want to ask a million questions about which actresses you got to bed.'

The naval officer led James to a boarding plank and he stepped inside the huge aircraft carrier filled with workmen. For a moment his thoughts of Julianna were overwhelmed by the feeling he had just come home.

★

It was September and Lieutenant Colonel Albert Ulverstone had finally been able to obtain the security clearance that would enable him to access the most sensitive military and political information within the South West Pacific theatre.

His wound had healed, leaving him physically fit for duty. However, as he stood in his office, hands behind his back, he was pondering the problem of being exposed as a traitor.

The dynamic of the war in the Pacific had shifted, with the Imperial Japanese armed forces now fighting desperately to hang on to the territory they had seized in their initial thrust south and east. But the Japanese were far from beaten and were still a formidable force to be reckoned with. Intelligence reports from Europe indicated that the Italians were on the verge of collapsing and coming over to the Allied side, and the situation for Germany was growing increasingly desperate, with the advancement of the Red Army.

Ulverstone glanced at the dossier on his desk, knowing it held vital intelligence that could assist his Japanese masters. The existence of the annoying Sydney solicitor worried him. From what Sir George was relaying to him the man was continually digging into the events surrounding the death of the man who had attempted to kill him.

The British officer walked over to his desk and read through the report, closed it and sat down at his desk. To relay the intelligence report to the Japanese required him to use a sympathetic radio operator posing as an American missionary in Brisbane. But Ulverstone knew that all radio transmissions were being monitored by a list of obscure Allied interceptors. It was time to make a decision, and the British aristocrat knew what came first – his own life and reputation.

He closed the folder, knowing that it would not be transmitted to the Japanese. It was far too dangerous to act now while Major Sean Duffy was covertly investigating him. Duffy had to be eliminated and he knew that his friend and ally, Sir George, had many reasons to see the solicitor killed. What worried Ulverstone even more than Duffy was the question of who had been behind the attempt on his life. Whoever it was must have some evidence as to his treachery. Whether they would do anything with this evidence was another matter.

*

Even as Lord Ulverstone contemplated Sean Duffy's death, Sean was reaching for his telephone. He did so with reluctance but it was time to call an old friend for a very big favour.

'Harry Griffiths speaking,' came a voice when the telephone call was answered. In the background Sean could hear the sound of boxing gloves striking leather punching bags.

'Harry, it's Sean Duffy,' he said.

'Boss! Good to hear your voice,' Harry answered. 'It's been a while since we had a beer together. I've heard a couple of disturbing whispers on the grapevine about you.'

'Cobber, that is why I am calling you. I need a bit of help.'

'You know you can rely on me,' the former soldier and Sydney policeman replied. 'About time we met at our usual watering hole.'

'How about this afternoon – around three?' Sean suggested.

'You can shout the first round,' Harry said, and hung up.

*

Sarah Macintosh was very pleased indeed. The grainy black and white photographs were exactly what she had ordered. The party that she had lured Allison to after David's transfer north had proved a great success. The spiked drink served to Allison had done the job and her private investigator and his accomplice had earned their pay.

Sarah looked down on the picture of Allison lying on her back, naked from the waist down on the double bed. The next photo showed the accomplice bending over her as if having sex. Sarah knew that he had not, but the series of photos looked explicit.

The following morning Allison had awoken with a terrible hangover, unaware of what had happened the night before. Sarah had soothed her with reassurances that she had passed out from too much alcohol and had been taken to one of the bedrooms in the Macintosh house to sleep it off.

'Oh, Alli,' Sarah crooned. 'What will David say when he finds out what a naughty girl you have been the moment he leaves town?'

PART TWO

Springtime in the Southern Hemisphere

1943

EIGHTEEN

The train journey north for Major David Macintosh took several days of gazing out at fields of sugarcane, where little locomotives tugged carriages spilling with the cut cane to the sugar refineries. The northbound train would occasionally stop at railway stations where the local ladies served up porridge and tasty sausages to the troops, accompanied by pots of coffee and urns of tea. There were occasional glimpses of the azure ocean between groves of tall palm trees. Approaching Cairns the vista changed as the engine pulled its carriages full of troops over tall wooden bridges with mountain streams rushing below. The vegetation had changed to great forests of tropical giants, and finally the troops were delivered to Cairns, where trucks met them to travel up onto the tablelands running parallel with the coast.

David found his transport vehicle, and after a few hours of climbing the narrow, tortuous road, the truck came to a stop at his old battalion's bivouac area. It was with a mix of excitement and happiness that he recognised the guard manning the gate to the camp. When he had last seen the man he had been a corporal, but now he sported the three chevrons of a sergeant.

'Sergeant Peene,' David said, stepping from the cabin of the truck and taking the salute. 'How the devil are you?'

The tough-looking NCO blinked and suddenly recognised David. 'Boss . . . er, I mean, sir, bloody good to have you back with the boys.'

'Bloody good to be back, Matt,' David said, slinging his kitbag over his shoulder. 'Where do I find BHQ?'

'Over there, sir,' Sergeant Peene said, pointing to a timber building. 'I know the CO will be glad to have you aboard again.'

'Congratulations on your promotion,' David said, this time extending his hand. 'Well overdue, in my opinion. You should have got your stripes back in New Guinea.'

'Thanks, sir,' the sergeant said, accepting the firm handshake. 'Hope you get the old company job as OC.'

'So do I, Sergeant Peene,' David replied before he marched off to report to the battalion HQ, where he was welcomed warmly by the respected and liked commanding officer, who told him his wish to have his company back had been granted.

'I do have some bad news, though,' the CO said. 'We were given notice that we were to be shipped out in a month's time. The reports that I have seen indicate that the boys up in New Guinea are up against stiff opposition, but the bloody powers that be have decided we are to stand down and continue with our training. I made the announcement yesterday, so morale is a bit low as the lads have been itching to have another crack at the Nips.'

After a briefing from the adjutant in the orderly room, David was allocated his quarters, and barely took time to throw his kitbag on the cot in his room before he marched over to his company HQ to meet his staff. The orderly room clerk stood quickly to attention when David entered the company HQ.

'Stand easy,' David said, looking around the sparse office. Clipboards with routine orders, signals and a portrait of the King adorned the walls. Only two men were on duty in the office, and David noticed a young corporal standing to attention by his bulky radio set.

'I am Major Macintosh, your new OC,' David said. 'Good to see the orderly room is manned.'

'Yes, sir,' the corporal by the radio said.

'I like to get to know the soldiers I work with,' David said. 'Who are you, corporal?' he asked the man now standing at ease.

'Corporal Andrew Paull,' the young man said. 'I'm your signaller, sir.'

'I have not seen you before, corp,' David said.

'I was transferred in with the last lot of reinforcements, sir,' Andrew said.

'Where did you get transferred in from?' David asked with genuine interest.

'I was with the Nackeroos before getting my transfer, sir,' Andrew answered.

'The Nackeroos. By any chance did you know Sergeant Tom Duffy?'

Andrew's face registered both surprise and consternation. 'Sir, it was Tom . . . sorry, Sergeant Duffy, who got me this transfer.' Andrew paused. 'After I cut off his arm.'

For a moment both men stared at each other, and then

David burst into a loud laugh. 'Bloody extreme way to get your senior NCO to give you a transfer,' he said. 'Hope it's not my head if you want a promotion.'

'Sir, I . . .' Andrew tried to explain.

'You don't have to explain how you saved Sergeant Duffy's life,' David said. 'I happen to know him, and I have already heard how your actions saved him from dying of a taipan bite. It is a small world indeed, and I can say that your quick thinking has proven you a bloody good soldier. Welcome to my team.'

Andrew realised that the major had extended his hand to him, and he was caught off guard by the gesture. There was something charismatic about the new company commander, and it was then that Corporal Andrew Paull knew he would follow Major Macintosh into hell if asked.

David then spoke with the orderly room clerk, and soon the word was out to the old hands that their former, well liked and respected acting company commander was back. The newer members wondered what all the fuss was about, until they heard that the legendary officer who had led his men from Africa to New Guinea was the best bloody boss they could have.

Before the day closed David tracked down his officers and senior NCOs to introduce himself, and after a few hours in the officers' mess he retired to his cot. The sweet and haunting sound of the bugles playing the Last Post drifted to him on the still air and was the last sound he heard before slipping into a dreamless sleep.

★

The newly fitted prosthetic lower limb hurt the stump of Tom Duffy's arm.

'You will get used to it,' Sean said, observing his friend's grimace of pain. 'Took me a while with my stumps, but it will get better.'

The two men sat in Sean's office, cups of tea between them.

'Just wonder how it will affect my shooting,' Tom said, holding up the arm and staring at the artificial hand.

Sean raised his eyebrows.

'I have some feral animals on my property up in Queensland,' he said, but his answer did not ease Sean's concerns. He had hoped that with time Tom might have lost interest in pursuing Jessica's desire to see Lord Ulverstone dead.

Tom had been able to convince his daughter to travel out to Bathurst to a small sheep farm he had in his portfolio of properties. She was still living under an assumed name, and Tom had been able to have her signed up in the Women's Land Army to work on the farm. The Land Army worked long, low-paid hours keeping food up to the nation. Even now beef was in very short supply to the civilian population, as it was needed for the armed forces of Australia and her allies. Tom had noted that his profits were going up with the shortage, as his Queensland stations supplied the much needed beef.

'I had a beer with Harry yesterday and he told me that the crooked copper, Preston, is snooping around asking questions about you, Sean,' Tom said, resting his artificial arm on the table.

'I would expect that,' Sean said, taking a sip of his tea. 'He is, after all, Sir George's man.'

'Watch your back, cobber,' Tom warned. 'If Macintosh is involved, you can bet Ulverstone also has an interest in you.'

'The odds are even,' Sean said with a short laugh. 'I have you and Harry on my side, and between us we have a fair bit of knowing how to stay alive when the bullets start flying and the whiz-bangs go overhead. Besides, I carry this.' He lifted the walking cane beside his leg. He raised it and pushed a button near the handle, and a wicked-looking rapier blade flicked out. 'Oh how I would love to have the excuse to slide this into Sir George Macintosh's throat and watch the life in his eyes go out.'

'And you are worried about me shooting Ulverstone,' Tom chuckled. 'At least it would be a head shot and his eyes would just blow out of his head.'

Even though they laughed at their macabre jokes, they both knew that the situation had probably come to the point of killing or being killed.

'I have an old mate at Vic Barracks who works in a department allied to Ulverstone's,' Sean said. 'He does not like the man, although I did not let on why I was asking about him. It seems that Ulverstone might be going up to Newcastle soon to inspect a couple of our coastal defence units.'

Tom knew what Sean was saying. 'Would you be able to find out when?' he asked.

Sean already knew. 'This time next week,' he said. 'He will be chauffeured in a staff car, along the main highway to Newcastle.'

'Day or night?' Tom asked.

'Day,' Sean replied. 'You would only get one chance.'

Tom nodded. 'I think it is time to head over the mountains to Bathurst to look at my property there and catch up with Jessie.'

'Be bloody careful, Tom,' Sean said. 'I don't have to warn you of the consequences if anything goes wrong. As it is I expect that there will be hell to raise if you succeed.'

'Put your faith in me, cobber,' Tom said, rising from the chair. 'I will be able to call you when I get to Bathurst.'

Sean rose and offered his hand. 'Good luck, old chap. While you are gone I will make sure things are covered at this end.'

With these final words Tom Duffy left the office and stepped out onto the streets of Sydney. The stump on his arm throbbed with pain and he knew he would have to take his rifle to Bathurst to practise his marksmanship away from prying eyes. Time was short, and Tom knew that he had only this one opportunity to execute a traitor.

★

The farm manager was a surly man in his sixties who did not exactly welcome the owner onto his property.

'We have not met before, Mr Duffy,' he said without extending his hand.

Both men stood in drizzling rain outside the small cottage with its lean-to verandah. It was late in the afternoon and already getting dark.

'I got a telegram from Major Duffy's office saying that you would be staying here for a couple of days. I suppose you want to take over the house while you are here.'

Tom hunched against the cold in his old greatcoat, his hat low over his face and a suitcase by his side. 'That will not be necessary, Mr Oldwell,' Tom replied. 'I believe you have a shed on the farm.'

'Yes, but a couple of Land Army girls are bunked down there,' Oldwell replied.

'I noticed it when I was driven in,' Tom said. 'It will do fine.'

Oldwell shrugged. 'It's up to you,' he said. 'I think the girls are in there now. You can't get much work out of them.'

'In this weather, Mr Oldwell, I don't see you out checking fences.'

'It's just that them not working every day bites into your profits,' he wheedled.

'I would rather see the girls safe and well out of this weather,' Tom growled. 'I will be doing a bit of shooting while I'm here,' he continued. 'So don't be alarmed if you hear shots. It's not the Japs invading.'

Tom picked up his suitcase and walked away towards the large shed filled with bales of hay and farming implements. He stepped inside and saw Jessica sitting on a straw bale, holding a steaming mug of tea. Beside her on another bale was a pretty young lady wearing overalls and an old leather jacket. Jessica peered at the figure standing in the entrance to the shed.

'Dad!' she exclaimed, jumping up from the hay bale. 'What the bloody hell are you doing here?'

'Don't swear, young lady,' Tom said with a grin, as his daughter embraced him in a big hug.

'Sorry, Dad,' she said. 'Working with stupid sheep you kind of pick up a few swear words.'

'Who is your colleague?' Tom asked, looking over at the other young girl.

'Oh, this is Maria,' she said. 'Maria comes from Griffith.'

Maria rose shyly when Tom walked over and shook her hand. He figured she must be only fifteen, and he could feel that her hand was hard with calluses. 'I am Jessie's father,' he said and noticed a puzzled expression on the girl's face. He remembered that Jessica had enlisted under her alias and had kept up the false name at the farm. 'It's a long story,' he said quickly.

'Are you hungry?' Jessie asked her father. 'We were about to cook dinner. Maria has been able to scrounge what she needs to make a delicious spaghetti and meatballs dish for us. Her family make their own spaghetti, and the meatballs are made from minced mutton. We were able to buy some fresh tomatoes for the sauce.'

'That sounds fine,' Tom said, holding his daughter's hand for a brief moment. 'I will be bunking down in the shed while I am here so we can catch up on everything.'

'I somehow think this is not a social visit,' Jessie said with a frown. 'What is going on?'

'I thought that while I was in Sydney I would take the opportunity of coming out to see the property and see you at the same time. I miss you all the time, princess.'

Jessie shook her head. She knew her father too well. 'Why are you really here, Dad?' she asked.

'To see you and our property,' Tom lied, although there was some truth in wanting to see his daughter. 'Anyway, I brought a gift,' he said, bending to open his suitcase.

Jessie felt a sick feeling in her stomach when she glimpsed the dismantled rifle but did not comment as her father passed a small leg ham to Maria, who squealed with delight at the luxury. She thanked Tom, and took it to a battered kerosene fridge in the corner of the shed, cleared to provide a makeshift living area.

'We will dine well for the next couple of days,' Tom said cheerily, but Jessica did not reply. She was in a world of dark suspicion and fear.

★

Detective Sergeant Preston eyed a few of the patrons in the pub. He saw one or two familiar faces of men he had arrested for petty crimes, but they steered well clear of him. He had chosen this sleazy hotel as a place to meet Sir George because he felt comfortable mixing with Sydney's underside and he knew Sir George did not. Cigarette smoke and the stench of unwashed bodies filled the small bar.

'The job needs to be done as fast as possible,' Sir George said quietly across the table. 'I will leave the details to you.' He pushed a folded newspaper across the table. Preston slipped his hand inside the fold, quickly withdrawing a wad of money, which he pushed into a pocket of his cheap suit. 'It is a generous amount. You can count it later.'

'I know that you are a generous man, Sir George,' Preston said. 'But I trust you have also provided for the help I will need for that bastard solicitor to have a serious accident.'

'I have,' Sir George said. 'I expect to read in the morning papers about the sad demise of Major Sean Duffy before the weekend is over.'

'I can promise you that,' Preston replied, lifting his large glass of beer topped by a head of froth. 'Duffy will be head-line news in the Sunday morning papers.'

NINETEEN

He was big, and sweat streaked his muscled body under a tropical sun. From his corner David Macintosh punched his gloves together, sizing up his opponent in the company's boxing ring. The CO had issued a standard operating procedure that physical fitness was to be maintained as they stood on standby for deployment back into the war. The men had access to many sports such as swimming, tennis and cricket. There was even a cooking competition between the battalions to see which catering section could turn out the best roast with potatoes, gravy and peas. The gravy proved to be the winning point in the fiercely contested competition.

David had been cajoled into the ring by the old soldiers who knew of his formidable reputation before the war as a heavyweight fighting in Sydney. There had been a time in the Dachau concentration camp that David had boxed for his life, but now he was fighting for the honour of his rifle company against the reigning champion from a sister company in the battalion. David had easily won his intercompany fights to reach the finals, and now money was changing hands behind the ring for the title of best heavyweight in the battalion. His opponent was a warrant officer from the quartermaster's stores, and he rippled with upper-body strength.

'C'mon, boss, show him how Charlie company are the best,' came the chorus of encouragement from the men and officers of David's unit. They were clustered around the boxing ring that comprised a piece of cleared ground with a rope around four padded pickets. The referee was the regimental sergeant major who had only a vague idea about the rules of boxing, but he had been appointed to adjudicate the match as no man would dare question his decisions.

The RSM made his grand announcement of the rules – as he saw them – and introduced the two fighters. David rose from his wooden crate that stood in for a stool, and it was whisked from the ring by his company second-in-command, Captain Brian Williams. The two men fought in sandshoes, shorts, singlets and head gear. It would be a three round match, and David knew in that time he had to deliver as much power as possible for a knockout.

The two fighters touched gloves and a bell sounded. Neither fighter spent any time probing for a weakness in their opponent's defence; this was purely a slugging match, and David could feel the power of the other man's punches as they found their marks on his face and body.

The bell rang and David lurched back to his corner. Captain Brian Williams shoved the wooden crate under him, and he slumped down onto it gratefully.

'The big bastard can punch,' David gasped as water was spilled into his mouth. Blood was trickling from a cut above his eye.

'I noticed that he keeps his guard up,' Captain Williams said. He too had spent a lot of time in the ring and had been a good light-heavyweight fighter in his state of Victoria. 'You need to get under it and have a go at his stomach and ribs.'

David glanced over to the opposite corner and could see the smile on the other fighter's face. He appeared confident and relaxed.

The bell rang again, and this time David came out wary of the power of his adversary. Remembering Williams's observation, he moved in and hammered the other fighter's midriff before he could deliver any punches of his own. David took heavy blows to the head but made sure that he was close enough that the blows did not have much leverage behind them. David thought he might have cracked his opponent's rib when he heard the man grunt with pain. The distraction was enough and David stepped away to concentrate on blows to his opponent's head. He remembered the man's overconfident smile and now he could hear the roar of the spectators baying for blood. He continued his barrage of bone-breaking punches, and when his opponent reeled away, David was sure he was weakening. The bell rang to signal the end of the second round, and both men staggered back to their respective corners.

'You have him!' Captain Williams said. 'I think you might have broken one of his ribs.'

David splashed water over his face. The tropical humidity made fighting uncomfortable. He glanced across at the other fighter and could see that his second was checking the man's ribs.

David stood up and walked over to the other corner and raised his opponent's hand as the victor. The stunned silence that followed David's noble gesture was broken by a roar of approval from the spectators – but not the bookmakers.

'When your ribs heal, we will have a rematch,' David said. 'But I figure you had the edge until the second round, so I am conceding the fight to you.'

The quartermaster warrant officer gazed up in surprise at David. 'No, sir, you won fair and square.'

'Sorry, sergeant, but I outrank you and the RSM, so I am declaring you the winner,' David said with a grin. 'Besides, this way you might be a bit more generous towards my company with stores.'

The warrant officer grinned and stood to touch gloves with David. 'You might be right on that, sir,' he said.

David returned to his corner where he saw Captain Williams shaking his head in disbelief. 'I know, Brian,' David said. 'I could have won, but we would have had a senior QM out of action, and we need more supplies for the company.'

'I suppose I see your point, boss,' Captain Williams sighed as he helped David remove the gloves.

The men of his company congratulated him on his display of both boxing and sportsmanship and then they drifted back to their duties. Charlie Company did not win the heavyweight title that day, but they did win the respect of the other companies and battalions when word got around.

David returned to his quarters to prepare for a shower. The cut above his eye did not require stitches, and he sat down at his desk in his shorts and singlet, sweat covering his body and bruises already starting to show. The mail delivery had been distributed and David saw a small pile of letters for him on the desk. He recognised Allison's and Sean's handwriting and the letterhead of the Macintosh enterprises. The business letter from the Macintosh enterprises simply reaffirmed his allowance. He set it aside and kept Allison's letters until last, so that he could savour them. Amongst the pile was a bulky letter with no return address. Puzzled, David opened it first to see a short typed letter.

Dear Major Duffy

As one concerned for our men at the front I feel it is my duty to inform you of the despicable behaviour of a woman by the name of Allison Lowe who I believe has won your affections. It is my sad duty to inform you that she has been having affairs behind your back. I do not wish to be forced to prove what I am telling you, but I feel that I should forward photographic evidence of her treacherous behaviour.

A Friend

His hands shaking, David drew out a set of grainy black and white photos and immediately saw what they represented. He felt physically sick and an old adage came to mind . . . *a picture says a thousand words.* These said a lot more.

David stared at the two letters from Allison, leaving them unopened on his desk.

*

Sarah was nervous. Her father had intimated that he would be going into full retirement due to his health issues. If that was so, he would have to nominate a head of the Macintosh enterprises. So far, Sir George had sided with her, and she should have been confident in getting the nomination. But her father could be irrational, and there was always the chance that he might name Donald instead.

She sat in her office pondering the upcoming announcement which Sir George said would be made in November. As far as she knew, her brother was preoccupied with matters outside the realm of making money. She had heard rumours that her brother might even be working some kind of covert operation with the prime minister's people. His trips away from Sydney could often not be linked with direct business concerns. Could that be used against him? Sarah knew she would need assistance to find out, and the private investigator she had hired to take the photos of Allison had proved to be discreet. Now she needed his services again. The appointment had been made, and Sarah's assistant announced his arrival.

'Come in, Mr Chatsworth,' Sarah said.

John Chatsworth, a former police officer, was a tall, dour man in his early forties. He had left the police force under a dark cloud but retained links to a circle of crooked police. That made him very efficient at his job of collecting 'the goods' on many so-called reputable businessmen.

He entered the room, took off his hat and sat down without invitation. 'I believe that you require my services again, Miss Macintosh.'

'I have a rather sensitive job for you, Mr Chatsworth,' Sarah said, annoyed by the man's apparent arrogance. 'I need to have my brother followed to see who he meets and why. It may require you to travel interstate.'

'That will be very costly,' Chatsworth said, raising an eyebrow.

'I can pay,' Sarah replied. 'My brother takes trips to Canberra and Brisbane. I want to know why.'

'I already know about your brother,' Chatsworth said. 'It's common knowledge that he works on committees for the prime minister.'

'It's his trips to Brisbane that I wish to know about,' Sarah said. 'None of the past journeys appear to be related to any of our business interests.'

'Maybe your brother has a love interest in Brisbane,' Chatsworth said.

'If he does, I want to know who,' Sarah said. 'I want you to see if you can gather any dirt on my brother that may be considered scandalous.'

'Are you sure?' the private investigator asked. 'What I might learn about your brother could be very damaging to the Macintosh companies.'

'I am sure,' Sarah said. 'There is a lot at stake for me.'

Chatsworth shrugged. 'Consider it done, but I will require upfront payment for expenses.'

Sarah reached inside a desk drawer to retrieve a cheque book. She filled in a cheque, and passed it to the private investigator, who raised both eyebrows this time as he slipped the cheque inside his suit pocket. 'That will do for a start,' he said as he rose from his chair, and replaced his hat on his head. 'I will be in contact.'

Sarah watched him leave her office and had a good feeling about employing his services as he had done an excellent job framing Allison.

*

Tom's left arm throbbed with pain. He held the forestock of the .303 balanced on the artificial hand and gently squeezed the trigger. The rifle bit into his shoulder as it had a thousand times before in his military life. The crack of the shot echoed around the rolling hills and at three hundred yards he saw the tin can bounce as the bullet ripped through it into the soft soil of the slight embankment at the back. Tom sighed with satisfaction. Minus an arm he could still take out a bullseye.

Still on his stomach he felt the vibration of the horse's hooves on the soft grassy ground.

'That was a good shot,' Jessica said from astride her mount.

Tom rose to his feet, ejecting the spent cartridge but not reloading the chamber. 'I was not sure if I could still do it,' he said, facing his daughter. 'Looks like I can.' He took a look at Jessica's horse. 'I might need your nag to ride into town this afternoon.'

'What are you up to, Dad?' she asked. 'I hope you don't have any silly ideas about shooting anyone.'

Tom had trouble looking his daughter in the eye and instead turned to gaze out over the hills already showing a blaze of colour from the many spring flowers on this beautiful sunny afternoon. The temperature was still crisp but the weather was improving. 'I just need to know I am not altogether useless.'

'How long are you staying?' Jessica asked.

'I will be leaving tomorrow,' Tom answered. 'I have to get back to Sydney for some business appointments.'

Jessica dismounted, and her horse put his head down and began munching on the lush pasture. 'I will come with you,' she said.

'That is not necessary,' Tom countered. 'Besides, you have your work here on the farm.'

'As you are the owner of the farm, you can excuse me from my duties,' Jessica said firmly. 'I will be travelling with you.'

Tom sighed. He knew his daughter too well, and if she did not travel with him, she would be on the first train after him. 'Very well,' he conceded. 'I will organise two tickets and inform the manager you need compassionate leave to travel to Sydney.'

Jessica broke into a broad smile. 'Thank you,' she said and threw her arms around her father's neck. 'Now I can make sure that you do not do anything silly with that rifle.'

Tom was sure his daughter knew what he was planning, and he wondered how he was going to keep her out of the firing line when they reached Sydney. It would not be easy.

That evening Tom rode into Bathurst to find a telephone box. He called Sean Duffy at his home.

'I am returning tomorrow,' Tom said when Sean answered. 'Is the job right to go?'

'I have a timetable,' Sean answered. 'I will see you soon.'

The call was short, but the mission had begun.

★

In a dark narrow alleyway beside a hotel frequented by wharf labourers two men stood head to head. One was a police detective sergeant, the other a well-known criminal who had joined the wharf labourer's union to ensure his exemption from military service.

'You do this job and I will make sure you are kept away from being conscripted for the army,' Preston growled.

'Yer askin' me to murder some coot,' the wharfie said. 'I just do a bit of pilferin', that's all, Mr Preston.'

'There is money in it,' Preston said, retrieving a wad of banknotes from his pocket and pushing them under the man's nose. 'If you ever say anything about our talk here tonight I will make sure you do not live to tell the tale.'

'I never saw you before, Mr Preston,' the wharfie said, eyeing the notes. 'I do you this favour an' you look after me in the future.'

'You make good money and I will be very grateful for your service,' Preston said. 'The man you have to do away with is a Sydney lawyer, Major Sean Duffy.'

'Duffy is pretty popular with the boys around 'ere,' the wharfie said. ''E's got a few orf in court.'

'That is why you will never tell anyone about our deal,' Preston said. 'Otherwise you might have a fatal accident of your own. I am sure that your commie mates are capable of dishing out a bit of natural justice to avenge a man they respect.'

The wharfie could see that he was trapped by the offer of money and retribution. 'When do I go after Duffy?' he asked as Preston peeled off a couple of banknotes and shoved them into the wharfie's grubby shirt pocket.

'You get the job done as soon as you can,' Preston said. 'It don't matter if it looks like murder, but just don't get caught. Make it look like a robbery gone wrong.'

As Preston briefed his hired killer, laughter from nearby prostitutes seeking out American servicemen drifted to them in the dark. Time was running out for Lord Ulverstone and Sean Duffy – although neither man realised how valuable time was becoming to them.

TWENTY

Captain James Duffy stood at ease in the small cabin allocated to his commanding officer aboard the USS *Enterprise.*

'Your record at Guadalcanal last year is impressive,' the naval officer said, perusing James's record of service. 'I see you have already accounted for nine Jap aircraft. One more will make you a double ace.'

'Yes, sir,' James responded.

'I have called you in to say that the marines need replacement pilots for their Corsairs in the Solomon Islands. I know you have not had time on the bent-wing birds, but I am sure with your record you could soon qualify with your old squadron in the Solomons – should you choose to accept the transfer.'

'When would I ship out?' James asked, excited that this would put him back in the air, hunting Japanese aircraft.

'We would put you on a transport plane in three days' time,' the commanding officer replied. 'I will give you until midday tomorrow to make your mind up about the transfer. I know it is not easy to leave the *Big E* once you have served on her.'

'Thank you, sir,' James said. 'I appreciate your consideration.'

'Personally, I would rather have you stay with us for when we ship out, but I know you jarheads like to stick together, and the Corsair is an excellent fighter bomber. Do you have any other questions?'

'No, sir, I will give you my decision tomorrow before noon.'

'If there is nothing else, Captain Duffy, you are dismissed.'

'Aye, aye, sir,' James said, snapping a smart salute and leaving the cabin to make his way back to his sleeping quarters.

When he did he found a note on his bunk. Lieutenant Guy Praine was in town and would like to see him that evening at a local bar frequented by sailors. James had the evening off and so telephoned Guy's hotel to confirm the meeting.

The bar was crowded with uniformed men and through the cloud of cigarette smoke James saw Guy sitting in an alcove in the corner. As he walked over, Guy rose to meet him and they shook hands.

'What the devil are you doing in this neck of the woods?' James asked.

'I was sent up from LA to do a story on the *Big E*,' Guy said. 'Can I buy a flyboy a drink?' he asked.

The drinks were ordered and both men settled down to chat. 'How is Julianna doing?' James asked, taking a sip of bourbon.

'Funny you should ask that,' Guy said with his character-istic lopsided smile. 'Not so good. She misses you, although she will not admit it.'

'All I ever asked was for her to wait for me,' James said. 'But she knows that all I have to do is say the word and I would be back in the world of civilians. Guy, I am a fighter pilot, and to return to being a civilian when we are fighting this war would destroy me.'

'I understand completely, but I am not a woman desper-ately in love with you. That's a totally different ball game, old chap.'

'I love her, but I have a duty to my fellow marines, and only a fighting man can truly understand that,' James said with a note of frustration in his voice.

'I have been able to wrangle you a week back in LA on a PR project,' Guy said with a broad smile. 'Maybe that would give you more of an opportunity to sit down and talk to Julianna. I know she would welcome it. It might even be enough time before the *Enterprise* puts out to sea. The scuttlebutt has that she should be ready by November, and there will be opportunities for you two lovebirds to get together. LA is not so far from here.'

James grimaced. The Corsair offer echoed in his thoughts. With more time he might be able to convince Julianna they had a future together. He realised he was facing a critical decision. He could turn down the offer to go back into combat, or request to remain with the *Enterprise* and have time to patch up matters with Julianna. He told Guy about the offer he had received earlier that day.

'Goddamned hard choice,' Guy said. 'But I think I know what your decision will be.'

'I could not live the rest of my life with Julianna if I chose *not* to transfer to a marine fighter squadron,'

James said. 'I know that is not something I can explain to her.'

'Damned right,' Guy said. 'She loves you and will do anything to keep you out of danger. You can't blame her for that.'

'I know,' James said with a pained expression. He glanced around at the sailors in their uniforms. They were so young, and in a matter of weeks would be in the firing line back in the Pacific. But he was young too, although combat had made him feel old. 'What would you do?' he asked in his desperation.

Guy finished his drink. 'It is up to you, James, not me,' he said. 'But I am fairly sure you have already decided to ship out for the Solomons.'

'I have to,' James replied. 'My marine buddies are out there, and I can do a lot more to keep them alive by flying than by staying here till the *Enterprise* is ready to sail.'

'I guess that when I see Julianna I will just have to lie and tell her that you had no choice about being posted to the Pacific,' Guy said with a sad sigh. 'Just make sure you don't do anything stupid, and come back in one piece.'

James toyed with his glass of bourbon, staring at the alcohol-stained table. He knew Julianna was the woman he wanted to grow old with, but at the same time he had a duty to his fellow marines. He was also aware that every hour in the air lessened his odds of coming home alive. 'Just tell her that I love her and hope that she will write to me,' he said.

'I will,' Guy answered, rising from the table. 'I have to leave you, I have an appointment with the XO of the *Enterprise* to plan out a story about her presidential citation.' He thrust out his hand. 'Until we meet again,' he said, and left James to his half-finished drink.

James remained for another ten minutes before returning to the carrier. He needed the time to pack and prepare for his transfer back into the war.

★

Night was descending on Sydney and the only two people remaining in the law offices of Levi and Duffy were Allison and Sean. It had been a court day and the two of them had stayed back to finish paperwork. Sean knew that young Patrick would have already arrived home from school and was most probably curled up in front of the radio, listening to his favourite programs.

Allison entered Sean's office with a folder of papers. 'That's it,' she said, placing the folder on the desk. 'You should leave all this until tomorrow morning.'

Sean glanced up at her. 'Thank you for staying back,' he said. 'Have you heard from David recently?' he asked, recalling that Allison had asked him if he had heard from David in North Queensland – which he had.

Allison sat down on a chair. 'I have written almost every day, but I have not had a single letter from him in return,' she said. 'I cannot fathom why.'

'Company commanders have their work cut out for them,' Sean said lamely, although he knew that David could have written at least one letter to her. 'I am sure he will write soon.'

'I just wonder what is going on,' Allison said sadly. 'David knows I love him.'

'Well, I think it is time to get a good night's sleep, and keep our worries for another day,' Sean said, rising stiffly from his chair. 'How about you head home and put your feet up whilst you can – we will need to prepare the brief for the Jackson case tomorrow and it may be another long day.'

'Yes, Major,' Allison said with a weak smile.

Sean watched her leave the office, then walked over to the clothes rack to retrieve his hat and umbrella. It was cold outside and he pulled on an overcoat. He walked down the stairs and out onto the street where he locked the front door. The city was coming alive as best it could to entertain the many American servicemen in town. Sean could feel a drizzle of rain and flipped open his umbrella to walk across Hyde Park to catch a train to his city flat. He used his walking stick to ease his pain, and inside the darkened park he walked carefully so as not to slip on the wet footpath.

From the corner of his eye he noticed a man rapidly approaching, but he took little notice as he had passed one or two other people using the park to get to the underground railway station. The shadowy figure fell into step behind him, and suddenly the hair on the back of Sean's neck stood up. He turned around with the umbrella above his head.

'Bloody hell!' Sean swore when the man closed the ten feet between them with a short rush. It was obvious that the fellow meant to do him harm because he had a long-bladed knife in his hand. Instinctively Sean thrust the umbrella between his would-be attacker and himself, as the blade came forward, catching the folds in the umbrella.

Flinging the umbrella aside, Sean stepped back and withdrew the long blade from his walking stick. The attacker threw off the umbrella and then hesitated when he saw the long deadly blade in Sean's hand. Sean desperately attempted to keep his balance on his two artificial legs and prayed that he would not fall over. The attacker came forward slowly and the two men faced each other in the drizzling rain in the dark park.

'C'mon, you bastard,' Sean snarled. 'Do your worst before I gut you.'

The attacker stepped forward warily. Sean could make out his face now and he could see the fear there. How many times had he seen the same fear on the faces of German soldiers when he and his men had poured into their trenches with bayonets fixed?

Sean knew that if he lunged at the man he might topple over, and so he had to wait for the man to come to him. 'Who the bloody hell are you?' he snarled. 'Did Sir George send you to kill me?'

The attacker did not answer but started to circle behind Sean as if knowing the man he was about to kill was hampered by his disability. Sean tried to turn to face him and in the attempt felt his legs go from under him on the slippery footpath. He toppled to the wet concrete of the pathway but did not let go of his sword stick.

Before Sean could roll over he felt a searing pain in his lower back from the assailant's knife. He cried out in pain but still managed to roll over enough to see his assailant bending over him, knife raised. Sean did not know how he did it but he was able to swing the point of the sword blade around to pierce his assailant in the shoulder. The man screamed in pain and fell back. Sean was aware he could hear voices and running footsteps. The attacker stumbled away, leaving Sean alone, bleeding profusely.

'You all right, buddy?' an American voice asked and Sean focused on the outline of a uniformed American soldier leaning over him. Beside him stood a young woman.

'Thanks, cobber,' Sean said, attempting to get to his feet. 'I think I might have to get to a hospital.'

The American soldier hefted Sean to his feet, and when he took away his hand he realised that it was sticky with blood. 'Did you have an accident?' he asked, startled.

'Something like that,' Sean replied, standing uncertainly and looking around for the sword stick sheath. The young woman bent over and retrieved it.

'Is this yours?' she asked, handing it to Sean, who quickly placed the blade back inside so that it once again became a functional walking stick, which he used to prop himself up.

'We need to get you help now,' the American said, realising that Sean was losing a lot of blood. 'I'll get a taxi.' With that, he rushed away, leaving the girl with Sean.

'What happened?' she asked, and Sean could see that she was young and pretty.

'I must have fallen over on something sharp,' Sean replied.

'We heard someone scream,' the girl said with a worried expression. 'As though they were being attacked.'

'It must have been me when I fell,' Sean answered.

'But we heard two screams,' the girl persisted. 'Did you get stabbed by someone trying to rob you?'

'I must thank you for your help,' Sean said, 'but all I need is to get to a hospital.'

The American soldier came hurrying back then. 'I got us a cab,' he said, helping Sean hobble down to the roadway where a taxi was waiting. 'We will get you to a hospital, buddy.'

Sean could feel the searing pain tear through his body with each step and he prayed that the blade had missed his kidneys as such a strike usually proved fatal.

The two young people accompanied Sean to the nearest hospital where a nursing sister helped him remove his overcoat and immediately called for a doctor when she saw the extent of his wound. Sean found himself whisked away on a trolley before he had time to thank the young couple waiting in the reception area.

As Sean lay on the trolley he turned to the nursing sister in her starched headwear and uniform. She had already questioned him to his identity and residential address.

'I am looking after a young fella,' he said through the pain. 'I need you to call a number and speak with a Miss Allison Lowe. Ask her to go to my place and look after my young fella, Patrick.'

The nursing sister took down the telephone number and left Sean to the doctor.

'You have a stab wound, Mr Duffy,' he said. 'But given who you are, I doubt that you provoked the assault. I have seen you in the papers.'

'Someone was trying to rob me,' Sean said, knowing that he had no proof the assailant had been trying to murder him.

The nursing sister returned to inform Sean that Miss Lowe had been contacted and was on her way to his flat. Sean thanked her warmly. What if he had been killed, he thought with a shudder. Who would look after Patrick then?

'The police have been informed of your attack, Mr Duffy,' the nurse said. 'They will be here shortly to interview you . . . Mr Duffy? Mr Duffy, can you hear me?'

Sean knew he was going into shock as everything around him became blurred. He closed his eyes, and the last thing he heard was the voice of the nurse saying, 'He could die on us, doctor.'

Sean saw the black void, and everything around him faded into oblivion.

★

When the light came back into Sean's existence he was aware that he could feel pain and that a face was looming over him.

'I see you are awake, Mr Duffy,' Detective Sergeant Preston said. 'You have a few questions to answer.'

Sean was not in the mood to speak with the corrupt policeman. 'I was attacked in Hyde Park and stabbed,' Sean said. 'I wondered if you had any prior knowledge of my assailant.' He could see the darkness come over the detective's face at his inference.

'Another man was brought into this hospital last night, suffering a severe shoulder wound,' Preston said. 'He claims that you attacked him – without any provocation – with a sword stick.'

'Don't make me laugh, Preston,' Sean said. 'Because it hurts when I do, and your statement might send me into fits of laughter. Can I guess and say that the man who attacked and stabbed me gave a false name and left before you arrived to interview him?'

'That is correct,' Preston replied. 'But we will find him. In the meantime I take the man's allegation very seriously.'

Sean wanted to sit up but the pain in his lower back prevented him doing so. 'You and I both know that your friend Sir George Macintosh was behind the assault,' Sean snarled. 'I would not put it past you to be the person who set this whole thing up.'

'That is an extremely serious allegation, Mr Duffy,' Preston said in anger. 'You had better have proof of what you are insinuating.'

'You bloody well know I have no proof – unless I can track down your man,' Sean answered. 'And I have means to do that, as you well know.'

He could tell that he was making the police detective uncomfortable, and also noticed that he was on his own. From Sean's experience, police usually travelled in pairs in such matters. It was obvious that the crooked policeman did not want any witnesses to this talk.

'You will be required to give a written statement to us concerning the incident,' Preston said. 'I expect your statement as soon as you are released from hospital.'

Preston turned to walk away.

'Tell Sir George that I will catch up with him eventually,' Sean said quietly.

The policeman stopped and turned around. 'Let us hope that you do not have another bad accident in the future, Mr Duffy,' he said and left the room.

Sean understood the veiled threat. He had friends in the police force who were honest hardworking men who despised this arrogant detective. But they feared him too, and Sean did not blame them – he was a dangerous and callous man.

TWENTY-ONE

Sean was ordered by his doctors to remain in hospital for at least two weeks. No vital organs had been penetrated, but infection was a concern and the new wonder drug, penicillin, was used to ensure the former soldier recovered.

His first visitors were Allison and young Patrick. The boy looked gravely concerned for this man who had treated him as if he were his own child, but Allison assured Sean she was happy for Patrick to stay with her until he was released from hospital. Sean was relieved that Patrick was away from his flat; he would be safer that way.

Sean and Allison discussed the police case whilst Patrick wandered around the ward, and Sean admitted that he thought the attack was related to the investigation into the murder at Long Bay Gaol. He had brought Allison in on the case so she could assist him with it.

'Major,' Allison said, taking hold of his hand. 'You need

to give up your investigation. None of us can afford to lose you – especially Patrick.'

'I am afraid it is too late,' Sean said. 'I am in a war again with Sir George, and he will not give up this time until I am dead.'

'Do you really think that Sir George is behind all this?' Allison asked.

'A long time ago he had a bent copper try to kill me,' Sean said. 'I could not prove it, but the circumstantial evidence was overwhelming. The Macintosh and Duffy war goes back a long time. I have heard that we have some kind of old Aboriginal curse on us for something that happened on a Queensland property many years ago. I have a dear friend, Tom Duffy, who has persisted in offering to purchase Glen View as he has Aboriginal blood linked to the land there. You have met Tom.'

'Yes,' Allison said. 'He came to your office a couple of weeks ago and you introduced us.'

'Tom is a good man, and his daughter, Jessica, a good woman. If anything should befall me, I want your promise that you will do everything in your power to help Tom and his daughter.'

'I am not sure I believe in curses, Major,' Allison said, patting his hand. 'But I do believe that Sir George Macintosh is a powerful man to have as an enemy. You need to recover and then lie low for a while.'

Sean smiled at her. 'David is bloody lucky to have you in his life,' he said, and then noticed the stricken expression on her face.

'I received a letter from David yesterday,' she said, fighting to control the tears welling up. 'He informed me that he would not be contacting me in the future. He did not say why.'

Sean gripped her hand, confused at David's decision. They had seemed so happy together. 'Maybe he
fears that he might not come home and in his clumsy
way is trying to spare you the experience of losing him to
the war.'

'His letter was only two sentences long,' Allison said,
tears spilling down her cheeks. 'It seems that he's furious
with me, although I have no idea what for. It is so horrible.
I've asked him to explain what's going on, but he has not
replied.'

Sean had received letters from David, but there had been
no hint of any problems with Allison. 'Maybe I can write to
him,' he offered. 'Sort something out.'

Allison held a dainty handkerchief to her eyes, wiping
away tears. 'I have Patrick to look after,' she said. 'Poor little
blighter has lost his mother to Changi and moved around so
much since the fall of Singapore. He must be suffering, but
he appears to be so resilient in the face of his terrible experiences. I should take a page from his book.'

Allison smiled bravely, then summoned Patrick from
the end of the ward where he was chatting with an old
man sitting in a wheelchair. She held out her hand, and
Patrick took it, then the two of them said goodbye and
left.

Within the hour Sean received a second visitor. It was
his old comrade from the Great War, Harry Griffiths. The
tough-looking gym owner plonked himself in the chair
vacated by Allison and deftly removed a bottle in a paper
bag from under his moth-eaten army-issue greatcoat. Sean
took the bottle and slipped it under his blankets.

'Thanks, cobber,' he said, knowing that the matron of
the ward would be furious if she found one of her patients
consuming alcohol.

'You are too old to go and get yourself into fights,' Harry said. He was about the same age as Sean, and the closest thing to a best friend he had.

'It looks like our old friend Sir George is up to his tricks again,' Sean said. 'And he has a new accomplice in Detective Sergeant Preston.'

'So, another Jack Firth to deal with,' Harry said quietly.

'This is different,' Sean cautioned. 'Preston is a serving officer, and if he gets killed, it will bring the wrath of the police down on us. Firth was out of the job when he met his unfortunate demise. There is also something else I need to tell you,' Sean continued and quietly explained the situation with Ulverstone.

'Bloody hell!' Harry said when Sean was finished. 'Talk about a one, two, three knockout blow.'

'Tom Duffy should be back in town,' Sean said. 'I need you to contact him on this number.' He passed his friend a slip of paper. 'I know that I can trust you, cobber.'

'Boss, you know you can,' Harry answered with absolute sincerity. 'When my missus was dying you were there for me and the family. You helped get my eldest boy a commission in the navy. You are my fair-dinkum cobber.'

'Ulverstone is a traitor, and while he lives men like your son and many others can be killed by what he relays to the enemy,' Sean said. 'Killing him is a legitimate act of war, although not recognised by the civil laws of this country. Tom will do the job, but he will need your help. I know it's risky – but so was it for us patrolling into no-man's-land in the last lot. I suppose we are fighting a war on two fronts – Macintosh and Ulverstone, aided by Preston.'

'I'm in,' Harry said. 'It's a bit quiet around the gym with all the boys gone off to war.'

'I'm hoping to get out of here soon,' Sean said. 'You are back on the firm's payroll as my investigator.'

'Just like old times,' Harry grinned, producing a couple of small glasses from under his greatcoat. 'I think we should toast our new war.'

Sean retrieved the small bottle of rum from under the blankets and Harry poured them a stiff drink each. Glancing quickly over their shoulders, the two men raised their glasses and took long drinks of the dark liquid. Dangerous times were ahead and both men were acutely aware of what could happen if anything went wrong.

★

The nightmares had become more frequent for Sir George Macintosh. In the middle of the night Wallarie would come to him and stand at the foot of his bed. His beautiful sister Fenella was often waiting in the dark too, her blood-covered face staring at him with questioning eyes. She would say nothing, only stare, and Sir George would shake with fear until he awoke into the silence of the real world. He knew that his time on earth was now counted in weeks, maybe even days.

Very early one morning, jerked from sleep by another nightmare, he rose from his bed and shuffled to his library where he had a stock of good liquors. He poured himself a drink and sat down in the big leather chair facing the grand window overlooking the driveway. It was still dark and Sir George wondered how many more sunrises he might expect to experience before the dreaded disease finally took his life. He so desperately wanted to live, and if he could use his vast fortune for just one guaranteed extra day of life, he would.

Sarah had proven ruthless enough to take his place, but she had a son whose father was the hated David Macintosh.

Donald had not yet produced any heirs, legitimate or otherwise, and he was not as business savvy as his sister. As for David Macintosh, he was not even a consideration, and with any luck he would be killed in battle as his father, Alexander, had been in the last war.

Deep in thought, Sir George took a sip of whisky. Suddenly he dropped his tumbler to the carpet, spilling its contents, and seized his chest in absolute terror. From the corner of his eye he had seen movement, and when he turned his head he saw plainly the semi-naked figure of Wallarie, an old, battle-scarred man holding a long, hardwood spear. Sir George knew that he was wide awake, and that this could not be a dream. He could feel his heart pounding in his chest and a single sentence floated across the room.

'You got any baccy?' Wallarie asked with a chuckle, before disappearing into the shadows.

For what seemed like an eternity Sir George remained transfixed in his chair until the sound of the servants starting their duties for the day broke his terror-induced paralysis. It had to be a hallucination, Sir George attempted to convince himself. The strange question ringing in his ears proved to Sir George that it could have not been the old warrior who haunted his family. After all, why would an old Aboriginal ask for tobacco? He doubted that the spirit of Wallarie would ask for something so mundane. The clatter of crockery told Sir George that the world would soon fill with light, and all would be well for the moment. He had made his decision as to who should be the next ruler of the family.

★

Captain James Duffy was acutely aware that the battlefront he had returned to was not the place many newcomers imagined from watching the very popular *On the Road* movies starring Bob Hope and Bing Crosby. The balmy tropical breezes swaying tall palm trees bordering pristine white beaches were quickly replaced by rotting vegetation and monsoonal drenching rain that turned the inland into a sea of mud. Under the canopy of tall rainforest giants insects sucked blood, delivering the deadly diseases of dengue and malaria. Where the rainforest finished, clearings of kunai grass with razor-sharp edges grew as high as a man and the temperatures soared to a hundred degrees every afternoon. That was bad enough, but the high relative humidity caused constant thirst, and the sluggish, jungle streams hid deadly intestinal diseases. Dysentery racked the soldiers who served in the Solomon Islands, along with fungal complaints and heat stroke. The story was similar to other battlefronts for the men who slogged across the islands towards the Japanese island.

James sat outside his tent, stripped down to his shorts. He wore aviator sunglasses to shield his eyes against the glare reflecting off the open area that formed the airfield, ripped out of the rainforest by the brave engineers and Sea Bees. At least he was not out in the bush patrolling as an infantryman. On the airfield they had access to a few luxuries the marines in the jungle did not have.

The distinctively shaped Chance Vought Corsairs were lined up under a baking tropical sun ready for action. James had quickly qualified on the Corsair in his first weeks in the Solomon Islands. He was impressed by the fighter bomber that had greater range and speed than his Hellcats, but did have a couple of disadvantages. Its long nose was hard to see over when landing, and it could not outmanoeuvre the nimble Japanese fighters. He knew the best way to destroy the enemy fighters was to get above them and then dive through their formations, firing the six .50 calibre machine guns mounted in the bent wings that gave it the nickname of 'bent-wing bird' to Allied personnel and 'whistling death' to Japanese soldiers unfortunate enough to be on the ground when the fighter dived on them. The distinctive whistling sound was caused by air rushing through the oil-cooling system.

James had quickly fitted in with his squadron, who were forever asking him about Hollywood celebrities and had given him the nickname 'Hollywood Jim'. He had flown two operational fighter bomber missions since his transfer. On his second mission the squadron had flown ground support for the marines in the jungle and had bombed entrenched Japanese positions on a hillside. He had dived on the hill and watched the enemy tracer rounds rising to meet him. They had flashed past his plexiglas cockpit window to trail off into the blue sky, and he had not felt any fear as he focused on a blackened clearing on the hill where log-covered strong points were identified by an earlier photo recon flight. He had released both his bombs so low, ensuring pinpoint accuracy, that he had put himself in dire peril. He could have easily been caught in the massive blast, and had immediately pulled hard and to the right to avoid the blast. Even so his Corsair had been rocked violently as he had climbed away to rejoin his squadron, flying cover above to interfere with any Japanese fighter aircraft. But none had appeared, and all the aircraft had returned safely from the mission.

When James had landed, his ground crew mechanics had come running over to help him out of the cockpit.

'You were goddamn lucky, Captain Duffy,' his armourer had said when James had stepped out onto the wing. 'Looks like you took a good burst of AA fire.'

James had jumped to the ground and seen where heavy Japanese anti-aircraft machine guns had ripped in around his cockpit. Had they penetrated the armour he would have been a dead man. James had felt a shudder of fear then, and had flashbacked to the previous year when he had been shot down.

'Got the devil's luck,' he had said. 'Looks like these birds can take it.'

'Goddamn right,' the armourer had said, poking his finger in one of the holes.

That had been four days ago, and now the young marine pilot sat in front of his tent, relaxing in the sun. He was thinking about Julianna. He had received letters from his sister, his grandfather and even one from Guy Praine in Hollywood – but none from Julianna. It was obvious that she was keeping her word to cut off contact with him while he was overseas on the battlefront.

James was about to amble over to the chow line when he noticed a sergeant from HQ hurrying towards him, a serious expression on his yellow-tinged face. The hue was caused by the Atebrin anti-malarial tablets they took, and all Allied servicemen in the South West Pacific theatre of operations had the distinctive 'suntan' – even James.

'Sir, you are wanted at HQ,' the sergeant said.

'Thanks, sarge,' James acknowledged. 'Any idea why?'

'You'll be told when you report to the CO,' the sergeant answered evasively and walked away.

James went into his tent to recover his shirt and cap. He walked quickly over to the tent housing their HQ and reported to the chief clerk, who told him to go straight to the CO's office.

The CO was a major only a year older than James. He had been a farm boy who had made it to college to study engineering, but Pearl Harbor had found him flying for the marines and he had proved himself a top ace and leader.

'Captain Duffy, at ease,' he said from behind his desk. 'I am afraid that we have received a signal with bad news from the home front.'

One thought reeled through James's mind – his grand-father was dead. 'Is it concerning my grandfather?' he asked quickly.

'Er, no,' the CO said. 'It is about your sister, Olivia. According to the message we got today, she was killed in a car accident in New Hampshire three days ago. I am sorry for your loss, and arrangements have been made from Washington to fly you immediately back to the States.'

Olivia! James stood swaying in shock. Olivia could not be dead. That was something that happened to brothers on the front – not sisters at home.

'Aye, aye, sir,' James said. He turned and walked out the door into the blinding tropical sun.

TWENTY-TWO

Jessica Duffy's two flatmates had followed in her footsteps and joined the Women's Land Army, so the house in Strathfield was empty. This was convenient for Tom and Jessica when they returned from Bathurst. Tom telephoned Sean's office and was informed by Allison of the circumstances of Sean's absence. She passed on the message that a Mr Harry Griffiths would be in contact with him soon.

That afternoon Tom and Jessica heard a knock on their front door. Tom was cautious and told Jessica to make herself scarce, as it might be the police searching for her as a deserter.

Tom opened the door.

'You must be Tom Duffy,' Harry Griffiths said, extending his hand. 'I'm the Major's cobber, Harry Griffiths.'

Tom invited him in and called to Jessica that it was safe to come out.

'Can I make you both a cuppa?' she asked after she'd been introduced.

'That would be fine, Miss Duffy,' Harry answered.

When Jessica disappeared to the kitchen to prepare a pot of tea, Harry took a seat in the living room on an old couch.

'I heard about you in the last lot,' Harry said, settling himself down. 'I heard the Hun called you the Butcher, for your sniping skills.'

'Yeah,' Tom said, trying to shrug off the old name. He did not want to think about how many German families still mourned the loss of a loved one because of a single shot from his rifle. It was still the stuff of his troubled nights when their ghostly faces floated before his eyes.

'The Major has briefed me on what you are planning to do,' Harry continued. 'I am here to help you.'

'Are you sure you want to be involved?' Tom asked. 'You know that we are acting outside the law.'

'I have a son on a destroyer out there,' Harry said. 'I see it as my duty to do anything I can to stop this Pommy traitor. In my mind, your mission is no different to the ones we undertook in no-man's-land during the last lot.'

'I could do with the help,' Tom admitted. 'The information I have is that Ulverstone will be travelling to Newcastle on the main road there in forty-eight hours time. I am planning to carry out an ambush on his vehicle. I have approximate times of where and when he will be on the road – thanks to Sean's intelligence.'

Harry stood up and produced a map from inside his coat. He spread it out on a low table in the living room. 'I reckon that this spot would be the best place to hit him,' he said, pointing to a bend in the narrow road from Sydney to Newcastle, at the top of a hill. 'Ulverstone's car will have slowed considerably before it comes over the hill and around the bend. A marksman positioned nearby would get a clear shot. I have information that the Pom travels in the back seat alone, which means there is little chance of hitting his driver. I could drop you off at the point there . . . and pick you up here on a side road not far away. We would be out of the area before the alarm was raised as we have surprise and ground on our side.'

Tom was impressed with the former soldier's tactical grasp of the situation and agreed with his plan. All that had to happen now was for Ulverstone to be punctual.

'You will need my help,' said Jessica, walking in with the tea tray.

Both men looked up at her in surprise.

'I want you to stay out of this, Jessie,' Tom said, and Harry echoed his agreement.

Jessica placed the tray on the low table and for a moment examined the map.

'I can improve on your plan,' she said.

'How do you know what we have planned?' Tom asked, assuming his daughter had been in the kitchen.

'You are both deaf old farts,' she snorted. 'Too much exposure to artillery fire in the last war, and when you think you are speaking quietly, you are talking so loudly that everyone can hear you down the street. I heard every word when I was making the tea.'

Harry and Tom looked at each other and shrugged.

'What can you do to help?' Harry asked.

'I could give early warning of Ulverstone's approach,' Jessie said. 'I can get hold of a car and sit off the road at a petrol station. I know what staff cars look like, and he will also have a tactical sign on his car. I can then pull out in front of Ulverstone's car and drive past your point a few moments before Ulverstone's car arrives – alerting you.'

'I really don't want you out there, Jessie,' Tom said.

'I think your daughter has improved our plan, Tom,' Harry said. 'We need precision, because if Ulverstone gets past you then we have lost the only real chance we have of eliminating him. We don't have much time to put all this into place.'

'Okay,' Tom sighed. 'But that is all you do, Jessie,' he cautioned.

'Good,' Harry said and stood to shake hands with Tom. 'I will contact you tomorrow morning and we will get ready to move out.'

Tom nodded and Harry left.

Jessica walked over to her father and placed her arms around him. 'I love you, Dad,' she said.

'I love you, too,' he said, knowing full well that they were now officially conspirators in murder. The outcome could easily be a hangman's noose around both their necks.

★

It had taken almost a week to reach his grandfather's home in New Hampshire. Captain James Duffy stood before the great entrance to the mansion, set amongst the beauty of tall trees whose leaves were taking on the russet colours of fall. The serenity of the New Hampshire countryside was so different to the world he had left behind in the Solomons.

James was met by his grandfather's old butler, who ushered him into the house and took his sea bag to his room.

James went to the vast living room with its great fireplace, and there he found his grandfather sitting in a chair, staring at the flickering flames of the fire.

'Sir,' James called softly, and James Barrington Senior turned his head to see his grandson standing in the doorway. He rose on unsteady legs and walked towards James, who noticed how much his grandfather had aged since he'd last seen him. It was apparent that Olivia's death had taken its toll on him.

Uncharacteristically, James Barrington Senior put his arms around James and held him as if he were a child. 'She is gone,' he said, tears rolling down his cheeks. 'She was so much like her mother.'

James gently disengaged himself from the embrace and led his grandfather back to his favourite lounge chair by the fire.

'I was told that Olivia was killed in a car crash,' James said quietly, sitting down himself. 'What happened?'

'Young Edgar was driving,' Barrington said, still staring at the fire. 'Sheriff Mueller told me that Wilson was drunk when they got to the crash site.'

'Was Edgar killed in the crash?' James asked.

'No, he walked away without a scratch,' Barrington said.

'Was he arrested?' James asked.

'No,' Barrington replied. 'You know that his family has as much influence as our own in these parts.'

'The goddamned son of a bitch should be behind bars – if he was drunk when he killed my sister,' James said savagely. 'Mueller should have done something. You helped him win the last elections and he owes us for that.'

'Wilson claims that Olivia was driving,' Barrington said. 'But everything Mueller saw indicates that was not the case.'

James felt a rage rising up in him and he recognised it as the feeling he experienced before gunning down the enemy. 'The son of a bitch will pay for killing my sister,' he said with cold fury.

'James,' his grandfather cautioned, 'you are the only one left in my life. If anything happened to you, I would have no reason left to live.'

'I never liked Wilson,' James said. 'You and I both know that his father got him out of the draft. He is a gutless coward.'

The following day Olivia's funeral service was held in the quaint nineteenth century church that she and James had attended before the war. James wore his uniform, holding an umbrella over his grandfather's head as the rain drizzled down and the wind whipped up the leaves that covered the graveyard. Olivia's coffin was placed in a grave beside that of her mother and grandmother. Only a handful of business acquaintances and the servants attended the funeral service, and James could not see Edgar Wilson or any of his family in attendance.

As the coffin was lowered into the ground, rain caused trickles of blood-red mud to follow, and James had a flash-back of combat. He stood trembling, wondering why he could not cry for the loss of his beloved twin sister. They had come into the world together, and now part of James's own soul was gone. Yet he could not cry. Was it that he had seen so many good friends die and he had used up his reserves of tears?

'Come, James,' his grandfather said gently, as if sensing his beloved grandson's emotional turmoil. 'It is time to go home.'

But for James, home was in the cockpit of a Corsair, on the other side of the Pacific.

★

Harry and Tom drove in silence in Harry's truck along the Pacific Highway towards Newcastle. The road was hardly more than a track through the bush and it took them past beautiful glimpses of the ocean and tiny little coastal villages, where fresh oysters were offered for sale. In the late afternoon they reached the point where Tom was to exit the vehicle on a crest covered by scrub trees and big rocks and with a view of the road below. Tom had with him a bag containing a few items of tinned food and a warm blanket. He also had his .303 rifle and was dressed in tough clothing suitable for the bush.

'We will RV two miles up the road at last light on that side road,' Harry said. 'Be bloody careful, cobber.'

Tom waved him away and climbed the slope of loose rocks and scrub until he found a small patch on the crest where he could look down on the bend in the road. With the truck gone a silence fell. A slight wind rustled the grass around Tom, and he hunched against the cold to wait out the night. He knew it was relatively safe to light a small fire, and he did so to heat the canned meat he had brought with him, along with the tea for a brew. According to all reports Ulverstone should pass this location just after lunch. Jessica would drive through ahead of Ulverstone when she spotted his staff car pass the petrol station down in a little fishing village on the coast. The plan was for her to continue on and then circle back to Sydney.

The night came with a chill and Tom wrapped the blanket around him as he sat by his fire. Eventually he let the fire die out and lay back to gaze up at a crystal clear sky of twinkling stars. How many times in his life had he done this? According to Wallarie, each star represented the spirit of a deceased person, and Tom wondered where in the night sky the old man's star would be.

'Wallarie, my brother, where are you up there?' Tom asked in a hushed voice as he continued to stare up at the heavens. Eventually he dozed off and was awoken by the sound of a vehicle on the road below. Tom sat up; the sun was starting to rise and there was enough light to peer down at the road. The vehicle was an army truck and of no interest to him.

Tom finished the remainder of his rations and buried any scraps left over. He was careful not to leave traces of his camp, and he settled back with the rifle lying across his knees as he watched vehicles pass along the road in either direction.

Midday arrived and the day was beautiful with just a touch of an early summer. Every now and then Tom would practise aiming at a vehicle coming from the south and conduct a dry run. He was pleased to see that vehicles coming from that direction came to an almost standstill at the top of the hard-packed dirt and gravel road. He had even stepped out the exact distance to where he calculated the staff car would slow, and set his rear sight accordingly. His artificial arm provided the rest for the fore grip, and the practice he had had at Bathurst proved to him he could still make the kill shot.

Tom leaned back against a rock that had warmed in the sun and waited. Just before one o'clock his attention was caught by a vehicle slowly crawling up the hill. He could see that it was Jessica at the wheel. She reached the crest and continued down the other side.

Tom moved away from the rock and lay on his stomach, his rifle ready for the shot. He controlled his breathing and waited calmly. Then he saw a dark green sedan crawling up the hill and could see that it was a staff car. There was a figure in the back seat wearing an officer's peaked cap. The sight was on the target and Tom expertly squeezed the trigger.

*

James Duffy knew he only had forty-eight hours of leave left before he was to be returned to active service. That was forty-eight hours to investigate the death of his beloved sister. From the little that he did know from his grandfather, Edgar Wilson's behaviour at the scene was far from fully explained. As far as James knew, his sister had never learned to drive a car. The first place he would start was with Sheriff Mueller.

James walked into the sheriff's office and was met by one of the deputies, who he knew from past experience was a good friend of Edgar Wilson. As a matter of fact, James had once been in a fist fight with Deputy Sheriff Ike Hausmann, when they were teenagers. Hausmann had been bullying a younger boy James knew and James had suggested he pick on someone his own size. James had won the fight and Hausmann had hated him ever since.

The deputy had his feet on a table and sneered at James. 'What do you want, flyboy?' he asked. 'I heard the hero was back in town.'

'I am looking for your boss,' James answered, ignoring the lawman's animosity.

'What for?' the deputy asked.

'None of your business,' James replied, fighting down the urge to walk over and punch the man in the face.

'I'm the law here, if you haven't noticed, Barrington. You answer to me,' the deputy said as he lowered his feet to the floor and stood up with his thumbs in his gun belt. He was heavy-set, but more fat then muscle. He had a pockmarked face, and was always bragging about his conquests of the local girls, which they vigorously denied with a shudder.

'I've been wondering whether you ever recovered from that belting I gave you,' James said in an icy voice. 'You know, you could take off the badge and have a go at me around the back of the office. Maybe you just might get lucky this time,' James goaded, but before the enraged deputy could respond, the sheriff walked into the office.

'Hello, James,' he said, placing his hat on a stand by the door. 'I am so sorry about your sister. I was unable to attend the funeral.'

'Good to see you, Sheriff Mueller,' James said. 'If you don't mind, I would like to speak with you in private.'

'Sure thing,' the law officer replied. Mueller was also a big man and he had a rugged, worn face. He gestured for James to follow him into his office and closed the door behind them.

James was invited to sit down and Mueller told him everything off the record. The lawman recognised that he owed his job to the Barrington family, and his loyalty was with James Barrington Senior and his grandson. The story that unfolded was not of an accident but of something far more sinister.

'My deputy Hausmann was first on the scene,' the Sheriff said. 'There was little damage to the automobile, and he said that he found your sister dead in the front driver's seat. I saw Olivia's body at the coroner's office, and her injuries did not look like they were the result of an automobile accident. They looked more like she had been bashed and then put behind the wheel. I can't prove anything, but the talk in the drug store is that Wilson was knocking her around. I wish I could do more but I don't have enough evidence to arrest the Wilson boy.'

When James left an hour later there was blood in his eyes. Wilson was going to pay for the death of Olivia.

TWENTY-THREE

'**O**livia was murdered,' James said. 'It was not a car crash that killed her.'

He stood by the great fireplace and his grandfather sat in his big leather chair.

'I was told that Edgar's family had employed the services of one of this state's best law firms after Olivia was killed,' Barrington said. 'I thought that strange, considering Olivia's death was reported as an accident.'

'Sheriff Mueller told me in confidence that when he saw Olivia's body he noticed she had bruises consistent with a severe beating rather than a vehicle crash,' James said, staring into the fire and pondering his next move.

'I will speak with Mueller,' Barrington said. 'I never liked the Wilsons that much.'

'I only have twenty-four hours of my leave left,' James said. 'Maybe I can make my own enquiries.'

'Leave it with me and Sheriff Mueller, son,' Barrington cautioned. 'I will get justice for my granddaughter.'

James knew that his grandfather was a formidable man, but he was also weak from his stroke and growing old. James knew that he could not pass the deadline for him to return to combat. But he still had twenty-four hours. If Edgar Wilson was behind his sister's death then he would pay.

*

'Driver, get us out of here,' Ulverstone screamed. He was aware that he had been hit by a bullet that had grazed his neck, opening a wound that bled profusely. Shattered glass covered his lap, and the panic-stricken driver almost stalled the car. He was good at his job, though, and the vehicle lurched over the hill to round the bend and commence its descent down the road.

Tom Duffy instinctively ejected the spent cartridge and reloaded. He did not know if he had been successful, but placed faith in his record as a marksman in the army. He had seen the side window shatter, and noticed the occupant in the back seat jerk, as if hit by a bullet. But Tom did not know that his bullet passing through the shattered glass of the side window had been slightly deflected, missing the centre of Ulverstone's head.

Tom quickly stripped down the rifle and picked up his few items in his hide. He was careful to cover any trace of him being there, and made his way down the hill to trek across country to his RV with Harry Griffiths, unaware that he had failed to kill the British traitor.

Lord Ulverstone held a padded handkerchief to his neck as the driver put as much distance as he could between the car and the ambush site. Blood oozed between the British officer's fingers and he shouted at the driver to go faster. He knew that he must get medical treatment or he might bleed to death.

'How far to the nearest hospital?' he yelled.

'Not far, sir,' the driver said over his shoulder. 'Just hold on.'

Ulverstone slumped back against the seat and found that he was actually praying to any god that might be listening. He did not want to die.

'Sir!' the driver shouted. 'Hold on. We have a problem.'

Ulverstone leaned forward to peer out the front window where he saw a stationary car parked across the road. He knew immediately that it was a trap.

'Go around it!' he screamed at the driver, but the car had been so well placed that any way forward was blocked by table drains. The driver swung the steering wheel, and the staff car slid sideways into a drain and stalled. Ulverstone was acutely aware how silent the surrounding bush was, as if holding its breath to see what would happen next.

The British officer carried a revolver in his briefcase and scrambled to get it out, but he was too late. A masked figure, wearing a balaclava was beside his shattered side window pointing a revolver at him.

A female voice yelled at the driver, 'Stay down and don't move.'

The terrified army driver obeyed, hugging the front seat, where he heard four rapid shots.

Ulverstone did not have time to consider that his killer was a woman. The four bullets found their mark: three in the head and one in the chest.

'Keep down for at least ten minutes,' the female voice commanded the driver. 'If you do not, the sniper will finish you off.'

The driver realised that it had been an unseen sniper who had fired the first shot, and he was not about to question the woman giving him the orders. He heard the car start up but did not see it depart as he remained huddled on the front seat with his head down. After all, he had accepted the job as a staff driver because it was safer than being shipped to the Pacific. He was going to make very sure that he did not die at home in Australia.

*

'He wasn't dead,' Jessica said as her father and Harry stood by the truck at the RV. 'But I am bloody well sure that he is now.'

'What in hell did you think you were doing?' Tom asked in his exasperation at his daughter's dangerous and violent act.

'I knew that we had to be sure Ulverstone was dead, so I made a contingency plan, and I was right to do so,' Jessica said. 'He might have lived if I had not ambushed him and finished the job.'

'Where did you get the pistol?' Tom asked.

'Better you don't know,' she replied, and Tom noticed Harry shift uncomfortably.

'We had better get out of here,' Harry said. 'I would say that the coppers will be swarming all over the scene pretty soon.'

Jessica took a route north to Newcastle while Tom and Harry headed south.

Harry was correct about police attention as he and Tom returned to Sydney, brazenly driving up to a roadblock manned by uniformed police. They were stopped but, after brief questioning, waved through. The old lorry did not attract any undue attention and by nightfall they had arrived back at Strathfield. The telephone rang a couple of hours later, and Jessica informed her father that she was in a Newcastle hotel. They had all made it safely.

The following morning Tom went to the hospital where Sean was still a patient. He made his way down the ward and found Sean sitting up in bed smoking a cigarette. A newspaper lay on the bedsheets.

'Hello, Tom,' Sean said by way of greeting his old friend. 'Pull up a seat.'

Tom pulled a chair up to Sean's bed, and Sean picked up the paper.

'I was reading the paper this morning and came across an article about a fatal car accident on the road to Newcastle,' he said. 'It appears a staff car went off the road, and one of Britain's lords was killed in the accident.'

Tom blinked. 'Is that what they're saying about Ulverstone?' he asked, hardly believing his ears.

'It seems that a government spokesman has declared the incident a tragic accident,' Sean said. 'No mention of any nefarious activity.'

'Why would they cover up the fact that Ulverstone was shot?' Tom asked, still unable to believe that the execution of such a high-standing British officer would be reported as a mere traffic accident.

'It is possibly because Donald Macintosh had a word in the PM's ear about what was known of Ulverstone's treachery,' Sean said. 'By claiming it was an accident, it can be written off without any embarrassment to the government, who had posted him to such a sensitive area in our intelligence services in the first place. I also have an idea the Yanks would have verified Ulverstone's treachery to our PM's department. No doubt our government would have eventually acted to remove him, but this is a better outcome for them because the thorn has been removed without any pain to our government.'

'What about the driver?' Tom asked.

'I am sure that he has been threatened with dire consequences if he ever attempts to talk about what really happened,' Sean replied. 'As for the police who were sent to investigate, I am sure they were threatened in the same way – in the name of national security. So you can sleep soundly tonight, knowing that you are not a wanted man, and I am sure if young Lieutenant Caccamo is looking down on all of this, he will be celebrating the conclusion of a mission that cost him his life.'

Tom did not tell his friend that Jessica had fired the killing shots. He wanted no one else other than himself and Harry Griffiths to have that information about his daughter.

'I have convinced the doctors that I can be discharged from here tomorrow morning,' Sean said. 'Then you, Harry and I can head down for a cold beer at the pub to celebrate.'

Tom nodded. His mind was still reeling at how lucky they had been in the matter of Ulverstone's death. Maybe old Wallarie had come to him the night before the ambush and touched him with his magic. Now Tom could safely return to Queensland and Abigail. But one thing disturbed him: Jessica was still wanted by the military and he knew they would eventually track her down.

*

'I know it is a big risk,' Donald said to Jessica across the formica table. 'But you have to return to MacArthur's HQ in Brisbane. We need you there.'

Jessica had received the telephone call to meet Donald at this cafe. The killing of Ulverstone had been playing on her mind and causing her nightmares. She felt she was adrift in a world where evading the authorities was her only purpose, but constantly looking over her shoulder was wearing her down, and she missed her old life in the WAAAF.

'I was told by my father that you might have tipped off the government about Ulverstone's treachery,' she said.

'I might have,' Donald replied evasively. 'But that is not why we are here. We need to get you reinstated in your old job. I know that you accompanied your father on his mission, but he has informed me you had no active part in the killing of Ulverstone.'

Donald was confused by Tom's account as the top secret police report he had read said that the body had been shot numerous times with a revolver and he had concluded privately that Jessica had killed Ulverstone. But he was not about to question the man who had risked everything to keep his daughter out of the conspiracy.

'If I return to Brisbane and show up at HQ, I will be immediately arrested and charged with desertion,' Jessica said.

A slow smile crossed Donald's face. 'Do you really think I would ask you to risk that?' he asked. 'I have pulled a few strings with the Yanks. Trust me when I say the best thing you can do is return to Brisbane.'

Jessica stared at Donald, pondering his words. Then he slid his hand across the table and took her hand. 'I have already spoken with your father, and he agrees that this is the best course of action.'

Jessica sighed and glanced out the window of the small cafe at the people on the footpath. They went about their daily routines, grumbling about the rationing, going to their dull jobs in retail stores, factories and offices. One thing about her life was that it was far from dull. 'I will do it,' she said and Donald squeezed her hand.

'I want you to be safe,' he said.

'Is that all?' Jessica countered, and Donald slowly withdrew his hand from hers.

'That is all,' he lied. He felt unable to express how he really felt about her, considering all that had occurred in the last few days. When the time was right he would do so, but when that time would come, he did not know. In war nothing could be planned for, not even love.

★

James Duffy knew the best place in town to ask questions was the drugstore. It was the gathering place of the town's youth; they would drink Coca-Cola and eat ice-cream sundaes whilst swapping gossip.

He stepped through the doors and immediately recognised a few faces. When the girls saw him in his marine air force uniform there was a squeal of delight from one of the pretty young ladies sitting on a stool at the counter.

'James!' she said. 'You look so handsome. We have all been reading about you in the papers.'

The girl's name was Betty, and for a brief time in college James had dated her. She had a blonde ponytail and a milky white complexion. James smiled at her and she slid from the stool to greet him.

'I am sorry about your sister,' she said in a grave tone. 'She and I were close friends while you were away.'

'Maybe I could buy you a Coke and you could tell me about her,' James said disarmingly, and Betty jumped at the invitation. James ordered two bottles of Coke and led Betty to an empty corner booth with a view of the street.

'How long are you home for?' Betty asked.

'I have to leave tomorrow morning,' James answered, taking a swig of the frosty drink.

'Oh, what a pity,' Betty pouted. 'I would love to hear all your stories about Hollywood. Did you meet Frank Sinatra? I love him.'

James had met Sinatra but was not impressed by the man who it was rumoured had got out of military service with the help of certain dubious Italian organisations. Now young girls swooned over him, forgetting boyfriends on the front lines. 'Yeah, I met him,' James said. 'What can you tell me about Olivia and Edgar?'

James's question caused a dark cloud to cross Betty's face. She looked around to ensure that they were not over-heard. 'He used to beat poor Olivia,' she said in a whisper. 'I heard that he beat her to death and made it look like she was driving and ran off the road. When they found Edgar, and your poor sister on the side of the road, he was drunk. He said that the shock of the accident caused him to drink a half-bottle of Jack Daniels while he was waiting for the sheriff. I hope the son of a bitch gets his own one day.'

'Betty,' James said, leaning forward. 'Do you know if there were any witnesses to the beating he gave my sister?'

Betty was about to answer when her attention was drawn to the doorway of the drugstore.

'Hey, flyboy,' said the deputy, and the place fell silent. He was not alone: another deputy that James did not know stood behind him. 'Your vehicle outside is defective.'

James felt his blood reach boiling point. He knew that the car he had borrowed from his grandfather was in perfect condition, so Deputy Hausmann must have done something to it. 'You had better come outside so I can write you up.'

James rose from the booth and walked over to the law officer. He knew he should not do this, but the sneer had to be wiped off the man's face. Hausmann did not even see the punch coming and it had enough force to send the deputy flying across the tiled floor. James was now looking into the barrel of a revolver pointed directly at him by the deputy's offsider.

Hausmann rose unsteadily from the floor, rubbing his mouth and spitting blood. 'That is a serious offence,' he spat. 'Assaulting an officer in front of so many witnesses, too. That can get you a long time in the county lockup.'

James looked around him and could see the fear in the faces of the customers – young and old.

'Okay, take me to the sheriff,' he said, stepping past the two deputies. 'We will sort this out down at the station.'

Both deputies followed James from the drugstore while James cursed himself for being so impulsive as he knew they now had an excuse to hold him until he caught his train out of town. He was pretty sure that Sheriff Mueller would let him go, despite the protests of his deputies.

They stood by the deputy's vehicle and James looked up to see Edgar Wilson only a few feet away with his arm around a young girl.

'You should have stayed away, James,' he said. 'I don't like you going about town alleging that I murdered your sister.'

'Pray that I get killed overseas,' James said as he was forced into the back seat of the police vehicle. 'Because if I live, I will come back and kill you. I swear on the soul of my sister.'

James saw a flicker of fear in Wilson's face, and afraid the coward should be because James meant every word.

TWENTY-FOUR

Detective Sergeant Preston sat in Sir George's library with his hat in his hand. 'I read the report on the death of Lord Ulverstone,' he said. 'Don't believe what you read in the papers. Ulverstone was murdered, but the bloody government has put a D notice on any report about his killing.'

'I appreciate you providing me with the facts,' Sir George said as he stood at the centre of the gloomy room.

'The driver said he thinks a woman finished off Ulverstone, but she was wearing a balaclava and he was forced to keep his head down when she fired the fatal shots into the car. The police at the scene had a visit from counter intelligence who warned them not to divulge anything about what they had seen on pain of very severe repercussions. Whatever your cobber Ulverstone was involved in is a very touchy matter. I hope it does not come back to you, as it is well known that you and Ulverstone met on a regular basis.'

Sir George felt a shiver of fear. Any hint of a scandal could easily bring the companies' government contracts to an end, but worse than that, if he was linked to Ulverstone's traitorous activities he could end up in the kind of trouble not even he could buy his way out of.

'Where was Sean Duffy during the unfortunate event?' Sir George asked.

'I asked the same question, and he has an alibi,' Preston answered. 'He was in hospital.'

Sir George paced the room. Had the hated solicitor conspired with someone to carry out the execution? After all, Sir George was certain Sean Duffy knew who had arranged Lieutenant Caccamo's death. Ulverstone had discovered the man's real identity from his access to top secret files. If Sean Duffy had organised such an audacious killing, what was stopping him from coming after Sir George?

Sir George turned to face Preston. 'The man you hired to kill Duffy failed,' he said. 'While Duffy lives, my life is in peril.'

'Duffy is a tough nut,' Preston shrugged.

'What about the man you hired?' Sir George questioned. 'You said Duffy was able to wound him. Is he still alive?'

'He is,' Preston answered. 'He is holed up in the Rocks recovering. As far as I know he has kept his mouth shut.'

'While he lives he is a threat to us both,' Sir George said. 'Should he reveal that you hired him it could be traced back to me. Neither of us can afford that, Sergeant Preston.'

'You are right, Sir George,' Preston agreed. 'I will have to make sure the problem goes away – but it will cost you.'

'I am not worried about the financial cost. Just get the job done,' said Sir George, 'and you will be well paid.'

'Consider it done,' Preston said. He replaced his hat and let himself out, leaving Sir George in a sweat of fear. This war was now between himself and Duffy, and it seemed the damned solicitor had a female assassin on his side. Sir George was deeply troubled. Who could she be?

*

Sean Duffy was sharing his kitchen with his friends, Harry Griffiths and Tom Duffy. It was mid-morning and they had skipped tea and gone straight to beer. The three sat around the table adorned with half-a-dozen large bottles of beer. It was a small celebration of the successful mission to eliminate a traitor.

'Well, that is one down,' Harry said. 'Is Sir George Macintosh next?'

'Harry, we are not murderers,' Sean said, taking a sip of his beer. 'We were once soldiers and probably killed a lot of men who did not deserve to die, but I still believe in the law. Killing Ulverstone was an act of war.'

'You bloody well know that attack on you had to be sanctioned by Sir George,' Harry said.

'I do,' Sean replied. 'But my best bet is to find the man who attacked me in the park and put him before a court where he can reveal who hired him. My real concern is for the safety of young Patrick. If I go after my assailant Sir George will do his best to stop me. I don't want Patrick caught in the middle.'

'I think I can help there,' Tom piped up. 'I am returning to my place in Queensland and Patrick could come with me. He would be safe up on the station.'

'He needs to be educated,' Sean said.

'I have the perfect answer to that – Miss Abigail Frost. She is a highly qualified governess. And Patrick would be living on the land of his forefathers. After all, the original Patrick Duffy knew the same lands.'

'Sounds like a bloody good idea to me,' Harry said. 'Up there the young fella would be well and truly out of danger from anything Sir George might be planning for you, cobber.'

Sean sat and thought for a moment while his two friends watched him in silence. 'I think that you are right, Tom,' he said finally. 'I will miss the little fella, but I have to think about his safety. He has already been threatened once, I don't think Sir George would hesitate to use him as a pawn in the war between us again.'

'Wise decision,' Harry said. 'I reckon the country air will do him good.'

'I will purchase another ticket,' Tom said, swilling down the remainder of his beer.

'And with your help, Harry,' Sean said, 'I can concentrate on finding the man who attacked me.'

'If we don't,' Harry said, 'I would bet it is a sure thing Macintosh will come after you again, and this time he won't fail.'

Sean did not reply but privately agreed with his old friend. Yes, he was still at war, but his enemy had more resources to win.

Late that afternoon Sean visited Allison at her flat and found Patrick there in his school uniform sitting at the kitchen table doing his homework. The boy looked up and the smile of welcome melted Sean's heart.

'Uncle Sean!' Patrick said, jumping up to hug him. 'Auntie Allison said you would be coming to get me.'

Sean glanced at Allison over the top of the boy's head. 'Patrick,' he said quietly, 'you are going on a big holiday to a property up north, in Queensland. It's a place with lots of dogs, horses and cattle. You'll have plenty of space to run around and play in, and you will be with Uncle Tom who is also another of the Duffy clan and a very nice man.'

Patrick stepped back from Sean with a frown. 'Will I see you and Auntie Allison again?' he asked. Since he had been separated from his mother he had been shuffled from one adult to another, and now when he said goodbye to someone he cared for he was never sure whether he would see them again.

'Of course you will,' Sean reassured, hoping that Patrick would not see the tears welling in his eyes. 'Now you have to gather up all your personal things into a suitcase and get ready for a very long train ride to Queensland. You will like it there because it is always warm.'

Patrick said nothing else and went to the spare room to gather up the little he had in his life. Just the clothes he wore, and a couple of notepads to draw in. While Patrick was packing his few possessions, Sean sat down at the kitchen table and Allison prepared a pot of tea. Tea always seemed to sooth the most emotional times, Sean mused.

'Have you heard anything from David?' he asked.

'Nothing,' Allison answered with her back to Sean. 'Something is wrong and I am at a loss to know why David will not answer my letters. And before you say it, he cannot be that busy he is unable to write me even a few lines. Maybe he has met someone else.'

When Allison turned to Sean he could see tears in her eyes, and her hands shook as she placed the teapot on the table. Sean rose to wrap his arms around the young woman he had grown so fond of. 'I am sure he will write soon,' he said, but without conviction. He was as much in the dark about David's silence as she was.

★

Sarah met her private investigator, John Chatsworth, in Hyde Park. He had done such an excellent job setting up Allison that Sarah had decided to employ him for another task – to keep track of her brother's movements. Sir George had indicated that he would be going into full retirement because of his ailing health and Sarah knew that he would have to nominate his replacement very soon. So far he seemed to be favouring her, but he could be irrational and manipulative and there was always the chance that he might name Donald to head the family companies instead. She knew her brother was preoccupied with matters outside the realm of making money. She had even heard rumours that he was working some kind of covert operation with the Prime Minister's people. She wanted to know what he was up to so she could use the information against him.

'I have followed your brother to a meeting at an inner city cafe, where he met with a woman,' Chatsworth said, producing a large brown envelope. He pulled out a large black and white photo of a woman leaving a cafe. 'Do you recognise this person?'

For a moment Sarah stared at the pretty face without recognising it. Then it came to her. 'Jessica Duffy!' she exclaimed. She had met Jessica briefly, when her brother Donald had been smitten by the girl.

'Your brother has been spotted meeting her twice over the last couple of days,' the investigator said. 'I followed her and last saw her getting on a train for Brisbane. Your brother saw her off.'

Sarah stared at the photo; she had to admit the Duffy girl was pretty. Since Olivia was out of Donald's life it was possible he and the Duffy girl had rekindled their relationship. Alternatively, Donald could be plotting to find a way to sell Glen View Station to Jessica's father.

'How much do you know about your brother's work in Canberra?' the investigator asked.

'We acquire contacts for our enterprises through his government sources,' Sarah answered. 'Why?'

'It seems your brother is involved in some very high security activities, although I haven't been able to discover exactly what,' Chatsworth said. 'Call me irrational, but my gut tells me it has something to do with this Duffy woman. Your brother moves in unusual circles. He seems to have some kind of link to the Prime Minister, but at that level it takes a lot of money to persuade people to talk.'

Sarah was intrigued. Donald's extracurricular activities could make it very difficult for him to take over the reins of the family enterprises. It was time to confer with her father. She slipped the investigator an envelope of banknotes and instructed him to keep following her brother.

That evening she sought out Sir George in the living room where he sat listening to the radio. An Australian broadcaster with a polished Oxford accent was droning on about events across the seas . . . *'Yesterday, Japanese aircraft attacked Allied ships carrying supplies to the Finschhafen bridge head, but only with moderate success. The Australian 20th brigade has broken through the Japanese line on the Bumi River north of Finschhafen . . .'*

Hearing the last part of the report Sarah briefly thought about David. Was he in action back in the Pacific? But her focus quickly moved on to what was most important: undermining Donald with her father.

Sarah walked up behind Sir George and placed her arms around his neck. 'Hello, Daddy,' she said and kissed him on the top of the head.

'What do you want?' Sir George asked with a wry laugh.

'Why would you ask such a question?' Sarah pouted, moving around to face her father.

'Because you are my daughter, and I know you better than you think,' Sir George replied.

'I am only ever interested in your welfare,' Sarah said. 'I have come across some disturbing news concerning Donald.'

'From your private investigator, no doubt,' Sir George said, stunning Sarah into silence. 'Nothing gets past me, my dear,' he said with a smile. 'I should compliment you on using John Chatsworth. He is very good at his job.'

Sarah sat down in a chair opposite her father. 'Is there nothing you do not know?' she asked with a note of respect.

'You are young but you have already shown initiative and the level of ruthlessness that is required in positions of leadership,' Sir George said.

Hearing her father's words gave Sarah hope that he would appoint her as his successor. It paid to be the dutiful and loving daughter from time to time.

'Do you know that my brother is seeing Tom Duffy's daughter?' Sarah asked and saw an expression of surprise on her father's face. 'And that he has been meeting with highly placed intelligence people in Canberra?' This time her father's look of surprise turned to consternation.

'How much do we know about Donald's contacts in Canberra?' he asked, leaning forward, and Sarah was pleased to hear him say 'we'.

'I have asked Mr Chatsworth to look into that,' Sarah said, 'but it seems he is doing more than just working with procurement committees.'

'Well done,' Sir George said, patting Sarah's hand.

'What is it that worries you about Donald's links with intelligence organisations?' Sarah asked. She was aware of the shady links the Macintosh companies had with the Nazi party through their involvement in German industry. The fruits of this association were, she knew, well and truly buried in Swedish and Swiss bank accounts.

'I do not like my children going behind my back,' Sir George snapped. 'If Donald is obtaining security information that might benefit this family, I expect him to let me know about it.'

Sir George was growing petulant now and Sarah knew she should not pursue the matter any further. She bid her father goodnight and went to her bedroom to change for the evening. She had a date with a handsome factory owner; he was married of course, but that suited Sarah perfectly. She had already booked a hotel room.

*

Sir George was no longer listening to the radio when the popular comedy hour came on. He was pondering his conversation with Sarah. His paranoia had been growing since the killing of Lord Ulverstone. Preston had said that a woman had fired the fatal shots. Was it possible that the Duffys had joined forces to conspire against him? Had it been Jessica Duffy who had shot Ulverstone in cold blood? Was it possible that his son was conspiring with her to kill him too?

Sir George was afraid. It was growing dark, and he feared the night with its shadows as his syphilis-ridden brain played tricks on him. Wallarie was coming each night to stand by his bed and taunt him with requests for tobacco. Fenella was with him too, and it was her words echoing through his waking hours that terrified him the most . . . *Your own blood will bring your death to you.*

TWENTY-FIVE

When Jessica Duffy stepped off the train at Roma Street in Brisbane it was a beautiful morning. Around her men and women in uniform scurried to retrieve luggage. She held her small suitcase in her hand and wondered whether she had packed the essentials for a prison sentence. Despite Donald's assurances she still felt sick with apprehension.

It was not a long walk to MacArthur's HQ in the city and when she entered the building she was quickly intercepted by two armed military policemen. Jessica explained that she wished to speak with her commanding officer and identified her section.

They told her to sit down in a chair in the foyer whilst they made a telephone call.

Jessica sat quietly, watching the uniformed people moving in and out of the building. Some faces she recognised, but she kept her head down to avoid them.

After some minutes one of the MPs came over to her. 'I will escort you upstairs,' he said. 'You can leave your suitcase here.'

Jessica stood up and followed the guard. Her hands were shaking and she squeezed them together tightly. She was not shown to her old section but taken to a room in a part of the building she was unfamiliar with. This made her nervous and she was left alone for some minutes sitting in a chair and staring at the blank walls. The only other things in the room were a small table and two spare chairs. It was an ominous place that appeared soundproof. The door opened behind her and the pungent scent of cigar smoke told her who was entering the room.

'Sergeant Duffy, you have returned to the fold,' the colonel said, taking a seat at the table.

Jessica rose from the chair as military protocol dictated. She came to attention as the form of salute when not wearing a head covering.

'Sit down,' the colonel said. 'We have been expecting you.'

'Yes, sir,' Jessica said, and did as she was told.

'It appears you have friends high up in the Aussie government,' the colonel said, ash falling to the table from his thick cigar. 'And it sounds like you have one hell of a tale to tell.'

'I am not sure what you have been told, sir,' Jessica ventured cautiously.

'Well, for a start, you were listed as a deserter,' the colonel said, staring at her pointedly. 'You know our attitude towards people who leave their post without permission. It usually ends badly when we catch up with them.'

Jessica felt the grip of fear at the colonel's words. 'I fully understand that I was foolish in going absent without leave,' she said. 'But I felt that I had to do something about Lieutenant Caccamo's mission.'

'That is what worries me,' the colonel said, leaning back in his chair. 'How did you find out about his mission? Did he spill the beans to you?'

'No, sir,' Jessica answered quickly. 'I had other means of finding out – which I do not wish to reveal.'

'You realise that under your code of military justice I can force you to reveal how you found out about Lieutenant Caccamo's mission?'

'I know that, sir,' Jessica answered, feeling her mouth go dry. 'But the important thing is that Lord Ulverstone is dead and cannot do any further harm to our security.'

'Did you kill him?' the colonel asked bluntly. 'The report I got said he was killed by an unknown assassin but that that the shooter was suspected to be female. Was it you?'

Jessica knew that to answer yes meant that she was admitting to murder under civil law. 'Yes, sir,' she said quietly. 'I killed Ulverstone to finish Tony's mission.'

Jessica sat absolutely still as the man on the other side of the table contemplated her words in silence. Eventually he leaned back in his chair and took a long puff on his cigar. 'You should go home and get back into uniform, Sergeant Duffy,' he said. 'You are to report to the swamp tomorrow morning at oh-seven hundred. We have arranged for you to return to your old accommodation. Do you have any questions?'

Jessica could hardly believe what she was hearing. It was as if nothing had happened. She had a thousand questions, but realised it might not be wise to ask any of them. She did realise that the transfer downstairs to tactical operations was a way of disciplining her, and that now she would be of no real assistance to Donald's intelligence gathering. Still, there was one question she needed to ask.

'What is the official stance on the death of Lord Ulverstone, sir?'

'He died in a car accident,' he said, rising from the table with a shrug. 'Happens every day.'

Outside, a guard escorted her downstairs to retrieve her suitcase, and a staff car drove her over to her old flat at Toowong. Her personal effects and uniform were in place as if she had never left.

*

Harry Griffiths asked a lot of questions – usually over a beer in the many public bars of Sydney. His gym had seen one or two heavyweights of the underworld make his acquaintance over the years. A lot of money could be won or lost on boxing matches, and although Harry had tried to prevent matches being fixed, he was pragmatic enough to know he could not stop the practice. As he had a reputation for being discrete about such matters, he was accepted by some of Sydney's toughest gangsters. So when he asked questions about an attack on a popular Sydney solicitor Harry received a sympathetic response from most of those he questioned. It was only when he found his way into the public bars frequented by the city's wharf labourers that he realised he was on dangerous ground. These were men with their own organised thuggery, but it was worth the risk for a man he viewed as a member of his own family.

'You don' wanna go askin' questions like that around here, Harry,' said the small wiry man standing beside him at the bar.

'The Major got you out of a bit of trouble if I remember rightly, Spencer,' Harry said, eyeing the tough and grime-streaked men coming in off their shifts on the wharves.

'I think you should piss orf while you can,' Spencer said loudly so that his work mates could hear him. Reluctantly, Harry finished his beer and took Spencer's advice. These were men with a reputation for not talking to anyone outside their circle. He left and returned to the empty gym.

Harry glanced around and wondered how long he would be able to keep the place open. Some of his best fighters had enlisted, and all he was getting were teenage boys who would sign up the moment they were old enough.

He heard the front door squeak open, and turned to see Spencer enter. Harry walked over to him.

'Yer right, Harry,' Spencer said. 'The Major has been a friend to a lot of the boys down on the wharf. I couldn't say much at the pub as yer can understan',' he said, looking furtively around the empty gym. 'The man yer lookin' for is Micky Slim. That's the name 'e is registered under with the union. I 'eard he is 'oled up in a place in the Rocks with a stab wound. The boys think he might 'ave 'ad a go at the Major. Yer know we can't dob in a brother comrade.'

'Thanks, Spencer,' Harry said. 'You might drop around soon if anything of interest falls off a truck. I might have a buyer or two.'

'Thanks, Harry,' Spencer said and turned to walk away. He paused for a moment and turned around. 'Yer might look fer 'im in the Hero of Waterloo. I 'eard he drinks there.'

Harry watched the little man leave, then he stepped outside and caught a taxi to the Rocks, the seedy area adjoining Circular Quay. He walked into the old hotel that had seen men shanghaied not so many years ago. He glanced around the bar filled with men in uniform, the odd old-timer standing at the bar and ruminating into his beer. Harry noticed one of the men had a heavy bandage around his shoulder. He pushed his way to the bar and stood next to him.

'Have an accident?' he asked after he'd ordered a beer from the buxom barmaid.

The man did not look at Harry. 'What's it to you, cobber?' he replied.

'I reckon you might have got it in Hyde Park a few weeks back,' Harry said, and this time the man turned to stare at him, fear flickering in his eyes.

'Are you a copper?' the man asked, gripping his beer.

'I was,' Harry replied. 'But now I work for Major Duffy – the man you tried to kill, Micky.'

Micky reacted fast, tossing the remains of his beer in Harry's face, and bolted for the door. Harry wiped the liquid from his eyes and decided that at his age it was not worth a foot chase through the winding alleyways of the Rocks.

Harry pushed his way out of the bar onto the sunlit street and stood for a moment looking up and down the tangle of laneways. Micky was not to be seen, but at least Harry knew he lived nearby. It was only a matter of returning to the gym and making a few telephone calls to round up some friends to assist him in his search of the surrounding tenement flats and boarding houses.

*

'Bloody good news,' Sean said when Harry relayed that he had identified his assailant. 'But we will need to pick him up ourselves. I don't know who to trust amongst the coppers any more.'

'Sergeant First Class Ward we can trust,' Harry said. 'We've both known him for years. He and I were constables together before the last war. I have a beer with Keith from time to time, and I know he has a strong dislike for Preston.'

'Okay, we get a confession out of the man you found and hand him over to Ward,' Sean said.

'Sounds like a plan,' Harry agreed. 'I have a couple of the boys on standby for a sweep tonight. I have a pretty good idea where our man lives.'

'I will come with you,' Sean said, and Harry shook his head.

'You don't need to be around when we catch up with Micky,' he said. 'There is the law and there is justice, and they are not always the same thing. I intend to make sure Micky gets the justice he deserves, and that may mean stepping outside the law.'

'I will leave it to you then,' Sean said. 'Just make sure that when you hand him over to the police he can still walk.'

Harry grinned, rising from his chair and putting on his hat. 'By this time tomorrow my old cobbers in the force will be knocking on Sir George's door at his fancy mansion to ask him a few embarrassing questions.'

Sean watched with slight trepidation as Harry left the office. Finally, after so many years, Sir George Macintosh might be brought to justice. But he knew Harry was good at what he did, and wondered if this was the breakthrough he had dreamed of for so many years. Sean had once loved Sir George's sister, Fenella, but she had been viciously murdered in Los Angeles, before the last war. Sean knew in his gut that Sir George had ordered the brutal killing, but nothing could ever be proved. At least now he could use the law he had worked with for so many years to finally make Macintosh accountable. Sean knew that it would be a long night as Harry hunted down the suspect. He just hoped he did not hurt him too badly.

★

Patrick Duffy had cried when he left Sydney on the train. Tom had seen his tears but was awkward in what he should do.

He knew that the boy must be missing his mother, and that he had been shunted from person to person since they had been separated. Eventually the tears subsided, though, and by the time the train reached Brisbane, Patrick seemed to have his feelings under control.

Patrick met Jessie in Brisbane for a brief moment at the railway station. She had a uniform on, and was introduced as Tom's own daughter. In Patrick's opinion she looked too old to be a daughter. Daughters were children like himself and it did not make much sense to him that she should be a grown-up. She was very nice, though, but before long they were on another train with the inevitable crowd of soldiers in uniform, cigarette smoke and clatter-clack of the great metal wheels on steel tracks. Whistles blew and coal smoke billowed past the window, giving off an acrid smell. Days seemed to stretch endlessly for the young boy, until they arrived in Rockhampton and Tom and Patrick left the train to be met by a tough-looking young man in a car. He was introduced as one of Tom's employees, and they drove on rough, dirt roads across endless plains as the sun slowly sank before their eyes.

They camped out the first night on the side of the track, and Patrick liked that. He had a vague understanding that the tough-looking young man had once been a soldier and had been wounded in some place called Tobruk.

Eventually the next day, after travelling over roads barely discernible in the scrub, they came to a single-storey house with a big verandah in the middle of a vast plain.

A pretty lady rushed up to Uncle Tom, kissing and hugging him when he got out of the car. Before Patrick knew it, she had turned her attention to him. She did not try to kiss or hug him, though, but bent down and looked into his face with a sweet smile.

'I am Abigail,' she said gently. 'Welcome to your Uncle Tom's house. I know you and I will become good friends.'

And so Patrick Duffy had arrived in the land of his Uncle Tom's ancestors, where he settled in remarkably well. His first friend was a young Aboriginal boy whose father worked as a stockman on the property. The boy spoke little English, and Patrick spoke no words of his new friend's language, but this did not interfere with their friendship.

Days turned to weeks and Abigail would insist that Patrick do school lessons, as well as her supervising domestic matters around the sprawling homestead on the brigalow plains.

'He is a grand boy,' Abigail said one evening after Tom had returned from a day of mustering cattle. The two of them sat enjoying the serenity of the dying day on the verandah. 'He is very intelligent, and I noticed that he sometimes changes from English to the local indigenous language. I will miss him when his mother finally comes to reclaim him.'

Tom gazed out over the scrub. The dust that had been stirred up by the hooves of the cattle had finally settled, and the beasts were in the yards awaiting shipment to the meatworks on the coast. 'What if she does not survive?' he said quietly, sipping his cup of tea. 'What happens to Patrick then?'

'Oh, that goes without saying,' Abigail answered. 'We adopt him.'

'But we are not married,' Tom said, and when he glanced at Abigail he thought he saw a flicker of challenge in her eyes.

'Well, Tom Duffy, why don't you do something about that?' she said.

'Are you proposing?' Tom asked.

'I think that since we share the same bed you should make an honest woman of me,' Abigail laughed.

'I suppose I should marry you,' Tom replied, and took another sip of his tea. 'What do I need to do?'

'You leave everything to me,' Abigail answered, 'as you have proven to be the least romantic man I have ever known. I think I should have the marriage banns posted in the church.'

'You know,' Tom said with a smile, 'I have never even asked you if you are a religious woman.'

'I am a Methodist, and I believe that you are a Roman Catholic,' she said. 'But we live in a part of the world where God is with us every day the sun rises. I think our religious differences do not matter here, but I would still like to be married in my church.'

'Makes no difference to me,' Tom shrugged. 'Just so long as you do not disapprove of the boys having a piss-up here, to celebrate our union.'

Abigail leaned over on Tom's shoulder. 'I love you, Tom,' she said. 'I think I started to love you when I was nursing you in the Gulf.'

'I have no idea how such a beautiful woman as you could love me,' Tom said, taking her hand, 'but I'm very grateful you do.'

'You do not see you through my eyes,' Abigail said with a sigh.

Just then Patrick appeared. He had been exploring the scrub near the homestead and was streaked with dirt, and his feet were bare. He looked exhausted.

'Patrick, you are to go inside and have a bath before supper,' Abigail said firmly but not unkindly.

'You look like you've had quite an adventure, son. Where did you go?' Tom asked.

'I went a long way to a place near the road over there,' Patrick said, gesturing vaguely west.

Tom knew he meant the road to Glen View. 'Were you on your own?' he asked. The boy was only new to a land where it was easy to get lost and die from exposure.

'No,' Patrick said. 'I met a very old man. He said he was one of the people who lived here, and said he knew you, Uncle Tom.'

'Did he have a name?' Abigail asked.

'He said his name was Wallarie.'

The hairs on the back of Tom's neck stood on end.

TWENTY-SIX

'Ithink Patrick must have heard the name of Wallarie from his Aboriginal playmates,' Abigail said. 'Even I know of his reputation as the boogieman around here. The old women tell children who are being naughty that Wallarie will come for them in the night.'

Tom was not convinced. She had been born in England and the mysticism of the Outback was not her heritage. 'I think it is time that Patrick had a day or two away from his schooling to go to Glen View,' Tom said. 'His grandmother was Kate Tracy, and she was the daughter of Patrick's namesake who was as a brother to Wallarie in the old days out here when Patrick and Wallarie were hunted in the Gulf country. I think Wallarie has a connection to him.'

'Tom, do you really believe in such things?' Abigail asked. 'The people of this land do not have our Christian beliefs.'

'I believe that the spirit of Wallarie is now our guardian angel,' Tom said. 'He kept me alive in two wars when by all accounts I should have been killed. I know of others in the Duffy clan who also believe in his power.'

'From the way you are talking we should be married in one of those stone circles I have seen in the bush,' Abigail said, shaking her head.

'It would be cheaper to do so,' Tom slowly smiled. 'Not such a bad idea.'

Abigail punched him in the arm. 'Tom Duffy! How dare you even suggest that. A proper wedding is something every girl dreams of.'

'Okay, a church it is,' Tom said with a chuckle. 'But I am going to take Patrick to a special place.'

'What special place?' Abigail asked.

'I cannot tell you,' Tom sighed. 'It's men's business.'

The next day Tom had the sulky hitched and he and Patrick drove the distance to Glen View Station. There he was met by the manager, Ross Woods, who was a friend of Tom's.

'Tom, you old bastard,' he said. 'It's been a while since we last saw you. Sorry to hear about your arm.'

'Yeah, a bit of a bugger but we get issued with two just in case we lose one,' Tom answered. 'I brought another Duffy here for you to meet.' He turned to Patrick. 'This is Master Patrick Duffy whose grandmother was Kate Tracy.'

'Pleased to meet you, Master Patrick,' Ross said. 'You have an impressive heritage.'

Patrick looked gravely at the station manager. He did not know what he meant, but he was smiling and the boy decided he must be a good man if Uncle Tom was friendly to him.

'How about you two come in and have a cuppa,' Ross said.

Tom and Patrick followed the station manager inside the house where a young Aboriginal girl dressed in a long white dress smiled shyly at them. Tom thought she was probably around fifteen years of age.

'Mary, fetch tea and cold water for our guests,' Ross said, and she departed the room to carry out the request.

Over tea and freshly baked scones, the two men chatted about cattle prices, the weather and the problems of labour shortages due to the war's demands for manpower. Patrick eventually asked to be excused and wandered out into the yard where he saw an old gnarled bumbil tree standing alone. Its green foliage provided shade over the dusty yard and Patrick was drawn to it. When he was under its shade he saw a butterfly fluttering on the ground. It appeared to be injured. Patrick scooped it up in his hand. 'Broken butterfly,' he said softly in sympathy for the delicate creature's suffering. After a moment its wings ceased moving, and Patrick instinctively knew the life had left it.

He knelt down and scraped out a tiny grave with the pocket knife that Tom had given him. 'Poor butterfly,' he said after he had buried the insect. 'You are gone.'

'Its spirit gone up in the sky,' a voice said behind him, and Patrick turned to see his Aboriginal friend Wallarie sitting cross-legged a few feet away. He was naked except for a human hair belt around his waist, and in that were tucked a couple of small, hardwood clubs.

'All things go away from this earth but live in the sky,' Wallarie said.

'Patrick, you should come inside,' Tom called from the verandah.

'Tom, he a good man,' Wallarie said. 'Tomorrow he take you to the place where we will meet again.'

Patrick looked over to Tom on the verandah, and when he turned his head back to speak with Wallarie, the old man had disappeared. Puzzled, Patrick walked back to the house, and when he reached Tom he said, 'Wallarie said we would meet him tomorrow.'

Tom stared over his head at the bumbil tree. 'When did Wallarie tell you this?' he asked.

'Just now,' Patrick replied. 'He talked to me under that tree. Did you not see him?'

Tom experienced the same eerie feeling he always had when Wallarie was around. He placed his hand on the boy's head in an affectionate manner. 'You know, Wallarie will always protect you,' he said. 'Maybe tomorrow I might even get to meet with my old friend again.'

Patrick hoped so, because Wallarie had once asked him if Tom could bring baccy – whatever that was.

That evening, when Patrick was in bed, Tom and Ross shared a bottle of whisky in the kitchen, as geckoes scurried along the walls, issuing their bird-like chirping challenges.

'What do you know about Wallarie in these parts?' Tom asked Ross as he poured the golden liquid into a couple of glass tumblers.

'I remember him – as do the other old-timers around here – but the young ones don't,' Ross said. 'He still frightens the blackfellas who work on Glen View. They reckon they see him in the bush when the curlews cry. They say he is an apparition of death, and you can't get any of them to go on up to the hill for anything. They avoid that dried-up creekbed down in the scrub, too, where I heard his people were massacred way back last century. It's said he once roamed Queensland killing whitefellas with your namesake, and I believe he was some kind of relative of yours.'

'My grandfather,' Tom replied, taking a swig of whisky. 'He was shot down by the coppers up in the Gulf country. His father, Patrick Duffy, is buried on Glen View – along with a few more of my mob.'

'It's no secret that you have been trying for years to buy Glen View,' Ross said.

'Don't worry, cobber,' Tom said. 'If that ever happens you can stay on as manager, and I might even give you a raise.'

'Thanks, Tom,' Ross said, lifting his tumbler in a gesture of a salute. 'That would be something. I am sure Wallarie would be pleased to know the land was back in the hands of one of his mob.'

Both men fell silent as a great moon rose over the brigalow plains and the curlews commenced their mournful song. Tom was sure that it meant someone was going to die, but in time of war that was inevitable.

★

When Sean Duffy received the news that the suspect in his attempted murder was in police custody at Sergeant First Class Keith Ward's station, he knew that he would have to identify the man and hope that he would confess. Harry had told him that Micky Slim had refused to divulge who had hired him, but he did confess to stabbing Sean in self-defence.

'Whoever put him up to it,' Harry said, 'has got him more scared of talking than facing a possible attempted murder charge.'

Sean caught a taxi to the inner city police station, where he found Sergeant First Class Keith Ward talking heatedly to Detective Sergeant Preston. He had a feeling of foreboding; why was Preston at the station?

Preston saw Sean and turned his attention to him.

'You here to identify your alleged attacker?' he questioned.

'That is why I am here,' Sean answered.

'Well, go ahead,' Preston said with a smirk. 'He is still hanging in his cell.'

'What do you mean, hanging in his cell?' Sean asked, and noticed the dark expression on Keith Ward's face.

'He went and hanged himself an hour ago,' Preston answered. 'It seems he must have had a guilty conscience. Some crims are like that. He is all yours now.' Preston placed his hat on his head and walked out of the station.

'What the hell happened?' Sean asked in a furious voice. 'How could your man hang himself?'

'Sorry, Major Duffy,' Ward replied. 'We are shorthanded, and I was on desk duties. Preston arrived and said he was to question the prisoner, but some time later he came to tell me that he had found the suspect hanging from a blanket that Micky had torn into strips and used as a means of strangling himself on the bars. I have informed the coroner and the matter is now out of my hands.'

'How long was Preston with him?' Sean asked, and he could see a flicker of guilt in the station sergeant's eyes.

'About twenty minutes, if I remember rightly,' he replied.

'Plenty of time to kill someone,' Sean said.

'Are you implying that Detective Sergeant Preston murdered my prisoner?' Ward asked. 'That is a serious accusation against a respected policemen.'

'You bloody well know he murdered the man,' Sean said.

'You need proof before we can act on that,' Ward countered. 'I don't like him but you of all people know we can't do a thing without proof. Between you and me, though, I reckon you could be right. I'm sorry, Major.'

Sean could see that the dejected police sergeant was not his enemy, but he also knew that when it came to it police officers would always stick together, despite any animosities they might harbour towards each other. It was a bond of blue that was almost impossible to break. 'I understand,' he said. 'We will let the coroner sort the mess out.'

'I will still need you to have a look at him and tell me if you think he was the bloke who stabbed you,' Ward said, and led Sean to the cells where the unfortunate man was still hanging from the bars. His face was blue and his tongue stuck out of a swollen face. Sean immediately recognised the man as his attacker, and could see the bandaged shoulder where his sword stick had inflicted the deep wound.

'That's him,' Sean said, turning to limp back up the concrete stairs and depart the dingy place of misery.

He stepped into the warm sunshine, aware that his war against the all-powerful Sir George Macintosh would go on until one of them was dead. He spent the afternoon with Harry in their favourite pub around the corner from Harry's gym, mulling over what had happened and what they would do next.

*

The small craggy hill rose over the expanse of dry scrub. Tom peered up at the bush-covered crest, Patrick beside him.

'This is a special place, young Patrick,' he said. 'It has a sacred cave that only men may enter, and from the top of the hill you can see for miles. How would you like to go up with me?'

Patrick gazed up at the hill and his boyish sense of adventure was in his reply. 'Yes, Uncle Tom, it would be grand.'

The man and boy set out along the well-worn wallaby track until they reached a point just below the crest where Patrick saw a small opening to a very dark place. The entrance was surrounded by low gnarled trees sprouting from the little soil they could penetrate with their roots.

'Our friend Wallarie used to live here,' Tom said, holding Patrick's hand. 'Wallarie was once a great warrior and brother to a man called Tom Duffy. Together they roamed the plains and had many adventures.'

'The same name as you, Uncle Tom,' Patrick said, mesmerised by the yawning dark opening. It was scary but also exciting. 'Can we go inside?'

'If Wallarie wants us to,' Tom replied, 'we will be allowed to enter his place of magic.'

Tom retrieved the flashlight he had brought in his pack, flicked it on and led Patrick inside the cave. It smelled musty and the beam of the torch settled on crude ochre paintings stretching along the inner walls of the cave. Patrick gripped Tom's hand, and Tom could feel his sweat. He was sure the boy was frightened, and who could blame him. The ancient paintings seemed to come alive as the flashlight's beam danced over them. The beam settled on one picture of a white stick-like figure holding a spear above his head. The picture had obviously been vandalised, as a large scratch had been ripped through it.

'Wallarie used to call this the cave of the white warrior,' Tom said, keeping his torch on the picture. 'He never said why, though.'

'Is Wallarie here now?' Patrick asked in a hushed voice, not daring to look into the dark shadows lest he see a monster lurking there.

'I don't know,' Tom answered. 'Do you think so?'

Patrick vigorously shook his head. He had no real understanding of the sensation he was experiencing, all he knew was that time had no meaning and he was in a place with memories he could not comprehend. He could hear children's laughter, and for a moment everything faded to a picture of naked, dark people – men, women and children – sitting by a waterhole surrounded by the bush. The picture in his head faded, and then it was replaced by something so terrible that Patrick screamed, startling Tom who immediately gripped the boy to him.

'I want to go home,' the boy wailed, and Tom quickly brought him out of the cave into the hot sunshine of the day. Patrick was trembling uncontrollably. He suddenly recollected the bloody scenes in Singapore when he had escaped with Uncle Cyril and his family. What Patrick had seen in the cave were the bloody, mutilated bodies of the men, women and children scattered around the waterhole in the semi-dark of an early morning and they had reminded him of what he had seen on the streets of Singapore.

'What is wrong?' Tom asked gently, bending to look Patrick in the face. 'Did you see something bad in there?'

Patrick nodded his head, too frightened to look back at the cave's entrance.

'Did you see black people being killed?' he asked and Patrick nodded again.

Tom turned to the entrance of the cave. Tom knew that Wallarie had revealed to Patrick the dark secret of the country's past. He guessed that he had done so to remind the new generations of where the curse had started, and why.

Tom returned to the Glen View homestead with Patrick, and after dinner put him to bed with soothing words that Wallarie would watch over him.

Then Tom walked into the moonlit yard and stood facing the bumbil tree.

'Wallarie, if you are here, you cunning old bugger, stop frightening kids,' he said loudly, and his challenge was taken up by a chorus of distant curlews.

Tom turned back to the homestead but had only gone a few steps when he swore a voice in his ear said, 'You didn't bring any baccy, Tom Duffy.'

Tom grinned. 'You won't get any if you scare Patrick again, you old bugger.'

But as Tom continued to stride towards the welcoming yellow light of the kerosene lantern inside the house, he experienced a wonderful sense of peace. He knew that there was another world beyond this one, and it was a world where Wallarie lived in the shadows and light of their lives.

★

Captain James Duffy sat on an empty ammunition crate under the wing of his Corsair fighter bomber, chatting with his ground crew. The wing provided shade against the blazing tropical sun and his armourer was draped in heavy belts of .50 calibre ammunition, ready to reload the wing-mounted guns. Behind him, another of his ground crew went over the fuselage searching for any tears caused by bullets or anti-aircraft shrapnel after the mission he'd completed only an hour earlier against Japanese log bunkers in the hills.

Although the ground support missions were not as thrilling as being in a life or death dogfight with enemy Zeros, James knew they were essential to the marines on the ground slogging through the jungle, mopping up any resistance from a fanatical enemy who asked no quarter and gave none in return.

James had been back with his squadron for a month now and felt at home once again. He missed the comforts of his life in Hollywood, but there was a real sense of purpose in what he was doing now. He still felt fear, but he had long adopted the fatalistic attitude that if his death was predestined fighting in this war, then so be it. This attitude helped keep his aircraft on course through a cloud of red hot shrapnel and bullets each time he dived on one of the concealed enemy positions in the jungle. He had earned a reputation for a steady nerve and was respected by his colleagues, and also liked by his ground crew for his easy manner with them.

Every day James thought about the death of his beloved twin sister. He swore to himself that he would live out the war to return home and wreak revenge on her killer. His grandfather was a constant correspondent and informed him that Sheriff Mueller had lost the election and that Deputy Ike Hausmann had won the office. James felt his rage rising at the news. He was sure that the deputy was complicit in covering up Olivia's murder.

James looked up to see the squadron clerk walking towards them. 'Got mail for you boys,' the clerk said, holding up the bundle, and when he was near he commenced calling out names. A couple of James's ground crew whooped and stepped forward to be passed the precious letters or small packages from home.

'Captain Duffy, mail for you,' the clerk said, holding up a letter and then sniffing it. 'You know some dame from Hollywood?'

James stood up quickly from his ammunition crate and took the letter from the grinning clerk. He quickly flipped it over to see that the letter had come from Julianna and had a Hollywood return address.

'Like her perfume,' the clerk said and James glared at him. 'Sorry, sir,' he said and retreated back to the shimmering heat of the airstrip, in search of other aircraft crews working on the returning fighter bombers.

James pulled his improvised seat further under the wing to keep pace with the sun high overhead. He carefully slipped open the letter and unfolded it. He realised that his hands were shaking, but fixed his eyes on the opening sentence.

My dear James,
I am writing to tell you how grieved I was to hear of your sister's terrible accident. I know this is not the best time to tell you, but I have met another . . .

James hardly read the rest of the letter. Julianna had said she would not wait for him, but deep down he had lived on the hope that she might. He had lost his sister, and now he had lost the only woman he felt he could have shared the rest of his life with.

TWENTY-SEVEN

The Melbourne Cup had been run and the soldiers of David Macintosh's company stretched away from the radios they had been huddled around. David rarely betted, but a tip from his radio man, Corporal Andrew Paull, had seen him put his money on the winner, Dark Felt, ridden by jockey, Vic Hartney. David donated his small windfall back to the company funds to assist buying a few creature comforts for the campaign ahead. They knew that they were finally being sent back into the Pacific war, but exactly where was still a closely guarded secret known only to the commanding officer and his closest staff.

The last big battalion parade was held in the tablelands of North Queensland. David marched onto the parade ground to take his place at the head of his company, while the company sergeant major took up the rear. A high-ranking guest officer took the salute at a dais erected for the occasion.

As the battalion marched past and David gave the 'eyes right' command he realised that the men following him, from his platoon commanders down to the riflemen, would depend on his skills to keep them alive in the forthcoming weeks and months. He felt that he had been born to be responsible for the men who followed him. The tramping of feet, and orders bawled to the respective companies of the battalion, was the only sound to echo in the surrounding bush. There were no families to see off their men as they were a long way from home.

The parade over, and the men dismissed to their duties, David attended a meeting with his fellow company commanders ordered by the commanding officer. The usual matters were given in a brief, and when it was over the CO announced that drinks would be on his chit for his officers that evening in their mess. The CO cautioned that he would be making any of the platoon commanders who took more than one drink on his chit the permanent duty officer for the duration of their stay in Australia. This raised a few chuckles amongst the more senior officers who knew none of the lieutenants would now dare take advantage of the CO's generous offer.

That afternoon, David received a letter delivered to his quarters. He could see it was from Sean and he sat down on his camp stretcher to read it. Sean's first main item was the fact that the annual general meeting for the Macintosh companies was to be held in a few days' time and that David, as a de facto member of the board, was entitled to cast a vote as to who should be the next general manager and second-in-charge, as only Sir George was authorised to appoint his successor. The second point Sean raised was that of the offer Tom Duffy had resubmitted for the purchase of Glen View. With Sir George resigning that would leave

David, Sarah and Donald in a position to decide if Tom could purchase the property. The last time such an offer had been made David and Sarah, along with Sir George, had declined the purchase, and only Donald had supported the offer. For David, the land held strong emotional ties as his mother was buried on Glen View. Sean stated that he hoped David would reconsider his position and agree to the sale. David had thought at length about the whole issue after he had met Tom Duffy on the Kokoda Track a year earlier. Tom had said that Wallarie was responsible for their unlikely meeting in the jungles of New Guinea.

The final part of Sean's letter questioned why David had not responded to Allison's letters. David squirmed. How could he tell Sean what he had seen in the photos he had destroyed?

'You heading for the mess, old chap?' Captain Brian Williams asked, popping his head around the door to David's room.

'Yeah,' David answered. 'Just finishing up here. I won't be long.'

Captain Williams disappeared to join the other officers of the battalion to celebrate the fact they were finally being posted off to rejoin the war. This would be the battalion's fifth campaign, and they had been annoyed to have to wait so long to be called on. Now the waiting was over.

David was late to attend the mess as he had sat down and written a letter answering each of Sean's three main points. That included why he had not answered Allison's letters and his decision on the sale of Glen View to Tom Duffy.

★

A week later Sean received David's letter. On the first point David said his proxy vote went to Donald. On the point of selling Glen View to Tom Duffy, that depended on Donald concurring. Sean was fairly sure that Donald would agree to the sale, although he assumed Sarah would oppose it because of her father's dogged resistance to the Duffy family ever owning Glen View. It was David's answer to his third question that stunned Sean. He leaned back in his chair and took a deep breath. Could David be correct when he said he had seen explicit photos of Allison having sexual intercourse with a man?

'David, you stupid, stupid man,' Sean said to the empty room. 'You've been conned.' He knew Allison loved only one man, and he was a good enough observer of human nature to know that she would never be unfaithful to the man she loved. If photographs existed of the alleged incident, Sean needed to see them for himself.

'Allison, could you please come here?' Sean called. 'Take a seat,' he said when she walked into his office.

'What is it, Major?' she asked with a look of concern. 'Has David been hurt?'

'No, no,' Sean answered, shaking his head. 'I have a letter from David on my desk. I promised you that I would ask him why he has not answered your letters, and he has finally given me an answer.'

Allison leaned forward anxiously and Sean took a deep breath.

'Have you ever been unfaithful to David?' he asked.

Allison was shocked. 'Of course not,' she answered. 'Why, has someone told him I have?'

'Not exactly,' Sean replied. 'David was sent a set of photographs showing you semi-naked and having intimate relations with a stranger.'

Stunned, Allison could only sit transfixed by the statement. 'That's impossible,' she said eventually. 'I have never been unfaithful to David, and if such photos exist, they must be fakes.'

Sean was watching Allison's reaction carefully. After many years in the court system he figured he could tell when people were lying; what he saw in Allison was a woman genuinely shocked by the allegation and he believed she was telling the truth.

'If you are the woman in the photos, how do you think they could have been taken?' he asked.

For a moment Allison searched her memory and then suddenly it all became clear.

'Sarah!' she gasped. 'I was stupid enough to believe that she was attempting to patch our friendship, and I accepted an invitation to a party at her place just after David left. I only had a few drinks and then I blacked out. The next thing I remembered was the following morning being in bed and suffering a splitting headache. Sarah told me that I had had too much to drink and had passed out. I thought it was strange at the time as I had only had a couple of drinks.'

'It would be easy to have someone pose you for photos while you were unconscious, perhaps from a Mickey Finn,' Sean said, using the popular American expression for a knock-out drug used in alcoholic drinks. 'I know that Sarah Macintosh has in her employ a private investigator, Chatsworth, who has a reputation for shady dealings. Do you remember who she had at her party?'

Allison went on to describe the few people she knew at the party, and suddenly it came to her. 'There was a man with a camera. Sarah said she had hired him to take pictures for the social pages,' Allison said. 'He had another man with him who was a kind of assistant. I thought that they looked like undesirable types, and wondered why Sarah had invited them.'

'Can you describe him?' Sean asked and Allison racked

her mind. She gave a description and Sean leaned back in his chair with his hands behind his head.

'You have described Chatsworth to a tee,' he said. 'I think we are getting to the bottom of this matter.'

'I was set up!' Allison exploded, and leapt to her feet, pacing the office in her fury. 'I am going to kill Sarah for what she has done.'

'That is not a good idea,' Sean said calmly. 'I will write to David and explain that the photos were staged, and that you are completely innocent. I am sure he knows how devious his cousin Sarah is, and to what lengths she will go to get her own way in life.'

Allison turned to Sean. 'Oh, poor David, thinking all this time that I had been unfaithful to him. I have to write and explain.'

'I think he will trust my words, so it might be wise if I explain first,' Sean cautioned. 'I am sure he will see sense. I have been told through my contacts at Victoria Barracks that David's battalion is currently being shipped back into the Pacific theatre.'

'Oh, God no,' Allison groaned. 'I would never forgive myself if anything happened to David whilst he still believed I had betrayed him.'

'David has survived so much in the past, and he is an experienced soldier,' Sean reassured. 'Nothing will happen to him.' Despite this reassurance, Sean knew full well that surviving in battle was just as much to do with luck as with experience. David's luck could easily run out, but he did not want to consider that possibility.

'Thank you,' Allison said. 'What would we do without you in our lives – all of us.'

Even as Allison thanked Sean he was troubled that he had underestimated Sarah Macintosh. From everything he had been able to glean about her, she was truly her father's daughter, and that made her very dangerous. If she took over the reins of the Macintosh empire she would be as ruthless as Sir George.

It was time to call Harry and ask him to take on a new job. He was to track down Chatsworth and get him to admit that he had framed Allison. That would not be easy as Chatsworth was a dangerous man in his own right.

*

For Sergeant Jessica Duffy life had returned to near normal, although she could not share with anyone her guilt over killing a man, even if he was a traitor and enemy of her country.

Captain Mark Carr had put her back at her old desk and she was continuing her work encoding and deciphering the reams of messages that came through each shift.

'Hey, Sergeant Duffy,' Captain Carr said one morning when she reported for duty. 'They want you upstairs.'

Jessica knew that could only mean her old office below General MacArthur's room. She fetched her cap and when she stepped outside she was met by two American armed police who silently escorted her upstairs. She felt that something ominous was in the wind and she began to feel very apprehensive.

Inside the familiar office she was told by a clerk that the colonel wanted to see her immediately.

Jessica knocked and was told to enter.

She stepped inside and saluted smartly, standing to attention.

'At ease, Sergeant Duffy. Sit down,' the colonel said, waving to a chair in front of his desk. As usual he was chomping on one of his foul-smelling cigars, blowing grey smoke in the air.

'Yes, sir,' Jessica responded dutifully, and sat down with her hands in her lap, awaiting whatever was coming.

'I have been asked who I thought might be the ideal person for a special assignment, Sergeant Duffy,' the colonel said, looking up from the file in front of him. 'Considering what I know about your levels of initiative, and your proven ability to carry out a difficult mission, I thought you would be the right person for the posting.'

Jessica breathed a sigh of relief but at the same time was intrigued. 'Thank you, sir,' she replied. 'I am humbled that you have that opinion of me.'

The colonel stared at her for a moment. 'I cannot tell you what your assignment is,' he said. 'If you accept then you do so on a voluntary basis, without knowledge of what is expected of you. Do you understand what I am saying?'

'I think so, sir,' Jessica answered.

'I can tell you that if you accept you could face great danger. But I also have to have your answer before you leave my office,' he said, taking a puff on his cigar. 'If you accept, you will be driven to your accommodation after our meeting, where you will pack a few things and then be taken to meet your new bosses.'

Whatever the colonel was offering sounded both mysterious and exciting. Jessica had come to find her work poring through cipher traffic less than challenging but, given her history, had not hoped for a transfer to something more interesting.

'Sir, I accept,' Jessica said, and the colonel blinked.

'As I said, it is a dangerous assignment, Sergeant Duffy,' he said with a slight note of surprise. 'Are you sure you want this?'

'Yes, sir,' Jessica answered. 'If it is something that can help us win this war, I am prepared to accept, no matter what the risks.'

'You are a truly remarkable woman, Sergeant Duffy,' the colonel said with a note of admiration. He rose from his desk and walked around to Jessica, extending his hand. 'Good luck, Sergeant,' he said, shaking her hand. 'We will miss you at Mac's HQ. Captain Carr has told me you have done a great job down in the swamp.'

'Thank you, sir,' Jessica said, feeling his firm grip. 'I hope that whatever I do makes our section proud.'

'I am sure you will,' the colonel said, walking her to his door.

Jessica stepped outside the office to be met by the two American military policemen. She saw the colonel nod to the sergeant.

'We will take you home to pack,' the MP said. 'Then we will drive you to your next destination, Sergeant Duffy.'

Jessica followed the two MPs, her mind swirling with a thousand thoughts. Only this morning she had risen from her bed, showered and changed into her WAAAF uniform to face another shift in her corner of the swamp. Tomorrow she could be anywhere, and facing the most dangerous mission of her life – whatever it was.

Before the day was over Jessica found herself standing on the side of an airstrip outside Brisbane with only her kitbag beside her. There she was met by her new boss and his team of one.

★

Sarah Macintosh forced herself not to chew her perfectly manicured fingernails. Tomorrow would be the meeting at which her father would make his official resignation from the board and name his successor. She was almost certain it would be her, but she had a niggling concern that was eating away at her.

That niggling concern brought her home in the late afternoon to the house she shared with her father and brother. Sarah told the staff that they could take the rest of the afternoon and evening off as a reward for their long hours of service, and they accepted with gratitude. Sarah now had the house to herself. Her father was in town, and Sarah sneaked into his library. She was sure she had seen him writing out his resignation speech a couple of days earlier, and had noted that he locked it away in his desk drawer. She retrieved the key to the drawer from the false bottom of a paperweight – she had known for some time that this was where her father hid it – and opened the drawer.

Sarah sat down in her father's big chair, rifling through the reams of papers until she found what she was searching for. Sarah scanned her father's resignation speech until she came to the sentence she knew was so critical to her future. When she found it she gasped.

'You bastard!' she swore softly. 'After everything I have done to prove myself worthy.'

Sarah placed the sheet of paper on the desk as if she were handling a viper and sat back in the chair in cold fury. Her father would pay for his treachery towards her. But first she had to take steps to ensure that the speech was changed to suit her. Sarah knew that she could not attempt a forgery, so her father would have to rewrite his resignation speech, naming her as his successor. Her fury was now replaced by a coldly calculated scheme.

She opened another drawer in the desk where she knew her father kept a pistol given to him by Heinrich Himmler when they had visited Germany for the 1936 Olympics.

Sarah held it in her hands, staring with fascination at the deadly instrument of death. She released the magazine from the handle to inspect the loaded clip, and then reinserted it. Donald had shown her how to use the pistol when war had been declared in the Pacific – in case she needed to use it in defence of her life in the event of a Japanese invasion. The silence in the house was broken only by the lazy tick-tock of the old grandfather clock that had always been a fixture in the hallway outside the library. Listening to the clock Sarah wondered how much it had witnessed in this house over the years.

All she had to do was wait for her father's return. Nothing would stand in her way now.

As she waited, her eyes roamed along the wall of the library at the array of Aboriginal weapons adorning the wall. She knew they had been gathered after a massacre of the native people who had once lived on Glen View. She wondered why her father would keep them when he was so fearful of some silly Aboriginal curse on the family. Sarah was not aware of the death that had haunted the family for almost a hundred years. The young woman did not believe in the superstitious beliefs of her father.

The old grandfather clock in the hallway continued to tick-tock the seconds of time, oblivious to the concept that human lives were sometimes critically measured in seconds.

TWENTY-EIGHT

Sarah heard the footsteps echo in the empty house and knew that her father would come straight to the library as was his habit. She continued to sit patiently with the pistol in her lap, waiting for him.

The door opened and Sir George entered the library.

'Hello, Daddy,' Sarah said, startling him.

'Sarah, you are home early, and where are our staff?'

'I gave them the evening off,' Sarah answered. 'I doubt that they will be back for several hours.'

'What are you doing in here?' Sir George asked suspiciously, walking towards her.

'I found your resignation speech,' Sarah said.

'But I had it locked away,' Sir George said in anger. 'How dare you go through my private papers!'

'I see that you have named Donald as your successor,' Sarah said, bringing up the pistol from her lap and pointing it at her father, who halted with a gasp. 'You know that I am the one who should lead the family – not my brother.'

'You should not point that gun at me,' Sir George said, realising that there was something in his daughter's expression he had never seen before. It was as if she was possessed by an evil spirit.

'I want you to sit down and write a new resignation speech, naming me as your successor,' Sarah said, rising from the chair and gesturing for her father to sit down at his desk. She walked to the big windows overlooking the driveway and glanced out. The chauffeur had already driven away, and they were truly alone in the house.

'I cannot do that,' Sir George said, regaining his composure.

'Then I will shoot you,' Sarah said calmly. 'I will call the police in a distressed state to say that I found you in the library – with the gun in your hand – and that I think you have committed suicide. I suppose that the idea of stepping down had become too much for you, and you decided to end your life.'

'You think that will pass a police investigation?' Sir George said.

'I think so,' Sarah said. 'You were right about Chatsworth being a very competent man. He has been able to obtain your medical records for me. You have syphilis, and I think that one of the symptoms of that is madness, in the end. Yes, I will get away with killing you if you do not rewrite the speech.'

'What is to stop me standing up at the meeting and simply saying that I wish your brother to take over from me?' Sir George asked.

'Because sadly you will be in hospital with a heart condition, and I will table your speech with your apologies for not being able to be there to read it yourself,' Sarah said.

'You would have to kill me to get away with this,' Sir George said. 'I had a premonition that this would happen. But I thought it would be your brother, who I thought had more reason to see me dead.'

'Not if you pick up your pen and do as I say,' Sarah said.

Sir George reached for the fountain pen, pulled out a fresh sheet of letterhead and commenced to write, while his daughter took a seat in the corner of the room. After he had finished he used blotting paper to dry the fresh ink. 'There,' he said, holding up the sheet. 'You are named as my successor.'

Sarah rose and went to his desk to examine the paper and saw her name duly noted as her father had said.

'Thank you, Father,' she said. 'I will arrange for you to be admitted to hospital tonight suffering a heart condition.'

'You are a ruthless bitch,' Sir George said. 'But you are my daughter.'

'Thank you, once again,' Sarah said. 'Let's go downstairs and I will call for an ambulance. I expect you to put on a good show for them.'

Sir George rose unsteadily to his feet and walked towards the door, Sarah following him. At the top of the steep stairs Sir George suddenly felt a hard shove in his back. He lost his footing and plunged forward down the stairs, coming to a hard stop at the bottom.

Sir George was not dead but he had experienced a sharp pain in his neck as he fell, and blood flowed profusely from a blow to his head and streamed down his face. When he looked up he could see his daughter walking down the stairs, a grim expression on her face. He tried to move – but could not. It occurred to him that the fall had snapped his neck and he was totally paralysed, at the mercy of his daughter now leaning over him.

'I'm sorry, Daddy, that it had to come to this,' she said serenely. 'I am sure you would have eventually reneged on our deal. I know you are not a fool, so I am sure you understand why I have to kill you.'

Sir George stared up, terrified, into his daughter's eyes, and could see an image of himself there. He did not want to die and she could still help him. Sarah stood up and walked away, giving Sir George the faintest of hope that she was going to call for assistance. He knew he was crying and he could not remember ever crying before in his life. Not for anyone but himself. In a moment Sarah had returned and was holding a cushion from the living room divan.

'No!' Sir George screamed, but his words were lost in the empty hallways and rooms of the house.

'It will not take long – if you don't resist,' Sarah said soothingly as she knelt down and placed the pillow over his face, pressing down.

Her father could not struggle and felt the breath being smothered out of him. In that time between life and death, his dead sister came to him, and standing behind her was the young woman he had murdered all those years before. He tried to scream but could not as his life drained away. His last experience as a living human being was sheer terror.

*

Sarah Macintosh, between fits of sobbing, was explaining to Detective Sergeant Preston that she had been in the dining room when she had heard her father's cry for help, but by the time she had got to him he was already dead from the fall.

The pair stood in the hallway as the covered body was taken on a stretcher out to the waiting ambulance. Preston was taking notes as Sarah sobbed and dabbed her eyes with a handkerchief.

'I must compose myself,' Sarah said with all the feigned dignity she could muster. 'Tomorrow, Father was to announce his retirement.'

'I heard that,' Preston said. 'My condolences for your loss.'

'I believe my father has at least left his last wishes in writing for his announcement at the meeting,' Sarah said, the tears drying up on cue. 'I should attend to those matters.'

Uniformed police were poking around the house but without much enthusiasm, as it was clear the deceased had died by accident.

'Nothing much to report, sarge,' a uniformed constable reported. 'Do you need us here any longer?'

'No, we are done here, I think,' said Preston. 'I will follow you back to the station.'

Sarah excused herself and said she would be in the library if anyone needed her. The officers packed up and left the detective alone in the house – except for his prime suspect. He might not be the most honest policeman in the force, but he was one of the smartest. Preston had not been fooled, and he walked around the many rooms of the house. They were all immaculately neat and tidy. He entered the downstairs living room and noticed the expensive divan. A pillow had been thrown down on it carelessly and looked out of place beside the other, neatly laid cushions.

'Well, well,' Preston muttered, picking it up. He could see fresh blood on the underside. He smiled. Sarah Macintosh had slipped up. No doubt she had intended to dispose of the incriminating evidence but had been unable to do so before the police had arrived.

Preston found his way to the library and entered without knocking. Sarah was at the desk perusing a pile of papers needed for the meeting in the morning.

Preston held up the pillow to her and noted that she paled and looked like she might faint.

'A nice memento of your father's death,' he said with a twisted smile. 'You could almost say it was a death mask – from the impression painted in blood – as if it had been held over his face to hasten his death. Could you possibly explain how it was on a divan next to the murder scene?'

'I . . .' Sarah was cornered, and at a loss for words.

'Don't worry,' Preston said, lowering the pillow. 'I am sure that you and I can come to an agreement. Your father once said to me that if he died under suspicious circumstances I was to look carefully at your brother. He never in his wildest dreams expected that his daughter would do him in. But in my experience women make much more devious killers than men.'

'How much would it cost me for you to be discreet in this matter?' Sarah asked quietly.

The detective named his figure, which was very high, and added that it was only the first instalment. Sarah did not hesitate to agree.

'For that price, I expect the pillow will be disposed of,' Sarah said.

'I will put it away carefully. But if you ever forget to make a payment, it will mysteriously turn up as evidence,' Preston said. 'Mark my word, I can make that happen.'

'I believe you, Detective Sergeant Preston,' Sarah said. 'I will honour my part of the agreement.'

'Good, then the evidence presented to the coroner will ensure a verdict of accidental death. Of course, the coroner can always override his own decision if new evidence is discovered.'

Sarah Macintosh stared him down. 'If that is all,' she said coldly, 'I would like to be alone to grieve my father's unfortunate death.'

'I will be in touch,' Preston said, and as he walked away he shook his head. That was one very dangerous and calculating woman.

★

The unfortunate death of Sir George Macintosh was spread across the pages of the daily newspapers. One such paper sat on Sean's office desk, although he had learned of Sir George's death from Donald before the papers hit the streets.

Donald was sitting in Sean's office, his hat in his hand.

'The annual general meeting went ahead this morning, despite my father's body lying barely cold in the morgue,' he said. 'His resignation letter stated that Sarah was to take charge. I must admit I was surprised, I always suspected that my father, deep down, thought it improper for a woman to hold such a high position. Nevertheless, that was his decision and I must respect it. I have tendered my resignation and intend to join up.'

'Isn't that a little hasty?' Sean said. 'I know it would be hard to play second fiddle to Sarah, but you have proved so competent in your job.'

Donald shook his head. 'I have always wanted to serve,' he said. 'Sarah taking total control is the straw that broke the camel's back. I have often envied David's courage, and doubted my own. No, it is my time to do my bit.'

'Courage is not something exclusive to a battlefield,' Sean said. 'Believe me. But if you are determined to enlist

I have no doubt that you will be commissioned with your background. What service do you favour?'

'I think I will join the army,' Donald said. 'Maybe I might even one day get a chance to serve with David.'

'Maybe,' Sean echoed. 'I have a feeling that the tide has turned against the enemy but the war is far from over. It could stretch out for several more years the way the Japanese are so tenaciously defending their territory.' The two men fell silent, pondering a future that held so much uncertainty. 'To get back to your father's death, do you know who the head detective is in the investigation?'

'My sister told me that it is Preston,' Donald answered and noticed Sean raise his eyebrows. 'Is that significant?' he asked.

'Preston was on your father's secret payroll,' Sean said. 'He had a lot to lose with the death of your father.'

'So, if anything was suspicious, he would be the first to stir up trouble for Sarah,' Donald said.

'I suppose so,' Sean said. 'Preston has just lost his meal ticket. On another matter,' Sean said eventually, 'I am sure Tom Duffy will be offering to buy Glen View when he learns of your father's death.'

'My sister will oppose the sale,' Donald said.

'What about you?' Sean countered.

'I will go with whatever David thinks,' Donald answered and Sean was pleased. Tom had told him about his positive meeting with David in New Guinea. 'The meeting to discuss sales will be held next week and I will be sure to attend. All you need to do is contact David, and ask him what he thinks about Glen View going to Tom Duffy.'

'I don't know if you have heard, but David has been posted back into the Pacific – whereabouts at this stage unknown.'

'Damn!' Donald swore. 'It may take time to get a reply from him, and if we do not before the meeting, I will be in the dark as to his views on the matter.'

'I am sure that David wishes Tom Duffy and Jessica to have the property,' Sean said.

'Speaking of Jessica,' Donald said, 'have you heard anything from her lately? I have attempted to telephone her, and all I get is that Jessica has left Brisbane, whereabouts unknown. I have even knocked on doors in Canberra, but I get the same answer, even from my contacts in the military – they do not know where she is. It is as if she has dropped off the face of the earth and I am very worried. Do you think she has been made to disappear because of her role in the Ulverstone matter?'

'I hope I am right in believing that matter has been put to bed, and Jessie exonerated,' Sean said. 'There has to be some other reason for her disappearance.'

'I hope you are right,' Donald said. 'Jessie and I have some unfinished business.'

Sean did not ask what that business was as he strongly suspected that Donald was in love with Jessica Duffy and there were expressions of this yet to be fulfilled.

★

White fluffy clouds billowed over a placid blue-green sea and set the stage for an idyllic holiday in Australia's tropical north. But not for Sergeant Jessica Duffy. She was wading from the water, wearing combat fatigues and towing a small rubber raft containing her .45 Thompson machine gun and spare magazines, along with a radio sealed in a greased tarpaulin.

Wet and exhausted, she just wanted to collapse on the isolated beach north of Cairns and sleep. But a man wearing combat dress strode down to her with a swagger stick in his hand. He had a barrel chest and powerful arms and sported a sweeping moustache. Despite the fact he was in his forties he looked as fit as a man half his age. His thinning red hair blended with a freckled face.

'I was expecting you before dawn, girlie,' he said when he reached Jessica kneeling in the hot sand. 'Not good enough if you want to stay with Z Special Unit. My granddaughters could do better.'

Jessica did not try to excuse herself, although she had been caught up in a rip as she had paddled through the night, navigating by compass and keeping out as far as she could from the shore. She doubted that the sergeant major actually had any grandchildren because he would have eaten them at birth. He was a hard man who had been assigned as her personal instructor in the art of guerrilla warfare.

'Go easy on her, sarn't major,' came the drawling English voice of another man. He wore the rank of captain and had a revolver in a canvas holder on his hip. 'It is not likely that Sergeant Duffy will be rowing into her RV.'

Jessica knew both men well. They were the only people she had contact with. Jessica had learned she was very close to the training camp for the men selected for special operations in the Pacific. She knew the top secret Z Special Unit was composed of the best of the best, and its operations not recorded for public information. The members were drawn from many nationalities, including British, Dutch, New Zealand, Timorese and Indonesian operatives. The Australian members were commando trained, and the special operations forces had evolved from the practices of the British Special Operations Executive and were also known as the Services Reconnaissance Department.

She knew this because she had once listened in to their mysterious messages as part of her role in Brisbane.

Jessica had been met at the airfield upon her departure from Brisbane by the captain and the sergeant major. They straightaway whisked her away to a farmhouse not far from the Z Special Unit HQ in the sprawling hilltop mansion on top of Ah Chings Hill near Cairns. She was kept well away from the others in the unit; in fact, the captain had told her she was not even on their parade roll, so sensitive was the mission she had been assigned to.

Jessica knew that the British SOE employed many women for work behind enemy lines in France, but their Australian equivalent saw the missions as purely men's work. This did not deter Jessica, and she strived to learn all she could from her two instructors. For the past two weeks, Jessica had trained without any knowledge of the mission she had been chosen for. The British captain standing on the beach was the only person she really saw – except when he released his sergeant major on her for one-on-one training in weapons, explosives, hand-to-hand combat, knife fighting, camouflage and stealthy movement.

Captain Mike Unsworthy was from the British Army and the tough senior NCO she knew only as sir or sergeant major. Despite his gruffness with her, she sensed that he cared deeply about her welfare, and drove her mercilessly to ensure she had a better chance of living through her top secret mission, of which she knew nothing at all.

'I have some good news for you, Sergeant Duffy,' Captain Unsworthy said. 'The sarn't major has briefed me that in his opinion you are ready for your mission.'

Jessica rose to her feet, weary with exhaustion, and tried to smile her gratitude.

'Tomorrow, we head up to HQ for a complete briefing,' Unsworthy continued. 'But tonight you stand down, and we will share the best steak and chips there is in this part of the world. I think a bottle of champagne would also be in order. So, gather your things and we will hitch a ride back to our digs.'

Jessica retrieved her Tommy gun, and the sergeant major secured the raft under palm trees growing at the edge of the beach. They walked through the scrub until they came to a dirt track where a jeep was waiting for them. The sergeant major drove, and when they reached the farmhouse Jessica staggered to her room to have a shower and as much sleep as she could catch before dinner.

Jessica stepped inside the room, with its fan whirling slowly overhead, and froze at what she saw laid out on her bed. It was a nun's habit. The white garb she had once worn as a Catholic missionary sister.

TWENTY-NINE

Harry Griffiths was an imposing man, with a reputation with his fists that Chatsworth was very aware of as the man sat down opposite him in his dingy office.

'What did you want to see me about, Harry?' he asked.

'Let's say my employer has asked me to look into a little matter of some photographs you took a few months back at the party of an illustrious Sydney family.'

'Don't know what you are talking about,' Chatsworth snorted. 'So, if that is all, you may as well go to the pub and have a beer.'

Harry shook his head slowly. 'I will ask the question again and you will tell me about the matter I am interested in.'

'Why the bloody hell are you asking me?' Chatsworth countered.

'Because I know for a fact you are on the payroll of Sarah Macintosh,' Harry answered.

'I heard her old man fell down the steps and broke his neck,' Chatsworth deflected. 'Sorry to hear it.'

Harry reached down and brought up a shotgun cartridge, placing it on Chatsworth's desk. The private investigator glanced at it. 'You threatening me, Harry?' he asked.

Harry placed a brown paper bag on the table beside the shotgun shell. 'Your choice, Chatsworth,' he said with a shrug. 'If I were you I would choose the bag. Better than having a bad accident one night while you are doing a stake-out on some poor bugger playing up on his missus.'

Chatsworth leaned back in his chair contemplating the offer. He had once heard whispers on the street that Harry Griffiths had killed a former policeman and got away with it.

'You know that what goes on between investigator and client is confidential,' Chatsworth said. 'Where would my reputation be if I dobbed in a well-paying client?'

'Put it this way,' Harry said, 'what if someone broke into your office and found incriminating photos? Nothing you could do about that, eh? You get my drift?'

Chatsworth eyed the brown paper bag, which had a healthy bulge to it, and nodded. He stood up and walked over to a metal filing cabinet, opening it with a key and produced a manila folder, placing it on his desk.

Harry leaned forward and flipped it open. The evidence was there, photos and negatives. He closed the folder and picked up the shotgun shell and slipped it into his pocket. 'See, we didn't even need to mess up your office,' he said. 'I can promise you that the file will disappear and my employer will be very grateful for your assistance in this delicate matter.'

Chatsworth well knew who employed Harry, and he respected Sean Duffy for also being a hard man in his own way. When the choice came down to being pitted against the formidable duo of Harry Griffiths and Sean Duffy or taking a payoff, the financial option was much preferred. After all, his employer, Sarah Macintosh, was a mere woman, with only one recourse to getting what she wanted – money.

Harry left the private investigator's office. When he stepped out onto the street, a car was waiting for him where Sean sat in the driver's seat.

'Move over, cobber,' Harry said with a broad smile. 'I don't trust your driving.'

Sean slid over to the passenger side, and Harry passed him the folder.

'It's all there,' Harry said. 'Chatsworth was very helpful, although he did not admit that Sarah Macintosh hired him.'

Sean flipped open the folder but closed it quickly when he saw the first lewd photograph. They would be burned – along with the negatives – when he returned to his office. As far as Sean was concerned the photographs in the possession of Sarah's investigator was all the circumstantial evidence he needed to completely exonerate Allison. It was time to make David see the truth.

At his office, Sean informed Allison that he had been able to obtain the incriminating evidence, and that he was one hundred per cent sure Sarah had been behind a devious plot to discredit Allison in the eyes of David. Allison burst into tears and Sean slipped the folder into a drawer in his desk and locked it, knowing he would destroy the folder and its contents that evening in his flat.

Sean excused Allison, and began to write a letter.

★

It was the first time that Jessica had visited the northern HQ of the Z Special Unit located at Fairview House. The grounds were deserted as she and Captain Unsworthy drove up in his jeep. There was not even a guard at the front entrance. Jessica thought this was unusual and said so.

'Your existence is a highly guarded secret, Sergeant Duffy,' the captain replied. 'We had the area cleared before you arrived. Most of the boys are out on training exercises.'

Unsworthy pulled up in front of the building and Jessica followed him inside where they were met by a naval officer in the uniform of a commodore. He greeted Jessica warmly after she and Captain Unsworthy had saluted.

'Sergeant Duffy,' he said. 'I have read Captain Unsworthy's report on the progress of your training and I am impressed. I am also aware of your rather unconventional activities whilst absent from General MacArthur's HQ in Brisbane. If ever a woman was destined for this mission, I am sure it is you. We should go into the conference room and provide Sergeant Duffy with her briefing, don't you think, Captain Unsworthy? I am sure Sergeant Duffy has a thousand and one questions.'

They followed the high-ranking naval officer into a large airy room adorned with maps and with a couple of tables strewn with aerial photographs.

'Could we organise tea or coffee for you, Sergeant Duffy?' the naval officer offered politely, but Jessica declined. The man perched on the edge of one of the robust tables. 'Right, I will get to the point then,' he said, withdrawing a silver cigarette case from his pocket and offering a cigarette to Unsworthy and Jessica, who both politely declined.

'You have shown remarkable courage in volunteering blindly for this mission. No doubt you are also wondering about the nun's kit we sent to you – well, for the next few weeks or months you will be a nun again. Oh, I can see the look of surprise on your face, Sergeant Duffy. Or is that a look of horror?' he chuckled. 'We know of your escape from New Britain last year, and how resourceful you have proved ever since. We are going to send you back to New Britain to your old mission station, and before you start asking questions, I am sure that you remember your mother superior, Sister Michael.'

'Yes, sir, I do,' Jessica said.

'Good, because she has not forgotten you,' the naval officer said. 'We have had contact with her through one of our coastwatchers. You will be dropped into New Britain by one of our subs leaving tomorrow. You will not be alone on your mission, you will be accompanied by another Z Special Unit operative. You will have paperwork to identify the pair of you as a nun and Lutheran pastor. Four weeks ago an American army air force colonel decided to go on a bombing raid with a US squadron, to see what air combat was like at first hand. Unfortunately he found out when the Boston bomber he was crewing was shot down off the coast of New Britain. Natives saved him and took him ashore. The natives lived near your old mission station, and reports were carried to our coastwatcher that he was given assistance by Sister Michael at great risk to her life and those of her good sisters. Sadly, we have lost contact with the coastwatcher whose last report was that the Yank colonel is hiding out on the island crawling with Japs. You and Pastor Heinz, also known as Warrant Officer Roland Porath of the commando company, are tasked to get him out from under the Japs' noses, because he has a secret in his head that, if it came out under torture, could change the course of the war against us. He was forbidden to fly but still did so, so I suspect our American brothers will not act kindly towards him when you get him back.'

'It's about Ultra, isn't it, sir?' Jessica offered boldly, causing the commodore to look at her sharply.

'I presume you picked that up in your work with the Yanks, Sergeant Duffy,' he said sternly. 'I think we owe that much to you to say it is a secret related to Ultra. If I were you I would do your best to forget you ever even heard the word.'

'That is all I ever knew, sir,' Jessica replied. 'I only ever heard the word said in hushed tones around the office when I was working on codes.'

'Maybe, if we win the war,' the naval officer said, 'the world will know about the vital importance of the word itself one day.'

Jessica did not tell the commodore that she had worked out that the term related to some place called Bletchley Park in England, and the information was so sensitive that it went beyond the highest standard classification of *most secret* to *ultra secret*.

'What word, sir?' she said and brought a broad smile to the naval officer's face.

'Good girl,' he said and continued briefing her on the details of her mission. He concluded by saying that she would be driven to Cairns where a sub would leave that night with her and her colleague aboard. More detailed briefing would be provided on the sea journey to New Britain.

'Good luck, Sergeant Duffy,' the commodore said, stretching out his hand in a gesture that took Jessica by surprise. Naval commodores normally did not shake hands with lowly NCOs.

'Thank you, sir,' Jessica said.

'Unfortunately, this mission is so sensitive that we cannot even recognise your existence if anything goes wrong,' he said. 'This is one of the few missions that will never be recorded. However, our prime minister knows who you are and what you are doing. He wanted me to tell you that he personally wishes you luck and hopes to have a cup of tea with you when you return.'

Jessica was stunned to learn that Prime Minister Curtin had been briefed on the mission. She knew that the country's respected wartime leader was aware of her existence, and she had once been introduced to him in Sydney at a conference. It was uplifting to know that the highest office holder in the land knew the risks she was taking in the name of patriotic duty, and if anything happened to her she had a feeling her beloved father would be quietly told of what she had done. If she did not return she hoped that he would be proud of her sacrifice.

That evening, dressed in combat fatigues and with her long hair cut off and her head shaved, Jessica was taken out to an Australian submarine at anchor in the estuary bordered by crocodile-infested mangrove swamps. With her was a kitbag containing her nun's habit, a razor-sharp dagger and a small pistol. She had also been given a small pill in a tiny metal case. Unsworthy had handed it to her on the wharf before she departed.

'I think you know what this is,' he had said.

'I know,' Jessica had confirmed, accepting the tiny container and stepping into the boat that would ferry her out to the submarine.

'But you know it is against my religion to commit suicide.'

'You have already disclosed that you know of the existence of Ultra,' Unsworthy said. 'Any act to take your life would be to protect the safety of many others you do not even know.'

Jessica pondered this as the boat approached the hull of the submarine, where a small party of sailors stood, awaiting her arrival. There was no turning back now.

★

Just ahead of the Australian submarine steamed a troopship setting sail from Cairns. Major David Macintosh leaned on the rails gazing at the rainforested hills behind the town. The sea was calm, and the regimental band played tunes on deck to entertain the men of the battalion, who only knew that they were going back into action once again; where was yet to be revealed.

They steamed until the vessel was about seven miles from shore and then dropped anchor to await further crew the next day. This was the calm before the storm, and David guessed that most aboard would be reflecting on what lay ahead. For the veterans of the battalion they already knew, and the new reinforcements dared not ask them lest they reveal their fear.

'Hey, David, are you coming down to eat?' Captain Brian Williams asked. The informality between company commander and company second-in-command was reserved for moments like this, private and out of hearing of the troops. 'I was told that we have been able to buy the ship's stock of chilli con carne to supplement our rations. Have you ever had that Eytie food before?'

David smiled. 'It's not Italian, it's actually a dish originating in Mexico,' he said. 'Hope you like spicy food.'

'I like hot English mustard on ham,' Brian replied. 'Is it hot like that?'

'It can be,' David said, pushing himself away from the rail. 'Well, cobber, let's go and find out.'

They negotiated the narrow passageways of the ship to find their mess and try the exotic dish that most had never heard of before.

Just ahead of David's ship, the Australian submarine carrying Jessica to New Britain cruised on the surface of the moonlit sea as both crossed the tropical waters into dangerous and uncertain futures.

THIRTY

The conditions aboard the submarine were cramped, smelly and without privacy. Jessica, however, had been afforded the privilege of her own bunk, and she was grateful for that. She dumped her kitbag and went to meet the sub's captain in his tiny cabin. There she met her colleague, Warrant Officer Roland Porath who went under the assumed name of Pastor Peter Heinz.

Roland Porath looked out of place as a Lutheran pastor. He stood over six feet tall and had such broad shoulders that he was forced to turn side-on to pass along the narrow corridors of the sub. He was in his early thirties and had a face that was appealing in a rugged kind of way.

The captain produced marine charts and indicated the drop-off point.

'We are to go inland and meet up with another Lutheran pastor at this village,' Roland said, pointing to a dot on the map. 'He will take us to your old missionary station, Sergeant Duffy – or perhaps I should say Sister Camillus?'

'I suppose we should get in the habit of addressing each other by our assumed titles,' Jessica answered. 'Do I address you as Pastor?'

'Yes,' Roland replied. 'When we reach your old missionary station run by Sister Michael we expect to find that the Nips have also brought in a few captured Australian nurses. Our intelligence indicates that the original Jap guards have all been posted away and a new lot is in place, so you should not be recognised . . . Sister Camillus.'

'Is Sister Michael aware that I will be meeting with her?' Jessica asked.

'Not that I know of,' Roland replied. 'She is our critical contact as she knows where the Yank officer is hiding out. We would have used our nearest coastwatcher to extract him, but he has gone silent. We suspect the Nips have either captured or killed him. So it is up to you and I to get the Yank out. No matter what happens, it is vital that the Nips don't get their hands on him. If it looks like they might, and we are unable to extract him, one of us will have to take steps to prevent him being interrogated.'

Jessica knew exactly what that meant. If there was a chance they could not escape the island, then they would have to execute the American officer. She did not want to dwell on that possibility.

Further arrangements were discussed in minute detail. Jessica felt confident – but frightened. Not by the threat the Japanese posed, but by meeting Sister Michael again. Jessica knew it was irrational to think so, but the older nun had been such a wonderful influence in her life. She had practically been the mother Jessica had never known.

Over a meal Jessica got to speak with Roland. They sat knee to knee in the small messing area, alone as the rest of the crew had been given strict orders not to mix with them.

'Are you really a Lutheran pastor?' Jessica asked.

'I almost was,' Roland replied, buttering a slice of stale bread with tinned butter. 'My parents were from Bavaria and they emigrated to South Australia before the last war. They were very religious, and always felt out of place living in the predominantly Catholic province of Bavaria. The Bavarians are a funny mob,' Roland said with a warm smile. 'They don't identify as being German. They see themselves as Bavarians – aloof from the Prussians and others.'

'Do you have your own family?' Jessica asked.

'Do you mean am I married? The answer is the only family I have are my aged parents. What else would you like to know, Sister Camillus?'

'Oh, I am sorry if I appear nosy,' Jessica said. 'And I am not comfortable in the role of a nun anymore.'

'I was briefed on your past,' Roland said, biting into the buttered bread. 'You have led an interesting life for one so young.'

'Considering the nature of our mission I would rather you call me Sergeant or even Jessica, for that matter,' Jessica said. 'I do not feel right being addressed as a nun again.'

'I suppose we can do that when it is safe to,' Roland answered. 'In that case, you can call me Roland but not Rollie. I hate that name.'

'Thank you, Roland,' Jessica said. 'I am sure that everything will go smoothly.'

Within a couple of days both Jessica and Roland found themselves on the deck of the submarine sitting off a darkened coastline. Sailors spoke in whispers as they prepared the inflatable dinghy to be rowed ashore to a small beach. It was important not to make noise and alert any enemy who might be in the area to the submarine's presence.

Jessica was dressed in her combat fatigues for the transfer to shore, and wore an American baseball cap to hide her shaved head. Roland was also dressed in his jungle uniform, and at their feet in the dinghy were the items they would need for the mission. Inside her kitbag, Jessica had her nun's habit and headpiece. She also had an Owen submachine gun with many loaded magazines of ammunition. There was also a flare gun with different coloured projectiles, and three hand grenades, and a compass and maps of the region. The most important piece of equipment would be ferried to the beach on a second run. It was the bulky radio transmitter/receiver required for them to establish communications when they were in a position to get the American officer out. All these supplies would have to be very carefully concealed when they left the beach to strike out for their RV with the Lutheran pastor. Neither Roland nor Jessica could afford to carry anything incriminating in the way of Z Special Unit items. They would travel unarmed and maintain their covers as Catholic nun and Lutheran pastor – should they be intercepted by any Japanese patrols.

With the gentle hiss of sea water on sand the dinghy beached. Jessica and Roland slipped overboard, and the sailor who had rowed them in whispered his good luck wishes. Their supplies were thrown onto the sand, and the dinghy immediately set out to retrieve their vital radio from the cargo of the Australian submarine.

Jessica and Roland pulled their kitbags up the beach. They could not use torches to examine their equipment, and when they gazed out to sea they had to adjust their eyes to see the faint shape of the submarine. The world was silent around them, until they heard the low throb of a marine engine in the distance and suddenly the submarine was gone from the surface, leaving only a small eddy of white water in its wake.

'We've got to get off the beach,' Roland hissed just as the probing finger of brilliantly white light flicked across the water. Jessica could see that a small vessel had appeared from behind the headland that bordered the beach, its searchlight seeking out targets for the machine guns mounted on its decks.

The two pulled back into the jungle that ran down from the hills behind them to the beach itself and lay on their stomachs, watching the Japanese patrol boat slowly cruise past. Jessica could even hear the chatter of Japanese voices across the water as the boat passed by.

The two lay side by side for an hour until they could no longer hear the engines of the patrol boat. Dawn would be on them very soon and both understood that they were not going to get their most important weapon – the radio. Things had already gone wrong, and Jessica had a sick feeling about what lay ahead.

They concealed their fall-back supplies, changed into their civilian garb as Lutheran pastor and Catholic nun, and set out to make contact with the missionary at his station in the hills.

★

Sarah could almost taste the tension in the boardroom as the members assembled for the monthly meeting. She sat at the head of the board table in the seat her father used to occupy and stared down at the faces on either side of her. Some still could not hide their hostility, and Sarah reminded herself to review their roles very soon. Most of the members, however, had fallen quickly into line to keep their well-paid jobs.

'Gentlemen,' Sarah said sweetly, 'we have on the agenda this morning the offer for the sale of Glen View to Mr Tom Duffy. I am sure that this is a matter you are all familiar with, as it has reared its ugly head before. You know how I feel about respecting my late father's wishes, and I submit that we should decline the request, and any requests in the future.'

The door to the boardroom opened and Sarah looked up to see her brother enter. She was surprised as she'd thought he was already in training with the army.

'Donald, what brings you to this meeting?' she asked.

'If I am not wrong, today the matter of Tom Duffy's offer for Glen View is on the agenda,' Donald said. 'Although I may have resigned from the board I have had legal advice to say that the company's constitution states I still retain de facto rights to vote as a member of the Macintosh family. So, here I am, dear sister, to cast my vote.'

'You are too late,' Sarah snapped angrily. 'Besides, how do I know what you have said about your right to vote is true?'

'It is,' a voice piped up. It was one of the board members who was also a company solicitor, and the oldest member of the board. 'It was inserted during the time of your grandfather, Patrick Duffy, before he was tragically killed in the last war. Young Donald can cast a vote.'

'Sadly, he has arrived too late to do so, and we have voted that the offer be rejected,' Sarah said dismissively.

'Oh, I forgot to mention that I have David's proxy vote,' Donald continued with a smile. 'We both choose to accept Mr Duffy's generous offer to purchase Glen View.'

Sarah could feel the rage rising up in her, and she glared at the board members, who knew that their jobs depended on agreeing with her. Some tried not to catch her eye, cowered by her obvious anger. 'The matter has been final-ised,' she resisted stubbornly. 'We are moving on.'

'Did I mention that in the constitution there is another clause our grandfather had included?' Donald said, moving away from the doorway and into the room. 'It appears that Glen View was singled out by Grandfather Patrick Duffy as a special case that only blood members of the family could vote on. That means you, David and myself, and that makes the vote two to one in favour of selling to Tom Duffy.'

Sarah could see that she was trapped. Someone had briefed her brother very well. She suspected that the damned solicitor, Major Sean Duffy, had given him counsel. Oh, if only her father were here . . . then she remembered she had murdered him.

'The rules say that the matter has to be held over to the next management meeting,' the old lawyer interjected. 'Then we can settle the matter with a vote.'

Sarah quickly considered this advice. Maybe, with any luck, her brother would get killed in the army, and David Macintosh too. 'I agree,' she stated. 'Until the next meeting.' Sarah was pleased to see the expression of disappointment on her brother's face.

'Please stay around and have a cup of tea with us at the end of the meeting, Donald,' she offered courteously. That would enable her to determine who on the board was still friendly towards him. Donald could opt to resume his place on the board at any time, and Sarah did not want that to happen.

★

The tropical downpour washed the blood of both enemy and Australian diggers in little rivulets until it became just another element of the great rainforest of New Guinea.

Major David Macintosh had moved his company HQ forward when his platoon commanders had eventually overcome the series of well-concealed log bunkers the Japanese had constructed. The clearance had been vicious and at close quarters as the enemy had fought to a man in their attempt to slow progress of the battalion towards its final objective of the main enemy HQ outpost.

David gripped his rifle as he moved cautiously forward with his radio man, Corporal Andrew Paull, beside him. They passed the body of a dead Japanese sniper who had been located in a tree, positioned to fire down on the Australians.

Ahead David knew he would find one of his platoons that had signalled they had destroyed the last bunker. That did not mean they had found all the enemy in the thick undergrowth growing under the rainforest giants. The early morning mist lay in the gullies and low spots of the battlefield, and this made David nervous.

'I don't like this, boss,' Andrew said in a whisper.

'Neither do I,' David replied, scanning the mist for any sign of his forward platoon positions. The radio that Corporal Paull was carrying crackled, and David recognised the voice of the commander of his rear platoon. David took the mike from Andrew to accept the sitrep and was told that they had spotted movement to their rear. David immediately realised this could mean a section of the enemy was attempting to encircle them. That also meant that he was most probably amongst them.

A sudden jerk on his shoulder by his radio man brought David's attention to movement only fifty yards away in the mist. Andrew pointed to their left flank, and David could see the figures of five Japanese soldiers. At the same time rifle shots rang out, and both men immediately went to ground as the bullets ripped through the air above them.

Andrew straightaway commenced a contact with battalion HQ, informing them of their situation. David pulled the map from inside his shirt so Andrew could transmit a grid reference. Battalion mortars were their only hope of getting out of the situation, but David hesitated. He was not sure where his platoons were on the map, and he knew he could not risk their lives to save his and his signaller's.

Suddenly out of the mist a Japanese soldier appeared within a few feet of their position, a samurai sword held above his head. David fired his rifle from the hip, and the bullet took the enemy officer in the face. He pitched backwards and before David could chamber another round a second Japanese soldier emerged, aiming a long bayonet at David, who had not yet seen him.

'Look out, boss!' Andrew yelled, leaping to his feet. In an attempt to parry the bayonet, he took it in his chest instead.

David swung around and saw his signaller had dropped his gun and was clutching the barrel of the Japanese soldier's rifle, vainly trying to withdraw the long blade. David leapt to his feet and swung his rifle by the barrel like a club. The butt took the enemy soldier in the side of the head with such force it split his skull. The Japanese soldier fell to the muddy earth with a groan.

David saw that Andrew was on his back still holding the attacker's rifle with its bayonet sunk deep in his chest. Shots cracked past David's head as he dropped to the ground beside his signaller.

'Got a bad one, boss,' Andrew groaned as blood rose from his mouth in frothy bubbles. His eyes glazed over, and he made one last gasp as he died, his lifeless fingers still gripping the rifle barrel. David was acutely aware that Corporal Andrew Paull had saved his life.

David heard the distinctive chatter of a Bren gun ahead and guessed that his rear platoon had moved back to lend support. Using fire and movement tactics his platoon broke up the encircling manoeuvre and the remaining Japanese were killed or fled into the forest. David had trained his company well, but it did not compensate for the death of the brave soldier beside him, who had once chopped off Tom Duffy's hand.

Only the courage of his company signaller had saved David from death this time. Courage and a lot of luck, too much luck for a man who had already had his fair share. For a fleeting moment David Macintosh thought about the spirit of Wallarie watching over him.

THIRTY-ONE

From the edge of the rainforest Jessica and Roland crouched, and surveyed the mission station in the valley. Jessica's clothing, like Roland's, was torn and dirty from their trek from the Lutheran mission station they had left miles behind them and now they were looking down on Jessica's former home as a nun.

'The Nips have guards everywhere,' Roland said. 'We will probably get a bit of a warm welcome.'

'It's now or never,' Jessica said and stood up. Roland followed her down a path, and they were almost at the edge of the barbed wire surrounding the main cluster of buildings, when they heard the excited chatter of guards rushing towards them brandishing rifles.

Both Jessica and Roland froze as the Japanese soldiers surrounded them, pointing bayonet-tipped rifles in their direction.

'Pastor Heinz and Sister Francis,' Roland said, holding up identification papers.

One of the soldiers they recognised as having the rank of a senior non-commissioned officer stepped forward and snatched the papers from Roland's hand. It was obvious that the Japanese NCO could not understand the English written papers, but he did understand the forged, Japanese papers they had given to them at their RV from the sympathetic Lutheran pastor who had been their initial contact upon arrival on the island.

He gestured towards the main buildings of the mission station and yelled, 'Speedo!'

Jessica and Roland tentatively dropped their raised hands and walked towards the office Jessica knew was that of the mother superior, Sister Michael. The native people they passed stared curiously at the newcomers, but quickly went back to work tending vegetable gardens when threatened by the escorting guards.

The small party stopped at the steps of the main building and an officer appeared. Jessica thankfully did not recognise him and the senior NCO who had taken their papers handed them to the officer who quickly perused them. One of the forged papers was a travel pass explaining that Roland and Jessica were to travel to the mission station where Jessica was once a nun.

'You not have permission to come here,' he snapped. 'Why you come here?'

'I have come to minister to the needs of my people here,' Roland answered. 'I heard a rumour that there are members of the Lutheran church in your care and if you look carefully you will see that we have written permission to be here.'

The officer turned to Jessica. 'Why you come here?' he

asked. Jessica took a deep breath, knowing that her answer could be a matter of life or death.

'This used to be my mission station before the war,' Jessica said. 'I was cut off when your soldiers came to New Britain, and now I have taken the opportunity to travel with Pastor Heinz to return.'

The Japanese officer stared at Jessica and she could feel absolute fear under his steady gaze. He was a short, solid man in his thirties with cold, dead eyes. 'You know Sister Michael?' he asked.

'Yes,' Jessica replied. 'She is my mother superior.' Jessica knew it was a gamble and her life now depended on the other superior validating Jessica's membership of the community, and also realising that Jessica was not what she pretended to be.

The officer said something in Japanese and Jessica saw a soldier hurry away.

She and Roland stood under the tropical sun, surrounded by the guards and the sweat under her long white dress was not all from the heat. After a few minutes Jessica saw that the soldier had returned in company with Sister Michael.

It was now or never that Jessica would live or die.

'You know this woman?' the Japanese officer asked Sister Michael who bowed and turned to face Jessica. Both women stared for only a second or two, and it was Sister Michael who spoke first with an expression of absolute shock.

'Sister Camillus!' she gasped. 'It has been a long time.'

'It say here that woman is Sister Camillus,' the officer said with a note of suspicion.

Jessica gave the slightest of nods, and the officer turned his attention back to Roland.

'It say in papers you good member of Nazi party,' he said and Roland immediately raised his hand in the Nazi salute. 'Heil Hitler, heil the Emperor.' His act caught the Japanese officer by surprise.

The officer reacted with the cry, 'Banzai!' three times, which was chorused by all the Japanese soldiers surrounding them.

Jessica hoped that the smile on her face would not be noticed. Roland was doing a grand job of convincing the Japanese he was a loyal ally of the Imperial Japanese army. When the voices of the Japanese guards died down the officer turned to Roland and Jessica, handing back their papers.

'You go,' he said in a loud voice and issued orders for his men to disperse back to their duties. He himself disappeared back into the office that once belonged to Sister Michael, leaving the three standing outside under the sun.

'I thought that you might have been killed when you left us last year,' Sister Michael said, and Jessica thought that she could see tears in the stern old nun's eyes. 'I also sense that you are no longer a nun anymore.'

'It is a long story, Sister,' Jessica said. 'But we will have time to talk.'

The older nun stepped forward and placed her hands on Jessica's cheeks.

'God bless you, Jessica,' she said. 'I think I know why you have returned to us, and if I am right, your life will be in great danger. We need to go somewhere out of hearing of our Jap captors and talk.'

Sister Michael led Jessica away from the guards to a place on the hill leading up to Jessica's old school hut. 'A loyal native boy from our coastwatcher informed me that there would be a mission of some sort requiring my assistance.

I never dreamed that it would involve you returning to us,' she said.

'I cannot tell you what our mission is,' Jessica said. 'But we must make contact with the coastwatcher – if he is still alive.'

'He is,' Sister Michael said. 'He was put out of action by a bad bout of malaria but has since recovered.'

'I guess that you have contact with him,' Jessie said.

'I have,' Sister Michael replied. 'He is located very near us and his boys keep an eye on our situation.'

'That is good news,' Jessie said. 'Pastor Heinz and myself have a great need to get in contact with him as soon as possible.'

'I can arrange that,' Sister Michael said. 'In the meantime it would be nice if you met the rest of the girls with us. We have had a group of army nurses interned here with us since you left. I will brief the sisters to remain quiet about the circumstances of you leaving us.'

'Thank you, Mother Superior,' Jessica said and realised at that moment how much she had missed this intelligent and compassionate woman who had such a strong influence on her past life.

When Sister Michael returned with Jessica to the missionary station – now acting as an internment facility – Jessica greeted her former sisters in Christ and they smiled their welcome. All did except one. Sister Clement bridled at the warm reception Sister Camillus received after betraying her vows. Sister Clement had never liked Sister Camillus. She considered her arrogant and heretical in her views of Christianity. She stood in the doorway of her medical dispensary glowering at the nun walking with the mother superior as she introduced Jessica to the Aussie nurses. Something should be done about Sister Camillus's treachery to the Church and her desertion of the missionary station the previous year. She would get a message to the English-speaking Japanese intelligence officer in the next village who also knew Sister Camillus.

★

The days passed and soon became a week. Jessica returned to her duties teaching the local children in her little shelter on the hill and Roland made himself known to the non-Catholic nurses as a spiritual adviser if they felt the need. Jessica and Roland avoided contact to allay any suspicions from the Japanese guards who generally appeared to be satisfied with their duties away from the battlefronts where so many of their comrades were being killed by the advancing Allied forces. Not all Japanese soldiers shared the ideals of Bushido.

Jessica was chalking up some arithmetic on her well-used blackboard to the small class of native children when she noticed Sister Michael climbing the gentle grassy, slope to her outdoor classroom. Jessica told her students to write down the answer to the numbers she had left on the board and walked down a way to meet the mother superior.

'I have just had a message from our coastwatcher,' Sister Michael said, after catching her breath. 'The message was that the package is with him awaiting an RV with a sub. The message also goes on to saying that your mission here is over and that you are invited to link up with him on the coast for transfer back to Australia.'

Stunned, Jessica stared at the old nun. 'We were not really needed,' she said with a sigh and for a moment was confused as to what she should do next.

'I know that you will have to leave us again, Jessie,' Sister Michael said. 'I hope that you are still acquainted with your rosary beads.'

Jessica smiled. 'I am still a Catholic, Sister Michael. All I have done is recognise that I was never really suited to be a bride of Christ.'

'That is all I needed to know,' Sister Michael said, taking Jessica's hand in her own. 'I know God will understand. But now you and Pastor Heinz must make plans to go to the coastwatcher, and return to Australia.'

Jessica glanced back at her class waiting patiently for her return. 'Will our absence put any of you in danger?' she asked.

'That is not in your hands – nor the Japanese,' Sister Michael shrugged. 'Our fate is in God's hands.'

Jessica was not reassured by the mother superior's confidence in the Almighty's protection.

'It is possible that one of my nuns might run off with the Lutheran pastor so they could be together,' she said with just the faintest of smiles. 'After all, we are still women under our skirts with, God forbid, carnal desires.' Jessica's sudden expression of shock turned the mother superior's slight smile into a broad grin. 'It will be just a little lie and I am sure I will be able to confess my transgression the next time my confession is heard.'

Jessica's appreciation of the remarkable woman shot up. She may live in a spiritual world but she also had her feet firmly planted in the secular world. 'Thank you, Mother Superior,' Jessica said. 'I will brief Pastor Heinz on the message you received.'

'The coastwatcher's boy will be able to guide you to his location tonight,' Sister Michael said. 'There is a place in the wire you are able to get through at night. The best time is around midnight when the guard changes sentry duty. They tend to spend some time having tea before swapping over shifts.'

Jessica thanked Sister Michael and returned to her class.

It was hard to concentrate when her mind whirled with thoughts of escape that night. It would not be easy, and anything could go wrong.

★

The Japanese officer was taller than most of his people, and had a studious look with the spectacles he wore. He stood before Sister Michael under the pale light of a kerosene lantern on the verandah of her quarters. Great moths flitted around the lantern in the oppressive tropical night. The nun was dressed in a neck to ankle nightgown which she pulled around her neck.

'They are not here,' he said almost mildly in near-perfect English. 'My men have searched their quarters and they do not seem to be anywhere to be found.'

'I have no idea where they could be,' Sister Michael replied in her most sincere tone. 'I am as shocked as you are that they are missing. I shudder to think that my suspicions of Sister Camillus may have been correct. Oh, poor girl, she has placed her immortal soul in jeopardy.'

Sister Michael suspected the Japanese officer of being a Christian from her previous experiences with him but he dare not admit his religion as an officer in the Imperial Japanese Army. This had made him a little more sympathetic to the plight of the missionary nuns.

'What do you mean, Sister Michael?' he asked.

'I have suspected that whilst together before returning to the station Pastor Heinz and Sister Camillus may have been possibly intimate.'

The Japanese officer took off his spectacles and rubbed his eyes. It was after midnight and he had just reached the missionary station with a small detachment of his men to arrest the two newcomers. 'Sister Clement has told me that she does not believe Sister Camillus is really a nun anymore,' he said, replacing his spectacles. 'That would mean you are harbouring spies.'

'Sister Clement suffers mild dementia,' Sister Michael said. 'She is prone to imagining things.'

'She appears lucid to me,' the officer said. 'She has gone to a lot of trouble to pass on a message to my staff. You are aware that if you do not co-operate with me then I will have no choice but to turn you over to the Kempeitai.'

Sister Michael felt the icy cold fear of the threat. The dreaded Japanese military secret police were known for their torture methods to extract information. She knew the threat was not a bluff. 'I have been reluctant to raise the issue concerning the Lutheran pastor and one of my nuns as I am sure you could appreciate. If they are missing I can only conclude that my suspicions were correct and this could bring great shame on my nuns. I am sure that you understand the gravity of shame.'

Sister Michael knew that she was not only fighting for her survival but of all those in her care. She knew that if their Japanese captors believed that a plot had been formulated in the missionary station then all could be executed – regardless of innocence. But she also knew there was a spark of decency in this particular Japanese officer.

'I think I understand,' he finally replied after a short silence, as if contemplating what he should do as right and what was his military duty to the emperor. 'I will mount an immediate search for them. You may return to your sleep, Sister Michael.'

The Japanese officer stepped off the verandah and rallied his men. Sister Clement had told him about a break in the wire and that was where he would commence his search.

★

Jessica had exchanged her nun's garb with one of the Australian nurses for slacks and a shirt before she and Roland had made their escape. The night was pitch black and the going in the dense undergrowth of the tropical forest was slow. The young, native man led the way and they often had to stop to ensure they were still together in the dark.

'How far?' Jessica had asked in the local dialect, and the native boy informed her that they should be close by dawn. As fit as she was the need for water was causing her some distress. The march through the tropical forest was taking a toll on her physical reserves, but the young native man informed her that they had to keep going to place distance between themselves and the mission station. They slogged through the night, climbing steep slopes and sliding down ravines. When the first rays of the sun appeared through the jungle foliage they finally dropped to the musty floor of the great forest giants. Sweat poured down Jessica's body and all she could think of was water.

'Are you okay?' Roland asked and Jessica nodded. Their guide had disappeared.

'Where is he?' Jessica croaked.

'He's gone to make contact with the coastwatcher,' Roland replied, wiping sweat from his brow with the back of his shirt sleeve. 'The coastwatcher has a policy of not leading anyone to his hide-out lest the Japs be tracking. He told me that he will make contact with us here.'

'Hope he's got water,' Jessica said and leaned back against the buttress roots of one of the tall trees. Around her the forest was coming alive with the sound of the diurnal creatures of the Pacific.

★

The Japanese intelligence officer had not believed the mother superior's story about the nun and pastor eloping. It had no ring of truth, and he had struggled with his duty to hand over the old woman to the cruel secret police. But his Christian morality nagged him to spare her as he had already formulated what was happening. He held a dossier on Sister Camillus and it was when he had been informed by Sister Clement's message of her sudden reappearance at the mission station that he had immediately activated his section to track her down. Unconfirmed reports from his native sources had implicated the nun in assisting the evasion of an Australian soldier the year before and, somehow, she had mysteriously returned. As far as he was concerned she had to be on a mission for the Allies and her companion, the Lutheran pastor, her accomplice.

He stood watching the sun rise from the verandah of the mission station knowing that his prey had a good lead on a detachment of his men out in the jungle.

The Japanese officer had directed them to follow a course to the sea as he knew an Australian coastwatcher was active in that area. If he had surmised right, the pair he sought would no doubt be attempting to make contact and finally the intelligence officer would be able to bag three birds in one swoop.

The intelligence officer called for his radio man and sent a message to the nearest navy outpost. He gave them the good news that it was possible that an American or Australian submarine was in the vicinity of a grid reference he provided. If he was right and his mission successful he would no doubt receive praise from his superiors for the killing or capture of a dangerous coastwatcher, two spies and the sinking of an Allied submarine.

★

'You look like you could do with a drink,' the voice said to Jessica as she dozed beneath the big tree's shade. At first she thought that she was dreaming but when she opened her eyes a bearded face met her gaze and a broad smile reassured her.

'Thank you,' Jessica said, accepting the offered water canteen which she almost emptied in her thirst.

'I'm Kevin Jones,' the coastwatcher said, retrieving the metal canteen. 'I got a message about you, Sergeant Duffy, and Warrant Officer Porath being tasked with getting the Yank colonel off the island.'

Jessica looked behind the coastwatcher to see an emaciated man wearing the rags of an American flyer. 'Is that him?' she asked and the coastwatcher nodded.

'He has malaria and God knows what else,' he replied. 'We have organised for you to RV with one of our subs tonight in the cove that you were dropped off at. You and Porath will escort him with one of my boys guiding you to the RV. I believe the sub will surface around twenty-three hundred hours tonight. It's pretty straight forward. Do you have any questions?'

Jessica shook her head and the young native man who had guided them through the night stepped forward with cooked plantain and grilled fish in a banana leaf. Jessica ate everything and was almost tempted to eat the leaf as well. Refreshed she joined Roland.

'Looks like we will be out of here by this time tomorrow,' he said, wiping his fingers on his trousers. 'I was given the briefing by Captain Jones as soon as he arrived. He saw you sleeping. He's a good bloke. He was telling me that the navy made him a captain in case he was ever captured by the Nips. He said he hoped the navy were paying him for his rank as before they commissioned him he was a civvie managing a copra plantation, and in the last lot, a corporal in engineers.'

'I remember monitoring the coastwatchers when I was in Brisbane, and they should make them all admirals for the danger they face,' Jessica said.

'Time to go,' Captain Jones said quietly. 'You need to be in position before last light. Good luck, God's speed and have a beer for me back in Australia.'

They shook hands with the bearded coastwatcher who passed them water canteens, some rice wrapped in banana leaf and a hand torch for signalling. They were then introduced to the American colonel who hardly reacted and it was obvious that he was badly in need of medical attention but was able to walk. They gently guided the tall and skinny American officer with them as they struck off into the dense jungle, following the guide who they had learned was once a native policeman. He carried the only weapon, a .303 bolt-action rifle.

They trekked cautiously all day, following the coastline, and just before sunset they came in view of the cove. Resting on a hill top they could make out the inlet through the trees.

'All going well our supplies are still hidden down there near the beach,' Roland whispered. 'I think that we should retrieve them.'

Jessica agreed and told the guide what they were going to do. He was apprehensive as night had not yet fallen but eventually agreed to accompany them with the American colonel closer to the small beach.

The sun was just about on the horizon when they arrived at an outcrop of rocks. Roland quickly dug with his hands in the sand, retrieving the weapons wrapped in cloth. He handed Jessica a Thompson sub machine gun which she quickly inspected, working the bolt to ensure it had not rusted. The copious quantities of covering grease had helped protect it. She retrieved spare loaded magazines, a couple of primed grenades, and a commando dagger. Similarly armed, she and Roland felt a little more secure. Retreating back off the beach they joined the guide and the American colonel.

★

The Japanese officer lowered his field glasses. The two figures on the beach had retreated to the jungle and it had been very hard to resist having his detachment fire on them. His commanding officer had given strict instructions not to engage the enemy until a possible submarine came for them. He outnumbered the enemy by four to one and knew his next step was to order his detachment to move from their present location to a position that would block any retreat deeper into the jungle. Night was almost upon them and it was time to set the trap.

He turned to his second-in-command and issued the order to move out. He had surprise on his side, and the enemy were as good as dead.

★

Roland and Jessica had taken turns to strip their weapons, ensure that they were in good working order and sit back to eat the remaining fish and rice mix from the banana leaves. They fed the American colonel who still remained listless and Jessica guessed he was recovering from either malaria or scrub typhus.

It was now very dark and the eerie noise of the jungle's nocturnal inhabitants came to provide a symphony of sound. Jessica gripped her Thompson, her nerves on edge with the waiting, whilst Roland stared out to the water of the bay. He also gripped the torch, ready to signal. He knew it would be very difficult to see a submarine surface on the placid dark shrouded waters so the signal from the sub had to be seen when it came.

Suddenly, the guide grabbed Roland by the shoulder and hissed, 'Jap man out there.'

Roland had not seen or heard anything but trusted the guide's instincts. He knew they had a sense for the subtle changes in the jungle night. He raised his weapon, scanning the darkness. Jessica had overheard the guide's warning and was also alert. At the same time when Roland turned his head he saw the flicker of a light from the bay. The sub had arrived on time and now they were possibly trapped between the two. At the same time he heard the distinctive sound of a small mortar being fired from close by and the distant hiss of a parachute flare that clearly outlined the surfaced sub. Roland could see the outline of sailors on the deck and see a couple quickly preparing their deck gun.

The second mortar bomb was not a flare but a high explosive projectile and it fell short in the bay, throwing up a small spout of water.

'Bloody hell!' Roland cursed. They had been so close and yet the chances of being picked up had dropped to almost zero. The sub would be forced to dive and leave them behind lest it fall victim to the Japanese.

'We have to get down to the beach now!' Jessica said, tugging at Roland's sleeve. 'We either get the Yank off now, or we leave him behind dead.'

'You take the colonel down and hope that the navy hang around long enough to pick you up while we try to find that bloody Nip mortar and put it out of action.'

Jessica felt a chill. She knew that if Roland went off into the jungle he would not be coming out alive. She did not argue because she had been trained in the deadly consequences of Z Special Unit missions. What words could she say leaving him to fight a rear guard action? Jessica struggled for words and finally said weakly, 'Good luck, Roland.'

'Just leave me your spare mags,' he replied. 'And maybe a grenade.'

Jessica passed Roland some of her .45 magazines and one grenade. She kept a spare grenade and the loaded magazine on her own weapon. She grabbed the American by the arm and commanded him to stick with her as they made their way towards the cove.

As she almost reached the beach she heard the distinctive sound of the Tommy gun and crack of the .303 and knew that Roland and the guide were engaging the enemy behind them. But the mortar continued to rain bombs down on the bay as they walked towards the surfaced submarine.

To add to the botched rescue the thump-thump of a small naval craft engine appeared from nowhere. Its searchlight masking the Japanese patrol boat as it appeared from behind the headland. Already its heavy machine gun was in action and the big bullets easily penetrate the sub's hull.

Jessica was now down to the water's edge and waded into the placid surf up to her knees, dragging the unresisting colonel with her. She had a torch from their supplies and flicked off the signal to those on the sub now desperately engaged in a fight from two sides. Behind her, Jessica could still hear the chatter of small arms fire and the occasional crump of an exploding grenade. Roland was still fighting, she was standing in the surf with a torch and the sailors occupied with their own survival. The deck gun now turned its attention to the patrol boat, and with more luck than accuracy, were able to land a shell directly on target.

The patrol boat exploded with a great roar of its depth charges exploding.

Jessica wanted to cheer but became acutely aware that the sound of Roland's sub machine gun had been silenced. She was aware of the foreign chatter of Japanese soldiers advancing through the jungle to her position in the surf.

The submarine's deck crew were scrambling to go below and it was obvious that they were not hanging around. Standing in the water to her knees and feeling its gentle swirl around her Jessica knew it was only a matter of time before the enemy reached her and the American officer.

She also knew that she could not be taken alive and remembered the terrible order in Cairns – kill the American if there was a chance of him being captured.

Jessica raised her weapon, lining it up with the unsuspecting colonel's head. She would use the grenade to end her own life and found herself quietly praying . . . *Hail Mary, full of Grace* . . .

Something bumped her leg in the dark and she realised that it was a log of driftwood. The submarine was almost gone from the surface and Jessica made a wild decision. She threw away her sub machine gun, tucked the knife and grenade into her trousers, and leaned down to push the log deep into the bay's still waters.

'C'mon, sir,' she said to the officer beside her. 'Give me a hand.'

The American realised what she was doing and pushed with all his strength until they were up to their necks in the surf. Then Jessica began paddling, using the log as a support. The inky blackness of the night was only lit a distance away by the burning wreck of the Japanese patrol boat but Jessica knew they were safely in the shadows of the night. Her plan was crazy but something in her mind told her this is what she should do. None of it made sense because the best outcome would be when the sun rose they would be drifting in the open ocean. She already had a dread of sharks from a previous experience escaping New Britain but death in their jaws might be preferable to death from exposure and thirst.

Both paddled with their legs until a current caught them and caused the log to ride it along the coast in the dark. If what she was doing failed then she still had a grenade and her knife to kill the colonel and herself.

Exhausted by dawn after pushing the log away from the shore, Jessie draped herself over it and found that she was drifting into the world between life and death, where dreams were also reality.

She was a little girl and her beloved father had purchased her first horse. He was now standing with her at the foot of that strange and eerie hill on Glen View. It was warm and dry and she felt at peace.

But an old Aboriginal man appeared from the entrance of the cave on top of the hill and was disturbing her blissful memories of better times before this death came to her. She knew it was Wallarie and mumbled that he should go away and that she would see him in the spirit world.

He was annoyed and told her to wake up or she would drift away from the hill.

Jessica shook her head and suddenly felt as if she was choking. Saltwater flooded her mouth and nose.

A hand gripped her shoulder and Jessica opened her eyes. It was the American colonel and he was trying to point at something. Using the water-saturated log, Jessica pulled herself partially out of the water to see the outline of a submarine only a hundred yards away.

Fear gripped her. These waters were the hunting ground of Japanese boats and this left only one choice. She felt for the grenade and its pin. They would die a lonely death in a lonely sea.

Then she noticed the sub's many scars from bullets and hesitated pulling the pin.

'It's one of your Aussie subs,' the colonel beside her croaked through saltwater-soaked lips.

Jessica allowed the deadly grenade to slip from her fingers. Her mission was almost over and she would go home.

EPILOGUE

December 1943

Sarah Macintosh had it all; her father's house and now she alone oversighted the management of the Macintosh financial empire. But there was just something Sarah could not control. It was the nightmares she often experienced. They were not of the murder of her father, but stupid and irrational dreams of an old Aboriginal warrior.

It was Christmas Day and Sarah sat alone in the spacious dining room.

The only sound Sarah could hear in the empty house was that of the old grandfather clock upstairs, ticking off the seconds of time and life.

★

The summer sun of central Queensland blazed with its shimmering heat on the vast, inland sea of semi-arid lands, providing thermals for the great wedge-tailed eagle, soaring aloft of the plains in search of prey.

Tom Duffy stood at the apex of the sacred hill on Glen View, gazing across the plains at the endless horizon. The letter had arrived from Sean Duffy, that the offer of purchase had been accepted and that everything had gone ahead to place the title in Tom's hands.

So he now stood alone on the hill – but soon he would be joined by his beloved daughter as she received special leave from whatever mysterious mission she had completed. They would sit down to Christmas dinner at Glen View; he, Abigail, young Patrick and Jessica, and remember those who could not be with them.

As Tom surveyed the great lands of Glen View there was no real sight of the war ending soon. Only Wallarie knew what lay ahead – and he was silent.

★

I see Tom Duffy on the sacred hill as I soar in the sky above. I am a spirit man and I can see all upon the earth. Whitefellas say they don't believe in ghosts, but say they believe in an after life, where you either go to heaven – or go to hell. Me, I never see heaven or hell, but the stars in the sky where my people live. The old people tell me my job is to keep an eye on that Duffy people, and the Macintosh mob.

It has been a long time since I was a feared warrior and magic man, walking the lands below. While they live in the world of the sun and moon, I live in the world of spirits. One day, the whitefellas will say I am the spirit of the land, and heart of Australia. But that is a long way off yet, and I really miss my baccy.

I suppose that this is not the end of the story, because families do not end. They just die and get born again.

AUTHOR NOTES

Despite the setbacks the Japanese suffered in 1942, the war in the Pacific was far from a victory for the Allies. The great Australian Prime Minister still considered Australia under threat from the Japanese as they had been able to demonstrate they were still capable of attacking the mainland. Darwin alone was bombed more than sixty times as well as other northern Australian places such as Broome. My father served as an anti-aircraft gunner at both Darwin and Broome before transferring to the RAAF where he was a mid-upper gunner on a B24 Liberator bomber in the Pacific campaign. I was fortunate to be able to talk to him about his experiences in both locations. Sadly, he has passed since.

In Britain, the Special Operations Executive used many women to work behind enemy lines in Europe but my role for Sergeant Jessica Duffy in the Pacific is a work of fiction.

I remember when I was training for my captain's exams reading of a British officer executed by his own troops for being in treasonous contact with the advancing Japanese just before the fall of Singapore. He became the inspiration for Lord Ulverstone as it is recorded there were a significant number of British aristocrats sympathetic to the Fascist cause, who were never brought before a court on charges of treason.

I have loosely followed the battalion history of the 2/1 Battalion and had the honour of sharing time with the legendary Paul Cullen, AC, CBE, DSO & Bar, ED in the 1/19 RNSWR Army Reserve officers' mess back in the 1980s. He had eventually became the Commanding Officer of the 2/1 Battalion in the Pacific campaign, and was truly loved and respected by all who served with him. After the war he founded Austcare and continued service with the Army Reserve. The interesting thing is Cullen was not his real name. He was born Cohen, but because of Hitler's directive to execute any soldiers of Jewish blood in North Africa he changed his name. As it was, the German general Rommel ignored Hitler's directive. I was also fortunate to meet Charles Anderson VC, MC in the same officers' mess around the same time. The 1/19 RNSWR was the postwar combining of the 2/1 battalion and the 2/19 battalion colours and both commanding officers would dine with us. Both men are true Aussie legends.

I could continue with historical notes but my stories are written to entertain, and simply remind this generation of those who came before us, of the suffering, and sacrifice endured by our parents, grandparents and great-grandparents both on the battlefield and at home. There are just too many research books to list and this is not meant to be a history lesson – just a reminder.

ACKNOWLEDGEMENTS

Thanks to my publisher Haylee Nash and the hard-working team at Pan Macmillan, Publishing Director Cate Paterson, editor Libby Turner, and publicist Lara Wallace. Thanks also to Alex Lloyd for his great assistance, and to Alana Kelley and the other support staff of Tracey Cheetham, Publicity Director, and Roxarne Burns, who organises my royalties. And not to forget Maria Fassoulas, Natika Palka and all the hard-working team from sales.

I would also like to acknowledge my Aussie agent and friend, Geoffrey Radford, and my American agent, Alan Nevins. On the *Frontier* TV project, Rod Hardy, Paul Currie, Brett Hardy and Brett's wonderful family.

A thanks to Angela Clarke at the Maclean Library, and all the staff there for their help in my research. Thank you also to Paul Shanley and Jan Martin for their kind assistance with the family tree.

At a personal level the continuing thanks go to all my friends in the Clarence Valley Rural Fire Service and others in the volunteer emergency services I have met during the course of my duties.

There has been the ongoing friendship supporting the task of writing from Mick and Andrea Prowse, Kevin Jones OAM and family, Dr Louis Trichard and Christine, neighbours, Jan Dean Peter and Kaye Lowe, Daniel Huddleston, Kristy Hildebrand, Graham Mackie, John Carroll and Jason and Melanie Walker who made Anzac Day special. A special thanks to Betty Irons OAM and her brother, Bob Mansfield for our good times at the Saturday Maclean Markets. Not to forget my great brother-in-law, Tyrone McKee, who can be found cruising Australian waters in his yacht, *Sahara*.

A special thanks to John and June Riggall. A couple of years ago I approached John with the idea of having a national memorial and legacy for emergency service volunteers killed in the line of duty to be recognised with an inscribed memorial in Canberra. As John was a former federal member of parliament I knew he had the skills to get the project off the ground. With the assistance of local federal member of parliament, Kevin Hogan, this project appears to be going ahead. Just volunteer firefighters in NSW and Victoria alone can count over 160 killed or died since 1950. Add to this the other states and organisations who have lost members and the wall would reflect the ultimate sacrifice made by men and women to protect their communities.

To three veterans of World War II, my aunt, Joan Payne, and Maclean RSL members, Vera Montague and Mick O'Reilly, go my thanks for your courageous service to this nation.

To all my extended family, the Duffy boys, my sister, Lyn and Jock Barclay in Tassie, brother Tom and his wife,

Colleen and my nieces, Shannon, Jessica, Charlotte and Sophia. To my family in Queensland, Luke, Virginia and Tim.

Not to forget my friends in the world of writing: Tony Park and his wife, Nicola, Dave Sabben MG and his wife, Diane, my old mate, Simon Higgins and Annie, Greg Barron and Karly Lane.

A special thanks to all my readers who buy the books for allowing me six months of volunteer bush-fire fighting each fire season.

MORE BESTSELLING FICTION BY PETER WATT

Peter Watt
Cry of the Curlew

A stark and vivid novel of Australia's brutal past.

An epic tale of two families, the Macintoshes and the Duffys, who are locked in a deadly battle from the moment squatter Donald Macintosh commits an act of barbarity on his Queensland property.

Their paths cross in love, death and revenge as both families fight to tame the wild frontier of Australia's north country.

Cry of the Curlew is the first bestselling novel in the compelling Duffy and Macintosh series depicting our turbulent history as never before.

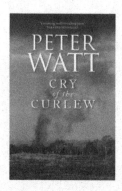

Peter Watt
Shadow of the Osprey

A riveting tale of love, death and revenge.

Soldier of fortune Michael Duffy returns to colonial
Sydney on a covert mission and with old scores to settle,
still enraged by a bitter feud between his family and the
ruthless Macintoshes.

The Palmer River gold rush lures American prospector
Luke Tracy back to Australia's rugged north country in his
elusive search for riches and the great passion of his life,
Kate O'Keefe.

From the boardrooms and backstreets of Sydney to the
hazardous waters of the Coral Sea, the sequel to *Cry
of the Curlew* confirms the exceptional talent of master
storyteller Peter Watt.

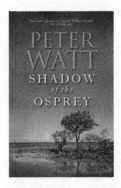

Peter Watt
Flight of the Eagle

A deadly family curse holds two families in its powerful grip.

Captain Patrick Duffy's passions are inflamed by the mysterious Irishwoman Catherine Fitzgerald, further pitting him against his father, Michael Duffy, and his adoring but scheming grandmother, Lady Enid Macintosh.

On the rugged Queensland frontier, Native Mounted Police trooper Peter Duffy is torn between his loyal bond with Gordon James, the love of his sister, Sarah, and the blood of his mother's people, the Nerambura tribe.

Two men, the women who love them and a dreadful curse that still inextricably links the lives of the Macintoshes and the Duffys culminate in a stunning addition to the series featuring *Cry of the Curlew* and *Shadow of the Osprey*.

Peter Watt
To Chase the Storm

When Major Patrick Duffy's beautiful wife Catherine leaves him for another, returning to her native Ireland, Patrick's broken heart propels him out of the Sydney Macintosh home and into yet another bloody war. However the battlefields of Africa hold more than nightmarish terrors and unspeakable conditions for Patrick – they bring him in contact with one he thought long dead and lost to him.

Back in Australia, the mysterious Michael O'Flynn mentors Patrick's youngest son, Alex, and at his grandmother's request takes him on a journey to their Queensland property, Glen View. But will the terrible curse that has inextricably linked the Duffys and Macintoshes for generations ensure that no true happiness can ever come to them? So much seems to depend on Wallarie, the last warrior of the Nerambura tribe, whose mere name evokes a legend approaching myth.

Through the dawn of a new century in a now federated nation, *To Chase the Storm* charts an explosive tale of love and loss, from South Africa to Palestine, from Townsville to the green hills of Ireland, and to the more sinister politics that lurk behind them. By public demand, master storyteller Peter Watt returns to this much-loved series following on from the bestselling *Cry of the Curlew, Shadow of the Osprey* and *Flight of the Eagle*.

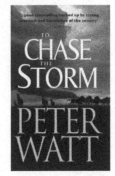

Peter Watt
To Touch the Clouds

*They had all forgotten the curse . . . except one . . . until
it touched them. I will tell you of those times when the
whitefella touched the clouds and lightning came down on
the earth for many years.*

In 1914, the storm clouds of war are gathering. Matthew
Duffy and his cousin Alexander Macintosh are sent
by Colonel Patrick Duffy to conduct reconnaissance
on German-controlled New Guinea. At the same time,
Alexander's sister, Fenella, is making a name for herself in
the burgeoning Australian film industry.

But someone close to them has an agenda of his own –
someone who would betray not only his country to satisfy
his greed and lust for power. As the world teeters on the
brink of conflict, one family is plunged into a nightmare of
murder, drugs, treachery and treason.

Peter Watt
To Ride the Wind

It is 1916, and war rages across Europe and the Middle
East. Patrick and Matthew Duffy are both fighting the
enemy, Patrick in the fields of France and Matthew in the
skies above Egypt.

But there is another, secret foe. George Macintosh
is passing information to the Germans, seeking to
consolidate his power within the family company. And half
a world away from the trenches, one of their own will meet
a shocking death.

Meanwhile, a young man is haunted by dreams of a
sacred cave, and seeks fiery stars that will help him take
back his people's land.

To Ride the Wind continues the story of the Duffys
and Macintoshes, following Peter Watt's much-loved
characters as they fight to survive one of the most
devastating conflicts in history – and each other.

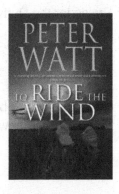

Peter Watt
Beyond the Horizon

It is 1918, a year when war will end, but an even greater killer arises.

On the bloody fields of the Western Front and the battle-scarred desert plains of the Middle East, Tom and Matthew Duffy are battling the enemy in the final year of the Great War. Even as they are trapped on the front lines, they must also find the courage to fight for the women they love when all hope is lost.

Back in Australia, George Macintosh is outraged by the stipulations of his father's will that provide for his despised nephew, and is determined to eliminate any threats to his power. And in a sacred cave in the far Outback, old Wallarie foresees a tide of unspeakable death sweeping through his homeland.

As all nations come to terms with the devastating consequences of the Great War, a new world will be born. But not everyone will live to see it.

Praise for the Duffy/Macintosh series:

'excellent "faction" books'
HERALD SUN

'good storytelling backed up by strong research and knowledge of the country'
COURIER MAIL

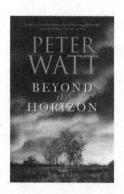

Peter Watt
War Clouds Gather

Against the backdrop of impending war and the rise of
the Nazi Party, the epic saga of the Macintosh and Duffy
families continues.

It's 1936. While Europe is starting to feel the shadow of
the upcoming turmoil, George Macintosh is determined
to keep control of his business empire. He takes extreme
measures to prevent his nephew David from taking a seat
on the Board. Meanwhile, George's son Donald is packed
off to the family station Glen View in Northern Queensland
in an effort to curb his excesses.

In Iraq, Captain Matthew Duffy doesn't escape the stain
of growing fanaticism. Recruited by British Intelligence,
he once more faces a German enemy, although this one
has a more pleasing aspect. Matthew is confused by his
attraction to Diane and finds himself having to make a
hard decision. And just as he is coming to terms with his
choice, he meets his estranged son, James Barrington
Jnr.

In the middle of all this upheaval,
the two families experience loss,
love, greatness and tragedy, and find
themselves brought closer together
and pulled further apart. Romance
blooms in the unlikeliest of hearts
under the gathering clouds of war.

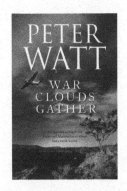

Peter Watt
And Fire Falls

*It is 1942 and the war in the Pacific is on Australia's
doorstep, changing the lives of the Duffy and Macintosh
families as never before.*

In Sydney, siblings Donald and Sarah Macintosh battle
for their father's approval, and control of his empire, while
their cousin David fights the enemy across the continents.

US Marine Pilot James Duffy defies his grandfather's
wishes, and, a number of times, death, protecting
Australian skies from the Japanese. Trapped in the jungles
of Malaya, Diane Duffy is caught between saving the lives
of hundreds of orphaned children, or that of her son.

While Tom Duffy finds himself enlisting in yet another
world war, his daughter Jessica narrowly escapes
slaughter at a mission station, causing her to revoke her
vows and follow in her father's footsteps.

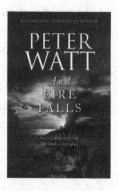